SOFIA'S STORY

BOOK FOUR IN THE PORTRAITS IN BLUE SERIES

PENNY FIELDS-SCHNEIDER

PFS

COPYRIGHT

SOFIA'S STORY

PART I

Eltham

CHAPTER 1

*W*e're *moving today... we're moving today... we're moving today!* Sofia's heart beat an excited rhythm as she leaned across the bed, hugged Jack, and kissed him on the back of his neck. Rising, she tiptoed around the cabin on this last morning they would wake at Montsalvat, and she hoped Scotty might stay asleep for a few more minutes.

Sofia had been looking forward to this day for weeks now, but had not expected the sense of elation accompanying each movement: folding her nightie for the last time, placing the kettle on the gas burner for their last day's early morning cup of tea, peering out the window at the morning sunshine while she waited for the water to boil. Nor for the surge of sweetness she feels when she hears the padding of tiny footsteps and sees Scotty emerge from the bedroom. She smiled and hugged him, making him squeal joyfully.

Finally, they were moving to a home of their own! Tonight she, Jack and Scotty would be in the little cottage in Eltham they'd found to rent.

Sofia considered how pleased her papa and Andres would be to see her with her little family. Her thoughts turned to the second child she and Jack both longed for. Perhaps, away from the stresses of Montsalvat, she would fall pregnant again. But considering she and Jack had waited five years for Scotty to arrive, she knew she must be patient. For some women, squalling babies burst from their wombs with annual regularity, wanted or not. For others, all the longing in the world was met with a monthly crimson flow and heartbreaking disappointment for years on end.

Their new house was barely a mile away from Montsalvat, but that small distance would be sufficient.

Close enough for Helen and Sonia to pop in with the babies they were soon to deliver, and for Sue to visit and share recipes. Over the years, she and Sue had become close as they'd worked together in Montsalvat's kitchen dividing and conquering the tasks to create weekend banquets to appease the voracious appetites of guests— anywhere from five to twenty-five of the who's who of Melbourne— that would arrive at Montsalvat without notice.

Sofia sighed. She couldn't deny she would miss those afternoons in the kitchen, herself in fits of giggles as she diced carrots and shelled peas and listened to Sue swear and curse Justus for his disregard for the residents of the retreat as he generously extended invitations for dinner. Each weekend was the same; at about five PM, the cars would start arriving, and counting them off, Sue's and Sofia's skills to extend the stews they cooked would be tested. And far too often, there were so many guests, the Montsalvat residents would have to go without so the visitors could eat. Then, Sue would be really furious.

But the one-mile distance was far enough to escape Justus' critical gaze and patronising manner. In their new home, she and Jack would be beyond the reach of his cruel tongue and no longer a captive audience to his dinnertime monologues espousing long winded, philosophical diatribes about society, psychology, and art; orations Sofia had once found fascinating, but now saw as obnoxious and condescending.

Of course Sofia knew Jack would visit Justus; he admired the older man—found him inspirational, and certainly, Justus was extraordinary. His vision for the artists' retreat, his designs for the Gothic-style buildings they'd constructed over the last few years were genius and his intellect was remarkable. The problem was that Sofia spent her days at Montsalvat, and by doing so, she was a first-hand witness to the effects of Justus' scathing criticisms on her friends: his malicious teasing of Mervyn and the heartless way he dominated Helen, now pregnant with his child.

Most upsetting for Sofia was Justus' treatment of Lil. The appalling way he had manipulated his wife and the mother of his child—not to mention a significant contributor to financing his dreams—into believing that if she truly loved him she would understand his need to take Helen as his lover. That he expected the two women would coexist on the retreat. Yet in return, he showed little regard for Lil's needs, nor a husbandly concern for the recurring malady which could render her blind one minute, unable to walk the next. Symptoms Justus described as psychosomatic and attention seeking, hence justifying his callous lack of sympathy.

Sofia knew Justus felt her disdain. Rarely did he speak to her anymore, and for this she was glad. While Jack might want to come back to Montsalvat and visit Justus, she didn't anticipate returning any more than she had to.

'Nearly ready, love? Anything you would like me to do?' Jack's words broke through Sofia's reverie. Today, he looked, as excited as Sofia felt and she was glad. She knew it was for her sake that he'd agreed to leave the cabin which had been their home for two years, leave the community they had lived in for nearly four years.

'No, my sweet husband!' she replied, raising her arms around his neck and nuzzling into his shoulder the way he liked. In response, he lifted her off the ground.

'Put me down, put me down.' At her laughter, Scotty put his hands up, anxious to join the fun.

'I'll put you down tonight, don't you worry,' Jack whispered mischievously, his eyes twinkling.

Sofia flapped at his shoulder with her tea towel. 'Off you go! You've got boxes to sort!'

She looked at the accumulation of belongings stacked in the middle of the cabin floor. All of their clothing, their linen, most of the kitchen items, Scotty's toys, and Jack's paints, brushes, oils and canvases were packed in wooden crates, waiting to be loaded onto Mervyn's truck.

After delivering them to their new address, Mervyn, Matchum and Jack would return for the furniture: their own bed and Scotty's little cot and chest of drawers, the larger cupboard used for Jack's and her clothes, her Spanish chest and the table and chairs they ate their breakfast from. It didn't seem like much, but with most of their meals prepared and eaten in the community dining room, their weekends spent outdoors and Jack's weekdays spent at the office in Melbourne, they'd never needed too many belongings.

'I want to finish cleaning here, and then I will wash the windows. Later, after you have moved the furniture, I'll mop the floor again.'

'Sof! You've been cleaning these two rooms all week! You'll be washing the mud off the walls next!'

Cleaning mud off walls might make sense if they lived in the style of home most Australians owned, but the cabin walls, like most of the buildings at Montsalvat, were made of mudbrick.

'I am not going to have Justus telling everybody I left the place filthy.'

'He won't think anything of the sort. Look at the community room, the Great Hall and every other building at Montsalvat. Nobody can keep mud-brick buildings clean. A little dust and dirt is healthy! It's the Australian way!' Jack laughed and reached for Sofia, and giggling, she flicked the dusting cloth in her hand toward him, pretending to be irritated.

'Well, it's not the Spanish way! Just because we live in a cabin built from mudbrick, it doesn't mean we can't be clean.' Sofia still bristled at the memory of the time she'd laughed when Justus had insisted the kitchen's floor tiles should be washed in milk. At the time she hadn't known how sensitive to criticism Justus was and had been shocked when his response had been a scathing comment inferring the Spanish were ignorant and dirty. She shook off the memory; nothing was going to spoil this day.

'Sonia's coming over soon. She's going to take Scotty and Max for a walk while I finish up here. But before I start, I will slip into town and get some Bon Ami and some vinegar for the windows. Perhaps you could get me a couple of buckets of water from the tank?'

'Would you prefer me to go to town?'

'No, I'll enjoy the ride.' Sofia peered out the window, where a clear blue sky foretold a beautiful winter's day was ahead of them. A perfect day for moving.

'Okay, then. If you don't need me here, I might slip over for a chat with Justus. He'll be painting at the Great Hall. I don't want him to feel we are abandoning him by moving into town. You know how sensitive he is when people leave his retreat!'

This time, Sofia's flash of irritation was no act. It was one thing for Jack to be inspired by Justus, but to hear him sympathise with the mean-spirited older man was more than she could tolerate.

'Don't get me started on Justus' sensitivities, Jack! But yes, go and see him. Mervyn will be back at ten, and then we can load the truck.'

Sofia stewed over Jack's words. Justus and his sensitivities! Really! The man never cared when he poked and jibed at others, brandishing his words like nasty little swords, cutting and fraying everyone's nerves while all the while grinning in his smug manner. Sofia would have loved nothing better than to lash out at him, but knew her English, as good as it was after five years of living in Australia, was not up to it. She chuckled, wishing she could let loose at him in Spanish. But if she started, she mightn't stop! Wouldn't Jack get a shock to see his sweet little Spanish wife screaming like a banshee at his precious Master?

'So, I will grab water for you, then?' Jack's wry smile made Sofia chuckle. She knew he hated to see her annoyed.

'Yes, please. Then you can go and appease your Master. Tell him he is still adored by us both, but if he wouldn't mind, could he refrain from visiting our new house!'

'Alright, Mrs Tomlinson, if that's what you want me to say to him, then I will.' Jack said, chuckling as he dodged the towel Sofia flicked toward him.

Five minutes later, Jack returned and set two buckets of water by the wall. He grinned at Sofia and then reached out for another kiss and squeeze. Some days were like this, she and Jack kissing for the sheer joy of being together, and Sofia knew she was lucky. Some women's husbands had no interest in their homes or families. For them, life was all about pubs and horse races or football. Other men's lives were all about work. And then there were men like Justus, egotists who poured all of their time and money into their own interests at the expense of their families.

Happily, Jack was different. Not only did he see it as a duty to care for his family, in the same way his father had, but he loved the time he spent with Scotty and her. She never doubted Jack was most contented when they were all together.

'Okay… off you go… I need to get to the shop!' Sofia laughed as, once again, she felt Jack's arms reaching for her.

CHAPTER 2

'Yoo-hoo!'

The call from the front door was typical Sonia. Her sister, Helen, never came to their cabin, and their brother, Matcham, rarely preceded his arrival with a call—he simply knocked and barged in like a large puppy, knowing Sofia would have one of her sugar biscuits for him, or she'd make an omelette or a tortilla at a moment's notice!

'¡Hola, Sonia, come in!'

With Sonia, Sofia always felt free to be her Spanish self. Her *hola*s and *sí*s and *graciases* did not worry Sonia, nor did they worry Matchum or their father, Mervyn, whose gentle manner was so sweet, you could never be upset by him.

Sofia smiled as Sonia stepped through the door, glanced at the pile of crates ready to be moved, then reached for Scotty.

'So you are leaving, you little rascal,' she grumbled as she swung him into her arms.

'Put him down, Sonia! Scotty is much too heavy for you to be lifting now.'

'Ha. These muscles have been carting rocks and belting stone for years. A little tacker like this is nothing!' Sonia tickled Scotty, causing his fit of giggles to fill the room.

'Well, it's high time you stopped carting rocks, too!'

Although Sonia, at almost seven months pregnant, would do well to heed the advice, Sofia knew her words were wasted. Sonia was a law to herself. One of the few people living at Montsalvat who had the courage to stand up to Justus when he was being overbearing. And Sofia was so impressed with the way Sonia had stood up to Arthur, the reluctant father of the baby she carried. She felt less sure about the way the young woman was so fearless in her disdain for the sneers of the world at large as she strode about the village in her men's overalls and work boots, swollen belly and ringless fingers. Perhaps it was a good thing Sonia so easily cast off the judgements of others, Sofia concluded. Her future as an unwed mother would not be an easy path to tread.

'Is there anything I can do to help?' Sonia offered.

'No, thanks. We've got most things organised now. Taking Scotty for a couple of hours will be wonderful.'

Listening to Sofia's plans for him, Scotty set up a howl.

'Scotty! What's wrong? You are going to go walking with Sonia and Max. There will be lots of lizards and you might even see a lyrebird! It will be fun!'

'No, no... I want you...'

Sofia was surprised. Scotty always loved ambling around Montsalvat with Sonia, and he adored playing with Max.

'I think he knows change is in the air, and he's out of sorts,' Sonia said, and Sofia agreed. Scotty loved Montsalvat and would find life in the small cottage, without Max or any one of a dozen adults to entertain him, quite an adjustment.

'Shh... shh... what's wrong, mi tesoro?' Rather than calming at her question, Scotty's wailing increased in volume. Sofia picked him up. As he snuggled against her, his thumb went to his mouth and his large brown eyes looked at Sonia defiantly, as though daring her to separate him from his mother. It was then Sofia noticed the dribble which had soaked his shirt, and his eyes, puffy from crying, were pink, as were his cheeks.

Resting her forehead against his, Sofia detected a slight fever. Scotty's two-year-old molars had been slowly coming, and for weeks they'd caused this same reaction. A drop of almond oil and sleep would be the best solution, she decided.

'Sonia, Scotty is teething again. He's got a temperature. I think it would be best if I put him down for a rest. He didn't sleep yesterday, what with all the packing going on. Perhaps he needs to catch up. A nap will do him good.'

'Okay...' Sonia sounded dubious. Sofia knew she'd be torn between wanting to stay and help with the packing and needing to keep the arrangement she'd made to collect Max from Lil, who was working at her office this morning. Yesterday the plan to take the two little boys for a walk down to the dam, after which she'd give them morning tea under the trees, had seemed a good idea. Now she'd have to cater to the demands of Max alone.

'It's alright. Scotty will be asleep in no time. He can have a walk with you and Max another day.'

As Sofia anticipated, Scotty was breathing the deep sleep of exhaustion within minutes of being returned to his bed. He'd be out for an hour at least. After giving him a final pat, she retreated from the room and closed the door. She glared at the smeared window panes and dusty sills, but there was little she could do without Bon Ami and vinegar. When the windows were dirty, the whole place felt dirty, and she wanted them clean! She glanced at the closed bedroom door and decided to slip into town, after all. She'd be there and back within twenty minutes, and Jack was barely a hundred yards away. She'd ask him to listen out for Scotty while she was out.

The morning sunshine was pleasant, but a wintery chill bit against Sofia's bare legs as she wheeled her bicycle across to the Great Hall. Already a breeze had sprung up, and she clutched at the skirt of her dress as it was captured by the wind. She could see through the upstairs window, to where Jack was standing, and rather than walk up the stairs and contend with social niceties with Justus, she called out from below.

'Ja-ck, yoo-hoo!'

He noticed her straight away and stepped out onto the balcony. Recently finished, it offered a sweeping view of the valley: the dam, the vegetable gardens where she and Helen worked, and Lil's House, the first building ever constructed at Montsalvat. Shielding the sun from her eyes, Sofia was surprised at how far up he appeared.

'Jack,' she called, 'I am going to go to the shops; I will be quick...'

He leaned forward in an effort to hear her. Realizing the breeze was carrying her words down the valley, she raised her voice and tried again. 'Jack, I am leaving now. Scotty is not so well. I put him back to bed. He is fast asleep. Can you check on him in a few minutes? I won't be long!'

Jack smiled and nodded before waving back at her, as did Justus, who'd joined him on the balcony.

As she turned away, the phrase 'No shoes!' filtered through the breeze, and Sofia chuckled and gave a final wave before pedalling off. He loved to remind her of the moment of madness three years earlier when she'd purchased those lavishly embroidered slippers on a whim —they'd been so beautiful she couldn't resist them. She'd never forgotten Jack's astonished expression as he'd gazed at the shoes then asked her where on earth was she planning to wear them. Nor had she forgotten her fiery response, which had been followed by two days of silence. Jack had been right, though. To this day, those slippers had lain wrapped in the tissue paper they'd come home in, for never had Sofia had an opportunity to wear them. Tonight she would, though! She'd wear them, and very little else! Wouldn't Jack be surprised!

Smiling, Sofia navigated the gravel path up the hill. She paused as, from her left, a flickering of embers from the camp fire caught her attention. Tiny flames had erupted and Sofia noticed a scattering of dry leaves had drifted against the coals. The previous night, the Jorgensens, Skippers, Jack and herself had sat around the fire—the men, Sue and Sonia sipping on beer, Sofia and Lil drinking red wine. The evening had been a farewell to Jack and herself; and after eating the lovely dinner Sue had prepared for them they'd taken their drinks and proceeded outdoors. There, they'd admired the spectacular array of stars against the inky sky, gazed into the campfire's flames and inhaled the aroma of eucalyptus emitting from the burning logs as they'd chatted until after midnight.

Although the rule at Montsalvat was for the embers to be covered in soil before they left the fire at night, this was rarely followed, and more than once they'd battled flames licking along the grass when coals escaped the confines of the fire pit.

Sofia steered her bike towards the flames and stomped on them, careful not to burn her legs, and wishing she'd worn her leather boots rather than the light shoes she'd chosen for the ride into the village. Next, she checked the bucket near the fireplace, and was sorry to find it was empty, for it would have been good to douse the coals in water.

Never mind, she thought. In the next hour, someone would be glad for the hot embers at the core of the fireplace, for they'd be wanting to cook some sausages or heat a bucket of water. In fact, Sofia thought, a final wipe over the windows with steamy hot water would finish them off nicely; when she returned from the village, she'd get the fire going and place a pot of water over the coals herself.

The ride into Eltham was quick: down Mount Pleasant Road, a right turn, and then barely a mile to the village. Once at the hardware shop, it only took a few minutes for Sofia to find the articles she needed. Nonetheless, in the way of small towns on Saturday mornings, with the sky clear and a weekend stretched out before them, the local residents were relaxed and keen to chat. Sofia waited at the counter for the plumber, Stan, to obtain some guttering clips which Mike was sure he had out the back of the store. While she stood in line, she talked to Valerie, who had her little girl with her. Valerie had given birth to Jane close to the time Scotty was born, and they often met in the street or at the baby clinic. Jane and Scotty had occasionally played together as their mothers talked. In a couple of years, they'd go to kindergarten and then to school together.

Valerie was surprised to learn Sofia was moving into town, and Sofia gave her the address of the cottage, pleased when Valerie promised to visit with Jane one morning in the following week. Scotty would be thrilled to have a special visitor.

Finally it was Sofia's turn to be served, and she passed over her ha'pennies for the vinegar and Bon Ami. She placed them in the large wicker basket on the front of the bike, then stopped at the bakery for some bread rolls and a Boston bun, a treat for morning tea. Setting out on the return journey, Sofia happily found the trip all the quicker for the wind gusts nudging the bicycle forward and was relieved she was not riding against it. The final turn, taking her up the hill to Montsalvat, was more difficult and it took all of Sofia's strength to rotate the pedals. She squirmed, tucking her dress beneath her seat to avoid the billowing fabric from getting caught in the bicycle's chain. She would have been better to have worn her work trousers, but her choice of the dress had been deliberate. More than once she'd been on the receiving end of the strange looks the people of Eltham directed towards the Montsalvat women when they entered shops dressed in overalls and work boots. Today, right before her move into town, she'd wanted to be viewed as a respectable villager, not one of the strange Bohemians from the artists' retreat.

～

As Sofia turned into Montsalvat's carpark, she saw plumes of black smoke billowing down into the valley. The fireplace! It was hard to suppress pangs of guilt, and Sofia wished she'd been more careful in stomping out the live embers she'd seen. She hoped they had not caused too much trouble. In the distance she saw the Skippers, Jorgensens, Arthur and Sue were standing in a huddle. Before them, flames emanated from the far end of the students' quarters. Surely the cabins were not on fire! Her heart lurched in her chest and her legs faltered as she tried to pedal faster.

CHAPTER 3

*A*s she turned the pedals Sofia's mind churned. Was the fire in her and Jack's cabin? Good Lord! Scotty was in there! Her feet felt like lead as she dismounted and ploughed forward, pushing the bicycle along the gravel path. Jack was standing with Justus in front of their cabin and Sofia's heart erupted into wild palpations as she saw the smoke billowing from the doorway.

'Scotty, Jack! Did you get Scotty?' she called as she got closer.

Faces turned toward her, and Sofia saw looks of bewilderment pass between them. Again, she yelled out, before dropping her bike and running. The pile of boxes and suitcases lying in a huddle on the road before their cabin revealed a salvage effort had taken place. But it was Scotty who Sofia was desperate to lay eyes upon; surely the harrowing fear coursing through her was unwarranted!

As she reached them, Jack gave Sofia a reassuring nod towards their belongings then stepped toward her.

Ignoring him, a stabbing sensation filled Sofia's chest as she ran to the doorway. She was immediately blinded by the black smoke billowing out, and leant over, coughing. *Where was her baby?*

'Where's Scotty! Did you get him out? Is he safe?'

'Scotty's not in there—he's with Sonia?' The questioning tone in his reply was unmistakable; Jack didn't know where Scotty was.

'No, Jack, I told you. He was sick. I put him in his bed.' Sofia heard the high-pitched ring of hysteria distort her voice and took a deep breath. She again tried to enter the cabin, but the heat of the flames beat her back. Her legs seized with terror as a trembling overtook her and she could barely hold herself upright. Her eyes frantically searched, trying to look everywhere at once; where was Scotty? All she could see was air thick with smoke and darting tongues of fire working their way along the kitchen's window frame.

A babble of anxious questioning accompanied a flurry of movement as the Skippers and Jorgensens scanned the buildings for a sign of the little boy.

Staring at Sofia, Jack's eyes widened in horror as comprehension sunk in, then with arms flailing, he ran through the open door.

'Scotty! Scotty!' he roared, his arms beating wildly against the flames that licked against his shirt.

Matchum got to him first, and joined by Justus, they held him back. And in that moment, Sofia's world collapsed as she grasped the extent of the tragedy that had befallen them, confirmed by the horror in the eyes turned toward her, the voracious tongues of fire raging within their cabin, and the pathetic huddle of suitcases and remnants strewn on the ground.

'I'll find Sonia,' Lena cried. 'Perhaps he's with her!'

'She's coming now. Just her and Max,' Sofia heard Helen's reply.

Oh, dear God, no! Please, this can't have happened. Not her darling little boy, trapped in that terrible inferno. The pounding in her head drowned out her thoughts and she gasped for air. No, he had to be here among them somewhere; but where? He'd been in her arms barely an hour ago. He'd smiled at her, even as he'd drifted off to sleep with his little teddy tucked under his arm. And she'd left him, believing he was safe, sure that sleep would be good for him. Why didn't she let

Sonia take him? Why was she so determined to go to town? Why did she walk past the glowing embers and fail to see the danger they presented?

'Scotty,' she cried, as if by hearing the desperation in her voice, he might appear at the door, whole and well, and this nightmare would end. But of course, he didn't.

She was barely aware of the sobbing that filled the air, nor did she react when Lil gripped her arm and spoke, unable to keep the sob from her voice.

'Sofia, he would have been asleep. The smoke would have sedated him.'

Sofia shook her head and again searched the crowd, sure she'd see Scotty tucked among the arms and legs, or perhaps cowering in the shadows of a building, terrified by the heat and shimmering smoke.

Her eyes landed on the items dragged from the burning building. Among them was the chest Jack always called 'Sofia's Spain', for it held the treasures she'd transported across the world five years earlier. The mantilla her mother had worn and the silver candlesticks—a wedding gift to her parents three decades earlier. In addition, it held hundreds of paintings. Those which had been painted by her father and Andres, as well as her father's collection: Picassos, Sorollas, Matisses, and others. In the time taken for Jack to drag this out, he could have gone into the back room and found Scotty sleeping!

In a split second Sofia could see it all. How pleased would have been to have rescued the chest; he knew how much it meant to her. But what did its contents matter? Why had she thought it so important? Did her mother's spirit dwell in the candlesticks or her mantilla? Of course not! Did its canvases hold Papa's and Andres' spirits? No! They were paintings! Paintings! Nothing more than pigments on canvas.

But even so, the chest had survived! Fury rose within Sofia as she recognised its malevolent intention. The chest taunted her with its hoard of relics—the cold embers of lives once so precious to her. How dare this soulless collection endure, when the treasures of her heart—

the priceless flesh and blood of those she loved—were taken one by one?

And what now? Was she supposed to feed it again? Was she supposed to empty the small suitcase which held Scotty's belongings and transfer them to this insatiable fiend—squeeze into its recesses his little toys and the tiny baby blankets infused with the aroma of his soft hair? Was she to fold up the beautiful white shawl Marian had bought for him, and perhaps add the little pair of leather work boots he'd been wearing these past months which now lay forlornly on their boot stand at the front of the cabin?

Looking at Jack, Sofia's hatred for the chest found an outlet. 'You saved this, Jack. The paintings! But not Scotty!'

The words sliced through the air and Jack winced as they pierced him. Sofia knew how irrational they sounded, but her self-control was gone. A terror rose within her; a fury for all she'd been robbed of, at the unfairness of it all. And now, her baby too was taken from her.

Sofia felt the howl gathering from deep within as one feels the rumble of a train in the distance; a collision of her overwhelmed heart beating frantically, her heaving lungs strained for air and her exploding brain which could barely comprehend that before her. She tried to step forward, and her legs thrust first one way and then the next in an attempt to stay upright, while her arms flailed at the flames as though they might sweep them from existence.

Falling forward, she landed against the chest. At the feel of its sturdy frame her fury spewed forth. Blind with rage, she pounded against it, and as her nails broke and her knuckles grazed, a torrent of grief poured from her throat, its gut-wrenching howl filling the air sounding as terrible to her as it must to those who heard. Scotty! What had she done?

If only, if only... The words roared through her mind, and were surely the most futile phrase ever formed.

'Sofia?' The voice was Jack's, and she saw his face, white and twisted, in an agony of sorrow.

Unable to bear the guilt of failing to act when she could have, of losing their baby, Sofia couldn't face him. And when he stepped towards her, she raised her hands against him in a bid to deflect the weight of his pain.

CHAPTER 4

*T*he days after the funeral were a blur. Each morning, at Lil and Lena's insistence, Sofia rose, dressed, forced down a mouthful of porridge and sipped tea before moving to the veranda, where she spent the morning in silence. What was there to say? Nothing!

Each day, Jack arrived and tried to talk to her.

'Sofia, please, come to the caravan with me. Margaret helped me to get it in order and it is quite cosy.' Jack's voice sounded stronger and he gave her a smile and squeezed her hand as he spoke and Sofia almost believed that perhaps she was imagining things. Perhaps he wasn't going to die after all. But then she thought about the van.

It had been their first little home together in Australia, after a year spent living at South Yarra with her in-laws, and they'd both loved the cosiness and privacy it offered. Sofia recalled how it was there, on its tiny bench seat, she'd straddled Jack's lap and shared the news they'd both longed for: after four years of marriage, she was finally pregnant. Oh, to remember his joy! She'd always known Jack's heart's desire was to have a child of their own. And his desire had become their desire, and finally they'd been blessed with Scotty.

Sofia shook her head and closed her eyes, trying to escape the memory. How could she have given Jack so much, and then by her own negligence, see it taken from him and break his heart? How could he think she might return to the van— sit in the same seat and look at the ceiling—to be reminded of the evening he'd lifted her so high her head had nearly touched the roof, and then he'd hugged her to him, as though he might crush her with the joy of it all.

And, when Lil heard Sofia sobbing at the memories, she came to the veranda and spoke to Jack.

'Perhaps it is better if you stay away for a few days, Jack. Let Sofia rest... allow her mind to settle. You have both had a dreadful shock, but I am concerned that Sofia remains so withdrawn. I think that utter quietness would be good for her. Don't worry, we will look after her. She will be ready to see you soon.'

Sofia wondered at Lil's words. Would she be better soon? Do women who lose their children ever get better? Who could say? She glanced at Jack as he took in Lil's words. It was then she saw his shoulders sag and the light leave his eyes and the lines collapse into his drawn face. And she knew for certain he'd been pretending to be strong for her benefit. She could see how Death hovered around him, wanting to make him another victim of the curse which took everybody whom she loved.

As Lil had said, Sofia's mind did clear, and her voice returned. But from morning to night her thoughts were for Scotty and her need to apologise to him and for Jack, whom she needed to avoid.

'Where is Scotty? I need to see him,' she asked repeatedly, wondering where the little graveside might be, but Lena's answer was always the same.

'Can you speak English, Sofia? Then we will be able to understand you.'

Sofia couldn't, though; her thoughts were Spanish, and so too were the words she spoke.

She waited for God to come to her and offer His comfort. Surely, when He'd said 'Let the children come to me,' He didn't intend them to consign their mothers to a living Hell. Over and over, Sofia repeated under her breath the phrase, '*Venid a mí todos los que estáis fatigados y cargados, y yo os haré descansar*' — 'Come to me, those of you who are heavily laden, and I will give you rest...'

But for as much as she tried to turn to God and seek the rest He promised, to lay open her heart and soul and mind to Him, be as an empty vessel for Him to fill, all she felt was a gaping hollow within. Her whole world was a silent void, offering no words of peace nor rest for her weary mind, nor answers for what to do about Jack.

And then it came to her, and Sofia knew what she needed to do. She must go to Him. And where would she go? To St Patrick's, of course!

～

It was a Thursday afternoon when Sofia rose from the veranda. Lil was at work in her office, and the Skippers had slipped into the village for some grocery shopping. Helen was collecting vegetables from the garden for dinner, and Sofia could hear Sonia's hammer as it whacked the chisel against the rock she was carving, its repetitive clang echoing from her workshop.

It only took twenty minutes for Sofia to take the same path she and Jack usually walked together each Monday when they left Montsalvat to spend the night with William and Marian. Today she found it tiring, and by way of a test to see if God was listening to her, she called for his strength to be with her as she forced one foot in front of the other.

The station master knew her, of course, and he took her penny and gave her a return ticket with a gentle smile and barely a murmur. *He knows*, she thought, and was glad he did not try to offer words of condolence.

When the train's familiar rattle and sway paused at South Yarra station where she usually disembarked, Sofia remained on board. Exiting instead at Flinders Street Station, she walked up the ramp, through the turn-style, and out under the clocks. The street was busy; it always was. After crossing the road and veering right, she felt breathless as she ascended the hill. The church was only three blocks away, a journey which she'd normally walked with ease, pushing Scotty in his pram before her, but not today. More than once, she needed to sit and rest.

Not only was Sofia's body exhausted, but so was her mind, and when she saw a low stone ledge beside a stairwell, she stopped and sat. And when she leant forward to rest her head on her arms, she fell asleep. Sofia only knew this when, opening her eyes sometime later, it was obvious the sun had moved across the sky and clouds had formed. Sofia struggled to her feet and then continued walking towards the church, whose towering steeple was visible against the backdrop of heaving black clouds.

Jesus, Mary, Mother of God, please look after my baby... Jesus, Mary, Mother of God, please keep Jack safe... The words repeated themselves, a chant whose rhythm matched the clip of her heels against the pavement as she made her way up the hill.

But when Sofia ascended the final rise and looked across the street to the main entrance of St Patrick's, she was filled with disappointment. The iron gates of the main entrance were closed, as were the arched doors leading into the cathedral. In disbelief, she walked around the block. St Patrick's had many entrances, and Sofia hoped to see another of its doors standing open. Or if not, perhaps a gate into the garden might be ajar, which would allow her to access the beautiful garden where she could rest on a bench or sit at the base of one of the saints' statues and pray.

The sky seemed darker, and not only because of the heavy clouds overhead. The sun was sinking and Sofia realised it was late afternoon. Again, she walked the periphery of the church and noticed a flickering light through the stained-glass windows.

"Father, are you there?" Her voice sounded feeble, and Sofia knew even if someone was inside, they wouldn't hear her.

As the grey sky deepened into twilight, Sofia waited, hoping perhaps there'd be an evening mass. But as time passed, there was no sign of people arriving, or movement from within the church. Moisture filled the air, and Sofia knew a shower of rain was barely minutes away. She pulled her cardigan around her shoulders and brushed her tear filled eyes. Was it possible even God had abandoned her?

Sofia looked down the road where the shadowy silhouette of the gateway into the Fitzroy garden was visible. *Perhaps the conservatory might be open, or even Cook's Cottage?* Either would offer shelter from the rain.

She wandered through the park until she heard the voices of two men arguing. One seemed determined to sleep on the bench he lay upon, and the other voice belonged to a policeman who was trying to move him along. The coarseness of the exchange caused Sofia to shudder in fear, and she gathered her arms across her body and retreated in the direction she'd arrived as quickly as she could. She stumbled trying to follow the path in the darkness which had descended, and balked more than once as the shapes of the bushes surrounding her appeared threatening. The familiar walkways of the park, lovely by day, were now shadowy and menacing, and Sofia knew it was not wise to shelter there.

Reaching the road, Sofia turned leftward and stumbled towards Flinders Street Station, and was glad when the lights of the intersection in the distance came into view. Droplets of rain felt like chilly darts on her forehead and she tried to walk faster. A chant from within her again picked up the repetitious pace of her footsteps. *What to do, what to do.... Jesus, Mary, Mother of God.... Please care for my baby... Jesús, Maria, madre de Dios... Please keep Jack safe.*

Just as the rain set into a steady downpour, Sofia arrived at the building opposite Flinders Street Station whose stairs led to a sheltered doorway, and Sofia climbed them. Once out of the rain, she sank down and pulled her now soaking cardigan tightly around her shoulders. What next? Return to Montsalvat? Go back to Jack? Bring the curse of death to him? Sofia desperately needed direction from God.

As she gazed at the lights of the station across the intersection, her eyes felt heavy. She knew what she would do. She'd wait here on the steps until sunrise, and then she'd return to St Patrick's. Here the street lamps offered safety, and in the morning she'd walk back up the hill to the cathedral. Surely the priest would be there then! She'd speak to him of the curse and he'd offer her some guidance and they could light a candle and offer prayers for Scotty and Jack.

~

'Miss, miss, are you alright?'

'You can't stay here, love. This is no place for a lady. Where do you live?'

Coming awake, Sofia was startled by the vision of a woman with a halo bending down over her and the shape of a second figure alongside her. Were they a pair of spirits here to guide her?

'Miss, please. It's raining… you're getting a bloody soaking.'

Sofia realised these were not spirits, but earthbound creatures. Women, one with fair hair and a strong fragrance of perfume, the other, taller and with a raspy voice possibly caused by the cigarette whose tip glowed as she took a deep drag.

'I'm waiting for the priest,' she told them.

'What did she say, Shirl?'

Sofia attempted to repeat the words, but her tongue felt thick and the dryness of her mouth made her voice raspy.

'I don't know... has she been drinking?' the voice to her right asked.

'I can't see any bottles, nor can I smell anything…'

Sofia pulled herself upright, and looking around her, she tried to make sense of why she was sitting on these steps in the dark with these two women.

Jesus, Mary... Mother of God... please keep me safe.... Where was God? Where was Jesus and Mary?

Loneliness shrouded Sofia like a damp fog, and she shivered. She scrubbed at her cheeks with the back of her hand to mop up the salty tears she could feel trickling into the creases of her mouth.

'She's crying—has she been hurt? I hope no bastard's got at her!'

'Love, can you tell us your name? Where do you live?...'

'Vivo en Montsalvat.'

'I don't think she's speaking English. What do you think? Should we call someone?'

'Not the police, the mongrels.'

'Certainly not. What about Mrs Whyte? She might have a bed.'

'It's late... after ten... Here, love, take my coat, you're freezing!'

The coat was prickly and reeked with the overpowering odour of stale perfume. Nonetheless, Sofia leaned forward, welcoming the warmth of the fabric around her shoulders and the softness of its fur-lined collar against her neck

'Should we check if she's got money, Lydia? There's a handbag there.'

'Yes, do it. If we don't, you can bet your life someone will, and they'll be happy enough to take it for their own.' She said then to Sofia, 'Love, we're going to check your purse. We're not here to rob you. You don't need to worry. We just want to get you off the streets—get you into a taxi and take you somewhere safe for the night.'

'Yes, there's a pound note here. Do you think she'd mind if we use it?'

'Can't see she has much choice, to be honest. Wait, there's Frank over on the corner. He'll take her to Mrs Whyte's. Perhaps we should go with her... anything could happen!'

'Yoo-hoo, Frank!'

'Ladies—a quiet night for you?' The man's voice came from the base of the stairs.

'You know how it is. Give it another hour and the johns will be prowling the streets.'

'Who have you got there, Shirley? Hasn't been drinking, has she? I don't want vomit in my taxi. You know it takes weeks to get rid of the stench!'

'No, Frank, nothing like that. We've never seen her before. She's not one of the usual girls, and look at how she's dressed. Perhaps her husband's thrown her out, or something. We think we should get her to Mrs Whyte's place.'

'Whatever you say, Shirl. I hope you've got some money tonight! I am not a charity, you know.'

Sofia allowed the women to guide her down the steps and across to the taxi resting at the curbside.

'We're coming too, Frank,' Shirley said before encouraging Sofia into the back seat. As they squeezed in, Shirley on one side of her, Lydia on the other, Sofia's sense of disconnection from the world increased. She fought to regain control. *No*, she should be saying. *Not this way! Take me to Saint Patrick's; take me to God.* But the words were lost somewhere between her mind and mouth. Instead, she stared out the window into the blackness of the night, wondering what she was doing, enveloped in the warmth of a stranger's jacket, seated between these ladies who seemed intent on protecting her, riding through the dark streets with the pounding of raindrops drumming on the rooftop of the vehicle.

'God, look at this rain now! It's really coming down!'

'Yes. Well, we can kiss goodbye any chances of earning a pound tonight! There will be no decent customers out in this weather.'

Frank grunted, and their voices fell into silence as the taxi driver and working girls alike accepted that the wet night ahead offered slim prospects of trade for them.

Finally, the taxi turned into a quiet street, and weaved left and right before coming to rest. The back door opened, and the resourcefulness of the girls seemed limitless as the fair one—Shirley—rummaged in a large bag for an umbrella, which she opened and held over Sofia before enticing her along a narrow pathway towards a front porch.

'Come on, Sofia. This is Melrose House. You will be dry and warm here, and Mrs Whyte will find a bed for you for the night. She's marvellous. She'll get you sorted.'

CHAPTER 5

*N*othing could describe how strange Sofia felt the following morning when she woke between crisp, clean white sheets, in a strange room. Aside from the bed, its furnishings included an old-fashioned dressing table with a cracked mirror and a mismatched wardrobe.

'Ma'am, would you like a cuppa?' The face peering at her was dark, belonging to a young Aboriginal girl, perhaps fourteen years old.

Sofia stared at her, bewildered, and without saying anything more, the girl placed a floral cup and saucer on the bedside table and then left the room.

Minutes later, a second person appeared. This time it was a woman of perhaps sixty years of age, who introduced herself as Mrs Whyte.

'Good morning, lovey. Have you got a name? We've got more than one "love" here, and it can get a little confusing. Names can be very helpful...' She chuckled at her joke.

'Sofia...' The word felt strange as it crossed her lips. Her throat was dry, and she reached for the cup to take a sip of tea.

'Sofia. Pleased to meet you. Do you have a surname?'

Sofia stared back at her. Did she? Her mind was blank.

'Not to worry; it's not necessary. Sofia will do us fine. Do you remember anything about last night? A couple of the girls in the city brought you here. They were worried about you—you didn't belong on the corner where they found you. They'd know, of course. Quite territorial, they are, and they know where everybody belongs. You were in their spot. Lucky for you, Lydia and Shirley are good types. Some of the others may not have been so caring.'

Sofia's recollections of the previous night were a hazy blur of muffled voices, tumultuous rain, driving through dark streets, and then being brought into this room.

'Sofia... not Sophie...? Sofia. I don't want to pry, but I do want to make sure we have our bases covered. I'll ask you a couple of questions, if you don't mind. Firstly, are you in any pain? Have you been injured?'

'No... no...' Sofia could feel the words at the base of her throat, but they wouldn't come out.

'Is there anyone else we should be thinking about? Any children, perhaps?'

Children! Tears ran down Sofia's cheeks, and she shook her head before lying back against the pillow and turning her face to the wall.

'Okay, love. I will leave you to rest for a bit. We can have another talk later. Please be assured, you are safe here. Concentrate on getting some more sleep. Trust me, it's your best medicine.'

Sofia slept on and off throughout the day. Turning over from time to time, she was conscious of sunlight fading to grey to black and then to pink and gold.

More than once, Sofia sensed movement in the room. On hearing crockery rattling close to her ear, she opened her eyes to see a cup of tea and a plate of sandwiches resting on the bedside table. Later, when sunshine filtered through the lace curtains, Mrs Whyte appeared with the young Aboriginal girl, whom she introduced as Esther, and they encouraged Sofia to sit on the side of the bed and wash her face and hands in the basin they'd brought. She then changed into the dress they offered, pale blue with white flowers, and a broad belt.

'I don't mean to be cruel, Sofia but it's lunchtime. You've been sleeping for almost thirty hours and it's time for you to get up for a bit. Come and sit outside in the sunshine. A couple of our ladies are having a cuppa out there.'

Sofia knew Mrs Whyte was right. It was time to leave the bedroom. She followed her through the house to the garden, taking the vacant seat Mrs Whyte offered and accepting the plate of cold meat and salad Esther placed before her.

'Ladies, this is Sofia. Sofia, this is Marie and Vera.' The two ladies gave Sofia a quick nod before continuing their conversation. Marie had a black eye and plenty to say about the man who'd inflicted it, prefacing each sentence with "The Bastard, this" and "The Bastard, that," as she gave a detailed account of the many times his stray fists had left their mark on her.

'I'm glad the children were away this time. They didn't see anything.' However, it emerged her children were expected home from their boarding school the following day—perhaps her sister might take them for a couple of weeks. Her sister was no pushover Marie explained. If The Bastard turned up on her doorstep, he'd get his marching orders!

The second lady, Vera, was quiet, although as she picked through her meal, she offered enough nods of agreement accompanied by ahs and tut-tutting to encourage Marie with her story. Sofia noticed Vera's arm was in a sling. Surely it hadn't been broken by her husband!

After lunch, Mrs Whyte invited Sofia into the lounge and gently questioned her. Was there any family, perhaps a sister or parents who ought to be contacted? Told where she was?

Although Mrs Whyte's questions made perfect sense to Sofia, her mind was in turmoil. She couldn't remember anything beyond hours of walking around a church whose doors had been closed to her, and then shivering on the stairs in the rain until the ladies had brought her here.

Additionally, it seemed her voice had left her. Whenever she replied, her answers came out as a whisper of barely audible Spanish.

'No,' she tried to say. 'Nobody.'

The next morning Sofia rose early, dressed and made her bed. She then took herself to the kitchen, where Esther had the stove alight and a kettle bubbling away on the hob. When Sofia glanced at her, she gave a sharp nod towards the stove.

'Help yourself, Ma'am. The water's boiled and the teapot's on the bench. Here, I'll get the cosy for you; it's cold today.' Sofia realised Esther had thought she wanted a cup of tea.

A few minutes later, glad for the warmth of the hot cup between her hands, Sofia accepted Esther's offer to sit on a chair close to the fireplace. The room was chilly, with a draft seeping through the cracks in the wooden window frame, and the warmth the stove offered was welcome. Being in the unfamiliar kitchen felt peculiar, but in its own way comforting. Rows of cannisters were set on a shelf: flour and sugar and tea. These made sense to Sofia in a world where little else did.

Sofia watched the firm movements of Esther's hands as she kneaded and pounded a lump of dough in the manner of one who'd done it a thousand times. Beyond her, Sofia caught sight of a bowl of lemons, and beside the stove stood a bottle of oil.

Without speaking, Sofia took her cup to the sink where she found a stack of dishes and cutlery waiting to be washed. Feeling Esther's eyes upon her, Sofia paused. Perhaps she shouldn't be touching things in Esther's kitchen. The young girl smiled and nodded though, and Sofia proceeded, first filling the basin with cold water, then adding hot water from the kettle and using the brush in the sink, she washed the dishes.

Mrs Whyte appeared at the doorway and must have noticed Sofia eyeing the flour cannister as she washed.

'You are welcome to cook if you like, Sofia. Esther will give you anything you need. Perhaps you'd like to make scones or some biscuits for morning tea?'

Sofia nodded. She'd make magdelenas. They were the easiest thing

in the world to bake; she'd been cooking them since she was a child—
her father and brother loved the lemon flavoured muffins, and she
could never make enough to satisfy them.

The fourth morning, Sofia swept the house from front to back, finding
the busyness gratifying. When she finished the floors, she returned to
the kitchen, where Esther was cutting a slab of raw beef into cubes.
Without asking, Sofia lifted the basin of beans from the bench onto her
lap, then proceeded to top, tail and slice them. Afterwards she helped
tidy the kitchen, set out the lunch plates, dish up the meal and then,
again, to clean and tidy.

A number of times through the following days, Mrs Whyte tried to
draw Sofia into conversation.

'Sofia, I can see you love cooking. Do you have a job in a
commercial kitchen? Perhaps at one of the hotels, or at a hospital?'

'No... sí... Galleria Touloisie.' That had been her job. Work Sofia
loved, cooking for her café and managing the art gallery in Malaga.
The memories of days spent marinating olives and baking polverones
and roscos fritos in her large sun-filled kitchen blended with other
memories; hours she'd spent in another kitchen. One where she'd
chopped vegetables alongside a tall lady with blond hair, and together
they'd laughed and chatted as they floured bite-sized chunks of beef.
Was that her job, too? The confusion of memories bothered Sofia, and
her eyes filled with tears. Was there somewhere she should be?
Something she was supposed to be doing?

'There, there, love. Don't you worry about anything. You tell me
what I can do for you.'

But Sofia didn't feel she needed anything more than to be able to
help Esther in the kitchen.

Three days later, Mrs Whyte suggested Sofia might like to have a chat with Dr Michael, who was coming to the house to look at a child's ears. The poor mite had kept the household awake all night with his screaming. Mrs Whyte explained how, given the doctor lived on the same street, he often called into Melrose House on his way to his surgery.

When the doctor arrived, Sofia tried to answer his questions, but could only manage nods and shakes of her head, all the while wiping away the tears trickling down her cheeks. He conducted a brief examination, asking her to lift her dress and listening to her chest with a stethoscope. He'd then tapped across her back with his fingers.

'Sofia, I think you need rest. I can see no sign of injury, no physical symptoms. You have some congestion on your lungs, but it's not serious. Your speech has been affected, of course, and these tears seem to be a problem—something has upset you recently?'

Looking into the deep brown eyes gazing upon her, Sofia shrugged.

'The main problem is this memory loss. Some sort of amnesia, I am thinking. I could have you admitted into Kew—it's the psychiatric hospital—but really, if Mrs Whyte's happy for you to stay here for another week or so, that might be best. I hear you enjoy cooking?'

'*Sí*.

'Well, I think for now, cooking might be your best medicine. Cooking and cleaning. And then, resting. Sitting in the sunshine. Soon your memories will return, and then you can tell us what has happened. How does that sound?'

To Sofia, it sounded fine.

Melrose House ebbed and flowed with a constant stream of women arriving and departing, day and night. Sometimes the number of residents was down to perhaps a half dozen; at others the rooms seemed to overflow with yelling mothers, howling children and a stern Mrs Whyte trying to bring order to the chaos.

At night Sofia lay in bed hearing cars arrive, or she'd wake to the sight of families collecting daughters or sisters or friends. Often she'd hear loud voices of anger, or shock, or distress as they'd been confronted by the sight of their relative's haggard appearance or swollen-eyes blackened by the fists of men who'd told them they'd loved them when they were sober, then who used them as punching bags when they drank.

Some of the women at Melrose House were regulars, and Mrs Whyte would get cross at them. 'Muriel! What do you want? For Daniel to kill you? He will, you know, if you keep going back to him. Men like him don't change. And believe me, I can tell you now, I won't be coming to your funeral to stand and watch him blubbering over your coffin, claiming to be broken-hearted, after he hits you one too many times.

Funeral! The word sent Sofia spiralling into a deep depression, and she lay on her bed sobbing, her heart hollow, her arms aching with an emptiness she could not fathom.

CHAPTER 6

Sofia had been at Melrose House for over two weeks when a butcher arrived with a delivery of meat for the refuge's fridge. He was different to the man who'd arrived the previous week, Gerry, who'd been nice, smiling at Sofia and not seeming to mind when her answers were incomprehensible

This man was younger, with a booming, laughter-filled voice who teased and joked with Esther as they unpacked sausages and chops from his large wooden crate. Quietly, Sofia slipped passed them to open the oven door. As she'd expected, her biscuits were nicely browned. Withdrawing the tray, she placed it on the bench to cool. The spicy aroma of cinnamon filled the room, and immediately the butcher turned towards her.

'My, oh my! Don't they smell wonderful! Aren't you the clever one!'

'*Gracias*' Sofia smiled shyly.

'Sofia is a wonderful cook. I don't bother with biscuits anymore. Why would I, when Sofia produces food like this each day?'

'I tell you what, ladies. You get that kettle bubbling, and set me with a plate of those, and after morning tea, I'll reveal to you both the secret to creating the best roast lamb you'll ever taste.'

'Don't be so certain about that. Last week, Sofia took charge of our Sunday roast, and the way everyone raved, you'd think they'd never eaten a baked meal before.' Esther pretended to be grumpy, but Sofia knew she was joking.

'Well done to you. Sofia is it? I'm Jack. Jack Bacon. Pleased to meet you.'

Esther plunged into giggles as he said his name.

'Jack Bacon, Sofia! Imagine, a butcher whose surname is Bacon!'

Sofia hadn't noticed the butcher's surname; it was his Christian name which caught her attention. On hearing it, she felt as though she'd been struck by lightning. *Jack!* The man winked at her, and she froze. At once she was reminded of another Jack, who was also tall and had a nice, kind smile like this man. Where was he?

Throughout the week, as she swept and mopped and cooked and cleaned, Sofia's thoughts twisted and turned into ever tighter knots as she tried to make sense of her past. She remembered the man called Jack her brother had introduced her to. She pictured the two men painting together, teasing each other, teasing her. But her head ached as the images of him slipped away as quickly as they appeared, and tears spilled over as glimpses of a dark-haired boy skittered through her mind.

The following Monday, Sofia entered the kitchen to find Jack Bacon's large body and loud voice filling the room again. He was finishing a cup of tea and telling Mrs Whyte about the stylish new stoves being made by Metters, ones with controls on the front to regulate the cooktop's heat and a thermometer that was built into the oven door. He smiled at Sofia when she arrived and asked if she had any more cinnamon biscuits for him. She laughed, and from his cheeky smile, knew he was teasing her.

These days, she was feeling better. She'd found comfort in the memory of Jack and Andres painting together as well as other memories: the boys picking oranges in the orchard and she and her father setting up a series of trestle tables in the gallery. Although confusing, they made her life feel a little lighter, her mind a little clearer, and furthermore, some of her English words had returned.

'Sorry, no. But Esther and I, we made Anzac biscuits this morning.'

'So you did; I have already eaten a tray-full, and they are the best I've ever tasted!' Esther giggled and turned to Sofia.

'You can bet he says the same thing to all the housewives he delivers meat to. He probably scoffs down half a dozen morning-teas each day!'

'You know me too well!' Jack laughed. 'I'd better be heading off,' he said. 'One last delivery—over in South Yarra—and then I'll be done.'

The words were casual, the kind of details which were inconsequentially added to a million sentences every day. Details of no relevance to Mrs Whyte, or Esther or Sofia. He could have easily said, 'Well, I'll be off now; thanks for the cuppa,' or 'Nearly finished my deliveries, only one more stop!' But he hadn't. He'd added a detail, which could have been a reference to any of two dozen suburbs. But Jack's next stop was South Yarra, and the words ricocheted through Sofia's mind like a bullet trying to find its landing place, before exploding.

South Yarra! Copelen Street, South Yarra! It was a destination Sofia knew like her own name. She'd lived there! It was where Jack had taken her when he'd brought her to Australia.

For twenty-four hours, Sofia was consumed by the need to get to South Yarra. She was free to leave the refuge; Melrose House was no prison. Women came and went all the while. In fact, for some of the women, the day they left the confines of the refuge—ignoring the fear within them to take the brave step of walking the streets on their own—was considered cause for celebration, evidence they were almost ready to find a job, acquire their own accommodation and restart their lives afresh.

Copelen Street—14 Copelen Street. The address which had emerged from the depths of Sofia's mind repeated itself over and over as if calling her. She considered her options for getting there. A taxi would be the best. She had a few shillings in her purse. Phoning one would be easy. The phone number for Yellow Cabs sat by the handset in the hallway; it was referred to whenever Mrs Whyte sought transport to ferry women to their appointments with doctors and hospitals and lawyers.

The following morning, Sofia stood in the hallway wearing the nicest dress to be found in the pool of clothing available for the women's use, her handbag on her arm, some coins in her hands. Mrs Whyte had been curious about Sofia's sudden desire to travel to South Yarra, but happy to call the taxi for her.

'Are you sure you'll be right, Sofia?' she asked.

Sofia nodded, not altogether sure what the day might bring, but knowing Jack was at Copelen Street, along with Marian and William. The names of her in-laws had arisen from thin air, as did images of their faces. They were kind and caring people, and Sofia knew they'd all be at home, wondering where she was.

'I can come with you, if you like,' Mrs Whyte offered, but Sofia shook her head.

'No, gracias; I will be fine.'

'So it's Copelen Street, you say. Forty, Copelen Street?'

'No... four-teen...' The word was heavy on Sofia's lips. She wished Mrs Whyte understood Spanish.

'Well, in case it doesn't work out, here is our number. Keep it in your purse. If you need anything, call. I'll come and get you straight away, believe me.'

Tucking the fold of paper into her purse as instructed, Sofia nodded her thanks, and as the taxi drew into the kerb, Mrs Whyte walked out with her to meet it.

'Hi, Frank. I was hoping it would be you. You might remember Sofia—you brought her here a few weeks ago, remember? Late one night. It was raining…'

Sofia watched as Frank nodded, noting he was a man of many chins, all quivering in unison every time his large head moved. She listened as Mrs Whyte, ever in command, gave him instructions, and was glad for her assistance.

'I am wondering if you would run Sofia across the city. She tells me she wants to go to Copelen Street. Number fourteen. I am not sure what her plan is, but you'll keep an eye on her, won't you? We can never be too sure what sort of welcome our ladies might be returning to, unfortunately.'

'Absolutely, Mrs Whyte. If there is any trouble, I'll have her back here in a jiffy, don't you worry!'

Trouble? What on earth did Mrs Whyte mean? Not fear but excitement surged through Sofia at the thought of seeing Jack. Not the butcher, Jack, but her very own Jack with his smiling kind eyes. He must be terribly worried that she'd stayed away for so long!

'Now, Sofia, you look after yourself, and perhaps you might give me a call in a few days, and tell me how things are going for you. We are going to miss you, Esther and I. You have been a wonderful help here!'

'Gracias, yes, I will. Thank you for letting me stay.'

'I hope things work out well for you. You seem happy enough, so I guess you know what you are doing?' Mrs Whyte's words were as much a question as encouragement, and Sofia nodded. She was sure of what she was doing. She was going home to Jack, and knew once she was with him, all would be well.

As the taxi swung away from the kerb, Frank embarked on a steady stream of chatter, but Sofia found it difficult to focus on his words as there was so much activity beyond the windows of the vehicle to distract her. It seemed like a long time since she'd been outdoors, and it felt good to see the city streets again. She reached for the handle to open the window, hoping to get a better view.

'Are you alright?' Frank asked. 'It's a little chilly, don't you think! I don't mind, but I would hate you to catch a cold. Mrs Whyte would kill me if she thought I wasn't looking after you!'

His chortle made his chins quiver, and Sofia smiled back before leaning out to see the buildings. She recognized a few. The large yellow sign of the Commonwealth Bank, for one. She had an account there. An account holding a large sum of money, which Jack had insisted she keep for a rainy day. Not raining today, she thought, looking at the clear sky.

As they approached the corner of Flinders Street and Collins Street, Sofia looked to the left. It was a road she was familiar with, one leading up a hill, towards the large cathedral whose steeple towered above the buildings around it. Another image came to her mind: herself wheeling a pram along the very same road. Pushing it up the hill. An inexplicable shudder ran through her body, and she put her hand to her mouth and stifled a sob.

'Are you alright, love? You don't look so well. Are they tears? There, there! We can turn back if you like.'

By now the taxi had crossed the Swanson Street Bridge and was barely minutes from the turn into Copelen Street. Sofia shook her head and indicated with a wave for him to continue driving.

And with a turn to the left, and then to the right, they were gliding along the familiar tree-lined street. Sofia fought to control the pounding in her chest as she glimpsed the red-brick house with its large columns supporting the front porch she knew so well. As the taxi slowed, her view of the house became obscured by a vehicle resting at the curb. Passing it, Sofia looked into its windows, where a couple sat, their heads close together.

Breathing deeply, Sofia tried to make sense of the scene. Was it Jack? Jack and Margaret? Why were they holding each other?

'Here we are, love. Now, as Mrs Whyte said, I'll wait for you... You give me a wave if all is well, or a yell, if there is a problem, and I'll be right in.'

Sofia didn't answer him, instead straining to look into the window of the vehicle behind them. From it, a face lifted and gazed toward her. Not her smiling, happy Jack, but a Jack with a pale face, haggard and gaunt. At once, she was reminded of another moment, of his pain-filled eyes looking at her. It was then Sofia knew she'd been separated from Jack because something terrible had happened. Something she'd been responsible for.

'No... no...' Her hands gesticulated for Frank to drive forward. She tried to strangle the sobs rising from within, without success.

'Was that your husband there, love? Him with that woman? It's all a bit much, isn't it... Dear, dear... I daresay you are better off without him. Come on, let's get you back home to Mrs Whyte. You'll be right there.'

Sofia had very little recollection of the drive back to Melrose House, or being led to her room where she lay in her bed, tossing and turning in restless sleep or staring at the ceiling. Mrs Whyte tried to talk to her, telling her she was not alone; sometimes husbands did this, found other women. She assured Sofia she would help her to get legal support. From her words, Sofia knew Frank had told Mrs Whyte about the car they'd seen parked out the front of fourteen Copelen Street.

When after two days Sofia had not spoken in either Spanish or English, Mrs Whyte called Doctor Michael. Sitting at her bedside again, he asked her a series of questions, to which she had no answers.

Then he prescribed tablets, which Mrs Whyte was to give Sofia three times a day.

'It's her nerves,' the doctor said. 'Seeing her husband with another woman would be a shock to anyone. And now she's stranded here in a foreign country, far away from her people. As long as she's sleeping and eating, she should get better. Are her moods alright? No outbursts or anything? No violence?'

'No, not at all. I am just worried about the constant weeping,' she heard Mrs Whyte reply. Sofia was surprised; she hadn't realised she'd been crying.

'And you are happy for her to stay, you said?'

'Of course. Sofia is no trouble. In actual fact, she is a great help. Let's leave her here for the time being and see how she goes. I'd much rather she was in here with us than see her admitted to Kew.'

'Truly, you are a gem, Mrs Whyte. What these women would do without you, I don't know.'

CHAPTER 7

O ver the next two days, although Mrs Whyte tried to encourage Sofia to rise from the bed, she barely moved. She had a puzzle to complete, a string of disconnected memories, and she felt sure that if she rose from the mattress before she put them together, the pieces would scatter, and she'd have to start all over again.

These new memories revealed Jack was not the young man Andres had introduced her to, but rather he was an older version, a man with fine lines around his eyes, a tanned face and a body strong from working outdoors. She also knew they'd left her home in Spain to live in Australia with Jack's parents, and afterwards, they'd lived in the bush, in a little cabin, with the others, and it was there she'd had a child. The small dark-haired boy she'd occasionally glimpsed. Where was he? Sofia had no idea, but was sure something terrible had happened.

Her memories of Margaret were vague; she'd been the girl in Jack's sketchbook all those years ago, and now she was back again. Only she was no longer in the sketchbook, but in Jack's arms. So many gaps. So confusing. Thinking about it, trying to make sense of it all, made Sofia's head spin. In the end, she knew the pain that filled her was best relieved by being busy. Arising from her bed, she went to the kitchen.

Flour. Sieve, shake, lightly tap on the side of the bowl. Add eggs and milk, stirring carefully. Knead, mix, blend, rub. Wash pots, check the oven, sweep the floor. For as long as she kept busy, Sofia managed to deflect her thoughts from their relentless but futile pursuit to solve the puzzle of her life.

Nothing, however, offered relief from the gut-wrenching hollow sensation running to Sofia's core, that had developed since she'd made the trip to Copelen Street, and which now accompanied her from the moment she woke until she closed her eyes each night. And it was there, Jack's sorrow filled eyes swam before her. *Andres*, she cried, her arms reaching out, seeking consolation from her brother in the moments where wakefulness and sleep blurred. *Andres, move your knees and your elbows and let me lie against you.* How glad she was to have a twin. Although their mama had died when they were born, at least she and Andres had each other, and together, they had Papa.

As the days passed, Sofia became consumed by her memories of her home in Spain. Vivid images of the orchard overlooking the sea and the magnolia tree in the centre of the courtyard returned. She could smell the scent of orange blossom and hear the laughter in her papa's voice as he tasted her marinated olives and suggested she'd oversalted them. How he loved to tease her! But Sofia never minded because she knew for all of his teasing, he was very proud of her. Proud of her efforts in taking on the family's cooking at such a young age, and for the way she'd cared for the art gallery, rehanging the paintings to display them to advantage, and procuring the works of local artisans to be sold to tourists. And even though Sofia didn't paint, her insightfulness had often impressed him, and he frequently included her when he and Andres discussed their work.

When Sofia glanced at the open newspaper on the backroom table, an advertisement caught her attention, and she knew it was no accident. *Last Chance to Travel to London for £35,* she read. The P&O Cruise Company was offering tickets on the *Strathnaver*, departing Port Phillip Bay on Friday. Interested parties should contact the Collins Street office immediately.

Spain to London to Australia. Sofia had made that journey before. *Australia to London to Spain* would be easy. Surely, this advertisement had been placed to beckon her home.

Yes, of course she must go; once she was home, the aching void in her soul would be filled. There, she'd marinate the olives and make almond cake for Papa and Andres. She and Papa would work in the garden, and afterwards the men would paint, and she would attend to the gallery.

Thinking about her plan, Sofia was excited. Now she had a purpose, where before she had none. She tore the advertisement from the paper and considered her next move. She would need to go in to the city soon, if she was to purchase a ticket on the Strathnaver. While Sofia considered telling Mrs Whyte about her decision to return to Spain, a part of her resisted, sure she'd be discouraged from making the journey.

As it emerged, the following morning Mrs Whyte had other things on her mind. Mavis, the solicitor's wife, had returned to Melrose House after breakfast, with not one, but two black eyes and a nose so swollen, she could barely breathe. Additionally, she had a bald patch on one side of her scalp, and a faded yellow discolouration down her left temple. Sofia assisted Mrs Whyte as she attended to Mavis' wounds.

'He could have killed you, damn it! I told you this has got to stop.' Mrs Whyte said.

'He loves me…' The words were muffled through Mavis' blocked nose and the tears streaming down her face. Mrs Whyte asked Sofia to help by squeezing the bridge of Mavis' nose, in a bid to staunch the bleeding that was leaving bright red splashes on the kitchen floor as well as on Mavis' dress.

'Oh, he loves you, does he? Mrs Whyte said. 'Is this what you call love? Esther, get us the mirror, will you please? Let's show Mavis exactly how much her Harold loves her!'

Sofia continued wiping the blood from the floor while Mavis sat on a chair in the kitchen, allowing the extent of Harold's love to be assessed. She knew from the curses flowing from Mrs Whyte's tongue, that today she was furious. Furious at Harold for his beatings and furious at Mavis because she kept going back for them. Furious at the government, whose laws said if a woman left her husband, she'd be abandoning her children and her security. At the publicans who happily served pints of beer to a drunken violent man, fuelling his temper and dulling his reason. At the church who told women it was a sin to leave their husbands with whom they'd vowed to stay 'til death did them part', and at the priests who insisted women had no alternative but to remain faithful to their promise to 'love, honour and obey' the abusive men they'd married. Mrs Whyte was furious with the police, so quick to arrest a man for striking another in the street, but averting their eyes to those same men when they beat their women and children within an inch of their lives.

When the bleeding refused to stop, Mrs Whyte decided Mavis needed treatment at the hospital. 'And after that, Mavis my dear, we are going to pay a visit to Sergeant Davis. Let him make what he will of your black eyes and broken nose'.

On and on, she went, berating the multitude of systems who conspired to protect men and fail women, and Sofia was sure if Mrs Whyte could, she'd have marched Mavis through every institution through to Parliament House and the high courts to display the indisputable testimony of the crimes far too many men inflicted upon their wives. Sofia knew the sergeant, his men and anyone within earshot were about to get the fullness of Mrs Whyte's fury.

Although Sofia felt dreadful for Mavis, and disturbed to see Mrs

Whyte so very angry, her decision to remain quiet about her plans for the day seemed sensible; Mrs Whyte had far more important things to be thinking about than Sofia making a trip to the city. It was after nine when the women left the house and at ten AM, dressed in a clean frock, Sofia made her own call for a taxi then stood outside Melrose House, waiting for it to arrive.

It wasn't Frank who drove the cab today, but rather a small, dark-haired man with a friendly manner. He leapt out and, with a gallant sweep, opened the door for Sofia. Her instructions for him were straightforward: she'd rehearsed the words over and over in her mind. To board the ship, she needed only two things, money and a ticket, and today she intended to get both.

'Please sir, can you take me to the Commonwealth Bank in Flinders Street?'

The drive into the city took barely fifteen minutes, and as the taxi drew to the curb, Sofia thrust a slip of paper before him, showing the address of her next destination: the P&O Cruise Company's office in Collins Street. She was disappointed when he shook his head.

'Sorry, Ma'am,' he said. 'I am not allowed to wait here. But when you've completed your business at the bank, walk down the road— there, you will find a dozen taxis, any of whom would be pleased to take you.' Sofia looked at where he was pointing and was relieved to see, barely one hundred yards away, a row of cabs awaiting customers.

The creak of the glass doors sounded loud to Sofia, as did the sound of her footsteps echoing through the large, empty space as she approached the long counter that separated clients from the tellers. Through the glass of one of the cubicles, Sofia could see a young woman with a thick black fringe who was examining her fingernails.

'I'd like to withdraw two hundred pounds, please.' Sofia's request seemed to startle the girl into wakefulness.

'Oh... ah... Have you got your passbook with you?' the girl asked, her alert eyes scanning Sofia's face with interest.

'Sí, yes... here.'

'Good-oh. Nonetheless, I'll have to get the manager for this.' The girl vanished before Sofia had time to respond.

The manager! Really—this had never happened before. A tremor of anxiety flickered through Sofia. Was the manager going to deny her *her* money? For it was hers. More than once, Sofia had come to this very branch and withdrawn money to buy a present or shoes or a winter coat for herself, and never before had her request been questioned. Certainly, those had been small amounts, five pounds or perhaps ten. Two hundred pounds was a large sum, but she was travelling across the world.

The manager introduced himself as Mr Stevens and invited Sofia into his office. As she walked with him, she sensed the eyes of the teller watching her. Sofia felt self-conscious. The dress she wore was green and slightly oversized, for the yellow one she preferred was in the dirty laundry basket, and her brown shoes—also from the 'communal property', as Mrs Whyte referred to it—fitted well enough, but in no way matched her dress or handbag.

'Good morning, Mrs Tomlinson. Thank you for seeing me. I won't keep you a minute. You wish to withdraw two hundred pounds today, is that correct?'

'Yes, Mr Stevens, thank you.'

'And do you have some identification beyond the passbook? A formality, of course, but for amounts over one hundred pounds, we like to have proof of identification. Perhaps a utility bill or some such?'

Identification? Trying to control her breathing, Sofia rummaged through her bag, doubting she carried anything remotely like a utility bill. There was a comb, a neatly folded handkerchief and a small change purse. She opened a side pocket and found two slips of paper. One was an old dry-cleaning bill for Jack's work jacket, the other the note Mrs Whyte had given her recently, with the telephone number of Melrose House printed on it.

Still searching for a document to please the bank manager, Sofia opened a second pocket, where she found a small purple booklet. Of course, it was her passport. It had been a permanent fixture in this handbag since she'd first arrived in Australia, along with her bank passbook. Jack had told her to keep it close in case they ever found themselves in a situation where her nationality was questioned.

'Let's have a look at those couple of papers, Mrs Tomlinson. I'd say they'll do us.'

Sofia passed over the documents on the table in front of her, and watched as Mr Stevens carefully filled out the withdrawal form, ticking a box saying identification had been sighted. After saying 'So this is your phone number?' to which Sofia nodded, he jotted down the digits.

'I don't wish to pry, Mrs Tomlinson, but you are alone... Mr Tomlinson has not come in with you today?'

Sofia stared at the manager and inhaling deeply fought down the urge to weep which had been steadily rising along with a dozen memories of Jack, ever since she'd entered his office. Words failed her, for his question was like sandpaper grating against her heart. Tears welled up as she shook her head.

'No, estoy aqui solo.'

'Sorry, Mrs Tomlinson. I don't speak Spanish!' Mr Stevens laughed as though he'd made a joke. 'However, two hundred pounds is a large amount of money to be carrying about in your handbag. Are you sure you'll be alright with it?'

'Sí. Yes, I will be fine.' Thankfully, Sofia's English had returned; however, her voice seemed to have vanished, for the words came out in barely a whisper.

'How would you like the notes, Mrs Tomlinson?'

Sofia shook her head, unsure of his meaning.

'Let's say I give you four five-pound notes for your purse, and we put the remainder in an envelope which you can put in your handbag?

Tuck it away in one of those side pockets. It should be safe there…
What do you say?'

'Fifty pounds for my purse, please.'

'Of course. As you wish, Mrs Tomlinson,' he said, adjusting the
numbers he'd recorded on the withdrawal form.

To Sofia's relief, Mr Stevens returned his pen to its stand and
pushed back his chair. The inquisition was over. He stood, assisted her
from her chair, and walked her to the door.

'Okay, Mrs Tomlinson. Give this note to the teller; see Patricia over
there—she'll get you sorted. You take care now, won't you?'

'Sí, gracias.' Sofia gave him what she hoped was a calm smile, but
even so she felt his eyes upon her as she walked towards the counter
and passed the form to the woman.

'All sorted now, are we, ma'am? Very good… You'll be able to buy
a few pretty frocks with this little stash, I'd say!'

Accepting the envelope filled with the notes, Sofia replied,
'Gracias.' She followed Mr Stevens' recommendation, tucking the
envelope into her handbag alongside her passbook and passport, then
folding the ten-pound notes, she placed them in her purse. It was a lot
of money, certainly, and dividing it this way seemed sensible.

Sofia stepped out into the sunshine, walked to the taxi rank, and
minutes later, she was set outside the P&O Travel Agency.

Already three booths were occupied with people seeking travel advice,
and Sofia hoped the advertised tickets were not all taken. A young man
greeted her, and she handed the now well-worn newspaper clipping to
him. He studied it and nodded.

'So, madam, you would like a berth on the *Strathnaver*, leaving for
London on the thirteenth of July—tomorrow?'

'Sí, gracia. I'd like to go to Spain,' Sofia replied.

'Spain! It's really much too late for me to organise your passage
through to Spain; you will have to make those arrangements once you

are in England. For now, we'll just get you over to London, if that's alright. Come and have a seat, here, while I jot down a few details. Lucky you! There are barely a dozen tickets left, and at a good price too, I must say!'

'Gracias…thank you, sir.'

'So, have you got your passport with you?'

If it hadn't been for her search for identification in the bank, Sofia would not have remembered the passport tucked into the concealed pocket of her handbag. Confidently she reached for it; reassured such a coincidence could only mean she was destined to take this trip.

'Hmmm,' the man muttered as he flicked through the booklet before turning it over in his hands. 'I don't see too many of these! Spanish—very well, now for your ticket. I need to record a few details and then you'll be cruising, so to speak.'

All it took was ten minutes for the paperwork to be completed, Sofia to add her signature, the ticket to be drawn up and inserted into a cardboard fold, and the transaction of thirty-five pounds to take place.

'Now, madam, you realise it is an early departure—you'll need to be at the docks by seven AM. Will you manage? It's very important we get everybody on board by nine so the ship can be on its way. I can't promise they would wait for late arrivals.'

'Sí, I'll be there. I will catch a taxi.'

'Very good. Here are a few pamphlets you might like to look at. A bit of general information about P&O's trips, and also some information on travel to France and Spain you might find helpful. Bon voyage and all that! I wish it were me… I'd love to be out of this office and seeing the world!'

'Gracias, señor. Thank you for your assistance!'

As she returned along Swanson Street, Sofia felt dazed. She could barely believe she held a ticket which would take her back to Spain, or at least nearly there. London was more than halfway, she concluded. Once there, she could be home in a matter of days.

CHAPTER 8

The following morning, when Sofia rose from her bed and glanced out of her window, the last of the stars still twinkled in the breaking dawn sky. Ten minutes to five, the clock in the kitchen told her. It was too early for Esther to be up; she usually arrived to light the fire in the kitchen stove at six AM, and Mrs Whyte rarely appeared before seven.

Methodically, Sofia laid out the garments she'd been wearing over the last few weeks. They were hers, but not hers. In her first week at Melrose House, Mrs Whyte had shown Sofia the collection of dresses, underwear, petticoats and shoes kept in the storeroom for emergencies, all neatly folded on the shelves which were beside other shelves, ones Sofia always ignored. The shelves holding stacks of snow-white nappies, tiny singlets, baby nighties, knitted garments and piles of children's wear. When Sofia first arrived, she'd been reluctant to wear the dresses in this room, sure they belonged to someone else. But Mrs Whyte had been insistent.

'No, Sofia, take whatever you like. These clothes are for anyone who needs them. I keep them here because, like you, many women arrive here unexpectedly.'

And when on the previous evening Sofia had collected two more dresses for her journey, she'd found a small suitcase amongst the shelves of shoes. She was sure that, like the other garments, Mrs Whyte would be glad to see the case prove useful to someone. Taking it, she'd returned to her room and packed her belongings.

Now, she removed the sheets and pillowcases from her bed and took them to the laundry. Returning, the kitchen clock revealed it was five forty-five; time to phone the taxi.

Before making the call, Sofia returned to her room and emptied her bag of the pamphlets and dockets she'd accumulated from the travel agent the previous day. She then checked that her ticket, passport, passbook and envelope of cash were safely stored in the side pocket.

As she sorted out the documents, Sofia was torn, wanting dearly to wake Mrs Whyte and tell her she was leaving and to thank her for the kindness she'd shown. But she didn't; she knew taking a trip to Copelen Street, and even into the city as she'd done the previous day, was one thing, but to venture across the world, was altogether different. And having set her mind on going home, she couldn't risk being stopped by anyone, including Mrs Whyte.

Instead, taking a ten-pound note from her purse, Sofia set it upon the folded blankets she'd placed on the end of her bed, where she knew it would be found by either Esther or Mrs Whyte later in the morning.

Next, she called for a taxi. Then quietly she opened the front door, walked to the front gate and waited. She listened to the melodious morning song of magpies and the sounds of bottles clinking to the sway of the Clydesdales pulling the milkman's cart along the street. Her taxi arrived to collect her within minutes, and rapidly navigated the quiet streets, delivering Sofia to Port Melbourne's docks at six twenty-five.

PART II

The *Strathnaver*

CHAPTER 9

*D*espite the early hour, Sofia was not the first passenger to arrive at Station Pier. Dozens, perhaps even hundreds, of people were present, resting beside their portmanteaus, valises and hatboxes in readiness for their voyage. Others walked up and down the length of the pier, gazing at the enormous ship. Already its drawbridge was lowered, although the chain across its entry prevented the Melbourne passengers from boarding.

Sofia approached a small office labelled 'Embarkation', the place where she knew her ticket would be checked before she could board the vessel. She sat on a small bench and looked at the upper reaches of the ship, where she saw movement. On closer examination, she realised a number of people stood along the rails, looking towards the city from their vantage point on the high deck.

For every minute that passed, perhaps a hundred more people were added to the crowd on the dock, and by seven-thirty, it felt like thousands of people were gathered, all excited about the voyage ahead. Nonetheless, Sofia might as well have been alone, for she felt utterly disconnected from the laughing and jostling all around her. She didn't feel lonely; rather, she didn't feel anything as she sat there. Merely a person in a line, waiting for the small window to open, her ticket in hand, ready to be presented and hence gain permission to board the ship and be on her way.

Twenty-five minutes later, with her ticket stamped, Sofia followed the instructions of the porter, heading up the gangplank where two stewards greeted her with warm smiles. She declined their offer to help with her bag, but accepted the pamphlet they gave her which outlined the layout of the ship and services she might enjoy.

'Ma'am, if you would take the first staircase, see? Go up three flights to B Deck and then walk towards the front of the ship. Your cabin is B201. You will find it at the end of the corridor—right beside the dining room.'

Sofia tried to mirror their smiles, but felt it come out as a grimace. All she wanted was to find her cabin and be alone, away from the excited bustle of people clamouring to board and explore the ship.

The stewards' directions proved straightforward, and finding her cabin, Sofia placed her case in the cupboard and looked around. The room was pleasant enough, with a small bed, wash basin, chest of drawers and a writing desk. Returning her attention to the door, she placed the 'Do Not Disturb' sign in the slot provided, and closing it, was pleased at how the sounds beyond were instantly muted.

The room proved restful, and Sofia closed her eyes, sinking into a light sleep, only to be awakened by the sound of movement outside her door. She waited for it to subside and then opened her door. As she'd thought, lunch was being served.

Emerging from the cabin, Sofia sat at the small table near the kitchen door and positioned herself so her back faced the majority of diners. Within minutes of being seated, an attentive waiter appeared and offered suggestions from the menu, but Sofia settled for a sandwich, which she ate quickly before returning to her room.

Over the following days, Sofia remained in her room, resting on her bed and only emerging for meals. Thankfully, she usually found the table she liked unoccupied. Other diners seemed to prefer tables by the windows with ocean views or those in a ring around the dance floor.

And although the waiter—usually the same one—entreated her to try some of the chef's special meals on offer, Sofia never varied in her choice.

For breakfast, she had tomato juice, buttered toast and a poached egg. For lunch she had a sandwich, usually something simple: ham and pickles or tomato and cheese. If the waiter was persistent, she could be persuaded to try chicken or turkey, or perhaps a small salad. Any such deviation was due to the waiter's enthusiasm rather than Sofia's interest; food held no appeal to her, particularly as she was now victim to a mild but constant queasiness caused by the ship's motion. Her evening meal was always the same: roast lamb or beef or pork, roast pumpkin and potato, and a serving of green vegetables.

Although some aspects of the ocean crossing reminded Sofia of a past journey, she noticed differences, too. On the previous trip, the ship had forged eastward towards the rising sun, while this time it moved towards a setting sun. Then, her days had been filled with the entertainment of deck games or listening to those passengers with musical skills who'd provided small concerts. On this journey, passengers had no need to make their own entertainment, for a constant stream of music filtered through the ship. In the evenings professional singers, three-piece bands, and even a small orchestra provided entertainment and with much laughter and loud voices, passengers congregated on the dance floor to sway to the music.

And on that past trip, Sofia knew she hadn't spent her days in the cabin, but rather she'd walked the decks in the company of a man with a friendly face and a cheerful manner. Jack, of course. Jack, who'd been excited because he was taking her to Australia, and who day and night would tell her about the things they'd see and do when they arrived.

After the third day, with a mild dose of sea-sickness persisting, Sofia adopted a habit of walking to the front of the ship and standing at the rail for a few minutes to inhale the fresh air before returning to her room. As she stood there, she'd say to herself, 'Australia to London,

London to Paris, Paris to Spain.' In less than two months, she'd see Papa and Andres!

~

'Miss—or is it Madam? Do you mind if I join you?'

It was dinnertime, and the tables were full. Sofia had been a little late to the dining room, for she'd slept heavily through the afternoon and the sky had been grey when she'd woken. It had been a relief to find her small table remained vacant.

She looked up to find a man frowning apologetically.

'All the tables are full... I should have come earlier.'

'Sí.' Sofia shrugged. Why should she mind?

Seating himself, he smiled at her. 'It's very busy this evening. I think everyone claimed their seats early, ready for the concert tonight. I hear there are some very good performers.'

Sofia returned the smile he offered and looked around at the people seated nearby. The women's hair-dos and dresses were more fancy than usual. Many of the men wore suits, or, like the stranger opposite her, a smart jacket and necktie. More than one was dressed in military uniform.

Sofia wore her yellow dress. It was one Mrs Whyte had given her when she'd first arrived at Melrose House. She had others, but this was the most comfortable, and every second day she washed it in the laundry situated halfway along the hall. After wringing it, she hung it in the airing cupboard, where the warmth of the large water heaters had it dry in no time.

'Marcus Edmund,' he offered, extending his hand towards her.

'Sofia,' she replied as she accepted it, surprised at how hoarse her voice sounded; but then again, she'd barely spoken since she'd boarded the ship.

'Pleased to meet you, Sofia. How are you enjoying the journey so far?'

'Good, thank you.' The question disconcerted her. She was happy enough to share the table, but really, she had no wish to converse.

'Are you travelling to visit relatives, or returning home?'

'Home. Home to Malaga.'

'Southern Spain, really? You do have quite a journey ahead of you!'

Sofia wasn't sure how to reply, so she didn't.

'How is sea life agreeing with you? I haven't seen you out and about very often.'

Very often? The words insinuated the man had seen her before.

'It is alright. I will be glad to be home.'

'You are right there.'

Their conversation was interrupted by a man's voice reverberating through the dining room's speaker system, asking if they were all ready for a night of jiving and swinging, to which cheering and clapping broke out. Sofia pushed her chair back; it was time for her to go.

'You're leaving?' Marcus said.

'Sí, good evening.'

That night, Sofia slept poorly, and when she finally awoke, the sun was higher than usual. She assumed she'd missed breakfast, but wasn't worried, for she felt too ill to eat. Hugging a pillow to her stomach, she closed her eyes. When she next awoke, sounds of movement in the corridor indicated it was meal time once again. Deciding that food might make her feel better, she rose, dressed and went to the dining room.

'Oh, there you are.' It was Marcus.

'Yes, here I am.' Today her voice sounded different. Light, as if she were joking. It was as though another woman had invaded her body and was speaking. Someone able to act polite and friendly while the real Sofia remained hidden deep within herself, watching from afar.

'I didn't see you in the dining room this morning. May I join you again?'

'Certainly, if you wish.'

Sofia noticed his hair, how it was a little grey at the temples, and she watched as his hands constantly reached up to touch his glasses. As the minutes passed, she saw his eyes upon her and watched his mouth move, but the words he spoke seemed to fall short, landing somewhere between them, not quite reaching her, and she didn't have the energy to try to capture them. Nonetheless, she fixed what she hoped was a pleasant smile on her face as she finished her sandwich and then excused herself, leaving him to finish his meal.

Perhaps it was two days later, Sofia wasn't sure, when Marcus asked if he might join her again. She stared back at him, wondering if he planned to make this a habit.

'It's okay. We don't have to talk. We can sit here in silence. No worries. By the way, my name is Marcus. Marcus Edmunds, in case you had forgotten.'

Sofia hadn't forgotten, and decided she didn't mind the company. She listened as he told her he was a doctor and explained how he'd been in Australia for four months; he'd been visiting a colleague, a man who'd trained alongside him in London and who now worked at the Ararat Asylum, which was northwest of Melbourne. The place was quite dreadful, he told her. Its doctors practised very dated methods of care which did nothing to improve their patients' lives. To add to its horror, it also housed J Ward—a division of Pentridge, Victoria's largest jail: a locked and heavily guarded unit for the criminally insane.

Sofia didn't react to his comments, and he kept speaking.

'It was interesting to see, of course, and the setting was quite beautiful. My friend encouraged me to visit there because he thought a senior doctor from London might persuade staff to adjust their methods of treatment. I doubt it, though. They all seemed very set in their ways.'

Sofia listened politely, glad that there was no need for her to contribute, for the man had plenty to say. After he'd finished describing the hospital at Ararat, he asked if she'd travelled through inland Victoria. Taking no notice when she didn't reply, he continued with an account of visiting the mines around Ballarat and his failed attempts to pan for gold.

At the end of the meal, Marcus invited Sofia to walk on the deck with him for a few minutes. She hadn't walked for days, and would have preferred to return to her cabin, but he was insistent, promising they would not walk too far. 'I feel sure that if you join me, you'll feel much better.'

'But I feel fine,' she replied, wondering how he could know she'd been feeling seasick Even as the words left her, Sofia knew he was right; a walk in the fresh air would make her feel better, and so she accepted his offer.

As they walked, Marcus asked Sofia about herself, but she had little to share other than she was anxious to return to Malaga and be with her father and brother. He turned the conversation to her Spanish origins and asked how she'd come to live in Australia.

His question rekindled memories of the previous journey, where she hadn't been alone.

'Sorry, but it was a long time ago. I don't remember it well,' Sofia attempted to wipe away the tears which pooled in her eyes, blurring her vision. She didn't feel women crying on ship decks was acceptable.

'No? That is perfectly normal, Sofia. Sometimes I forget what I ate for breakfast, so don't apologize. And furthermore, don't you go worrying about those tears. People cry all the time, for all sorts of reasons. It's quite common.'

Accepting the handkerchief Marcus offered, Sofia dabbed at her eyes and nodded. She wasn't so sure he was right, but she appreciated his efforts to appease her.

CHAPTER 10

*A*s the week wore on, Marcus frequently joined Sofia for meals and a walk, and she discovered a sense of peace when she was with him. He was undemanding and happy to follow her lead. If she felt like talking, they did; if she preferred silence, then he didn't pressure her to speak.

Time spent listening to him chatter about the places he'd worked and his home north of London, where his sister trained horses, offered a distraction from her bleak thoughts and the confused images tumbling in her mind. And while some of the passengers looked at her strangely or even approached to ask if she was okay, Marcus barely reacted when she cried, or when she spoke in Spanish, as she knew she often did. Nor did he seem bothered when she couldn't hear his words or find her own to answer him.

After one particularly companionable walk along the deck where they'd stopped at the front of the ship to watch the roll of the ocean and Sofia had even laughed when a seagull had landed on the rail within a few feet, Marcus again asked Sofia about her decision to leave Spain. She tried to remember and shared her scattered recollections of the voyage she knew she'd taken in the company of Jack. Her replies prompted further questions about her life in Australia. Where did she live? Where was Jack now? The questions made Sofia's head hurt, and tears to threaten.

'Jack is with Margaret.' Sofia could offer no explanation, for she'd forgotten why. However, from the sense of dread that accompanied many of the memories that skitted around the periphery of her mind, she knew something awful had happened.

There were frequent periods where Sofia felt her mind steeped in a heavy grey fog, through which the world felt distant. At such times, although she could see Marcus' mouth move, she could barely comprehend his words, nor reply. One morning, after an extensive period of silence following Marcus' attempts at speaking to her, she tried to apologise, but he brushed her concerns away.

'It's fine, Sofia. Some people need to chatter constantly, others are happiest when there is quiet and they can hear themselves think. You do not need to apologise to me.'

'Gracias,' she replied, and wondered if she should tell him she could never hear herself think, so full were her thoughts of things which made no sense at all.

~

In her second week on the *Strathnaver*, Sofia had finished her sandwich when one of the ship's stewards approached her.

'Good afternoon, Mrs Tomlinson. I am sorry to interrupt you, but the captain has asked if I could take you to his office. He would like to speak with you about a matter. It should only take a few minutes of your time.'

Startled, Sofia shook her head. Her mind froze in a paroxysm of anxiety. Had she done something wrong?

'Madam, please don't be concerned. The captain has received a telegram, the contents of which he needs to share with you. It happens frequently. I am quite sure it does not bear bad news.'

'Is everything alright?' Sofia was relieved to hear Marcus' voice from behind her right shoulder. His words held an edge she did not recognize.

'I beg your pardon, sir. I hadn't realised you were travelling with Mrs Tomlinson.'

'Well, I am not travelling *with* Mrs Tomlinson, but I am her friend. Sofia, would you like me to help you with anything?'

'Perhaps Mrs Tomlinson might permit you to join her in the captain's office, sir. There is a matter he needs to discuss.'

'Would you like me to come along, Sofia?'

She nodded, and standing, took the arm Marcus offered and they followed the steward through the ship's passages until they stood outside a panelled door.

At the steward's light tap, the door opened and the tall man ushered them in with a sweep of his hand.

'Thank you for coming, ma'am. I am sorry to interrupt your day. Please, have a seat. How are you? Is everything to your satisfaction?'

Still confused by his request to see her, Sofia had no words in reply to the captain's barrage of questions.

'I think, if I may speak on your behalf, Sofia, we could say your journey is going quite well?' Marcus turned to her as if to confirm his statement before continuing to the captain, 'Mrs Tomlinson is eager to get home to her family in Spain, but she has no complaints about the service she is receiving on board, Captain.'

A good reply, Sofia thought. Marcus had summed up her feelings well, and the captain seemed pleased with his answer, too.

'Very good. The reason I have asked you here, Mrs Tomlinson, is because I have received a telegram from Melbourne. This is quite common—every day we get messages on behalf of our passengers. This one is a little different, though, as it has come from the Victorian Police Department.'

Sofia jolted at the captain's words. Memories of a grim-looking man in a blue uniform sitting across from her at a large table came to mind. A man with a large notebook, asking her dozens of questions to which she'd had no answers.

Sofia's throat closed as she struggled to inhale, but couldn't. Instead she panted, short, sharp breaths that made her head spin.

'Mrs Tomlinson, please, it's alright. There is no need to be concerned. Can I get you some water?' The captain's voice sounded like it came from across the room, even though he was sitting right before her. Marcus sounded much closer.

'Sofia, take a deep breath and count to ten. You will be alright. You are safe here. Would you like to take my hand?'

Sofia grasped the hand Marcus held towards her and did her best to follow his instructions: 'Now, close your eyes and inhale slowly. Carefully breathe out, in time with my counting—one... two...' All the way to ten. Soon she felt her mind clear and her muscles relax.

'Perhaps you could tell us what the telegram says?' Marcus asked, turning his attention back to the captain as if nothing had happened.

'Err, yes. Mrs Tomlinson, are you sure you are feeling up to this? Let me assure you, it's not bad news.'

Sofia nodded.

'It has been sent by a Sergeant O'Neil, and he is requesting you return a message to your husband. It would seem Mr Tomlinson is very worried about you.'

Mr Tomlinson! Jack! Images of him returned to her. Not those of him and Andres painting together at the finca, nor glimpses of a time past when she'd travelled across the ocean with him to Australia. These were a return of the terrifying memories of his drawn and haggard face contorted with anguish; his eyes filled with sadness; a tiny box set out in the front of a roomful of people, and a stranger speaking words of eternal life and how the Lord said, *Suffer little children, and forbid them not, to come unto me: for of such is the kingdom of heaven.* She saw his face looking toward her from where he sat in the vehicle with Margaret. Jack and Margaret. Margaret and Jack. Of course, he would find consolation in Margaret's strong arms. Sofia's own arms were not strong, nor were they safe.

'I can't go back,' she said in a whisper.

'You don't want to go back to Australia?' Marcus asked. 'What about your husband? What are we to say to him?'

Sofia shook her head. Marcus conferred with the captain. They spoke of her husband and another woman, the shock Sofia must have experienced when she'd learned of the relationship, what reply might be sent to the scoundrel. Marcus then turned to her.

'Sofia, what message would you like to send so we can reassure your husband that you're safe? Shall we tell him you're returning to your family?'

In a flash of clarity, words came to Sofia, that emerged as a whisper.

'Tell him going to Australia was a terrible mistake. I should never have left Spain. Margaret will be good for him. I wish for him to be happy.'

The captain nodded, but his expression was dubious, and again he conferred with Marcus, whose sympathy filled eyes never left her.

Unable to bear his pity, Sofia turned her gaze to the window. Just outside, a seagull scampered along the ship's railing. Its image blurred as tears filled her eyes and she felt the soft fabric of a handkerchief being pushed into her hand.

'At least this man will know his wife is safe and where to look if he wants to find her,' she heard Marcus say. 'Seems he's got another woman in his sights, though. All very well for him to be worried about Sofia now. If only he knew the damage he's done!'

Sofia shook her head and fresh tears fell. No. It wasn't like that, she thought. Marcus had it wrong.

Marcus did not mention the discussion in the captain's office again. Instead, when they walked on the deck after the meals they shared, he questioned her about Malaga. Sofia enjoyed these conversations where memories of her childhood seemed as if they were only yesterday: long days playing in the sun with Andres, afternoons working in the orchard with their father, cooking biscuits in the kitchen for their afternoon tea, and then calling Andres and Papa from their studio to join her in the courtyard. As she described these events, Sofia's excitement at returning home increased. She couldn't wait to see her gallery again, to fix the paintings on its walls—she knew her father would not do it in the way she liked. And again, she would visit the craftsmen and women who'd once supplied the gallery with their products. It would be good to see them again.

Sofia did not always enjoy Marcus' company, though. Sometimes his conversation became probing and inquisitive, and he'd want to know more about her life in Australia: her marriage. Each time this happened, her breathing quickened and her mind froze. Sometimes she'd feel his questions coming and deflect them. 'I'm cold now. I think I'll go inside.' Or, without speaking, she'd rise and walk to the front of the ship. There she looked towards the horizon, willing land to appear so she could continue her journey to the place where she knew peace awaited.

And of course, land did appear from time to time, as the *Strathnaver* made stops at Aden, Port Said, Naples and Toulon, where passengers left the ship for a few hours, returning with their arms full of souvenirs and their voices lively with excited chatter.

Despite Marcus' encouragement for Sofia to leave the ship at these stops, she always said no, preferring to remain in her room, glad for the silence the ship offered when everybody left.

Finally, the captain announced they would arrive in London within the week, filling Sofia with excitement. She was almost home! All she needed was a ticket to travel to Spain.

CHAPTER 11

*A*s the *Strathnaver* navigated the English Channel, hugging the coastline northward on its final leg of the journey, Sofia became agitated by a turn in Marcus' conversation.

'What are your plans when we arrive in London, Sofia? Do you have somewhere to stay?'

'I will be okay. I will go to a motel, and then I will find a travel agent,' she told him, remembering how simple it had been to purchase her ticket for this journey.

'So, you plan to cross the Channel? Travel to Paris and then on to Spain? Where will you stay while you are in Paris?'

'No—I mean yes, I will go to Paris, and then I will go to Spain.'

'But I think you might need to stay in Paris, if only for a night. You should stay near the station. From which station does the Malaga train depart?'

The questions were needling, demanding details Sofia had not thought about. It was enough for her to remember to wash her clothes each day and to walk to the dining room for her meals. In response, Sofia's irritation grew. She knew where she was going, and she was sure a travel agency like the one in Melbourne would make the arrangements for her, but Marcus' probing made the task of travelling to Spain feel overwhelming.

'I will stay with my aunt. She is in Paris.' Even as she said the words, Sofia knew they were a lie. Her aunt had left Paris years earlier, and she had no idea where she was.

'Very well, then. Have you heard from your brother and father? Are they expecting you?'

'No... but of course they will be expecting me. They will wonder where I have been all of this time.'

Sofia wanted Marcus to stop asking questions that made her confused and tongue-tied. *Why was he so anxious to know about her plans?*

'Do you realise Spain is not altogether safe for travel? I've been listening to the news reports on the radio in the ship's lounge each evening. There is less fighting at present, but still, tensions between the Nationalists and the Republicans are high. In fact, there is a lot of unrest all through Europe, with the German Chancellor, Hitler, making threats on Czechoslovakia. Do you think you might delay your journey for a few months?'

The political nuances of Europe were irrelevant to Sofia, and she felt sure he was trying to upset her.

'No, no.' Despite Marcus' negative talk, her destination was Malaga, and nothing would deter Sofia from getting there as soon as possible.

'Sofia, I am worried about you. I believe you've had a terrible shock. I am not sure if you agree, but I don't think you are so well. I've had some experience with these things, as you know, and I believe you may be suffering from depression. Perhaps even something more serious. Do *you* think you are well?'

'I am fine.' Damn him!

Despite her defiant reply, Marcus' question made Sofia uneasy. No, she wasn't well. All around her, people laughed and were full of humour. They chattered non-stop, while she found words difficult. They were immersed in a world where everything fascinated them: the food, the view from the front of the ship, the entertainment on the decks and in the dining room. Although Sofia dwelt in the same environment, she felt nothing of their excitement. Worse, though, blank hours in her day had become a regular event—periods of time she could not account for. Sometimes the bright rays of morning sunshine filled her cabin, and then, barely moments later, darkness filled the room. No, she definitely was not well, but when she was home, she'd be better.

Finally, the ship turned into the Thames. And as the expanse of water became enclosed and the rolling ocean waves became dappled waters, the atmosphere on the ship also changed. Voices seemed louder as they called to each other, conversations took on more urgency as though the things which hadn't been said during the voyage needed to be said now, and even the clothing people wore seemed a little more formal. And when Marcus looked at Sofia across the breakfast table, he looked serious and broached the subject of her health.

'Sofia, I know I have mentioned this a few times, but I feel I need to say it again. I really do not think you are ready to continue such a long journey through to Spain. Please would you consider staying in London for a few weeks and perhaps seeking some treatment?'

'I will be fine when I am home,' Sofia told him.

'Yes, but getting home will not be easy. You will need to be buying tickets, finding accommodation, navigating Paris, all alone.'

'Sí.'

'There is a place—a hospital—near my home. There, you could rest and regain your strength, ready for your journey home. It has an excellent reputation.'

His words made Sofia fearful. She must be vigilant. She'd been mistaken to believe Marcus was her friend. He was something else— someone who wanted to take control of her life, who wanted to stop her from returning home.

Keeping her guard up, Sofia agreed with all of Marcus' suggestions, nodding when he said he would find a motel for her in London, after which he would organise some tests so they could be certain she was well enough to make the journey home. However, even as she agreed, Sofia's mind plotted and planned. And as the *Strathnaver* approached the Tilbury docks, its passengers jostling for position along the rails to view outer London sprawling before them, she sat in her room, her packed case on the floor beside her. And when the great ship bumped with a force that made her bed shudder, she ventured down the stairwell, not stopping until she reached the lowest deck. Once there, she pushed through the passengers, who were packed and lined up, waiting for the call to disembark. Finally, she reached the empty corridor beyond the end of the line, and found the open door of a vacant cabin. Slipping inside, she shut the door and lay on the bed.

What to do… what to do, what to do?

Marcus was somewhere out there, certain that she needed some sort of treatment—a plan which would stall her journey home. Staring at the ceiling of the cabin, Sofia lost track of time. She tried to plan her next move, but her thoughts became confused and the sound of her heart pounding filled her ears. *Count to ten*, she reminded herself, but only got to six before sleep took over.

Waking with a start, Sofia was conscious of quietness pervading the ship. She guessed the passengers had left, but because the cabin had no windows, she had no idea how much time had passed, if it were day or night, nor what was happening beyond the cabin. And so she remained still, paralysed by fear and unsure of her next move.

What if Marcus was out there? Sofia knew he would not give up on her easily.

CHAPTER 12

The quiet was broken by laughter and loud voices echoing through the hallway. Startled, Sofia fixed her eyes upon the door, wondering if she should barricade it. Perhaps she should try to hide somewhere in the cabin. There was nowhere to hide, though. The tiny space held four bunk beds and a small cupboard for clothing. There was no bathroom as there had been in her own cabin; on this deck, passengers shared the communal facilities farther down the corridor.

Without warning, the door opened, and a lady in the striped uniform of the ship's cleaning staff burst through the door and gaped at her.

'Good lord, miss! You gave me the fright of my life! What are you doing here? You're in London now. Everybody left the ship hours ago! You need to go, too.'

Without replying, Sofia leapt to her feet, slipped on her shoes, reached for her handbag and case, and fled. A second lady, working in the room across the corridor, stared at her as she raced past.

At the stairwell, Sofia slowed, her mind buzzing with the possibilities of what she might encounter at the top of the stairs.

Would Marcus still be around, waiting for her to appear? What a mistake she'd made! She was now alone and would stand out to anyone searching for her on the upper decks. She berated herself for not remaining in the thick of the crowd; she should have attached herself to a group and stayed close. Found a coat in the lost property to wrap around her, so Marcus wouldn't recognise her yellow dress. Damn, damn, damn.

But Sofia needn't have worried, for when she reached the top of the stairwell, the deck was vacant and the gangplank unsupervised. It only took her seconds to scamper down the ramp to the port, where exit signs guided passengers to the right. If she followed these, they would take her to the main terminal. And if Marcus was searching for her, he might be waiting there.

Looking around at the empty dock, Sofia noticed a road veering to the left of the main building, following the wharf's stone wall. Carrying her suitcase and with her handbag strapped over her forearm, she headed towards it while remaining in the shadow cast by the ship. Probably this was the entry route for dock workers and the trucks delivering supplies to the port; it would surely take her to the main road leading to London.

Walking along the isolated roadway, Sofia was relieved to think she'd outsmarted Marcus; foiled his plan to keep her in London. However, a different need emerged, for the sun was setting rapidly, and heavy storm clouds cast a menacing shadow along her route while a heavy mist cloaked the river beside her. The road was dark, quiet and dank with the rank odour of rotting fish. She jumped at a movement to her left, among large metal bins overflowing with rubbish. With a loud screech, a cat dashed past her.

Sofia realised she may have escaped Marcus, but her nerves tingled with fear of a different kind. She needed to find a route away from these docklands before darkness descended. Increasing her pace, she stumbled on the uneven pavement. Gathering herself, Sofia tried to look purposeful as she walked. And when a couple of heavy raindrops fell, she knew she needed to move quickly.

A whistle split the air from somewhere close by, the familiar sound of a catcall, making Sofia flinch. Out of the mist, two workmen appeared. Passing them, she averted her face to the ground, but nonetheless could feel their eyes roaming over her. To her relief, the dim glow of lights shone through the windows of a building ahead. She approached it and read the sign hanging over its doorway: *The Captain's Tavern.*

Through the glass of an old oak door, Sofia saw a dozen or more men scattered through the room with large mugs of ale before them. There was not a woman in sight. Knowing she had little choice, Sofia stepped inside and approached the bar. It was hardly the sort of place she was looking for, but with night falling and the patter of raindrops increasing in strength, she needed shelter and a place to sleep. Tomorrow, she would find a travel agent and buy a ticket for a train to Spain.

'Evening, love. What can I get for you?'

Happily, it turned out Sofia *wasn't* the only female in the room; the words came from a woman perhaps as wide as she was tall, whose round eyes peered through plump red cheeks.

'I need somewhere to stay,' Sofia answered, forcing volume into her voice even as the men's voices quieted and she could feel their eyes upon her.

'Stop gawping, you pack of hyaenas. Haven't you ever seen a lady before?' the woman shouted before returning her attention to Sofia. 'Somewhere to stay! Did you come off the ship just now? You must have taken a wrong turn, lovey, for here is the place for the likes of those who build the ships, and mop the ships, and service them. Not for those like you.'

'I need a bed for the night.'

'Yes, love. But not here. Our rooms... well, they are for the men. Look, wait a minute and I will see what I can do. Would you like a pint while you're waiting? I could even rustle up a cuppa, if you'd prefer. I always have a pot brewing out the back.'

Sofia nodded, not because she wanted to drink beer or tea, but because she wanted to know how to escape the dark, shadowy streets.

'Come along here and sit where it's quiet. Give your feet a rest, and I will be right back.'

Sofia took in the array of tables and the large fire burning in a grate, thankful for the dim lighting which obscured her presence from the men in the room. It did not help, though, for a new group walked in and their brazen gaze made her squirm.

Sofia was glad when the bar-lady returned.

'Eyes off, lads. This lady's not here for you to run your dirty paws over!'

'Give us a break, Sybil! We was just wanting to be friendly like!'

'Yeah, Jimmy, and the last time you were being friendly like, we had a woman with a busted cheek, and the police on our doorstep.'

'It wasn't my fault!'

'No, Jimmy, it never is. Now shut up and get out of my way. Me and the lady need to talk.'

She continued in a gentler tone, 'So, miss, I've had a chat with Cecil, my better half. He reckons he can manage here, so now I'm free to go home to the young ones. I'm thinking you should walk with me. I live in Tebbutt Lane. Just around the corner from there is a bus stop and taxi rank. There will be a few people about at this time of day, so you should be safe. From there, you can catch a bus into London, where you will find plenty of accommodation far more suitable than what's on offer here.'

'Gracias. Thank you.'

'You don't need to thank me, love. It's what any Christian woman would do. It's not safe for you to be walking around here alone. I wouldn't even trust the cab drivers who come this way. Only last week a girl was found floating in the Thames, and she wasn't the first, believe me.'

Safe... safe... safe... The word pounded through Sofia's mind. *Where to be safe? Safe from Marcus? Safe from the night shadows?*

PART III

London

CHAPTER 13

*S*ofia was glad for Sybil's company as they made their way along the dimly lit street where the sheds and workplaces attached to the docks gave way to ramshackle houses. The rain had stopped, but the pavement beneath their feet was slippery, and several times Sybil caught Sofia's arm and gently manoeuvred her around the oily puddles. The older woman was clearly well known in this street, for every few minutes a voice called 'Evening, Sybil,' to which she replied, 'Evening, Mick,' or 'Hughey,' or 'Pete' amid her barrage of chatter, explaining how she and Cecil only planned to run the tavern for two years—three at the most—before selling up and relocating to a nice country village. But here they were, twelve years later, and still no plans to leave. She told Sofia about her four children whose hungry bellies would be waiting for their dinner, and how she hoped the eldest —Sally, who was a good girl—would have the fire lit, ready for their stew to be heated. As they walked, Sofia could hear traffic, the sound growing closer until she saw a stream of cars driving under flickering streetlights ahead of them.

'Okay, love, now this here is my corner. Ahead is Calcutta Road— when you get to the end, turn left. Barely half a block up, you will see the bus stop. Buses will arrive every fifteen minutes or so. They're all heading into London—any one of them will get you there. Now, don't go right into London, though, but rather, get out at Stratford or even Whitechapel. There, you'll find hotels on every corner. They might not all be spotless, but at least you will be dry and safe for the night.'

'Thank you for helping me.' Sofia tried to smile, even though terror filled her at the thought of being alone again.

'No worries, love. You alright, then? Move quickly, because I think this rain might start again. You'll find some shelter at the bus stop.'

'Alright. Thank you.'

As Sybil's footsteps retreated into the side street, Sofia fought back the rising fear which threatened to immobilize her and continued toward the busy street. After four weeks of being confined to the *Strathnavers* decks, the openness of the dark street felt disorientating, and the rustling and chirping that emitted from the shadowy foliage draping the fence beside her made her heart race.

Taking a deep breath, she hurried towards the corner. There, as Sybil had described, Sofia saw the bus shelter crammed with dozens of people awaiting transport home at the end of their workday.

As Sofia approached, splashes of rain fell against her hands and face. Without looking up, a weary-looking woman squeezed further along the bench, opening a small space at the edge for Sofia to sit. With a nod, she accepted it and tucked her suitcase beneath her legs.

Barely ten minutes had passed when the lights of a double-decker bus swept against the sidewalk. The vehicle parked and released a dozen people onto the pavement, who were immediately replaced by those alighting the bus. It displayed "London" above its windshield.

Sofia watched, overwhelmed by the bustling movement, and when she finally considered that perhaps she should also be alighting the bus, she was too late, for with a loud ding its door swung closed. As it veered onto the road, its wheels swished through the water-filled gutter, splashing onto the pavement and causing cries from those waiting on the curb.

When the second bus arrived, Sofia was ready. Rising quickly, her purse in her hand, she was one of the first to ascend the stairs.

'Whitechapel? That will be a ha'penny, Ma'am.'

Sofia handed him a coin, which he looked at in surprise.

'What's this? I need a British penny, ma'am. Can't accept issue from the colonies.'

Sofia stared at him, confused. All she had was Australian currency —the copper and silver coins and the pound notes in her purse, as well as those notes carefully concealed in the side of her handbag. She didn't know what to do.

'Ma'am, you need to pay your fare or hop off—I don't mind which, but there is a line of people behind you, and they won't be thanking you for leaving them standing in the rain!'

Still Sofia stared, immobilised by her predicament, and her breathing became short.

'Allow me, Madam, if you please.' The words came from behind her, and an elderly gentleman reached around her to drop two coins into the bus driver's outstretched hand.

'Thank you. Your lucky day, ma'am. Now perhaps you would like to take a seat and we can get this show on the road.'

Sofia nodded to the driver and turned around and muttered 'Gracias' to the kindly stranger before moving down the aisle.

Gracias! No, she mustn't speak Spanish; she must speak English, she chided herself, gripping the rail on the seat before her and gazing into the flickering tail-lights on the road ahead as the bus veered into the traffic.

Finally, the call came: 'Next stop Whitechapel.' Sofia scrambled to her feet and left the bus, automatically offering a 'Gracias' to the driver as she stepped onto the curb.

If she felt confused and nervous as she'd walked through the dark dockside streets and sat amongst the passengers at the bus stop, now she felt terrified.

The noise of the roadway—honking horns, tyres on wet cobblestones, torrents of raindrops beating the pavement—was deafening. To add to the confusion, she was captured amid pedestrians rushing past her, umbrellas clutched low over their heads. The deluge of water falling from the sky blurred the flashing red, green and yellow of the neon signs which seemed to be everywhere; on buildings and roadways and corners, advertising names of taverns and shopfronts, both open and closed, and promoting all manner of goods to be purchased, from cigarettes to soft drinks.

Trying to focus on her immediate needs, Sofia forced herself to shut out the images and noises. A bed. She needed a bed. She needed to escape this frenzied commotion; she needed quiet.

A red tubular light flashed on a building ahead: *The Royal Hotel*. Sofia pushed open the glass door and approached the lady who sat at the reception desk, where she was making notes in a large ledger by dipping an old-fashioned nib into a pot of ink.

'May I have a room, please?' Sofia's words came out as a whisper, however, the lady wasn't perturbed; she barely paused from her note-making, and her brusque reply was automatic.

'Sorry, madam, we are full.'

She didn't so much as lift her head to acknowledge Sofia's presence. After standing silently before her for a minute, Sofia reluctantly turned back into the street. Walking a few doors down, she discovered another hotel. Again, she entered the foyer, but without even speaking to her, the receptionist shook his head and pointed to the, 'No Vacancy' sign above the desk.

Sofia continued her walk along the street, passing two more hotels with 'No Vacancy' signs clearly displayed. Entering a third, she received the same response to her request for a room; however, this time the young man who greeted her was courteous, and he explained the circumstances she was up against.

'Between the cricket match—England's playing New Zealand, you know—and the opening night of some play at East End, the inns are full, to coin a phrase! You might do better to hop on a bus and head north. Shame about the rain—it's an awful night to be out on the streets!'

'I need somewhere to sleep,' Sofia insisted, sure this enormous building with its dozens of floors must have one small room available for her.

'You and everybody else! I am really sorry. If I had anything at all, I'd give it to you, but I haven't. The bus stop is only two doors up, or if you'd prefer, there is a taxi rank a few yards yonder. I'd be heading across to Wanstead. You'd have a better chance for a room there. In fact, if you like, I could call you a taxi.'

After mulling over the options he'd presented, Sofia shook her head. She couldn't bear to ride another bus. And she had no money for a taxi—it would be too much to hope for a second stranger to rescue her when she was asked to pay her fare.

Sofia walked to the exit, but was dismayed to see rain falling even heavier than it had five minutes before. Spying a couch in the lobby, she sat down, clutching her handbag on her lap. The young man nodded to her with a sympathetic smile. She tried to concentrate and think what she should do next. She'd go to a bank the next morning and exchange her notes for British ones and then she would find a travel agent. But still there was the problem of a bed for tonight. Perhaps she would stay here, on this seat. Closing her eyes, Sofia moved her lips in prayer. *Dear Father in heaven, please keep me safe. Please, take me home to Papa!*

A high-pitched ding jolted Sofia awake. Where was she? Had she slept? She reached to the floor where her bag had dropped, and saw to her left, a square light revealing the door of the hotel's lift had opened. She watched in surprise as a tiny boy with blue overalls ran out of it, closely followed by a man with sandy coloured hair.

As he scampered after the child, the man called teasingly, 'You come back right now, you little rascal!'

Barely feet from her, he glanced in her direction with a smile, then grasped the child, scooped him up and swung him around. The boy erupted into paroxysms of laughter. Sofia stared, as the man paused, reached back to the giggling woman who followed them out of the lift and pulled her to his side in a tight hug.

Something about the scene, the man and woman and their child—their little boy—so happy together, tore at Sofia. Her throat closed over and she sought desperately for air, as she rocked back and forward on the seat.

No, no, she thought, shaking her head now filled with a throbbing pressure so strong she thought it might explode. Trying to relieve the pain, she thumped her forehead with the heel of her hand.

'Ma'am, are you alright? Can I help you?'

Sofia's eyes took in the young man, his face a picture of concern, his mouth moving like a fish in a tank. His words seeped into her consciousness like a noise travelling through water and blended with the blood surging across her temples. She tried to reply, *No, I'm not alright—something is dreadfully wrong,* but her effort to speak was overshadowed by the pounding, and the only sound from her mouth was involuntary: a low keening she couldn't stop. Her hands went loose, letting her handbag drop to the floor. The crushing pain in her head intensified and Sofia clutched her hair, then pushed her fist into her mouth before an awful muffled cry escaped. 'Jack, oh Jack, oh Jack!'

CHAPTER 14

*H*ours, days or weeks might have passed before the squeaking of a metal trolley penetrated Sofia's thoughts. Looking around, she found herself sitting in an open room, surrounded by assorted tables and lounge chairs on which sat the same disparate group of men and women she saw each time her eyes opened.

A lady wearing a white dress approached her, holding a small cup in her hand. 'Here, missus, your pills. Let's try to swallow them today. Much easier than me having to force them down your throat, don't you think? And certainly much nicer than the baths, I'm sure!'

Baths? A hazy memory of a large room with tiled walls came to Sofia. She'd been naked and surrounded by a sea of faces—men with expressionless faces who watched while two women restrained her in a bath filled with the coldest water Sofia could have imagined. Another woman poured a bucket of ice into the already freezing tub. She shuddered, reliving the experience of the chill which had seeped into her bones: the initial ache, followed by an agonizing numbness that made her shriek in terror.

But the horror hadn't ended there. For when Sofia had thought she could stand it no longer, the women dragged her to her feet, pulled her over the side, and then compelled her to step into a second bath, this one so hot it felt it would boil her raw. Sofia remembered screaming as her stinging, frozen flesh was assaulted, only stopping when her screams became a dreadful gasp as her lungs struggled to draw breath from the steam-filled air.

Other images came to Sofia: being held down by half a dozen brutally strong hands while a needle was forced into her arm. And then there was the sense of large, rubbery fingers pushing capsules to the back of her throat, followed by volumes of water, making her choke and splutter as a voice shouted into her ear, *'Swallow, Mrs Tomlinson! Swallow!'*

Trembling at the memories, Sofia lifted her head and opened her mouth to accept the red and white capsule and a mouthful of water from the cup placed before her lips. Tears started from her eyes, flowing down her cheeks and dripping from her chin to her neck.

'There, there, don't cry... Lord knows there's enough tears in this place without you adding to the flood, don't you think? And between you and me, here's a little warning: if we can't stop you from crying soon, I fear for what treatments Doctor Hasluck will want to try. He's back this week and who knows what he'll make of you. These tablets are by far your best option. Come on, there's a good girl. Doctor will be in to see you shortly, and we don't want you weeping all over him.'

Sofia rolled the capsules around her tongue, then swallowed, and the woman who watched her nodded and smiled, then patted her on the shoulder.

Whether Sofia slept or merely fell into a daze, she couldn't say, but she stirred as a warm, tasteless mush was forced between her lips. Opening her eyes, she pushed her tongue forward, then clenched her teeth and tried to stand.

'Sit down and open your mouth, in the name of God, or I'll strap you down, and then you'll know you're alive!' The voice was rough, as was the metal of the spoon being pushed against her teeth. Looking into the hardened expression of the woman standing over her increased Sofia's determination to resist the onslaught.

'Bloody hell! Starve then, for all I care. I've got thirty others who need my attention without trying to feed the likes of you.'

From the smell of toast and the sound of the ladle clinking porridge into bowls, Sofia knew it was morning. She gazed about. Opposite her was the familiar rounded face of an elderly gentleman; today his head was covered by a chequered cap, his eyes closed. By the window, the woman wearing her neat red bonnet was eating her breakfast. Sofia admired the delicate way she cut her toast into small pieces and then, one by one, placed them in her mouth with a dainty toss, alternating each mouthful with sips from a floral teacup.

A noise drew her attention towards the doorway, where three men, two wearing white jackets, the other in a suit, approached her. The man leading the group looked familiar. He glanced at Sofia with a nod, as he spoke to the man in the striped blue suit.

'Severe complex depression, it would appear. We don't know much about Mrs Tomlinson's history. The police found her in the lobby of a hotel in East London and brought her in to us. She hasn't spoken since she arrived, but all the crying suggests she is deeply distressed by something.'

'Where is her treatment up to, Dr Timms?'

'She's had three sessions of hydrotherapy and a week of insulin coma therapy. The crying has subsided somewhat, and she seems to be more alert,' Dr Timms continued, 'But as you can see, she's got a way to go. She barely eats, which is a problem. She's not violent, thankfully. Usually she is happy to take Thorazine, and it has had some effect calming her, but I recommend we increase the dose and add vitamin supplements.'

'I say she is the perfect candidate for cortex excision.' The man in the suit's words came as a decree, rather than a negotiation.

'No, Doctor Hasluck, surely not. Let's give her a little more time!' The comment from the younger man was ignored.

'And have we found any family to help us establish what caused this breakdown?'

'No. We know Mrs Tomlinson has both a passbook and a Spanish passport in her possession as well as a large sum of money—Australian currency—now held in the hospital's safe; it would appear she has recently arrived from Australia, but there is no trace of any relatives here in London. Nonetheless, I don't think we should rush into radical treatments. I'd like to give her another week or two on Thorazine, and if there is no improvement, we can start Metrazol treatments. If we can get Mrs Tomlinson conversant, we will be able to commence psychoanalysis.'

'My dear Timms, look around you. For every person you can see in here, there are hundreds of others begging for treatment. There are not enough lifetimes for us to go delving into the history of each person, forensically examine the woes of their childhood, their family sagas, the real and imagined traumas inflicted upon them, their genetic dispositions. We need solutions, not analysis—I know you are full of psychological theories, but you must realise these are highly impractical.'

'Psychology is far preferable to surgery!' The statement came from the younger man.

Doctor Hasluck barely glanced at him as he replied, 'Not necessarily so. The treatment of the mentally ill has been in the hands of you psychologists for decades, and look where we are. Our hospitals are overflowing with the poor beggars, and we offer them nothing but a lifetime of institutionalization. And this at great cost to our public funds, I might add. Surgical intervention—transorbital lobotomy— offers an immediate solution to their misery.'

'Yes, but the surgery is so new! We still don't know what its long-term effects might be.' Sofia studied the patches of red blooming over Doctor Timms cheeks.

'Humph... New to the United Kingdom, perhaps. Portugal is five years ahead of us, and now Freeman in the USA is going with lobotomies, too; he's performed hundreds of them over the last year and has refined the technique. Ten minutes of the correct surgery, and a life is changed!'

Again, the young doctor protested, 'That may be so, sir, but Freeman's work is not without complications—even he admits that. I think Doctor Timms is right, we should not rush into anything with Mrs Tomlinson. She has already improved a little. Can't we at least try one of the new psychotropics?'

This time Doctor Hasluck turned to him, peering over a pair of small rectangular glasses. 'And you are going to tell me *they* don't have complications!'

'Yes, but with regular adjustments, we can get them right. We need to be patient!'

'I am losing patience with this conversation, that I can tell you, doctor! I will give Mrs Tomlinson one more week, and then we need to make some decisions. You must realise, the thing about the surgery is, the earlier we intervene, the greater our chance of success.'

Doctor Hasluck didn't wait for an answer; instead, he turned on his heels and crossed the room to see his next patient, and the two doctors in white jackets followed him.

The shuffling of furniture beside Sofia made her open her eyes. A young man was pulling up a chair beside her. She watched his mouth move but couldn't hear what he was saying for the din in the room had reached new heights. She turned her attention to the cause of the ruction. Earlier that morning a new lady had been brought into the room and although the nurses had tried to make her sit, she wouldn't. Instead she'd walked backwards and forwards murmuring words which made no sense. Her incessant pacing had created an energy in the room which was discomforting, causing others to mutter or cry or call out for her to sit. As the collective sounds had escalated, the voice of the woman causing the commotion became louder, and angrier, until she was shouting. A short while ago, she'd come close to Sofia and catching her eye she'd leaned forward and patted Sofia's shoulder.

'They've got you, too!' she'd hissed into Sofia's face. Frightened, Sofia had closed her eyes and pretended she was asleep. Now opened, she was glad to see a man and woman had arrived and were attempting to lead the ranting woman out of the door at the far end of the room.

The man beside her paused and watched as the woman left before turning to Sofia.

'Mrs Tomlinson, do you remember me? I am Doctor McDougall. I was here earlier today, with Doctor Hasluck, and Doctor Timms.'

Sofia gazed back at him. He looked familiar.

'I would like to ask you a few questions. It is very important you try to answer them as best you can, because we need to make some decisions about your treatment. You want to get better, don't you?'

Sofia wanted to nod, but her head did not obey the command of her brain; instead, she stared at him.

'Is there anything you can tell me about yourself? How about I ask you questions, and if you agree, just nod. Here is an easy one. Is your name Sofia? Sofia Tomlinson?'

She tried to answer; to tell him he was wrong. Sofia Sánchez-Lopez was her name, but her throat was dry and the words she uttered were unclear.

'We have two documents with your name on them. Your passport lists Sánchez-Lopez as your maiden name and has a second, your married name as Tomlinson. This is the same name listed in your bankbook—an Australian document.'

Australia? Sofia was confused. She was Spanish, not Australian.

Sofia felt her shoulders make a slight movement.

'Was that yes, Mrs Tomlinson?'

When she said nothing, he sighed and asked, 'Do you have family here in London? You are wearing a wedding band... Did your husband come to London with you?'

After a brief pause, the man tried again. 'Do you remember when you had a last menstrual period?

'I see you were born in Spain. Can you recall what town you lived in?'

'According to your passport, they issued it in Malaga. Do you remember Malaga?'

Malaga, Malaga, Malaga... Sofia tried to frame the word, but it came out as a hoarse whisper. Leaning forward, the doctor frowned.

'You remember Malaga?'

'Mrs Tomlinson, if you don't mind, I would like to get an opinion about your health from a friend of mine. He's a very skilled psychiatrist, and he might offer some suggestions to help us get you better. Is that alright?'

Sofia stared out of the window, her mind fixed on a place far away, where an orange orchard grew on the side of a steep hill and fishing boats sailed against the brilliant turquoise sea. She did not care what the fellow did.

Two days later, Sofia was sitting in the same place beside the window, he returned, this time accompanied by a tall man with a tanned face, whose keen eyes peered at her from behind steel-rimmed glasses before widening in surprise.

CHAPTER 15

'Sofia! Heaven forbid! Whatever happened to you?'

The words fell upon her ears like a police officer's baton. She looked to the left and right, pulling herself forward, searching for an escape, but the man stood in front of her and she had nowhere to move.

'Sofia, it's alright! I will not hurt you!'

'You know her?'

Sofia's heart raced at the sound of the voice. It was Marcus, who'd said he was her friend but then wanted to stop her from going home!

'I do. Sofia Thompson… no, that's not right. It will come to me soon enough. She was on the ship when I returned from Australia earlier this month. She caught my attention because she was so withdrawn. I knew then she was unwell, but heaven help me, she was not in this state!'

'It's Tomlinson. Mrs Sofia Tomlinson. Did you speak to her? Do you know what triggered this?'

'I spoke to her every day. It was easy to see something troubled her. Serious depression, I was certain. She exhibited all the usual signs: no appetite, little interest in life, withdrawal, disconnection. Not only from the people around her, but even from reality. I rather hoped it was temporary, thinking if I could draw her into daily events, she'd emerge from whatever had overtaken her. Seems there was some trouble with her husband. My impression was he'd run off with another woman and Sofia was returning to her home. She has family—a brother, I think she mentioned, perhaps a parent, too—in Spain. I tried to pass time with her, monitor her, and hope I could get her to undertake treatment in London before she continued her journey. She was in no fit state to travel! Sofia wouldn't hear of it, though. Every time I raised the subject, she shut down. In fact, towards the end of the journey, she developed symptoms of paranoia. You know the look a patient gets when they lose trust in their doctor. And I was right, for she vanished just before we disembarked. I searched everywhere for her, but it was as if she'd been spirited away I felt dreadful; at the very least, I would have helped her find accommodation and organised her ticket to Malaga.'

The words Marcus spoke describing events on the ship stirred Sofia's memories. Moments when she'd sat across the table from him, or stood at the side of the ship's rails and gazed out at the expanse of ocean formed in her mind.

'So what you are saying is Mrs Tomlinson, Sofia, was lucid on the ship? She was speaking then?'

'Well, not much. Like I said, she was extremely withdrawn. Cried a lot. Often, she ignored my questions. I suspected she was being evasive. She seemed to manage the ship routines okay, keep up with a bit of washing and things, although she didn't mix with anyone. She spent most of the time alone in her room. I'd meet her in the dining room for a chat and encourage her to walk a bit, or at least sit outside for a few minutes. You know—fresh air and exercise!' Marcus breathed heavily and shook his head.

'I feel terrible. In fact, I have felt dreadful ever since I last saw her; worried about what might have become of her! Who would have thought it was Sofia I'd be seeing when you asked me down here?

Look at her! Something terrible has happened! I should have tried harder to find her.'

'Never mind, Marcus. You are here now, thank God. Doctor Hasluck's talking lobotomy, of course. He's been desperate to sink his scalpel into someone's brain for months, and now, since he returned from America, he's even worse. Sees every patient as a candidate for surgery! Thank God the psychologists still have some authority at Bellavue, but I am worried Mrs Tomlinson will be his first. Especially since she has no family to advocate for her.'

'Can you tell me again what happened, Angus?'

Sofia listened as the young man explained how the police had brought her to Bellavue Hospital on a wet night a month earlier. How for weeks she'd been non-responsive, but now, the medications seemed to rouse her. Not enough, though. Still she cried throughout the day and barely spoke.

'What treatments has she had?' Marcus sounded grim. Angry, even. Angry at her?

'Oh, the usual tricks. The hydrotherapy and insulin comas. We increased her Thorazine yesterday. I think it is helping.'

'And what about fresh food and exercise?'

'I know. I only came in on her case ten days ago, and I've done my best to get the nurses onto it; I outlined a daily schedule for her, walks and fresh food, vitamins and dairy, but I am sure they look at it and laugh. Doctor Hasluck's giving her a week. I suspect in the meantime, he'll be sharpening up his instruments and getting all the permissions in place. My feeling is he will get a win with Mrs Tomlinson. She's not a British citizen, and there is no one here to advocate for her. Doctor Hasluck can't wait to bask in the glory of being the first man in the United Kingdom to perform a lobotomy.'

'No way—it won't be happening. I need to get her out of here. Give me half an hour to make a few calls; I'm sure I can get her into Napsbury.'

'Can you? Doctor Hasluck will have a fit if he finds he's been robbed of his guinea pig!'

'Well, the medical profession's influence may be increasing in the psychiatric sphere, but for now, we psychiatrists are still in charge. We'll tell him a relative signed Mrs Tomlinson out and transferred her to another institution. Say they were insistent and there was nothing we could do to stop them.'

'Napsbury Hospital will cost a fortune. But then again, Mrs Tomlinson has a passbook; in addition, she arrived with a large sum of cash in her purse, although it is Australian currency.'

'We won't worry about money for now. Sister Clare at Napsbury is a friend of mine, and she'll be happy to let us sort out the fees in due course. I want to get Sofia out of here as quickly as possible! I'll make the arrangements, but in the meantime, can you get me copies of her records? Napsbury will need them, and I'd like to read them, too—find out what sort of damage was inflicted upon her while she's been here.'

Marcus crouched down before Sofia.

'Sofia, do you remember me—Marcus, from the *Strathnaver*?'

Looking into the warm brown eyes gazing into her own, Sofia saw the concern in them. Tears slid down her cheeks, but words failed her.

Ignoring her lack of reply, he continued speaking. 'I don't know if you understand this, Sofia, but I am arranging for you to be moved. I need to make a telephone call, and then I'll be straight back. We need to get you away from here, to a place where you will get more suitable treatment. Afterwards, I will help you get on your way home to Malaga. I promise you! How does that sound?'

Sofia shifted in her seat. More than anything, she wanted to go to Malaga. She felt the warmth of Marcus' hand on hers.

'Just wait here for a little longer, Sofia. I need to make a call, and then I will be back.'

Marcus rose and left with the young doctor. Fifteen minutes later, he returned, this time accompanied by a man dressed in the white overalls of an orderly.

'It's all organised, Sofia. We need to go. I have signed you out, but Doctor Hasluck will not be pleased. He's in the hospital now— Hopefully, we won't meet him on our way out. Do you think you can walk with me like we used to on the ship? You will be quite safe, I promise you.'

Safe. Safe, safe, safe. Sofia couldn't remember when she last felt safe, but perhaps it was when she was on board the ship. Standing, she felt the familiar warmth of Marcus' arm against hers on her right side, the arm of the orderly on her left.

'All right, now. We are going to walk straight through to the foyer, where they should have your belongings ready for us to collect, and then we'll keep going. I've got a car waiting out the front.'

Although she felt strong on her legs, the thought of walking through the far door, an exit unfamiliar to her, made Sofia falter, but Marcus urged her forward. 'Don't stop now, Sofia. We need to get you out of here before anyone creates a fuss. I promise, this time I will get you better.'

CHAPTER 16

$\mathcal{I}$t only took minutes for them to collect her suitcase, handbag and a green folder from the office and then Marcus led Sofia outside. To Sofia, the lightness of the sky and the expanse of the outside world felt disorientating, and she turned to re-enter the building they'd just left.

'No, Sofia, we need to go to Napsbury Hospital. Come on, now. I promise you will be alright.' Marcus held her arm as they went down the stairs, where she could see a vehicle waiting.

'As well as the car, I've managed to steal a couple of staff members to join us; lucky the charge nurse on the medical ward here is a good friend of mine and she said we can have them for an hour.' At the base of the stairs, a nurse and an orderly joined them, and after a brief discussion, they agreed Sofia would likely feel better sitting in the back seat between Marcus and the nurse, while the orderly drove.

As they sped away from Bellavue Hospital, Sofia was glad Marcus, seated to her right, and the woman, Nurse Farley, to her left, provided a buffer against the world outside, which appeared as a chaotic and menacing blur. Every bump on the road made her jump, and Sofia wondered why she'd been persuaded to leave her chair in the dining room. However, since the young doctor had mentioned Malaga, her determination to go there had resurfaced. Did Marcus truly mean to help her get home? She analysed his words and expressions and tried to recall the conversations they'd had on the ship. Things were changing so fast, it was hard to be sure of anything.

A mild trembling overtook her hands, and she joined them together, trying to still them. Her breaths came in short gasps, and butterflies filled her chest. More than anything she wanted to believe that all Marcus had promised was true, but it was impossible to be sure. Marcus must have recognised her fear, for he reached for the window blind and lowered it, allowing only a couple of inches of light to penetrate the vehicle's rear seat, and gestured for Nurse Farley to do the same.

After about twenty minutes, Marcus lifted the shade. Sofia saw they were driving along a narrow road lined with rock walls and hedges.

'See, Sofia, it's nice here. Peaceful. We are nearly there now. You will like Napsbury Hospital. It's quite large, but the staff are very kind, and the setting is beautiful. Lovely gardens in which you will take walks and sit outside in the sunshine. Tomorrow, I will review your treatment, and all things being well, we'll have you better in no time.'

Sofia listened and attempted a smile.

The words rang through her head: *she'd be better in no time, and then she would go to Malaga.*

The vehicle slowed and turning right, passed through a gateway. The driveway was long, and lined with trees. Between them, a range of smaller buildings were visible. The rural setting surprised Sofia; beyond the colour-filled flower beds and expanse of lawn, the hospital was surrounded by fields for as far as she could see.

Finally, the vehicle came to rest before the entry of an impressive two-storey red brick building. Looking up, Sofia considered the dozens of floor to ceiling windows arranged on each side of the doorway; they promised wonderful views. And should anyone be looking out of them, they would be sure to see any person who arrived, or departed.

To Sofia, the quiet in the foyer seemed eerie, for in recent weeks, noise had dominated every minute of her life. Disparate sounds she'd never heard before: the screams of someone overcome by terror shattered the darkness of the midnight hours. Moans started off like a series of slow waves, a humming which gathered speed and volume despite the softness of wheedling encouragement or the sharp crack of commands. Rushing footsteps, the clanging of trolleys, the clinking of keys, the slamming of doors, the finality of locks dropping into position. Warnings and threats, tutting, and swearing, and cursing.

Marcus seemed to notice the peacefulness of the foyer, too.

'I wonder where everyone has got to, Sofia. Let's see if we can find someone, perhaps down here...' As he had on the ship, Marcus easily maintained a one-sided conversation with her, as though Sofia's lack of response was of no consequence to him.

Walking along the corridor, he led her to an office. The door was closed, but in response to his gentle knock, a friendly voice called for them to come in.

Sofia paused, looking at the seat outside the office.

'No, Sofia, we are not here to talk about you. We are here to make a plan to get you better. It is important for you to be part of these conversations.'

Apprehensively, she stepped into the room.

'Oh, it's you, Marcus! That was quick. Sofia, is it? Miriam Clare. Pleased to meet you. Marcus phoned me earlier and said he was bringing you across.'

The woman extended her hand towards Sofia with a smile. She

appeared to be about fiftyish, small framed and with a neat athletic figure, suggesting an energetic disposition.

'Welcome to Napsbury, Sofia. I am matron here, and in addition, I look after some of the therapy groups—I am sure you will find them beneficial. Here at Napsbury, we specialize in treating depressive disorders. We like to believe our methods are the best in all of England. We favour a gentle approach with a focus on fresh air and good diet, although we are constantly under pressure to adopt some of the more drastic treatments. Nonetheless, while I am in charge and we have the benefit of specialists like Marcus, we will continue to handle things our way.'

'Absolutely, Miriam. Do you mind, Sofia, if I fill Sister Clare in on what I know? Feel free to correct me at any time.' Sofia listened as Marcus outlined the same story he'd shared with Doctor McDougall. As he spoke, he glanced at Sofia frequently, as if ensuring she agreed with his statements. And by the sorrow in Marcus's voice when he explained how she'd vanished at the time of disembarkation, Sofia realised how much he blamed himself for frightening her and causing her to hide from him. Sister Clare turned her attention to Sofia.

'So, Sofia, do you recall much about leaving Australia? Your journey to England?'

Sofia shook her head slowly, and Marcus nodded his approval. It had been the first response she'd made since they'd left the dining room. She didn't remember why she'd left Australia, but she did remember being on a ship, talking with Marcus, and that she was on her way to Spain.

Still looking at her, Marcus continued, 'Since leaving the ship, Sofia has had a decline. She wasn't this withdrawn when I last saw her. Hopefully, we can manage an equally quick turnaround. Thank God Angus called me. He was worried for Sofia, for Doctor Hasluck is desperate to get her into a theatre and wield his scalpel. Honestly! Lobotomies may be considered an ideal treatment for depression in Portugal and the United States, but I am yet to be convinced. And I certainly don't want Sofia to be his guinea pig.'

'Yes, I've had to listen to a few of our newer medical graduates suggest we tamper with our patients' brains. What they don't seem to understand is once you start chopping into the grey matter, there is no going back.'

'Exactly. I've heard some dreadful stories about such treatments in America. Dr Freeman's out of control over there! Can you believe he drives around with his mobile lobotomy unit and for $200, he'll operate on anybody? Even on young children at their parents' request! Anyway, enough of this—Sofia's had a big day, and she'd probably like some rest. Where are you thinking of placing her?'

The matron turned to Sofia. 'I think we'll start you over on Ward Four. It is crowded, but it is one of the quietest wards we have, and you'll get a good night's rest there.'

Marcus stood and picked up the folder he'd been carrying. 'Sofia, I will leave you with Sister Clare. She'll see you are settled. You are in the best of hands here, believe me. Tonight, I am going to have a read of these, and tomorrow morning I will be back, and then we'll talk again. How does that sound?'

What seemed most strange to Sofia was to be repeatedly asked her opinion. Nobody in Bellavue had ever asked her thoughts about anything. Instead, she'd constantly been told how she was feeling and what she might want.

'*You won't be wanting a blanket tonight, it's hot in here,*' said the nurses who'd settled her for the night, even when she was shivering with cold. '*Here are two sleepers—there you go—swallow them down; you've had a big day and you'll be needing a good night's rest.*' At the time, it hadn't mattered. Sofia hadn't cared what was happening to her. Now, though, since she'd been reminded of Malaga, Sofia did care. She desperately wanted to get well enough to leave the hospital.

That night, Sofia lay awake, her eyes wide open. The ward they had placed her in was not unlike the one she'd slept in at Bellavue—the pitiful cries of women calling out or shouting or sobbing filled the air. A young woman in a blue nightdress repeatedly walked to Sofia's bed and stood over her, saying, *'Mama, please! Take me home. I'll be good, I promise!'* Each time she crossed the room, Sofia held her breath, frozen in fear, and pretended she didn't hear until the night nurse rose from her desk and led the woman back to her own bed.

A rattling persisted from a bed close to Sofia's, where a woman of barely twenty rocked, ignoring the calls from the other patients in the room to lie still, to let them all get some sleep. And then there was the quiet weeping that wouldn't stop. Only when the night nurse shone her torch upon her bed, saying 'It's okay, love, would you like me to sit here with you for a while?' did Sofia realise the heartrending sounds came from her own mouth.

The following morning, Sofia was sitting in a dining room amid perhaps forty men and women when Marcus arrived.

'Good morning, Sofia. How did the night go?' he asked.

She nodded, and he sat across the table, encouraging her to finish her breakfast, chatting about the sunshine and how pleasant the drive to Napsbury had been.

At his insistence, Sofia completed every last drop of her tea and finished her toast. Only when she'd eaten did he assist her to stand and lead her to a small room with a desk. On the desk sat the file, he'd collected from Bellavue the previous day. Marcus flicked through the pages and outlined their contents to her.

'Sofia, I can see you were taken to Bellavue at nine PM on the thirteenth of August, the day the *Strathnaver* arrived in London. I'd dearly love to know why you vanished without even saying goodbye to me!' He smiled wryly and shrugged before continuing.

'It seems to me that after leaving the ship, something happened to upset you. Perhaps you were frightened by someone or traumatised by some sort of flashback. The records here say there was no sign of injury, and you had your suitcase and handbag with you, so there was no question you had been robbed.' He raised his eyebrows and looked at Sofia. 'Do you remember anything about that day?'

Sofia tried to think, but beyond the memories which had been stirred by Marcus's descriptions her mind was a blank.

'Not to worry. Memories often return when you least expect them. You may find it unsettling, but ultimately, it will be a good thing if you can put together some of these events. And remember, we are here to support you. Unfortunately, there was probably no worse place the police could have taken you than Bellavue; it would seem they took you to the hospital closest to where they picked you up.' He continued to scan the pages before speaking again.

'I can see references to the hydrotherapy and the insulin comas Angus mentioned yesterday. Of course they had no effect, other than to terrify you, I imagine. And here is your medical chart; you are taking Thorazine. Also, in the evenings you were given pentobarbital, heaven forbid—I suspect it was administered to give the nurses a good night's sleep, rather than for your benefit!'

Closing the folder with a forceful snap, Marcus took a sheet of paper from a drawer in the desk and began writing.

'At present, my suspicion is that you have exogenous melancholia; in other words, I think something happened—you had a terrible shock —and this caused you to shut-down. Believe it or not, this is a good diagnosis; it suggests your mind closed up as a way of protecting you, and I am confident it is treatable. Of course, with no prior knowledge of your life in Australia, it is difficult to know what we're dealing with. My plan is to wean you off the barbiturate; I doubt it's doing you any good. As Sister Clare said yesterday, our focus at Napsbury is a healthy diet, lots of fresh air, and group therapy. She likes to run therapy sessions where she can. I'm sure you will find them helpful. We don't like to rush things; routines and rest will go a long way towards getting you better.'

Sofia nodded and found herself relaxing. The staff at Napsbury were pleasant; the ward nurse had smiled at her when she'd put her dress on backwards, then helped her to fix it, and the orderly had joked as he cleaned the floors, dancing around the ward with his mop, trying to make the women laugh at his antics. Already, she knew Napsbury Hospital was a much nicer place than Bellavue.

Over the following week, Marcus visited Sofia each morning, and she looked forward to these visits. Within the routine at Napsbury, it was easy to forget about life beyond the hospital walls, but each time she saw him she was reminded of her bigger goal: to get better and travel to Malaga.

First, they walked in the garden for fifteen minutes, Sofia listening as he pointed out the various plants. Cats seemed to be everywhere, and she joined Marcus' laughter as they leapt from the path when approached, slept on the bench seats and stalked lizards resting on the pavement. Following their walk, he'd take her to a large room, a bit like a school classroom, where Sofia joined Sister Clare and her group of women in a circle.

Although in the discussions patients were encouraged to speak about themselves and the things bothering them, Sofia's main concerns were about a past which she couldn't remember, and she doubted anyone could help her. And though some of her words had returned, her voice barely reached above a whisper, her sentences coming as often in Spanish as English, so she didn't dare try to contribute. However, she did value the strategies Sister Clare shared each day. How to control her anxiety by breathing deeply and slowly, just as Marcus had encouraged her on the ship, or filling her lungs with air and then holding the breath for the count of ten. How to eliminate the tightness of her muscles by rolling her head from side to side and shaking her shoulders, elbows, wrists and fingers.

~

Over the week, Sofia relaxed in the comfortable atmosphere at Napsbury, though her stomach churned at the constant sensation of something forgotten, something haunting her. When she complained of this to Marcus, he was pleased, explaining it was a sign that her past was stirring. Still, he insisted she should focus on the present, gain strength from the daily routines, and practise speaking. He assured her the memories would return in time, when her mind was strong enough to receive them.

Once a week, Marcus took Sofia to the room with a desk, where he undertook a more formal analysis of her progress. Sometimes Sister Clare joined them. Then, Marcus asked lots of questions, sometimes about her past, other times about her future. He asked about her sleep patterns and dreams, and about any voices or instructions from within her head. For most of his questions, Sofia could only shake her head; she had memories of her childhood where she and her brother walked around the edges of a castle and played among orange trees, but all she knew about her future was her intentions to get home. And as for voices, one thing that Sofia was clear about, the only voices she heard were the fragments of past conversations, none of which made any sense. During each of these meetings, Marcus recorded lots of notes, and when he finished, he made recommendations about her treatment.

After the first week, Sofia began accompanying the dozen or so patients who walked around the grounds after their group therapy session was over and found she enjoyed it. By her second week, her voice returned. Still, her thoughts tended to be in Spanish, as did many of the phrases she uttered, and no-one understood her. However, as the days passed, her English gained fluency. Marcus was right, she thought, Napsbury Hospital was a pleasant environment, and with little to worry about other than appearing for meals, arriving at the group sessions by nine thirty each morning and discussing her progress individually with Sister Clare twice a week, she could feel her body strengthening and her mind clearing. And although Sofia preferred not to take the various capsules she was given each day, she accepted the medication gave her a sense of stillness. Every step forward was immensely encouraging, and as Sofia gained optimism, so too did her confidence that each day of improvement brought her closer to the day when she'd be well enough to go home.

CHAPTER 17

*I*n her third week at Napsbury, Sofia came across an elderly man seated in a quiet corner of the gardens, carefully applying paint to a large canvas.

Intrigued, she moved closer, peering over his shoulder. He was painting a cat of sorts. She looked around to find the source of inspiration, but no cats were visible seated on any of the benches, nor on the chairs nearby.

'Don't hover, come on over—have a seat.' The man spoke without so much as lifting his brush or turning his head.

Stepping closer, Sofia again examined the painting.

'You're very good, sir.'

'Why, thank you. It is very kind of you to say so.'

'No, but I am not just saying so—you are indeed very good.'

Sofia was not sure who was more surprised, the man whose space she'd invaded, or she herself, who'd initiated a conversation with a total stranger.

'And which wonderful critic do I have the pleasure of meeting?' He turned to look at her, his face heavily lined with a large, droopy moustache obscuring his lips so she didn't know if he was smiling or scowling.

'Sofia. Sofia Tomlinson.'

'Lovely to meet you, dear. And I am Louis. Louis Wain.' At Sofia's blank expression, he continued, 'No worries. I do not expect you to know me, although many did once. My cats have danced across children's books and smoked their way into inns and taverns and they've sung carols and fished and played cricket. Indeed, there's not much my cats haven't done, including making me a famous man—but that time has long passed.'

'You only paint cats?'

'Why, of course, dear. Whatever else would one paint?'

'This work is very interesting. Abstract surrealism, perhaps?' Sofia was surprised by the comment which sprung from her lips. The colours Louis used—ultramarine blue and cobalt yellow—were as familiar to her as the odour of linseed oil emanating from the tiny pot clipped to his easel. A memory of her family's gallery sprang to her mind, in the way her memories frequently arose when she least expected, and Sofia could imagine a painting such as this hanging on its wall would rouse considerable interest.

'Do you sell your work to galleries?'

'Well, who knows? Dearest Felicity tells me my paintings are rubbish, though that doesn't stop her from arriving to collect them each week!'

'They are wonderful,' Sofia said. 'Your colours are extraordinary, and those patterns are incredible. I imagine they'd be very popular!'

'*Were* popular, dear. *Were* popular. Sit down, if you wish. Tell me about yourself.'

And without thought, Sofia sat. As she chatted, more memories were unlocked, like a movie unfolding before her eyes. She told Louis about the finca and gallery, how she longed to be back there, and would be soon; Marcus had promised.

'Marcus?'

'Doctor Edmunds. He's been managing my treatment and when I am better, I will return to Malaga.'

'Wonderful! I'd love to go to Spain, but I fear the only place I will be going is heavenward, all being well—but then, maybe not.'

Sofia laughed when he rolled his eyes and pointed towards the ground.

'But aren't you going home, Louis? You seem well.'

'It would be nice, but not possible. I've been over a dozen years in one asylum or another, and don't tell anyone, but truly, I am very happily institutionalised. I couldn't manage on my own anymore. And one thing I do know—a position in a place like Napsbury is not easy to come by. Believe me, as I speak from my copious experience, Napsbury is by far the best. Besides, if I left here, I'd be at the mercy of my dear sisters, Claire and Felicity, and they're as mad as hatters. Worse than me, in truth, but they hide it better than I do. I'd be imprisoned if I had to spend as much as a week with them!'

'Anyone who paints as well as you do can't be too mad.' Sofia laughed, enjoying the man's humour more than she'd enjoyed anything in a long time.

And so a habit began where Sofia sat for a few minutes each day with Louis, listening to him speak as he worked on his paintings. While his subject was always predictable—his beloved cats, she soon learned Louis' moods veered towards the erratic. He seemed to be obsessed by the power of electricity; consumed by notions of electromagnetic fields and lightning conductors and of how electricity quivered in the air, passing from animal to object to person. Mostly, Sofia just listened and nodded; she found by saying nothing, he'd usually quieten and engage in more rational conversation. In these calmer moments she heard about Peter, the cat he and his wife had found almost forty years earlier, and how, as his beloved Emily had lain dying of cancer, he'd sketched and painted perhaps a thousand images of cats to make her laugh. He wept as he spoke sweet words of love for the woman who'd been taken from him after only two years of marriage. Then, without warning, his voice would transform into a snarl and he'd describe the pressure he'd been placed under to provide for five sisters, none of whom had married. Sofia learned that the five sisters had been reduced to two, as Louis explained how the youngest had been institutionalised with madness then influenza, while the other two had the good sense to succumb to illness and death before the madness got them.

One Friday, as she walked up the path towards Louis, Sofia heard a loud, berating voice. Puzzled, she entered the clearing and found him looking down while a lady shuffled through a sheaf of his recent works, mostly pencil drawings.

'More of your wallpaper rubbish,' she said, not bothering to temper her spiteful tone in Sofia's presence, then bundled a pile of the works into her carry bag. 'And what on earth is that meant to be?'

She pointed at his easel, where Louis was finishing the painting Sofia had told him the previous day was her favourite yet—an extraordinary image of feline eyes surrounded by radiating patterns, as colourful as they were detailed.

Louis didn't reply, but instead turned to Sofia and in a tired voice said, 'Sofia, meet Felicity.'

'Good afternoon, Felicity. The painting is wonderful, isn't it?' Sofia said.

'Huh. Only a crazy person would think that,' was her abrupt reply. Then, without saying another word, she closed her bag and strode off, with neither a farewell to Louis or a glance towards Sofia.

Feeling awful for Louis, Sofia tried to find something comforting to say, but it was too late. Louis seemed to be oblivious to her presence. She watched as he frantically moved his head up and down with sharp jerking movements that surely would be painful. Accompanying the motion, the air became infused with a strange sound as the pitch of his voice heightened and he vented a torrent of abuse, mixed with nonsensical phrases.

'Walls; cats on walls; everybody wants cats; nobody cares; damn you, Louis damn you, Felicity, Crazy bitch, crazy Louis, mad, mad, mad,'

As Louis spoke, his hands frantically snapped his paintbrush from one to the other; and with each switch, his manner swung also, calm one minute, tense and aggressive the next; his voice rising and falling, gaining pace then slowing down; his face reflecting emotions that jumped around like ants in a hot frying pan.

~

The following day, Sofia was glad to find Louis back to his usual self.

'Louis, I am sorry your sister does not like your work. Believe me, your paintings are truly wonderful!'

'Well, not wonderful enough is the problem, or perhaps they are wonderful and I am not. Copyright, nobody told me about copyright. What would I know. I just want everyone to realise how beautiful cats are. Most people just saw them as vermin that lived in alley-ways. Or they did until I set them straight. Beautiful cats, full of currents—you can see it in their fur...'

Sofia could see Louis was losing awareness of her as his conversation veered to the subject of electricity which seemed to obsess him. She attempted to refocus him. 'So your father, Louis. Was he a good man?'

'Yes, very good. Very kind. But sadly, he passed away and so Mother kept us. But then, she lost everything and so it was down to me. I was the breadwinner.'

'Louis, surely not! How could you be expected to look after five sisters?'

'Well, clearly, expected to or not, I couldn't. Well I didn't. And so it goes on. I almost killed Clare. I still might if she's not careful!'

He looked at Sofia and laughed, and she was relieved to see him smiling.

'Yes, I can joke about it now, but I wasn't laughing twenty years ago. Then, the demands and complaints were unbearable. I just had to strangle her!'

'Who did you strangle, Louis?'

'No, no. No, no, no. I didn't strangle her. Luckily they got me off in time. But that was the beginning. It was then, they put me in the pauper's institution. I suppose we'd all had enough of each other.'

'How awful,' said Sofia, thinking of her treatment at Bellavue.

'Thankfully, a bolt of lightning struck and its electromagnetic field drew Dan to me "Louis, my friend. This is wrong," he said. "You, the man who brought cats to the British, should not be living here!" Dan had connections; H G Wells and even the Prime Minister of England felt the force, and together they sponsored a nation-wide fundraiser. And that, Sofia, is how I came to Napsbury.'

Marcus was very pleased with Sofia's progress, and he enthusiastically told her so each week. Still, two things bothered her. Firstly, in response to her requests that she return to Malaga, he'd reply that caution was necessary, for it was a long trip and political tensions in Spain could make travel difficult. While Sofia found his excuses frustrating, she found Marcus' second concern offensive. Three times he'd raised the suggestion she might be carrying a child, which, of course, was ridiculous, and with increasing irritation, she told him so.

But the strangest conversation of all was when Marcus came looking for her in the gardens one Wednesday afternoon, a serious expression on his face.

'Would you mind if we had a chat for a few minutes, Sofia? I need to discuss something with you.' She wondered if he was going to apologise for the assertions he'd made.

'No, stay seated,' he said when she went to rise from the garden bench, expecting he'd want to talk in the privacy of the office. 'I'd prefer we had a little chat out here, if you don't mind.' Sofia was puzzled. If she wasn't mistaken, Marcus' usual calm manner was absent. Rather, he appeared to be nervous.

'Sofia, I want to speak to you about something which may come as a surprise to you.'

'What's happened? Are you going to tell me that I am not improving?—The treatment isn't working? I feel very well, you know.'

He must have detected her consternation, because he quickly continued, 'No, no, it's nothing for you to worry about. You are doing fine. Miriam and I are very pleased with your progress.'

'What then, Marcus? Has something happened?'

'No, nothing has happened. However, sometimes, for a range of reasons, there are times when doctors need to pass their patients on to colleagues. It's not about you, it's about me, do you understand? You have done nothing wrong. The thing is, I have asked a friend of mine, Doctor Spencer, to meet with you. If you like him and you agree, he will take over your treatment.'

'But I don't want anyone else to treat me!' Sofia felt alarmed, convinced it had been because of Marcus' steady guidance and the way he and Miriam Clare worked so well together that she'd found her voice, that her English words had returned, and she'd attained a degree of peace. Her calm was broken now only by occasional nightmares. If they continued on the path they'd been taking, it would only be a matter of time before she'd be fully well and ready for her memories to return, or at the very least, she'd be able to manage her life despite the terrible things concealed in the depths of her mind. Marcus waved away her protests.

'Sofia, I am afraid that's not possible. In fact, I won't be seeing you at all for a while. But if you agree, I will seek reports from Doctor Spencer from time to time. Naturally, I will be very interested to hear of your progress. Now, if you don't mind, he's waiting in the office. Let me take you to meet him.'

Doctor Spencer was very tall and very dark. Perhaps of Middle Eastern origin, Sofia thought. On their arrival, he ushered her to a seat with a welcoming smile. It felt strange to see someone other than Marcus seated behind the large desk.

'I am very pleased to meet you, Sofia. I have heard a lot about you. How are you today?'

'A little puzzled,' Sofia replied quietly. 'I thought I had been progressing well with Marcus, so I am not sure why I need to change doctors.'

'Ah, these things happen from time to time. I promise, I will give you the same dedicated attention as Marcus has, and we will have you better in no time.'

'Alright then.'

'And when is the baby due?' Doctor Spencer spoke with the assurance of a man who knew his medicine and was confident of his opinions.

'Baby! What? No, there *is* no baby!' Sofia glared at Marcus, but he wasn't looking at her. Rather, Marcus and Doctor Spencer were sharing a strange expression. Sofia was sure that Marcus had planted the idea of pregnancy in Doctor Spencer's mind, just as she'd been sure he had spoken to Sister Clare a week ago after she'd asked if Sofia could remember when she'd last menstruated. She couldn't, but as she'd told Sister Clare, she couldn't remember much of anything, so it was hardly surprising. However, a woman would know if she was pregnant, and Sofia knew she wasn't.

Sofia stood up, ready to leave. She would not be speaking any more today. Certainly not to Marcus nor to Doctor Spencer. And if anyone else wanted to be clever and insist she was having a baby, they'd get the same treatment.

Marcus looked at her entreatingly and caught her arm as she stepped toward the door. 'No, Sofia, please don't go. Doctor Spencer didn't mean anything. Come on, sit down. Let us talk some more.'

For fifteen minutes, Sofia was silent as the men spoke of her history and subsequent treatment. Repeatedly, they asked her questions, but she refused to answer. Not only was she annoyed by the reference to pregnancy, she did not appreciate Marcus' desertion of her.

She was glad when Marcus indicated the meeting was ending by standing.

'So, Sofia, do you agree to continue your treatment under Doctor Spencer's care?'

'I suppose I will have to, since you are leaving me,' was her answer.

Leaving the office, Sofia felt a level of nervousness she hadn't experienced in ages. It was upsetting, especially as she'd been feeling particularly well before Marcus arrived. In the space of an hour, her whole life had been turned upside down. She glared at the nurses as she stomped through the corridor and ignored Sister Miriam when she asked if everything was alright.

Determined to escape the inquisitive staff, Sofia exited the building and walked along the pathway, only stopping when she found Louis painting in his usual place.

'Sofia! Sit down! How are you today? You are looking a little flustered.'

'No, I'm not flustered. I'm angry. At least I am now; I was doing absolutely fine until I discovered Marcus won't be treating me anymore.'

'Really! Why ever not? Is he leaving? If he is, half the inmates here will be sorry.'

'No... he didn't say he was leaving. Just that, for personal reasons, he would no longer be treating me.'

'Personal reasons. Huh. You know what that means, don't you?'

'No. Personal means it's his private business. I wouldn't dream of asking.'

Louis lifted his head and guffawed. 'Sofia! Dear, dear! *Personal* means his feelings for you are affecting his professional conduct; his emotions are clouding his ability to treat you properly. The poor man. Every time he's looking at you across his desk, he probably wants to leap across and kiss you.' Louis laughed again as though Marcus' abandonment of Sofia was the funniest thing in the world.

'Louis Wain, what nonsense. Don't be so ridiculous.'

Louis shook his head. 'What is so ridiculous about a man falling in love with a beautiful young woman like yourself? Sounds perfectly natural to me! If I was forty years younger, I might be tempted to chase you around the gardens a time or two myself!'

Sofia glared at him before rising and flouncing off. What a lot of rubbish Louis spoke sometimes, she thought as she returned to the dining room. There she sat silently by the window, gazing to the south and counting the days until the staff would deem her well enough to leave Napsbury and she could continue on her way home.

Despite her initial reaction, Sofia adjusted to the routine of meeting with Doctor Spencer each Wednesday, where they discussed her childhood and memories of Malaga, which had returned with degrees of clarity, as well as the nightmares which persisted. She was feeling better than ever, but each time she raised the question of returning home his answer was always the same—one step at a time, Sofia, best not to rush things.

Once she recovered from her irritation with Louis, Sofia resumed her daily walks to his spot in the garden and sought his opinions on all manner of things: the behaviour of other patients, the tablets that made her feel nauseous, the weight she was putting on, and complaints about Doctor Spencer forestalling her return home. Thanks to his many years in institutions, Louis was a fountain of information, with answers to everything. His main advice though, was simple.

'Just play the game, Sofia, play the game!'

'What game, Louis? Whatever are you talking about?'

'Over the years, I've seen dozens of patients—hundreds, even— argue their viewpoints with the sisters and doctors, and all they ever achieved was trouble. Here at Napsbury, that might mean the lengthening of one's stay, or an adjustment to their medications, which nobody particularly enjoys. But in other places... ah.' Louis shuddered and shook his head. 'It could mean being shackled to one's bed for weeks at a time, or being forced medication or denied food, or a series of electrotherapy.

Sofia remembered the cold baths at Bellavue, of being held down as pills were forced through her lips; the glassfuls of water poured down her throat, making her gag and cough, chilly streams washing down her face and soaking her clothing. She could well imagine the horrors Louis referred to.

Occasionally she saw Marcus from afar, and he would wave or come to her and ask how she was, but no longer did he sit with her on the bench seats or walk with her in the garden.

Sofia's determination to comply with her treatment, and as Louis had advised, to 'play the game,' served her well, for in early December Doctor Spencer collected her from the common room where she'd been assisting with the distribution of morning tea, and took her to his office. There, he asked her the usual questions about her sleep, dreams, and memories.

'I am sleeping better than ever, Doctor, and only occasionally am I disturbed by dreams. Usually, I can get back to sleep. I think the sleeping pills help.'

'What I am thinking is that we could discharge you before Christmas. Find someplace nearby, where I'll continue monitoring you as an outpatient for a month or two.'

Sofia was thrilled with the news, but a little unsure of how she'd cope. She felt like Louis had described— institutionalised. Comfortable with her daily routines within the confines of Napsbury Hospital, but now, suddenly terrified at the thought of being alone, with nothing to distract her should moments of anxiety arise, and no nurse to come to her bedside in the night and reassure her when the nightmares filled her with dread. Doctor Spencer assured her he had faith that she'd manage.

'You have a number of options, Sofia. To my understanding, you are not without resources.'

Sofia looked at him blankly. What sort of resources was he referring to?

'Money, Sofia.'

She hadn't given a thought to money in months.

'When you were admitted to Bellavue Hospital, you had quite a sum with you, and also a passbook to an Australian bank. On your behalf, these were collected, and are now in the safe here.'

'Oh… and my fees, for being here? I will need to pay those.'

'Well, I don't know anything about that. It's a conversation you will have to have with Sister Clare. But to my knowledge, you could afford to rent a nice little apartment in St Albans, from which we could continue our weekly appointments. You wouldn't need to travel here to Napsbury; I have an office there.'

'I am not sure if I am ready to live alone,' she replied. 'Can't I go home to my brother and father? I will be fine once I am with them.'

'Sofia, we are moving into the height of winter, and a trip to southern Spain requires a week at the very least. One involving hectic train schedules and a number of stops where you would need to find overnight accommodation. It's quite a journey from here to Dover, and then you would have to travel across the channel to Calais, then to Paris. Once there, you would have to get across the border into Spain, and in Spain, as we've discussed numerous times, you may find the transport links are very disrupted. You need to travel to the Costa Del Sol; all the way to the south of Spain and I don't think you are ready to undertake so many challenges. And then, of course, there is the baby to think about….'

'The baby, the baby, the baby! What baby?'

Dr Spencer inhaled deeply and then shrugged. 'As you wish, Sofia.'

Play the game, Sofia reminded herself. Do as Louis said and go along with things for the sake of peace. Otherwise she might find her stay at the hospital extended. Perhaps she'd agree to taking an apartment in St Albans after all.

Doctor Spencer paused. 'There is, of course, an alternative you might like to consider.'

'Yes? What is that?' Sofia was open to all suggestions.

'I have a good friend... in fact, *we* have a good friend, who has suggested you could stay at his house for this final stage of your recuperation.'

'What friend? I don't know anybody in England.'

'You do: Doctor Edmund—Marcus. He blames himself for causing you to vanish when you disembarked at Tilbury. He's sure if he'd stayed with you, made sure you had accommodation, helped you to buy your tickets to Spain, you would never have become so ill. So you see, he feels responsible for all you've been through, and disappointed in himself for losing your trust. He still shudders to think about your treatment in Bellavue, how close you came to having brain surgery. How it was only pure chance he intervened. I think he believes that reconnecting with you like that was no accident. It was a sign that he was meant to cross your path—meant to look out for you.'

Sofia was amazed to think Marcus would make such an offer.

'You wouldn't be alone with him, of course. That wouldn't do. However, Marcus shares his home with his sister, Elizabeth. They've inherited the family seat, so to speak—a wonderful estate on the fringe of St Albans, which would provide a peaceful environment to prepare for your journey to Spain. Being part of a normal household, away from the hospital, would be very good for you. You could walk into the village each day and in doing so, you would regain your confidence as you adapt to a lifestyle on the outside.' Dr Spencer smiled as he wiggled his fingers in reference to *the outside*.

Sofia nodded, warming to the idea. It was a good thing to be deemed well enough to leave Napsbury and take a step towards 'the outside'. And as keen as she was to commence the journey to Spain, the nightmares of terror and darkness, of rain and loud footsteps and piercing screams, haunted her. Though she'd never admitted it to any of the doctors or nurses, she did harbour a fear she could once again be plunged into the depths of illness. Plus, Marcus had said he would help to organise her passage home.

'When would I leave?' she asked.

'As soon as Marcus hears you agree to stay at his home, I'm guessing he'll be here like a shot. He is quite fond of you, you know! There is nothing he wants more than to see you fully recovered.'

'Okay, then. I will go there and continue our weekly meetings in your office, if you wish. And then, hopefully, very soon, I will be ready to travel to Spain.'

'Wonderful. Let's plan for your discharge on Friday. That way, you will have time to adjust to the idea of leaving, and Marcus and his sister can prepare for your arrival.'

Sofia felt dazed as she left Dr Spencer's office. Rather than returning to the common room, she ventured into the garden. She wanted to speak with Louis.

'I am leaving,' she told him.

'Leaving! When?'

'This Friday! Doctor Spencer has organised for me to go to Marcus' house, where I am to live with him and his sister. From there, I will continue to receive treatment as an outpatient until they think I am well enough to travel home.'

'Good on you! Sad for me, though. I can't tell you how many friends I have seen come and go over the years.' Louis' hands began twitching, then frantically passed his paintbrush back and forth, and she knew her words had upset him.

'I will come and visit you, Louis; I would enjoy doing so.'

'No. Once you are out, don't look back. It's the best way. Go forward; get better and move on with your life. Don't worry about old Louis here!' His hand movements increased in speed, and Sofia watched as paint struck the canvas. Louis' work did not appear any the worse for his frenzied motions; if anything, its patterns became more detailed, his colours more vibrant. The image—a cat, of course—

would only be evident to people familiar with his art, for beyond the hint of feline eyes peering from the centre of the canvas, the work was entirely abstract.

Sofia shuddered for Louis, anticipating his sister's reaction to the painting when she came in on Friday. If he didn't paint more conventional pictures, Felicity had said last week, he'd have her and their older sister, Claire, starving on the streets. The scolding had plunged Louis into misery for days.

It was ridiculous that he had to endure her abuse. Sofia knew Louis' work was extraordinary. Furthermore, she knew she was not the only one intrigued by his art. His psychiatrist, Doctor Maclay, frequently came to see Louis paint. He seemed to be mesmerised by the complexity of Louis' designs; the less realistic the cats became, the more excited he was. However, Louis' doctor's excitement was not for the quality of his artwork she realised one afternoon when he appeared with a group of colleagues. Listening to Doctor Maclay's imperious analysis of the painting on Louis' easel Sofia was aghast.

'See how intricate the patterns are, surely a visual representation of the deterioration of the schizoid mind. I am gathering a collection of them—viewed side by side the works display an extraordinary continuum of the mind as it progresses from normality to madness.'

She'd watched Doctor Maclay pat Louis' shoulder.

'You keep up the good work, Louis. I will be back to see you again in another week or two. I have a colleague arriving from America next month. He would love to see your work.' Without waiting for Louis' reply, Doctor Maclay and his entourage left, leaving Sofia standing beside Louis, who continued to dab paint on his canvas. The words of the doctor hung in the air and she did not know what to say. After a moment of silence, her eyes met his and to her relief Louis erupted into his familiar guffaws, and she joined him. The intricate designs Louis' drew were no more the product of a mad person than Thomas Edison's invention of a machine on which he'd recorded his own voice singing 'Mary had a little lamb'. Like Edison, Louis loved to experiment, and his paintings were just that: explosions of complex lines and shapes which sought the fine line dividing realism from abstractionism. But perhaps only an artist could understand this.

~

Marcus greeted Sofia like an old friend when he arrived at mid-morning the following Friday. After hugging her, he turned and introduced her to the woman accompanying him.

'Sofia, I would like you to meet my sister, Elizabeth. Elizabeth, this is Sofia.'

'Lovely to meet you, Sofia! Marcus has told me so much about you!'

'Oh,' said Sofia, somewhat overwhelmed by the warmth of their greeting. Looking at the woman, it was like she was looking into a mirror of opposites. For where Sofia was small and dark, Elizabeth was tall and fair. Sofia returned her warm smile. 'Nice to meet you, too. Thank you for inviting me to stay in your home.'

'So you are all packed?' Marcus seemed eager to get her away from Napsbury.

'Yes. There isn't much. I need to do some shopping. I hadn't realised how few dresses I own. I've put on such a lot of weight since I've been here and outgrown anything I had when I arrived!'

'No doubt because of all the good food Napsbury Hospital is famous for!' Elizabeth's laugh was warm and friendly, and immediately, Sofia knew she'd like her.

'Yes. They have the most wonderful bread. Plus all the walks in the garden Sister Clare insisted I take gave me a tremendous appetite!'

In truth, Sofia was embarrassed by her weight gain. Never had she felt so bloated in all of her life—no wonder they all thought she was carrying a baby. Hopefully the Edmunds would have a good herb garden. One with peppermint and ginger and fennel. She would make herself some teas—they would make her feel better.

CHAPTER 18

$\mathcal{T}$he drive to the Edmunds' home took barely fifteen minutes, and as they passed through a stone entrance before an impressive two-storey house, Marcus said, 'Welcome to Talonsgate, Sofia.'

Dr Spencer had been right. The house was both enormous and stately. A mansion, really: a huge stone central building attached to what appeared to be a smaller replica of itself by an ornate glass corridor. Sofia had never been inside a house so large before.

'Come on, Sofia, I will show you to your room,' Elizabeth offered. 'It's near to mine, and we have a wonderful view across the fields towards St Albans.'

'While you do that, I will organise our lunch,' Marcus offered. 'What say we meet in the dining room in fifteen minutes?'

Following Elizabeth up the broad stairwell, pausing on the landing, Sofia was captivated by two enormous paintings in gilt frames. The one on the left showed a man in full military uniform, his hand resting on the small sword tucked into his belt. His piercing eyes bore into Sofia and she admired the portraiture skill of the artist. Beside it, in a matching frame, was a painting of a woman wearing a beautiful velvet dress. She sat at a writing desk with a pen in her hand and a cat curled upon her lap. Other paintings hung alongside them: family groupings and smaller individual portraits, people in garden settings surrounded by dogs, cats and pheasants. Together, they revealed a glimpse of the grand estate Talonsgate had once been.

'The ancestors!' Elizabeth laughed as she continued up the stairs. 'Marcus hates them. He says they depress him with their formidable expressions, the way great-great-great-grandfather Lawrence holds his sword as if challenging Marcus to a dual or daring him to be a real man and go to battle! If it were up to my brother, they'd all be stashed in the attic and replaced by landscapes or something a bit more modern.'

'I think they are wonderful,' Sofia said. 'And this, here...' She paused by a large painting at the top of the stairs. Though also a portrait, this one was different. It depicted a woman with dark hair standing in a grassy meadow, clutching at her cape which billowed in the breeze.

'Now that one is not so old. Well, perhaps a few decades, but not centuries old like the others. Marcus bought it a few years ago; I am sure he fell in love with the woman. The painting is called *Boreas*—a reference to the god of the northern wind—by Waterhouse. Have you heard of him? His works are quite wonderful.'

'A turn of the century Pre-Raphaelite, ' Sofia replied, surprised by the confidence of her response.

'You know about art?' Elizabeth asked.

'Well, yes. I do, I suppose. My father and brother both paint. We have a gallery in Malaga.'

At the top of the stairs, Elizabeth opened the door immediately to the right. 'Here is your room. Lovely, isn't it? Mine is exactly the same —a few doors down the hallway. We have the same view. See the steeple of the church at St Albans? And lucky for us, we get the sunrise. I do so love the early morning sunshine. It alone is enough to make you know the day will be wonderful!'

Sofia nodded. It was a beautiful view, and closer to the house she saw stone-edged fields which had been further divided by a series of white post and rail fences, where horses grazed the lush grass. It really was very beautiful.

'To the side here is a smaller room. Marcus thought you might like to have your own little sitting room, though of course, we hope you come and join us downstairs whenever you like.'

The room was sweet, wallpapered with a pattern of fine lemon and white stripes and containing a plump blue velvet settee with matching lemon cushions, a writing desk and a rocking chair upholstered with more blue fabric.

'Oh, this is lovely. Do you think it was once a study—the setting of the lady in the painting on the stairwell?'

'I'd never noticed. Maybe it was! It's been used for all sorts of things over time. It was once Marcus' and my nursery, would you believe?' Turning back to the main room, Elizabeth pointed out the rosewood furniture. 'Here are some drawers for your clothes and a wardrobe for you to hang things. I can lend you some toiletries and even some dresses if you like. They'd be a bit long for you, but we could make them work for a day or two. We'll go down for lunch now, and then afterwards I'll rummage around and find you a few things. Perhaps when you're feeling a little more settled, you and I can drive into the village and get you anything you need.'

'You are very kind. Thank you, Elizabeth. And yes, this is a beautiful room. How very lucky I am!'

Elizabeth led Sofia down the stairs, and, passing a formal-looking room with a long table and a dozen seats, she pointed.

'There's the proper dining room,' she said. 'It's awful. When we were young, we'd perch up on the chairs and our grandmother and aunt would frown at us for our table manners—or lack thereof! Marcus and I rarely use it. We much prefer the glass room.'

Arriving there, Sofia realised it was indeed made of glass and was the room connecting the main house to the smaller one she'd noticed when they'd arrived. Marcus was waiting for them.

'All settled in then, Sofia? Do you like your room? Say, if you don't find it comfortable, there are half a dozen others to choose from!'

'No, it's lovely,' Sofia laughed. 'Really lovely. It will do me perfectly!'

'Excellent. Now, I hope you are hungry, because I have got a feast here for our lunch. Pea and ham soup, followed by chicken pie, and then lemon pudding to finish. This will be our main meal of the day; tonight it will be the leftovers.'

'Dear me! I'm supposed to be losing weight, not putting it on,' Sofia said, but even so, she relished the thought of the meal ahead.

Looking around, Sofia understood why Elizabeth and Marcus liked the glass room, for it was particularly beautiful; long with heavy timber double doors mirroring each other at each end, and three arched glass doorways lining each side. To the left they opened onto the courtyard where Marcus' car remained parked outside the entrance where they'd arrived half an hour earlier. To her right, the windows opened onto a lovely colour-filled garden surrounding a somewhat overgrown lawn. Beyond, Sofia could see the same patchwork of fields she'd noticed from her bedroom.

'It's lovely, isn't it? This corridor and the lodge beyond was built over thirty years ago,' Elizabeth explained. 'Our great-aunt returned to Talonsgate after the death of her husband. She was over seventy, and to Marcus and I, she was both ancient and unbearably cantankerous. Thank goodness our parents made the decision to build the lodge. This passageway provided access between it and the main house, but also gave us a much needed buffer from the nit-picking she indulged in at every opportunity.'

Lunch was a pleasant meal, the soup was delicious, as was the chicken pie bought from the town bakery to which Marcus had added boiled potatoes and beans. As they ate, Marcus explained how Talonsgate had stood for almost six hundred years. Now he and Elizabeth were the last remaining Edmundses to live there.

'It's a dilemma, for these old places are terribly expensive to maintain. If Elizabeth and I had any sense, we'd sell it, and we could each afford to buy a modern detached house in London.'

'No way, Marcus! Who would want to live in London?' Turning to Sofia, Elizabeth continued, 'He's joking. We both love it here. We've managed to hang on to it by selling off most of the land. With the funds raised, we wired the house for electricity, fixed the plumbing and re-slated the roof. The kitchen is dreadful, though!'

'Not something to overly worry you, Elizabeth,' Marcus teased.

'Believe me, it doesn't bother me in the slightest,' she replied with a shrug. 'I'd far sooner we put a new roof on Gideon's stable than worry about a kitchen stove. We make do, and these pies from the bakery are wonderful, so we will never starve!'

After lunch they carried their plates to the kitchen, where Sofia saw evidence of the neglect Elizabeth had alluded to at the lunch table. Jugs and jars, some so old it was impossible to discern the contents, crammed the shelves. The aroma of stale air filled the room, making Sofia want to undo the brass latches holding the windows closed, but she doubted they'd work; they looked like they hadn't been touched in years. Dust clung to every surface and the only areas of the kitchen remotely clean were the porcelain sink, the benches around it, and the large central table. At the far end of the kitchen, a green enamel fridge looked brand new, and totally at odds with the rest of the room.

Although Sofia itched to fill a bucket with water, find a broom and begin throwing jars into the rubbish bin, she said nothing, but followed Marcus and Elizabeth outside for a tour of the grounds. First, Sofia was introduced to Elizabeth's own horses: Gideon, Benson, Storm and Christine. Half a dozen more horses were in the stalls.

'Patients,' Elizabeth said with a laugh.

'Patients?' Sofia was mystified.

'Well, horses with behavioural issues. Biting their owners, or refusing to be caught, or saddled or ridden. Often they are minor problems, but sometimes the behaviours are unpredictable and dangerous for their owners. Mostly, it's the owners who are the problem.'

'Yes, Elizabeth, but it is they who pay our bills, so we need to be nice to them, don't we?'

'Yes, Marcus. Right again, as always.' Elizabeth rolled her eyes at Sofia who laughed.

Unlike the kitchen, the horses stalls were in fine order; spotless, and with the smell of fresh hay filling the air. A clear indication of Elizabeth's priorities. Watching her face light up as she stroked her horses' noses and whispered into their ears, Sofia easily understood how much she loved them.

As the day progressed, Sofia felt relaxed in Marcus and Elizabeth's company. They laughed a lot and constantly teased each other, which reminded her of her life with Andres.

Elizabeth was engaged. Her fiancé, Joseph, was an officer stationed at Woolwich Garrison, east of London, although he frequently visited Talonsgate. 'Mind you,' Elizabeth said, 'I am not sure if he isn't already married.'

'What? You think that he might have a wife somewhere? Surely not!'

'Not to another woman, Sofia—to the army! It's his life. I am lucky to see him once a month!'

'Elizabeth, leave the poor man alone. If I am not mistaken, Joseph's been at Talonsgate at least once a fortnight for the last year, and by the creaking on the staircase, I'd swear there's been a late-night visitor on more than one occasion—unless, of course, there are other suitors hovering about in the midnight hours.'

'Marcus! What a terrible thing to say!'

Most days Marcus left for work by eight in the morning, sometimes returning home for lunch, sometimes not until four PM. Whenever he did, he asked Sofia if she'd walked that day, and regardless of her response or whether it was rainy, windy, or fine, he insisted she accompany him across the meadow.

On their third walk, Sofia slipped on the loose gravel, and Marcus was quick to steady her. Although she was absolutely fine, from then on, Marcus made a habit of holding her arm, insisting he didn't want her to slip again, and Sofia didn't mind. She found comfort in his presence and enjoyed the exercise, sure it was helping her get stronger. Not only were the walks good for her physically, but Sofia also hoped their afternoon conversations might help unlock the memories of her years in Australia. But for all Marcus' references to Melbourne—the theatres he'd visited, the train journey he'd taken to Ararat, his visits to Ballarat—Sofia's recollections of her life before Napsbury remained vague, beyond impressions of the ocean and of Marcus sitting across the dining room table from her, and although she didn't say it, most of these centred upon the fear she'd felt of him.

Though it meant leaving her bed before sunrise, Sofia was happy to accept Elizabeth's invitation to attend to the horses with her. Elizabeth cleaned out each stable then replenished the hay and oats while Sofia used the hose to fill their water troughs. The combination of the horse manure Elizabeth shovelled and the rich, sweet odour rising from the fresh hay reminded Sofia of working alongside her father in the garden. As she returned the hose, she longed for the time when she'd be with him again.

Afterwards, as a weak light captured the dew on the fields making it sparkle, Sofia marvelled at the beauty of the rays filtering through the mist. She watched Elizabeth heave a heavy saddle over Gideon's back, ready to take him out into the yard for exercise. When they walked outside the stable, white puffs of air emitted from both horse and humans as they exhaled. Elizabeth encouraged Sofia to come closer and pat the great black stallion. Sofia cautiously reached out, nervous when he responded to her wary pats by gently nuzzling her hand. The velvety softness of his mouth tickled her, and she laughed.

'Gideon, you sly thing, charming Sofia like that. I suppose you want her to give you a carrot. Well, guess what, I haven't got any today. An apple will have to do.'

Sofia accepted the apple Elizabeth passed her, and following her instructions, held it toward Gideon on the palm of her hand. She was amazed at the horse's delicate manoeuvre when, with flaring nostrils, he made a snuffling sound before grasping the apple between his lips and with a flick of his head, took it into his mouth, taking but a few seconds to devour it.

After watching Elizabeth ride for a few minutes, Sofia returned to the house and made for the kitchen. Two days earlier, she'd volunteered to prepare breakfast, and Marcus and Elizabeth accepted. They liked to eat light: fruit and yoghurt on muesli, a pot of tea and toast with jam or honey. As much as she enjoyed the meal, Sofia wondered if their preference was as much about avoiding cooking as anything else.

After her third day of preparing breakfast, Sofia prompted Elizabeth to return to her horses and Marcus to leave for work, leaving her to tidy up their breakfast dishes. She decided neither of her hosts would object if she made a serious effort to clean the kitchen. Likely neither Marcus nor Elizabeth would even notice. She began by taking one jar at a time and emptying its contents into the rubbish bin, then washing the container in hot soapy water. After the shelves were cleaned, she moved on to the cupboards and drawers of the main room before attacking the side storerooms, ridding them of dust, signs of a mice infestation and outdated supplies.

'So you've discovered our guilty secret,' Marcus exclaimed when he arrived home for lunch to find the stainless-steel bench in the centre of the room covered with jars, packages and cooking implements Sofia had retrieved from a huge oak sideboard. 'Not that it's any secret, I suppose! Neither Elizabeth nor I care much for cleaning. It's terrible, really. We manage the basics, shopping, cooking and washing up, but that's as far as we get. Although we make promises to each other to get in and do a really good tidy up of the house, our efforts never seem to extend to the kitchen.'

'I hope you don't mind me poking around these cupboards,' Sofia replied. 'I was washing up the breakfast dishes, and one thing led to another. I love kitchens. They are my favourite rooms!'

'Well, you've got no competition here, so go your hardest. But, don't overdo it, will you? Only a little at a time. On Saturday, I'll unearth the mop and bucket and do a really good top to toe—remove those cobwebs in the ceiling and wash the windows and floors! It makes me feel excited thinking about it.' Marcus' doleful expression made Sofia laugh.

'That would be wonderful. And perhaps we might even attack the old stove... I suspect that oven hasn't been lit in years, but if we can get it going, I will bake you the best *tarta de Santiago* you've ever tasted!'

'I can't imagine what that is, Sofia, but it certainly sounds too good to resist. The oven will be cleaned *stat*, I promise you.'

'Marcus, you're home early! Did you bring bread with you?' Elizabeth's cheeks were pink from the chill in the air.

'Bread, ham and pickles. Plus corned meat for dinner. I think we already have plenty of vegetables. If not, I will bring some back this afternoon.'

'Carrots? Potatoes? I will cook the meat if you would like me to.'

'No, Sofia, definitely not,' Elizabeth said. 'You are our guest, and here you are knee deep in cooking and cleaning. We usually give our guests at least a fortnight's grace before we set them to work!'

'It's no problem. There is nothing I would enjoy more. Consider it therapy for me.' Sofia laughed.

'Okay, but I will help you,' offered Elizabeth. 'You really shouldn't be lifting heavy things in your condition.'

'What condition?' Sofia frowned, but before Elizabeth could reply, Marcus intervened.

'Great,' he said, 'it will be a team effort. And I will do the washing up!'

~

A week later, Elizabeth drove Sofia to her appointment with Doctor Spencer.

'My, my,' he said as she walked through the door. 'Sofia, you look like a new woman! Country life certainly does agree with you.'

'Yes. Marcus and Elizabeth are very kind, and as you said, their home is wonderful. You will be thrilled to know I am eating plenty of fresh fruit and vegetables, walking for miles each day and sleeping like a log.'

'Excellent, I couldn't ask for more! I can see a big improvement already. Your speech is more fluent than ever, which is wonderful, and you look positively glowing. How is the... weight gain, if you don't mind me asking?'

Sofia slid her hands down her sides and grinned ruefully. 'I think you are right. Country life agrees with me. With all the stews and pudding I'm eating, I will be a barrel before too long. Andres and Papa will barely recognise me when they see me. So you think I'm ready to go home?'

'Oh, no!' He frowned. 'I don't think you should rush this, Sofia. It's only been a week. Marcus and Elizabeth are happy to have you, yes? And you seem to be happy there? Let's get through Christmas, and then we can talk about your trip to Spain!'

'After Christmas? I had hoped to be in Malaga *for* Christmas!'

'No Sofia. I can't support that plan. I don't know if you understand how very ill you were when you first came to Napsbury. I have been through your notes, and frankly, I think we should be thankful you've come as far as you have, given the state the police found you in. But with that said, we must make sure you are fully recovered before you embark on a long journey. Something triggered your breakdown, and we need to unearth the cause so we can avoid it happening again.

Travelling alone all the way to southern Spain could prove too much in your present state. Do you agree?'

'Well, yes, I suppose so.'

'And of course, there is the question of your pregnancy.' Doctor Spencer fixed unwavering eyes upon Sofia.

'No, doctor! Why do we keep going back to this? Certainly, I have put on weight, but you can't accuse every fat woman of being pregnant!'

'I agree, Sofia. Not all women who carry excess weight are pregnant. But you are. I would suggest you are about six or seven months along.'

'No! That's ridiculous, and I don't know why you keep bringing it up.'

Sofia fought to restrain her tears. Damn Doctor Spencer. She'd been going so well, and now he wanted to create problems for her. She wouldn't go back to him, she decided as she stood, clutching her handbag in front of her abdomen, and made for the door.

'Sofia, please, come back and sit down. We don't have to speak about pregnancy if you don't want to. I won't mention it again, I promise.'

Sofia paused. In truth, for as well as she'd been feeling physically, she knew her mind wasn't altogether right. Yesterday when she'd walked into the formal dining room in search of a milk jug to match the creamer she'd found in the kitchen sideboard, she'd had a vision of a large brown box resting on the long table. It was a coffin, she knew, and on seeing it, she'd gasped and stepped back. Then it had vanished. Today, on the narrow gravel road into St Albans, she'd recalled a similar dry, dusty road, where she'd been riding a bicycle. And these were but two of the many images randomly invading her thoughts.

Furthermore, there was the question of her time in Australia. Why was she ever there? It didn't make sense.

And much as she wanted to go to Spain, in truth she was overwhelmed by the thought of the train connections and overnight stays she'd have to manage. What if something happened along the way to cause an episode like the one which had placed her in Bellavue Hospital? It was only by extraordinary good fortune that Marcus had rescued her and taken her to Napsbury. Should such an event reoccur, perhaps she mightn't be so fortunate. It was vexing; if only she could get home, Sofia knew she'd feel so much better, but getting home was not proving easy. Without doubt she'd need help to arrange the trip.

Play the game. The advice Louis had given her. That was what she'd do—she'd be compliant and regain her strength. In a week or two, surely Doctor Spencer would agree she was ready to travel.

'Okay, then.' She returned to her chair. 'What would you like to talk about?'

For the next fifteen minutes Doctor Spencer kept his questions light. Familiar ones he'd asked numerous times before, about her childhood, her family and her friendships in Malaga.

Sofia was pleased with the answers she gave. She told him about her wonderful childhood playing with Andres in the orchards at the finca set high on the hill behind Malaga, overlooking the sea. About her father, who was a lovely man and passionate artist. Although she and Andres had both learned to paint, it was her brother who had the talent, while she'd developed her love for cooking and proved she had a head for business, managing the gallery her father had opened.

Doctor Spencer probed Sofia about her mother, who had died giving birth to herself and her brother—the burden of delivering twins had proved too great. As she spoke, Sofia ignored the tears flowing down her cheeks, and unlike his usual probing into her emotions, Doctor Spencer did not comment on them; he only passed a handkerchief to her. Sofia didn't mind these conversations about her past, for each time she spoke of it, it seemed her memories clarified. It was the questions about Australia for which she had no answers.

On the second weekend at Talonsgate, Elizabeth's fiancé, Joseph arrived. Sofia wasn't sure if it was the effect of the military uniform he wore, but there was no question: Joseph was tall, dark and handsome. As he stood beside Elizabeth, who was equally tall, but with a fair complexion, they made a fine couple.

Despite his obvious joy at being with Elizabeth, and his friendly greeting to Sofia, his dinner table conversation was full of doom.

His concerns stemmed from the actions of the German chancellor, who'd taken control of the Sudetenland on the border of Czechoslovakia. Land which had been taken from Germany twenty years earlier, following the Great War, and which Adolf Hitler had demanded back. It was an error of judgement, in Joseph's opinion, that the British government had submitted to the chancellor's demands.

'But what is the worry, Joseph?' Elizabeth said calmly. 'The Prime Minister agreed this should be allowed, didn't he? And after all, the Sudetenland population is mostly German. To me it makes perfect sense.'

'I don't trust the man. He's used terror to dominate German citizens for years, executed his political opposition, put together an army and navy and created alliances with Italy and Japan. They say he is committed to creating a master race; he believes in Aryan supremacy and intends to stamp out what he describes as the degenerates: those groups he believes are holding Germany back. Homosexuals, the disabled, Seventh Day Adventists and Jews. I was talking to my cousin Avner, this week, and he says the stories of the attacks from last month are not rumours after all. Thousands of shops across Germany have been destroyed, farms owned by Jewish Germans have been taken over by the government, synagogues have been burned. People everywhere are simply vanishing and nobody knows if they've fled to somewhere safer, or been taken by Hitlers men. It's shocking!'

'Has Avner heard anything about your relatives in Germany? Has anyone heard from them?' Elizabeth asked.

'Well, as you know, most are here in England, but my father's oldest sister, Aunt Lydia, is still in Berlin. Both Avner's parents and mine are trying to make contact with her, but even so, they have to be careful about what they write in letters. It's possible my aunt's family is avoiding drawing attention to themselves—to their Jewish heritage. Correspondence asking whether they're safe or enquiring about Jewish people being persecuted could be the last thing they'd want.'

'It must be a terrible worry for your family, Joseph. Thank God you are here safe in Britain,' Marcus offered.

'Let's hope so. You have to wonder, after Franco's move in Spain, and now Hitler in Germany, and apparently the Italian leader is also agitating for power, where it is all going to end. There are some who are predicting a war, one Britain won't escape from.'

Over the weekend, Sofia saw why Elizabeth was fond of Joseph. He was both funny and kind, and full of enthusiasm. He and Elizabeth went horse riding on Saturday, and then on Sunday, leaving at sunrise, they all piled into Marcus' car and drove west. Crossing the Welsh border, they came to a beautiful town snuggled between mountains called Abergavenny, where they stopped for breakfast. While they were in the café eating sausages and eggs accompanied by Penclawdd cockles and laverbread, Elizabeth heard St Fagans, a town barely twenty miles south, was celebrating its annual fair. Marcus and Joseph agreed it was a treat not to be missed, and they arrived at St Fagans at midday. Despite the chilly breeze, the sun shone and Sofia enjoyed meandering through the stores, where all sorts of handcrafts were being sold and samples of fresh produce were offered by smiling Welsh people with delightful accents. Meanwhile Marcus and Joseph called in at a tavern, insisting they had to sample the local pale ale the region was famous for. Meeting up afterwards, they surprised Elizabeth and Sofia by passing them each a pair of intricate spoons.

'Oh, this is beautiful,' Sofia exclaimed, her finger outlining the one Marcus had given her. It had been carved from a dark wood, its surface sanded to the silkiest of finishes. She studied its handle. Halfway along, the timber had been delicately worked to represent a knot, and toward the end was the shape of a heart. Within the heart sat two tiny birds.

'Do you know what it is, Sofia?' Elizabeth's eyes were teasing.

'A spoon?'

'A *love* spoon! They've been made by the men of Wales for centuries, carved especially for their sweethearts. Beautiful, aren't they?'

Given to their sweethearts? A sense of disquiet rippled through Sofia and self-consciously she glanced at Marcus who looked alarmed. Thankfully, Joseph filled the awkward silence.

'Yes, and the spoons are also a treat for tourists to buy for their friends and family, so don't feel you are compelled to marry this goose because he's presented you with a spoon. I am sure any modern woman would be looking for more than a piece of carved wood to convince her she'd found the right man. Mind you, don't go jumping over any brooms you find lying around the doorways of Talonsgate with Marcus, or indeed you might find yourself wedded to him!'

CHAPTER 19

*A*t least every other day through the following week, Elizabeth found a reason for herself and Sofia to drive to the village: the purchase of horse feed, fresh meat and bread for dinner, a visit to the vet to discuss a yearling's limp. On the third visit, Sofia noticed a shopfront displaying colourful posters: boats on the Seine with the Eiffel Tower rising in the background, the turquoise blue waters of the Mediterranean against the steep cliffs of Greek islands.

'Do you mind if we have a look here?' she said, and without waiting for Elizabeth's reply, Sofia entered. As she suspected, it was a travel agency. There was no harm in enquiring about the journey to Malaga, she decided, and waited for the young man at the counter to finish serving the customer he attended to.

'May I help you, madam?'

'Yes, please. I would like to organise a trip to Spain. Southern Spain. To Malaga.'

'Really? It's been a long time since we've had anyone go through Spain, what with the war and all. They say it's safe now, but I am not sure. When were you thinking of going?'

'Soon. I am not absolutely certain of the date yet, but I thought I would find out how to get there.'

'So all the way to the Costa del Sol, you say? Quite a journey! It will take a few days—will you require us to organise accommodation along the way?'

'Yes please.'

The man flicked between a series of pages, each bearing rows of times and dates.

'I would suggest you take an early bus to London, and at Victoria Station, catch the night train to Paris; book a sleeping carriage. It will take you through to Cardiff, and then the carriage is transferred onto the ferry to cross the channel. On the other side, at Dunkirk, the carriage will be rejoined and the train will continue to Gare du Nord, arriving at about nine AM.'

'You mean I only have to catch one train?'

'Yes, it's wonderful, isn't it? The Night Ferry has only been around for a couple of years. Makes the trip to Paris so much easier; you can sleep all the way if you wish. Of course, the train has a dining cart for all of your meals and a full porter service to assist with your luggage. Nonetheless, once in Paris, you'll be exhausted, I'm sure. I recommend you stay a night or two there, rest up a bit and prepare for the next leg of the journey. However, then it all gets a bit tricky.'

'Oh... why tricky?' Sofia felt excited to discover she only needed to travel on one train to get to Paris; that it wasn't the arduous trip Marcus and Doctor Spencer seemed to think it was.

'Well, it's easy to organise both your ticket to Paris and your accommodation. However, from there, booking your passage through to Madrid is difficult. I cannot guarantee the accuracy of the timetables or which trains are running. I suggest once you arrive in Paris, you find a travel agency and let them organise tickets to the border and then Madrid. They may even organise your tickets to Malaga. But you need to understand, it could be hectic, with disruptions occurring at a moment's notice.'

'I am sure I will be fine.' Even as she said it, Sofia felt a tinge of dismay. She would much prefer to have her trip home arranged all the way through to Malaga before embarking on her journey.

'Would you like me to jot down some of the costs, so you know what you will be up for?'

'No, it will be alright for now, thank you. I will be back in a few weeks, and then we can finalise the details.'

'Okay, miss. I suggest you don't leave it for too long, you know... with the baby coming.' The young man's ears reddened as he spoke.

'Thank you, sir,' Elizabeth interrupted.

Sofia had barely listened to the comment; she had no intentions of delaying the journey for long. She would have to focus on getting better: lots of fresh air, walking and healthy food, and carefully adhering to the medication schedule Dr Spencer had given her.

As they left the agency, Elizabeth spoke. 'Sofia, are you sure you should be thinking about all of this at present?'

'Thinking about what? Getting home to my family?'

'Well, yes. I don't think you should rush this. You've been home from Napsbury barely three weeks, and it *is* a long journey. Why don't you wait a month or two? Leave it until after Easter; till May even— then you can be here for my wedding!'

Sofia set her mouth in a firm line and did not reply. Easter was three months away! There was no way she could stay in England that long.

That evening, Sofia had no doubt Elizabeth had spoken to Marcus about her visit to the travel agency. They'd eaten dinner and were moving to the lounge room, where they liked to spend an hour chatting or reading before going to bed. The fire was cosy there, a pleasant buffer against the chilly winter evenings. Elizabeth excused herself for a few minutes to check on a horse who'd been delivered into her care two days earlier.

'You are keen to return to Spain, Sofia?' Marcus asked once his sister went out. 'Aren't you happy here with Elizabeth and me? We love having you stay with us, you know.'

'Of course I am happy here, Marcus. You and Elizabeth have been very good to me. But I *need* to go home. I will *feel better* when I am home!'

'Don't you think you could consider making your home here for a few months at least? St. Albans is a delightful village, and with everything going on in the world, it is safe.'

'Marcus, no. Spain is my home. I belong there with Andres and Papa. I have been away from the gallery for far too long. I am sure they could use my help.'

He reached for her hand. 'But what if I said I needed you here, Sofia? I know you need rest, and, well, peace, at present, so I don't want you to feel pressured. It does not need to be a conversation for now. But do you think one day you might consider making a life here with Elizabeth and me?'

'Marcus—Elizabeth is getting married soon.'

'Yes, but after their wedding, she and Joseph plan to continue living at Talonsgate in the lodge. Elizabeth has her horses, of course, and with Joseph frequently away with the military, it will be a good arrangement for them.'

'I don't know, Marcus. You and Elizabeth are very kind, but still...' Sofia felt her throat knotting, and her words came out muffled. Was Marcus going to try to stop her from leaving, again?

The pressure of his hand upon hers made Sofia tremble. She wished Elizabeth would return, for suddenly the space between herself and Marcus felt too small.

He must have sensed her discomfort, for he removed his hand. 'I am sorry, Sofia. I shouldn't have said anything. All you need to think about is getting better. You have been through so much, and you have come a long way. I won't mention it again. Let's focus on getting you well.'

Sofia nodded, but couldn't help a sigh escaping, or the frown settling on her forehead, or the trembling in her hand.

CHAPTER 20

*O*ver the next few days, although life at Talonsgate continued its same routines, Sofia couldn't shake a lingering sense of unease. Her longing to be home had escalated since speaking to the travel agent, but so too had a sense of foreboding that Marcus was conspiring with Doctor Spencer to stop her. The conversations which had come easily between them on their afternoon walks became stilted and when she overheard Elizabeth and Marcus discussing her determination to travel to Malaga, her fears were confirmed: they were plotting to keep her here! Sofia's mind spun in endless circles day and night, planning a course of action to get to Malaga, but nothing seemed easy. Hence she was surprised when, on the following Thursday evening, Marcus raised the subject of her journey home.

'Sofia, I am starting to think you might be right. Perhaps you won't feel truly well until you are with your family. It has been a long time since you've seen them, and I suspect much has changed in Spain since you left, but even so, maybe going home would be the best thing for you after all.'

Taken aback by his words, Sofia felt both elated and overwhelmed. She again thought of Louis saying how he was institutionalised. Had she too, become dependent upon the safety net offered by Marcus and Elizabeth at Talonsgate? Is that why now the opportunity to leave was causing her to freeze? Surely not? A second concern also sprang forth. Had Marcus decided that if she didn't want to stay with him, then she should go immediately? She nodded even as her heart raced with conflicting emotions.

Marcus had not finished. 'Elizabeth and I have been talking. If Doctor Spencer says its alright—and, of course, if you agree— Elizabeth could travel with you to Madrid. Once there, you will only have the final leg of the journey to make. In Madrid you can send a message to your family to let them know the time you will arrive in Malaga. Elizabeth can see you onto your train, and then your family can meet you at the other end. Could that work?'

Sofia could barely believe her ears. All of her fears evaporated as she looked at Elizabeth in amazement.

'You will come with me, Really? That would be wonderful! Are you sure you don't mind?'

'Not at all, Sofia. It has been years since I was last in France, and I have never been to Spain. It will be wonderful! Perhaps we can spend a night or two in Paris before going on to Madrid. I would love to do some shopping there! Plus we could visit the Louvre, and maybe we… well I could climb the Eiffel Tower.'

'Oh yes, certainly. It sounds wonderful. Thank you!'

The knowledge she would soon be home set Sofia glowing with delight, and when she visited Doctor Spencer the next day—this time accompanied by Marcus—she had no trouble convincing him she was well enough to undertake the journey in Elizabeth's company.

Doctor Spencer agreed with Marcus's suggestion this might be the step necessary to enable Sofia's full recovery. However, he insisted that before he could allow Sofia to leave his care, she must promise to continue treatment in Malaga. 'I will speak with my colleagues and see if I can identify a suitable doctor for you.'

Marcus smiled ruefully. 'I am a step ahead of you on this, Alex.' He took a piece of paper from his pocket. 'Here are the details of a Doctor Hernández, who has a practice in Malaga. He's written a few journal articles and his methods seem to be sound. I think he could be the right person for Sofia.'

'Thank you, Marcus. I'll put some notes together for him. There is no doubt about it, Sofia, the good Lord was watching over you when he put you in this man's path.'

'I am sure you are right, Doctor Spencer. And thank you for your care. And thanks to you, too, Marcus.' Sofia could not stop smiling, suddenly full of appreciation for the treatment she'd received from them both, now they'd agreed she was well enough to travel home.

'Not so fast… I would still like you to visit me each week until you leave. And of course, one day in the future, should you return to England, I hope you will come and see me! I will be very interested to hear how you get along.'

'My thoughts exactly, Alex. I rather hope Sofia decides to return to us, sooner rather than later!'

Thrilled by the knowledge she was going home soon, Sofia relaxed and enjoyed Christmas at Talonsgate. The fun began on Christmas Eve, when Joseph arrived armed with a plum pudding he'd purchased in London, as well as bags of sweets: liquorice all-sorts, barley sugar and marshmallows, and a box of beautifully decorated bon-bons he'd found in Harrods.

Laughingly, he placed them onto the table. 'As I'm Jewish, Christmas is not really my thing. But nonetheless, Elizabeth, I'm happy to indulge you by eating as much roast turkey and plum pudding as you wish!'

The making of Christmas luncheon was a combined affair. True to his word, Marcus was up first on Christmas morning, preparing what he'd told them would be the finest turkey they'd ever tasted. When Sofia entered the kitchen at seven AM, he had the bench covered in all manner of ingredients. With much hilarity, Sofia helped him adjust the recipe he'd found in an ancient cookbook which described how to catch, pluck and clean the turkey, before making stuffing using hyssop, parsley and sage. Marcus was comical as he described his efforts to catch the turkey and the difficulty he had plucking it, but the white paper tied with green string from which he produced the turkey made a lie of his claims. Together they blanched and chopped what herbs they could find. These were supposed to be added to a mix of tender, lean pork, bacon, the liver of the chicken and hard-boiled eggs, and the final touch, according to the recipe, was to add a powder created from a long black pepper, a piece of ginger, cinnamon and white salt. They only had half the ingredients, but made do.

At quarter to ten the turkey was in the oven, and Sofia set up the glass room table for a light brunch—serving her own special tortilla accompanied by sliced bread, a mix of finely chopped tomato, olive oil and garlic, and glasses of orange juice.

Following a leisurely hour over the table, they returned to the kitchen. Sofia and Elizabeth prepared vegetables to go with Marcus' turkey, while Joseph—who wasn't to be outdone by Marcus—got to work on a custard and brandy sauce recipe he'd found in Marcus' book to serve with his pudding.

At midday, they all agreed it was time for a present-giving ceremony, and they headed for the lounge room with glasses of a dark red port in hand.

'Good heavens, Marcus, what is that?' Elizabeth pointed at a small, slightly bent branch cut from one of the pine trees lining the driveway, which had been draped with tinsel and settled in the corner of the room.

'Our Christmas tree, of course!'

'Really? Well I hope our Christmas has a bit more life in it than that poor little thing!'

Beneath the tree sat the presents that had accumulated on the dining room table over the last twenty-four hours: an eclectic bundle of parcels from Joseph, wrapped in gold and red cellophane complete with gorgeous green ribbon; Elizabeth's in brown paper finished with red and green twine; and Marcus' and Sofia's sharing the colourful striped wrapping Sofia had purchased in St Albans' department store.

Sofia was pleased when Elizabeth, Marcus and Joseph appeared to like the books she'd bought them. She nervously eyed the rectangular parcel Marcus, who was playing Santa, handed her, hoping his gift to her wouldn't be too personal. Unwrapping it, she was relieved to find it was a box of Godiva chocolates, imported from Belgium: very select, but nothing she needed to feel embarrassed by. She immediately opened them and passed them around.

Their Christmas meal was somewhere between a very late lunch and an early dinner, as at three PM they sat before the fire Joseph had lit in the rarely used dining room and watched Marcus carve the turkey, then heaped their plates with roast vegetables and the beans which Sofia had peeled and sliced that morning. Joseph's pudding was delicious, though they teased him for his heavy-handed addition of brandy to the custard.

At the end of the meal, Sofia groaned and rubbed her ever expanding belly. She smiled ruefully when she saw Marcus watching her.

'Full, dear?' she smiled at the slight slur in his voice as he leaned close to her. He'd begun filling his glass with wine while preparing the turkey mid-morning, and it hadn't been empty, since. Though she too had accepted a small glass of the wine at the time, she'd only sipped on it, and with the addition of the glass of wine she'd drunk with their meal, felt pleasantly relaxed and clear-headed.

'Absolutely! Starting tomorrow, I will be on a strict diet!'

'Wonderful. That means the leftovers will be all mine. And never mind your weight, Sofia—you look beautiful. Furthermore, I am pretty sure those extra pounds will drop off in no time, just you wait and see.'

She ignored the softness in his eyes as he complimented her. 'Well,

I hope you are right, because if I keep eating at this rate, I will explode. I am sure Papa and Andres will barely recognise me when I step off the train.'

'You don't have to go, Sofia. You could stay here.'

'No, Marcus. I do have to go home.' Sofia squeezed his hand, knowing the wine had loosened Marcus' tongue. She was grateful for his kindness, but her home was in Malaga.

Sofia could barely believe it when, in the first week of the new year, she and Elizabeth purchased their tickets to Paris; they would depart on January 26th. This allowed time for Elizabeth to make arrangements for the care of her horses for the fortnight she planned to be away.

The same young man Sofia had spoken with weeks earlier served them. Again, he reiterated the potential for disruptions to train services in Spain, adding that skirmishes between the Republicans and Nationalists could erupt at any time, and warning them to stay safe. Elizabeth, like Sofia, was far too excited about their journey to feel concerned.

'We'll be alright, Sofia. Two women minding their own business on a train to Madrid shouldn't upset anyone. Once we have bought our tickets and are safe in our carriage, we'll be fine.'

During the following weeks, if Sofia had any reservations about the journey, it was nothing to do with the political situation; to her Spain represented safety and security at home with her father and brother. Rather, her concerns were about the emergence of disturbing images that seemed to be arriving with ever greater frequency, often when she least expected it. A memory of sitting at a large table surrounded by people, listening to a man speaking with authority about paintings and rules and philosophies. Of working in a large garden alongside a thin pale girl. Of gazing at a pile of cases resting outside a burning building. None of these images made sense to her but they did serve to remind her of how unwell she was, especially when they descended on her unexpectedly, and left her gasping for breath.

This had occurred last week when Sofia had left Elizabeth standing in a long line at the post office to go to the bakery. There, while she waited at the counter, a small child in a stroller had gazed up at her, then broken into a broad, toothy grin. Sofia had no explanation for the sense of dread that coursed through her body. Fleeing the shop, she'd stood at the corner, breathing in and out, slowing her heart rate, and focussing her thoughts on returning home to Malaga in a bid to calm down. She hadn't mentioned the episode to Elizabeth. To do so might raise concerns about her readiness to travel. And then, barely an hour later, she'd been overwhelmed by a similar dread when they'd wandered into a shoe shop, where Elizabeth thought she'd look for a pair of shoes more suited to the journey to Paris than the leather boots she usually wore. As they perused the shelves, dainty slip-ons, elaborately decorated with beads, caught Sofia's attention. She was captivated by them, sure she'd owned a similar pair, but unable to think of when.

'I can see myself stomping around the stables in those,' Elizabeth said when she noticed Sofia gazing at them. 'Really, it's hard to imagine any occasion that you'd wear those, isn't it?'

Her words, combined with a sense of déjà vu, almost knocked Sofia off her feet. She stumbled to a chair and held her head until Elizabeth declared they'd done enough shopping for the day, and they'd gone home.

Today they'd returned to town and Sofia hoped nothing would happen to spoil their shopping trip. Elizabeth was still fixed on buying shoes for the journey—something comfortable, yet attractive and which wouldn't look shabby while they were in Paris. Seeing a dress shop, Sofia decided she'd purchase a new dress or two for their journey.

'Elizabeth, I might pop in and see if I can find something

comfortable to travel in. This weight gain is ridiculous. Honestly, I don't know what to think.'

'Don't worry, Sofia. I put on weight every winter. The chilly weather is an invitation to stuff ourselves, and so of course the pounds keep piling on. However, soon it will be summer and we'll be back to salads, and our flab will all drop off.'

Sofia looked at Elizabeth's slim waistline dubiously, but was glad when she pointed out some dresses designed to fall from below the bust, unlike the majority cinched to show off the slim waistline Sofia had somehow lost. Thrilled at the find, she purchased a black, a blue and a red dress, a comfortable pair of shoes that would do for travelling, stockings, hat and a practical black handbag which would go with everything. She also bought a small suitcase, for the only one she owned was the tatty old case she'd brought with her from Australia.

After their purchases, Elizabeth took Sofia to her hairdresser, where a chatty lady called Lydia insisted she part her hair on the side. She'd then shaped Sofia's thick black curls into soft waves, long enough to be pulled back into the bun but also manageable if left hanging freely. Sofia was delighted with the result.

'My, my, don't you two look chic!' Marcus laughed when they returned home. 'I am not sure I should be letting either of you onto the streets of London, much less Paris. I pity the poor men who catch a glimpse of you and forevermore are prisoners to the memory of the mysterious foreigners who passed them by.'

Finally, January 26th arrived. Their train didn't leave until quite late in the evening, and even though Sofia and Elizabeth were quite happy to catch the bus from St Albans, Marcus insisted on driving them to Victoria Station. After weeks of teasing them about breaking hearts all over Paris, he was suddenly serious and full of warnings.

'You must beware of the charming mannerisms of French men;

they are renowned for luring foreign women into their arms and beds with their sweet talk.'

'Marcus! Really. I am quite sure Sofia and I will be quite safe, and well able to deal with any Casanovas who come our way, should we be so lucky. Besides, I might be engaged, but Sofia's perfectly free to be charmed by whomever she likes.' Elizabeth winked at Sofia; she loved to tease Marcus.

'Well, that being said, you need to watch out for any unusual gatherings. Conflicts, violence even, between the Nationalists and Republicans could arise anywhere.'

'Okay, Marcus. We will resist the urge to join crowds of protestors or to throw rocks at anyone,' replied Sofia, joining in the teasing. She knew Marcus's concerns had some basis; some of the conflicts Marcus had alluded to had been very nasty. A dreadful incident had occurred at Gandesa, south of Barcelona a few months earlier, where many people had been killed. Weighing up the event, they'd agreed it had occurred well south of their route, and if Elizabeth and Sofia minded their own business, remained inconspicuous and if questioned, showed themselves to be compliant and agreeable travellers, they'd be fine.

'Marcus, darling, stop worrying! I will be home within a fortnight, and Sofia will be safe with her family. She'll be back to see us sooner or later, I'm sure—unless, of course, you continue to harangue her. Now be a gentleman, will you, and get our suitcases from the luggage compartment?'

Marcus looked glum, as if suddenly doubting the wisdom of their trip. Sofia was sure that if he could, he would have ripped up their tickets and taken them back to Talonsgate.

At Victoria Station, as they prepared to board the Night Ferry, Marcus gave Elizabeth a quick hug and a repetition of the warning to avoid trouble. Then he turned to Sofia.

'Please be safe, my dear! You will write when you are settled, won't you? I'll look forward to hearing from you, and perhaps in summer, I could come to Malaga and see how you are going?'

'Of course, Marcus. I would love you to come and visit.'

To her surprise, he pulled her to him, wrapped his arms around her and kissed her on her forehead. This was more than a hug of friendship, she was sure.

'Come on, Sofia,' Elizabeth said. 'If we aren't quick, the train will take off without us. Bye, Marcus. Don't forget to keep up the horse feed, will you? Davy will look after them, but I did say you would make sure their feed bins remain full.'

PART IV

Figueres

CHAPTER 21

*I*t was hard not to feel excited as they boarded the Night Ferry at the carriage labelled with the number three, from where it only took minutes to find their cabin. It was a neat room with two bench seats that converted to beds, each with a small overhead lamp. After storing their luggage , Elizabeth suggested they make their way to the dining room before it filled up with passengers. There, they could pass an hour or so, before returning to their cabin. They agreed that since everyone had to alight the train at Dover, there was no sense in trying to sleep before then.

It was almost eleven when they reached Dover. Sofia and Elizabeth wrapped their coats around themselves and joined the other passengers in a waiting bay. There they stood, fascinated, listening to the clanging of metal ringing out in the darkness as the carriages were separated and loaded onto the waiting barge. Once they were in position, they were able to board and return to their cabins, where it was time to sleep.

Sofia was wakeful, though, and the carriage's constant shuddering and ferry's whirring motor didn't help. A small electric light allowed for reading, and she tried to concentrate on her magazine, but found it difficult to quell the nervousness rising within. She'd been here before, she was sure of it. The sense of floating, the swaying of the cabin and the sound of the motor seemed familiar.

'Sofia, are you alright?' Elizabeth asked.

'Yes… no… I don't know. I feel like I remember being here!'

'Here, on the Night Ferry? Oh well, perhaps you have. If you travelled to Australia in the last couple of years, you might well have been on this very train. Before then, you would have caught a similar ferry, but if so, you'd have changed trains along the way.'

Although Elizabeth's reply was quite logical, Sofia felt unnerved as more of her past unfolded, and she felt weighed by a sense of foreboding rather than pleasure.

'Here, love. Hold my hand. We have a long night ahead, and I really think you should get a good sleep. Marcus would never forgive me if anything happened to you, as you probably know!'

It was ten AM when they finally arrived at the Gare du Nord. Dismounting, they followed a string of fellow passengers carrying suitcases towards the exit signs of the enormous station, with no idea where they were going, and surrounded by French-speaking people who all seemed to be in a rush. Nonetheless, soon they emerged onto a busy street, and were pleased to see a row of taxis waiting.

'Thank God the travel agency booked our hotel,' Elizabeth said. 'I would hate to try to find a place to stay amid this chaos! My high school French isn't that good!'

Sofia agreed, especially because their taxi driver understood very little English. When Elizabeth passed a piece of paper with the name of their hotel to him, he nodded and smiled broadly.

'Oh, oui, Le Regina—Place des Pyramides.' He started the motor and veered out onto the busy street, barely glancing at the vehicle behind, whose driver honked with a blast of impatience.

Minutes later, in line before The Regina's reception desk, Sofia arched her spine, rubbing the ache in her lower back, and despaired at the heaviness in her legs, which made walking difficult. Surrounded by chatting women and couples hand in hand, she felt exhausted. Across the room, she saw a vacant chair.

'Elizabeth, do you mind? I need to sit for a minute.' Without waiting for an answer, she crossed to the seat. Falling into it, she rested her head against her hand, closed her eyes and breathed slowly and deeply as Sister Marie had taught her, trying to ignore the sensation of her heart pounding so hard it seemed it might explode in her chest. What was wrong with her?

Minutes later, Elizabeth returned, followed by a porter.

'Are you okay, Sofia? I have our key, and this kind man is going to take our luggage to the room.'

The ride up the escalator was quick—only three levels. After opening the door, the porter placed their cases inside and left with a slight bow and broad smile.

'Anything you want… ring!' he said, mimicking a gesture of using the telephone on the table near the door.

The room was beautiful, with a velvet settee, a vase of flowers on a coffee table and afternoon sunshine filtering through lace curtains.

Approaching the window, Elizabeth swept the curtain aside, revealing a view of a thousand city buildings. Below, dozens of market stalls with striped awnings formed an island in the middle of the street. Peering down with Elizabeth, Sofia saw vendors selling flowers, fruit and vegetables and books.

'We should go out for a walk,' she offered, although she wondered how long her legs would hold out.

'No! You are exhausted. We've been on the move for over twelve hours, and I know you barely slept last night. It is time to stop.'

'But we have only been sitting, Elizabeth! It's hardly tiring… Don't you want to see Paris?'

'We've got three days here. Tomorrow we can go out and have a look around, but for now we should rest. I insist.'

Sofia spotted a patch of green barely a block away. 'Okay then, Elizabeth. I *would* like to put my feet up—but afterwards, I say we take a stroll in that park? Perhaps we'll find a little café nearby where we could have our dinner.'

'Great idea, Sofia. Now you try to sleep. I might even have a little lie down myself!'

Sofia felt a little guilty. She should be generous and encourage Elizabeth to go out and see the sights, peruse the Parisian department stores she'd so looked forward to seeing. But the words refused to come. Sofia couldn't ignore feeling the only thing keeping her anchored to the present was Elizabeth's practical, optimistic presence. Left alone, she hated to think where the thoughts battering the periphery of her mind might take her.

Sofia felt much better when they stepped out that afternoon. The energy of the street was stimulating, and although the crowded pavements, clamour of shopkeepers and noise of the vehicles in Paris were similar to the atmosphere of London's city centre, it was also very different.

They walked along the Rue du Rivoli, allowing themselves to be swept along with the movement of people, not caring where it took them. Soon they were walking along the Right Bank of the Seine, enjoying the sight of the small boats bobbing on the water. Approaching a bridge, they crossed it, and continued walking along the river's edge. Along the way, they passed numerous artists who'd set up easels, some turned to the west to capture the Eiffel Tower, others facing Notre Dame.

Everywhere they went, the streets were full with vendors selling pastries and flowers, buskers playing violins and artists with rows of canvases set out on benches, hoping to make a sale.

There were cafés and restaurants everywhere, and as they looped back to the Champs-Élysées, they found a vacant table outside a delightful restaurant which specialised in seafood. It's black and white chequered tablecloths and red padded chairs formed a picturesque arrangement and because it was six PM, they were mostly vacant. A friendly waiter seated them, and very soon they received their order of a creamy oyster stew, slices of bread, and glasses of Chardonnay. They decided to complete the delicious meal with an apple tart and clotted cream.

'Oh, Elizabeth, I will need to buy new dresses again—I shouldn't have eaten so much!' Sofia said, patting her abdomen.

'Well, it's a good thing we bought ourselves decent shoes! We can walk off a bit of our meal on the way to the hotel, ' Elizabeth said, extending her leg and admiring the two-toned leather pumps she'd purchased—smart, but very practical for walking long distances.

'Yes, especially when the ground is so uneven! The French ladies certainly are chic, but I don't know how they manage in those heels.'

Elizabeth watched plaintively as two women in stylish hats and fur-lined coats passed by. 'I don't think Marcus has to be too concerned about a couple of country bumpkins from England breaking the hearts of French men when they are surrounded by such beauty. It's quite depressing, how oaf-like these mademoiselles make me feel!'

Sofia laughed. 'Elizabeth, you are not an oaf. What's more, you've got Joseph who adores you, so I wouldn't be feeling too sorry for yourself!'

In one way the walk proved to be a good remedy, for no sooner had Sofia climbed into bed and shut her eyes than she was asleep. It didn't last long, however; even in the midnight hours, street sounds filtered through the window, pulling her into wakefulness. For over an hour she rolled back and forth, struggling to get comfortable as her abdomen felt at war with her body and her mind coursed with memories of Andres and Papa; of them carrying buckets of oranges through the courtyard, of Papa taking one and throwing it toward her and laughing when she jumped high to catch it. She was consumed with longing to see them again, to hear the sound of her Papa's calm voice soothing her the way he had when she'd been a child.

Eventually, she fell back asleep, but it seemed only minutes before she was woken again, this time by the clanging of a bell and flashing lights from the street. Sofia leapt to her feet. Perhaps a fire alarm had sounded! The urgent repetitious shrieking grew louder, the flashing lights closer. It was then she realised the vehicle was not a fire truck but an ambulance. As she stood at the hotel room window, she found herself remembering a different night, when she'd been driven through the dark streets of Paris, following a similar vehicle. One with her brother inside.

Images of Andres fell on her in a cascade. Him on the floor of the restaurant, gasping for breath. Him in hospital, pale and very ill. He'd been hospitalised in Paris, she was sure. But worse were images of Andres lying in his bed in Malaga.

Sofia stumbled to the bed and fell into it, trying to make sense of what she was seeing. It was then images of a coffin came to her—large one minute, and then tiny—and her head ached as if it might explode.

'Sofia, what is it?' Elizabeth asked as she entered the room, but Sofia didn't know and couldn't speak. Instead she drew her legs up, reaching for a blanket, trembling and wide eyed.

'Sofia, talk to me!' Elizabeth's questions came fast. 'Are you alright? Can you hear me?' Sofia grasped the hand she offered and clung to it as tightly as she could.

Words seized in her mind, and she couldn't ask the question she wanted answers to. *What were these images? Was that Andres in the coffin?*

'Please, have a sip of water. Come on, perhaps it will help.'

Elizabeth held the glass to Sofia's lips, her hands firm, but the action reminded Sofia of another time when she'd had water forced down her throat, and she launched back, flinging the water away and staring at the woman before her.

'Heavens, Sofia! What is happening? It's me, Elizabeth. I am not going to hurt you. I don't know what to do! Should I call for help? Perhaps the hotel can find us a doctor?'

A doctor! Would she be returned to a mental hospital, then? Sofia gasped in fear. Her madness was returning. And yet, even as she closed her eyes and sealed her lips for fear of saying anything that would prove she'd lost her mind, deep within she ached for help.

For the next hour, Sofia sat huddled on her bed, trembling with fear, and although Elizabeth tried to offer a cup of tea, or words of assurance, Sofia couldn't bring herself to respond.

At Elizabeth's request, a doctor arrived. After a quick assessment of Sofia, he gave her an injection to sedate her. As Sofia's eyes closed, she heard him speaking with Elizabeth.

'Mademoiselle, I think she is suffering from exhaustion. Such a long trip has overtired her. A rest will do her good.'

'But what about the hallucinations? Her terror?'

'Perhaps she was having a nightmare. When she wakes, she may very well have forgotten all about it.'

'Will Sofia be right to continue the journey to Malaga? She is desperate to return to her family.'

'Yes, but perhaps you mustn't dilly dally in Paris. Rather, get her home, as quickly as possible.'

Sofia awoke exhausted and apprehensive, but improved. She felt dreadful for upsetting Elizabeth through the night and tried to apologise. 'I truly don't know what happened. I slept well for a while, but then I was awakened by an ambulance. I stood at the window watching, then the next thing I knew I was in a panic. My head ached something dreadful—I was sure it would split open!'

'Thank God it didn't, Sofia, but I think the best thing we can do is take the doctor's advice and get you home. If we board a train early tomorrow, we will be in Madrid the following day, and then you'll reach Malaga by Sunday at the latest.'

The bookings officer at the Gare du Nord looked grave as Elizabeth explained their intention to travel to Madrid and then Malaga.

'Miss, it is too dangerous to be going to Spain now. I really must suggest you reconsider this journey!'

Elizabeth was ready with her reply. 'Surely if we clutch our handbags and hang on to our suitcases, anyone will see we are mere travellers, neither aligned to any factions nor having any intention of stirring up trouble. Are the trains running?'

'Yes, at present the line through Barcelona and on to Madrid is open, but who knows for how long?'

'It only needs to be long enough for Sofia and me to get through. A week should do it. Sofia needs to get home, as a matter of urgency. We have already completed half of our journey and do not plan on turning back now.'

'Alright, alright—so you'll be wanting two tickets to Madrid, then?'

'Yes, please!'

'That will be thirty francs. The train leaves from Gare de Lyon. It will take you to the border at Cerbère, where the French railway line ends. I have never been there, but from what I hear, you exit the train and then walk down a tunnel to Spain's Portbou Station to continue your journey to Madrid. The Spanish have their own system of railway lines; sadly, these are not compatible with ours.'

'Thank you.' Elizabeth looked at Sofia and rolled her eyes as if to say, *surely this can't be too difficult!*

The following morning, with their suitcases in hand, yet again Sofia's heart pounded and the sensation filled her with dread; it was the same anxiety she'd been consumed with two nights earlier, which had led to her nervous collapse and increasingly was occurring whenever she thought of Malaga and tried to make sense of why she'd left.

She tried to practise Doctor Sinclair's recommendation: to look forward rather than behind, and allow the memories of her past to come to her when they were ready. She consoled herself by thinking that at least, all going to plan, she'd be home in three days and life would make sense again. In a few hours they'd be at the Spanish border, and by evening they'd be in Barcelona. There Sofia planned to make a telephone call to the dairy up the road from the finca, or maybe the small grocery shop on the hill. Either would be happy to take a message to her papa, to tell him she was on her way home. And, if that proved impossible, she'd just take a taxi up the mountain and arrive unexpectedly. How wonderfully surprised he and Andres would be to see her!

Nonetheless, for all of her efforts to look ahead, the feeling of unease grew by the hour, settling like a heavy rain cloud above her.

'Sofia, you are very quiet. Are you alright?'

'I'm not sure, Elizabeth. I can't explain how I feel. Yesterday was disturbing. Not only because of my... relapse, but because my mind won't rest. I am full of worries!'

'But what are you worried about? You are nearly home now, I thought you would be excited.'

'Andres—I had forgotten about his illness, how sick he would become. Sometimes he had to go to hospital.'

'Your papa would have let you know if anything happened to him, surely. Anyway, you will be able to see him for yourself in a few days. It will be wonderful! Don't let your mind deceive you into worrying about problems that don't exist. Minds love to play tricks on us, don't you think?'

Sofia nodded, but Elizabeth's words did nothing to ease how the memories of home shifted and shimmered elusively. Andres' face, white and resting against a hospital pillow, his body, thin and haggard. How could she have forgotten his bouts of illness? They had beset him ever since he'd caught influenza as a child. Even worse, though, was the difficulty she had recapturing her papa. The enthusiastic artist, the man who encouraged her to take control of the gallery and painted such beautiful works for her to sell in it, had become a shadowy figure.

Sofia found herself trapped in a repetitious battle, forcing herself to focus on the future one minute and the next trying to assemble the details of those last days in Spain. For all of her trying, memories of that time danced around the corners of her mind, just beyond reach, and nothing made sense. Andres had read the newspaper and insisted she leave Spain; it was he who'd said she should go to Australia, of course. But why didn't he and Papa come with her?

Frustrated, Sofia accepted that the more she tried to make sense of her past, the greater were her feelings of confusion. Elizabeth was right. She needed to relax, wait and see how things were at home, rather than distressing herself with imaginings.

CHAPTER 22

*W*hen they finally boarded the train to Cerbère, Sofia was pleased to find the carriage nearly empty. Sleep tempted her, but Elizabeth was inclined to chat.

'Tell me again about your childhood,' she asked, and in response, Sofia regaled details of growing up on the finca.

'How did your mother die, Sofia, if you don't mind me asking?'

'I don't know, really. Bearing twins, I suppose.' She wondered at Elizabeth's morbid fascination with her mother's death. 'It must have been hard on her body, and she couldn't cope.'

'Yes, twins would be very difficult, I imagine. But the delivery of babies is much safer these days than it was at the turn of the century. Did she have you at home, or in the hospital?'

'In hospital, I think. Apparently the midwife was worried when our mother became overly tired, and so an ambulance was called. My father always said he wished she'd stayed at home—perhaps then she would have regained her energy and survived. He had more trust in the midwife than he did in the doctors at the hospital.'

'Alright. But, you realise, in those days hospitals did not have all the modern equipment we have now. Lucky for us, labour is much easier, and we can have oxygen and even morphine and scopolamine should we need them.'

'Yes, I suppose it is easier.' Sofia wondered why Elizabeth was so fixated on the topic of modern day childbirth.

'Do you think because your mother died, you too might fear childbirth?'

'I have never really thought about it. I think it would always be a little scary, don't you? Nobody ever talks about all the pain, but I can't imagine giving birth is easy!' Sofia shrugged. It seemed a pointless conversation.

'And your father and brother are both artists? How wonderful.'

'They are both very good. Mind you, Papa's always said Andres is the more talented of them. He thinks Andres has the potential to be really... you know... famous... an important artist. He won the Prado's prize for portraiture, you know!'

The words were out of Sofia's mouth before she realised. Memories of Andres' submission to the competition, the painting of herself holding a tray of biscuits for the café, assailed her. Her startled expression must have worried Elizabeth.

'Sofia, we don't need to talk about this anymore. Let's look out of the window! We are nearly at Cerbère. Look at the tiny village over there—those houses with their steep roofs! Oh, how I love French villages. I would love to live here for a while. I'd eat turkey and croissants and baguettes spread with Camembert every day. Their champagne is to die for, I hear!'

Glad for the change of pace in their conversation, Sofia gazed out the window at the rolling hills dotted with steep-roofed farmhouses. The fields formed a picture of colourful striped patterns, and in them she saw men and women bent low over crops or riding carts up and down the rows.

Before long, the train began a descent into Cerbère. A whining metallic ring filled the air as it braked in readiness to stop at the station.

After the solitude of the carriage and the calm of the striped fields, Sofia was surprised to see a large crowd gathered on the platforms.

Even more surprising was the amount of luggage they carried: bags, boxes, suitcases and containers. It was as if these people were loaded with everything they owned.

'Wow,' commented Elizabeth. 'The concierge did mention it would be hectic here, but I wasn't expecting this! Are you right, Sofia? Here, let me help you.'

She slung her handbag over her shoulder and picked up her own suitcase with her right hand, Sofia's in her left. After stepping out of the carriage, she turned to assist Sofia onto the platform.

'Darn it,' Sofia said as she stepped down heavily, clutching at her rounded belly as she landed upon the gravelled surface.

'Be careful, Sofia. Hang on to my arm as we weave through. It looks like some of these people have set up camp! Heavens, I've never seen anything quite like it. I can see the exit, though... see, over to our right.'

Gingerly, they made their way through the crowd, Sofia gripping Elizabeth's arm as her forthright friend alternatively nodded *gracias* to those kindly strangers who parted to allow them through or glared at those who grumbled when they squeezed between them.

Sofia listened to the hubbub of voices, many speaking in Spanish, others speaking in Catalan. It seemed strange to be amongst Spanish-speaking people again.

'Retirado! Retirado,' more than one said when their eyes met hers, waving their hands as if to encourage Sofia to turn around, but Sofia was too focused on keeping up with Elizabeth to wonder why the people surging towards them were so intent on leaving.

Finally, they found a quiet spot by a wall and paused to collect their bearings.

'I can see the sign to Portbou over there, Sofia. See where it says *Border Crossing*? Looks like we'll need to head down this ramp to get across. Are you okay? I could try to find someone to help us with our bags, or at least search for a trolley. It's a long way to walk in your condition...' She looked at her with a dubious expression, and Sofia felt apologetic to think her collapse in Paris weighed so heavily on Elizabeth's mind.

'I will be alright. Don't you worry.'

There was no chance the station porters, already overwhelmed by the crowd blocking the platform, could help two able-bodied women make the crossing from the French to the Spanish stations.

'What do you think is going on here?' Sofia asked.

'I don't know, but I think we should get over to Portbou Station as quickly as we can lest we miss the connection to Barcelona. We don't want to be stuck here with this crowd for any longer than we have to be.'

'Definitely not. Come on. I will stay close. You're doing well as a battering ram—like Moses parting the Red Sea! Don't stop now!' Sofia hoped her attempt at humour would reassure Elizabeth she was indeed alright. Although their destination was quite a distance away, surely if she took one step at a time and clung to Elizabeth's arm, her legs would hold up.

Between Sofia's stoicism and Elizabeth determinedly pushing forward, they finally arrived on the Spanish side of the train line. Elizabeth had been right to hurry, for barely fifteen minutes after they'd stepped onto Portbou Station's platform, a train arrived. Sofia watched in amazement as, before it had even ground to a halt, the carriage doors were flung open and dozens of people spilled out, jostling and tugging to free their cases before racing to the exit gates.

'Good heavens,' muttered Elizabeth. 'I can't even imagine what's going on here!'

While they had to wait for over five minutes for the train to empty, it barely took a minute for the travellers taking the southern journey to settle themselves in the carriages. Sofia and Elizabeth exchanged glances of relief when they finally sat on a broad leather seat. Soon they heard the deafening roar signalling the train's pending departure, and felt the vibration of its engine stirring into action.

Looking around, Sofia realised they weren't alone. Halfway along the carriage, two men wearing dark suits and grim expressions sat talking, and nearer to them sat an attractive lady with blond hair.

'Okay, Sofia, first Barcelona and then on to Madrid. Can't say I won't be glad to get there. I wonder if there is a dining room on this train. Do you think I should go and see? I would kill for a cup of tea right now. What would you like?'

'Anything. Coffee, actually. Perhaps they might have a sandwich or something.'

While she waited for Elizabeth to return, Sofia gazed out the window and was amazed to see what she assumed was the main road leading into Portbou. It was dotted with hundreds, perhaps even thousands of people all moving in a northerly direction, towards France.

Had an avalanche rushed down from the snow-topped mountains to the west?

The blond lady must have noticed Sofia's worried expression, for, catching her eye, she smiled ruefully and shrugged in a knowing manner. Sofia was about to ask if she knew what had caused the Spaniards to flee north when, with two paper cups in hand, Elizabeth returned.

'This is all I could get,' she said. 'Lucky for you, it's coffee. Seems there is some sort of problem down south. We aren't going to make it to Barcelona after all, I'm afraid. There was some sort of attack there last night. The lady in the dining room said it happens all the time—the rail schedule is constantly being disrupted when skirmishes break out. I suppose we can't say we weren't warned this might happen.'

'So what will we do?'

'Get off the train at Figueres; we'll be there any minute.'

As if responding to Elizabeth's words, the train slowed its speed to a walking pace, creaking and swaying as it inched into a small town, then coming to rest.

'Quick, Sofia, swallow your coffee. We'll have to get out and then try to make our way north again.'

'Back to France!' Sofia exclaimed incredulously. 'No, surely not. I want to go home to Malaga!'

Her heart thudded with disappointment. Here she was, finally in Spain, but it was as though the world conspired to prevent her reunion with her family!

Elizabeth took her hand and squeezed it. 'I am sorry, love. It's so unfair. After all you've been through, and now we are finally so close —but there's no helping it. I suppose we should have listened to the advice everyone was giving. Clearly now is not the time to travel to Madrid! Perhaps we can try again in a few days.'

'Can't we take this train back to Cerbère?' Sofia asked, suddenly feeling stretched to her physical limit.

'Yes, but do you remember how chaotic it was? If we go back, we'd be stuck at the border overnight. We are better to remain here, get our bearings and find a taxi, or anything else travelling north. Good heavens, I hate to think of what Marcus would say if he could see us!'

Sofia agreed—Marcus would panic if he knew Barcelona had been attacked, even if it was a small skirmish. She couldn't help feeling a little guilty. It was her fault they were stranded in Figueres. Tears rolled down her cheeks, and she hung her head in embarrassment.

'Sofia, no, please. It will be alright. It's afternoon now. We have plenty of time to find a place for the night. We will get settled, and while you have a rest, I'll find transport back to Paris.'

Sofia nodded and gave in to a childlike longing. 'I need to see Papa and Andres! It's been so long, and...' She paused before continuing. 'Elizabeth, you know I am not well. *I know I am not well*! I feel so consumed by fear for Papa and Andres! I need to know they are safe; and when I see them, I will be well again too, I'm sure.'

Speaking the words, Sofia realized her greater worry was that she was losing her mind, that once again she would be plunged into the sickness that landed her into hospital, and perhaps this time she'd not recover.

Before Elizabeth had a chance to reply, a woman's voice interrupted them.

'Ladies, can I do anything to help you?'

The words came from the fair-headed woman in the carriage in a clear British accent. Sofia hastily wiped her face with her handkerchief and tried to regain her composure.

'Oh, thank you,' Elizabeth said. 'We do have a problem, actually. We've been travelling for days now—started in St Albans, through to London and then across the Channel to Paris. We are on our way to Malaga, but it would appear we've been stalled.'

'Yes, apparently there's been another bombing in Barcelona. Hopefully it's not too serious. What do you intend to do?'

'Find a place here in Figueres for the night, and then make our way north again tomorrow.' Sofia marvelled at Elizabeth's controlled, matter-of-fact tone.

'If you don't mind me suggesting it, perhaps you would like to come home with me. Judging by what's happening at Portbou, things could be extremely busy here. My husband and I live out of town a bit, towards Sant Llorenc de la Muga. It's quiet there and you will be safe. In a day or so, when things settle, perhaps the trains will be running again. If not, I will help you organise your return to France.'

'What do you think, Sofia?'

'That would be wonderful!' Sofia was thrilled. A few days in Spain could equally provide the means for a journey south, as it might north. Surely, there would be a passage to Madrid via the road, where they could completely bypass Barcelona!

'Looks like it's a yes, thank you,' Elizabeth said with a smile. 'How very kind! I hope we're not putting you out.'

'Not at all. I know what it is like to be a foreigner caught up in a pickle in a strange land. Laura, by the way. Laura Diaz. Not a native Figuerian, by any means; not even a Spaniard, as you may have guessed, but a fellow Londoner—well, I was, once upon a time! But I have been here long enough now to have learned a few tricks!'

CHAPTER 23

*S*ofia and Elizabeth introduced themselves as they followed Laura through the exit and to a small van, the only vehicle in the station's carpark.

Sofia quickly discovered Laura had a vivacious personality, a friendly disposition, and an enjoyment of chatting that matched Elizabeth's. For twenty minutes as she steered through the town and then towards the distant mountains, she shared a summary of her life. She'd worked as a research officer in the library of the University College in London, until a handsome Spaniard swept her off her feet and spirited her away. After a whirlwind romance they'd married and now lived between two homes, one in Roanne, France the other just outside Figueres.

After navigating the winding road into the foothills of an impressive mountain range—the Pyrenees, Laura told them—they arrived at a low-set stone building perched on the side of an escarpment, facing west towards an astonishing view of snow-capped mountains extending as far as the eye could see.

'Beautiful, isn't it? I often tell Lucien he can be assured I'll never leave him, for I couldn't imagine leaving this view. I am not sure which I love more, him or this place!' Laura laughed. 'No, I am joking —Lucien's a darling, and also very clever! You will meet him later. He's in meetings today.'

Laughing again, she took Sofia's case and led them inside the house, where she rested the luggage on the landing.

'When's the baby due?'

The causal question led to an uncomfortable silence.

It was mortifying to be constantly explaining her weight gain wasn't due to pregnancy, but rather her illness and indulgence in bread and potatoes over the winter. Sofia felt Elizabeth's eyes upon her as though she too was waiting for her reply.

When none came, Elizabeth filled the silence with disjointed comments, shaking her head.

'Pervasive denial... Sofia's not thinking about pregnancy yet, are you, love? Don't know why... Joseph and I can't wait to have a baby— Joseph's my fiancé. We are marrying in May. Hopefully there will be a bun in the oven by Christmas!'

'A May wedding, how lovely.'

As Laura and Elizabeth chatted about the upcoming wedding, Sofia remained silent. *Pervasive denial,* Elizabeth had said? Where had she heard the phrase before? It was an unusual coupling of words. At last Sofia recalled a conversation she'd overheard between Elizabeth and Marcus weeks earlier. They'd spoken in the stable while she'd been collecting eggs from the chicken coop to make an omelette for their breakfast.

'Alex says it's pervasive denial of pregnancy,' Marcus had said. 'When, despite all evidence to the contrary, a mother refuses to accept she's pregnant. The condition can last all the way through to delivery and beyond.'

'Yes, but when the baby is born, reality must surely set in,' Elizabeth said.

'Unfortunately, it's rarely simple; often the infant will be rejected altogether.'

As she'd returned to the kitchen, Sofia had thought nothing of the conversation beyond considering how fascinating the animal kingdom was, and wondering what Elizabeth would recommend to the owner of the troublesome horse they'd been discussing.

She was jogged out of her reverie by Laura's voice addressing her.

'Come on, Sofia, we'll go downstairs to the main house. This is the entrance; our living area is below.'

The stairway was narrow and steep, each step formed from an enormous timber plank with one end embedded in the exterior stone wall. Clinging to the rail as they descended, Sofia gasped with pleasure. The room at the base of the landing was large, with windows running its full breadth. Through them, the snow-capped mountains she'd seen from the road seemed closer, and the steepness of the hill more acute.

Removing her gaze from the stunning view, Sofia returned her attention to the rectangular room. Its timber floorboards were dotted with colourful rugs in the same style Sofia remembered from her childhood. She and Andres had taken those rugs outside, draped them over a rail, and belted them with a broom to shake out the dust hundreds of times.

At the far end of the room, Laura took slivers of fine kindling from a bucket, placed them in a neat stack in an enormous fireplace, then added larger pieces. She ignited the carefully constructed tower and the pungent odour of fresh burning wood drifted into the room.

'Sorry, it's always a bit smoky when first lit. It will settle soon,' Laura said, but her words were lost upon Sofia. Wisps of smoke drifted toward her. She flapped her hand toward them, but they refused to vanish. Again, she reached out, her open palm batting them away.

'Sofia, are you alright?' Laura's voice was infused with concern. 'Come here. Sit down, you are tired. I have some bread and a bowl of gazpacho for lunch. After that, I'll show you to your room where you can rest. You must be exhausted, you poor thing!'

'Yes, a lie down would be wonderful. Thank you, Laura. Sorry to be such a bother,' Sofia replied feeling silly for letting the smoke worry her. She was thankful for the offer to lie down; she'd be asleep in seconds.

Two hours later, Sofia awoke, feeling considerably refreshed and determined to behave as a gracious visitor. How wonderful people were! First Marcus and Elizabeth had invited her into their home and cared for her, and now Laura, a perfect stranger, had brought her and Elizabeth to this spectacular house.

As she made her way to the living room, Sofia's eyes landed on two paintings in the shadows of the hallway. A pair of Edgar Degas ballerinas. Wonderful, but surely not originals!

Laura caught her gaze and laughed. 'You are up, Sofia! I hope you had a nice rest. And yes, they are imitations—both of them! I love to paint, although these days I am more enthusiast than artist. Many years ago, Lucien and I spent a year in Paris, and while he delivered lectures to the students at the Ecole des Beaux-Arts, I was a student at the Louvre. "Imitations of the Masters," my course was called. We studied the history and techniques of counterfeit artists, and then our teacher guided us in painting our own replicas of famous works. Sacrilege, really, to allow a bunch of talentless amateurs to butcher such wonderful paintings, but still, it was fun.'

'They are very good!' Sofia replied. 'Our father loved—loves, I should say—all forms of art. He often took Andres and I to the Prado to see the exhibitions.'

A sound from above distracted them, and the feet, then torso, then body of a man appeared on the stairs.

'Here is Lucien! How are you, my darling?'

The man was older, perhaps fifty, with a thick crop of curly black hair; his greying temples only added to his good looks. His tread was heavy and his expression serious, but when he saw them his furrowed brow softened and his eyes lit with twinkling charm as he approached.

He kissed Laura, then turned to greet Sofia and Elizabeth. Though he spoke in English, his Spanish accent was unmistakable.

'Oh... so not just one lovely wife, but three beautiful women! How lucky can a man be?' He smiled at them warmly before returning his gaze to Laura and asking in a lower tone, 'Did you hear of the bombing in Barcelona?'

'Yes. They stopped the train at Figueres. Poor Elizabeth and Sofia were left high and dry, so I asked them here. I knew you wouldn't mind.'

'No, certainly not. Figueres is not out of danger, so you did the right thing, bringing them here. I am surprised you got here at all; I tried phoning a number of times to warn you, suggest you stay in France. It is hard to know what the next few days might bring!'

'Figueres in danger, really? Just how bad is it in Barcelona?'

'Very bad! It took us all totally by surprise. It seems this time Franco is determined to take control of Catalonia. I guess he knows so long as Barcelona is the home of the Government of the Republicans, he'll always face resistance. They dropped six bombs. Hundreds of people have been killed!'

Laura gasped. 'Six bombs! I had no idea it was so bad. There were, of course, many people making the crossing into France, but we see that a lot these days. Perhaps there was more than usual.'

Sofia's heart fluttered. Evidently the attack on Barcelona was more than just a small skirmish.

She sat quietly alongside Elizabeth while the discussion between Laura and her husband continued.

'The Republican government is here, in Figueres; they are sheltering at Sant Ferran. There will be a final sitting of parliament here, any day now, and then they, too, will go to France.'

'Our Government is leaving Spain? Good Lord, it is grim!'

'Yes. This time it is very serious, I'm afraid. And of course, as news that the government has fled has spread across Barcelona, the people are in turmoil. It is truly a dreadful mess. And we must be realistic; with what happened at Gandesa, and now Barcelona, there is every reason to believe Figueres will be targeted very soon.'

'So, is it time for us to make our move? What about the art collection?' Laura asked quietly.

'Well, of course, we cannot leave until we have secured it. Plans are in the making as we speak. They will be finalised tomorrow.'

Sofia tried to make sense of what she was hearing. Paintings! What art collection? She couldn't contain her fears.

'You mentioned paintings?' Sofia asked.

'Yes, we have quite a collection of important works in Figueres, in safe keeping,' said Lucien.

Sofia nodded with interest, and looking at Lucien, Laura continued.

'Lucien was a professor of art history in Madrid,' she said. 'We were there in 1936, when Franco started attacking the city. Nine bombs were dropped on El Prado, and another eighteen were dropped on Liria Palace; the home of the royal family. Thousands of irreplaceable artefacts were at risk of being looted or destroyed. Of course, at the height of the violence, people's safety and homes was a priority. However, groups like the Alliance of Antifascist Intellectuals—Lucien's a member—appealed to the government that measures be taken to preserve Spain's artworks, lest they be destroyed. The government listened, thankfully, and established the Committee for the Requisition and Protection of the Artistic Patrimony, which, of course, we joined.'

'Of course! I had never even considered what happens to museums like the Prado in war. Especially these days, when the weapons are so destructive. Joseph—he's my fiancé, and an officer in the British Army—told me a single bomb can collapse a whole building!' Elizabeth sounded genuinely intrigued.

'Most people don't think about the galleries,' Lucien said. 'Of course, when the lives of the people you love are at risk, or you are trying to find water and food to survive, it is hardly surprising. Nonetheless, hundreds of people stepped forward to help us to salvage paintings and sculptures after the churches in Madrid were bombed.

And we were none too soon, for quickly, vandals and looters were getting at it.'

'Vandals! Surely not.' Sofia couldn't comprehend anyone wanting to damage art.

'Oh, yes, sadly.' Laura said. 'When the fighting began, it was as though everyone went mad. Many Republicans expressed their anger at the churches by destroying their property. It was terrible. The churches, of course, own extraordinary items, some of which are more than a thousand years old!'

'Beyond trying to save what we could of the churches, our committee's major task was to rescue what we could from El Prado, including the Dauphin's Treasure housed there. It was good we made our move, for only days later, El Prado was bombed yet again.' Lucien shook his head, as if doing so could rid his mind of the terror, and Elizabeth picked up where he'd left off.

'For the last three years, committees across Spain have worked tirelessly to save paintings, books, tapestries and statues. Items that can't be moved—fountains and the larger public sculptures and so forth—are wrapped. We've saved the works of the Royal Armoury as well as the library of the Royal Palace, plus some astonishing pieces— over five hundred years old—from the House of Alba. Lucien and I have helped move collections from one place to another, as the fighting intensified.'

'Yes, it would have been dreadful if those pieces were destroyed! There is truly nothing like them in the world,' Sofia said, aghast at the thought of Madrid under such threat. While she was aware of the conflict caused by Franco and his men rising against the Republicans, she'd only considered the human interactions; it had never occurred to her that important buildings like the National Museum would be targeted.

'So how did you come to bring the collection to Figueres,' Sofia asked.

'Well, first the Government asked us to move the most important pieces: the crème de la crème, as the French would say—to Valencia.

So we moved the Dauphin's Treasure, and over five hundred paintings and drawings. It was a debacle, to begin with—the trucks could only drive at twenty miles an hour, lest the vibration of the vehicles damage the works. You should have seen Goya's pair of *Maja*s that had been loaded by a pair of enthusiastic helpers, being driven through the streets of Spain, teetering precariously in the back of an open truck!'

'But they should have been packed in crates!' Sofia couldn't imagine how such precious items could have been left exposed to the elements.

'Certainly,' Lucien agreed, nodding approval at Sofia. 'Thank goodness, our committee took over, and we made sure everything was crated properly; but even then I had my heart in my mouth while the works were on the roads!'

'All in all, over seventy thousand items have been saved,' Laura said, with a look of triumph.

'How incredible!' Elizabeth's voice quivered with excitement at the spectacle of the rescue.

Sofia's mind went to the collection her father used to take her and Andres to see.

'So you saved the Goyas and the El Grecos?' she asked. 'What about the international works—the Rubens and van Eycks? The Rembrandts? You took all of these to Valencia?' Sofia felt overcome with concern for the paintings she'd grown up admiring.

'Some of these, certainly, but not all. Thousands of works are still hidden in Madrid, but they are all safe, as far as we know. I see you have a love of art? You have had some training?'

'My father is an artist. He taught my brother and me everything he knew about the old Masters, and the Moderns, too. The Picassos, Matisses, Sorollas, my father loved them all. Picasso was his childhood friend.'

'Pablo! Then you will know he is now the director of the Prado.'

'I had not,' Sofia said, amazed. 'But I am sure he is worthy of the role.'

'He has no intention of letting the Nationalists anywhere near the collection. I suppose you've seen his portrayal of the cruel attack on Guernica? Mind you, Sofia, not everybody shares your appreciation for our efforts,' Lucien said.

'But surely they see you are heroes!'

'Actually, no; many in Madrid are outraged to think the best of their collection has been taken away. Some even share the view Franco likes to perpetuate, that we—the Republicans—are the looters, that we seized the opportunity to plunder Spain's treasures for ourselves. He even spreads rumours that we're selling Spanish treasures on the black market or sending works to the Soviet Union.' Lucien sighed and continued, 'Time, of course, will reveal the truth. People will be thankful when everything is returned to their rightful owners!'

Laura nodded in agreement with her husband. 'Every step of the way, we've documented the details of every single painting, tapestry, or sculpture in triplicate. It took forever, but we know who each work belongs to.'

'As long as nothing happens to them!' Lucien's mouth turned down.

'Nothing will happen, Lucien. You have had too many sleepless nights worrying! Think what might have happened if we hadn't moved the works.'

'You are right, of course, but it has been an enormous responsibility just the same.'

'It sounds like you have done a wonderful thing! So, you say the collection may be moved again? Even with Franco so close?' Sofia asked, excited to think it may not be lost to Franco, after all.

Lucien nodded. 'Yes, selected works from El Prado are hidden away at Sant Ferran and Peralada Castle. We also have some works at the talc mines in La Vajo. And...' Lucien looked at Laura and then, with a nod, at Sofia.

'Would you like to see some of our masterpieces?' he asked, a twinkle in his eye replacing the sombre expression he'd been wearing.

Sofia nodded, for of course she wanted to. Still, she hardly knew what to expect when Laura and Lucien led her and Elizabeth down the stairwell. At the base of the stairs, Lucien removed a padlock from a small arched door set into an otherwise blank stone wall.

The room they entered was dark, lacking the panoramic views of the living room above. Rather, it felt cavern-like, encased in stone with only one small window set high on the far wall. Lucien lit a gas lamp and then stepped aside, allowing Sofia and Elizabeth to see past him.

'My goodness,' gasped Sofia, spellbound by the sight of dozens of enormous crates, some so large they filled the walls they leaned against, surrounded by smaller wrapped boxes and parcels. 'There must be two hundred pieces here!' Although wrapped and crated, she had no difficulty envisaging the contents, or recognising the magnitude of the collection before them.

'Two hundred and forty-four, to be exact,' announced Laura. 'This lot includes three El Grecos and two Rubens, as well as two or three of the Dauphin's treasures. I can barely believe it, but the box over there holds the cup with golden siren!'

Sofia shook her head in amazement as she looked at the small crate set to one side of the room. She did not recognise the particular piece Laura referred to, but she'd seen the exhibition of the Dauphin's treasure on numerous occasions and knew the magnificence of the pieces.

'Why were they moved from Valencia to here?' Elizabeth looked every bit as amazed as Sofia felt to think the works had been moved not once, but twice.

'When the Republican Government was forced to flee to Catalonia, the Prime Minister insisted these most important artworks be taken too. Our castles in Figueres, close to the French border, were chosen. Then, just two months ago, this load arrived unexpectedly, and because we had space and are away from the town centre, Laura and I were given the dubious privilege of caretaking it.'

'Lucien, you said the paintings are to be moved again. Where will they be taken?' Sofia asked, quietly.

Lucien looked at Laura, then Sofia. 'There is talk that the collection will be moved to Switzerland.'

'Switzerland! Whatever for? It will cost a fortune to get them there!' Laura's voice was sharp, and she sounded as surprised as Sofia felt.

'Yes, it certainly will be both expensive and a major organisational feat. This morning Timoteo and I learned that representatives from art galleries across the world are offering their support. A new organisation, the International Committee for the Safeguard of Spanish Art Treasures is being created. It is they who'll pay the costs involved to get it to Geneva, Switzerland. There, it will be placed in the care of the League of Nations.'

'But what does the League of Nations know about art, Lucien?' Laura asked.

'The League of Nations' job is to protect the works, Laura. It is the International Committee who will provide the expertise for the care of our collection. Representatives from the Metropolitan Museum of Art in New York, the Louvre, the National Gallery and the Tate Gallery in London. We have to trust them. The details will be finalised tomorrow, and then an official agreement will be signed.'

'Why, how extraordinary!' Laura replied. 'Are you pleased, Lucien? At least, the responsibility for the collection can be shared with an organisation who hold some clout. And in the hands of the League of Nations, it will surely be safe!'

'Is there no other way?' Sofia asked. 'Surely the paintings could be kept in Spain—hidden in the mountains, perhaps, or even left here in Figueres?' As a fellow Spaniard, she wondered if Lucien shared her grief at hearing these jewels of Spain were being sent so far from home?

He shook his head sombrely and looked at her with an expression of recognition. 'You have a deep love for these works, as I do, sí?'

'Yes. Papa used to take us to the Prado every year. Our whole world was about art until...' Sofia stopped. What had she been about to say? *Until they died?* No, surely not! But the words had flowed so easily, and instinctively she felt they held a truth. *Until they died!* Could it be that neither her father nor brother were alive?

Sofia tried to continue, but her words tangled on her tongue as confusion seized her. Once again, haphazard memories flickered through her mind—the coffin on the dining room table, their family priest murmuring consolations, an ambulance ride, standing beside a hospital bed. But who lay in there, her father or her brother? Shaking her head, she gasped for air as tears rolled down her cheeks.

'Sofia, come on!' said Elizabeth, evidently assuming her sorrow was in response to learning the Spanish art collection was being moved to Geneva. 'Lucien and Laura have cared for these works throughout years of trouble. And now, they must do what is best, even if that means moving them to Switzerland. You should be thrilled!'

Sofia felt the sting of a rebuke in Elizabeth's words and nodded. *Yes. No.* She was glad the works were safe, but sorry they'd been moved from the beautiful rooms of the Prado, and sorry they were about to be moved again, this time leaving Spanish soil. She was sorry for the war dividing Spain, sorry thousands had died. But these concerns were suddenly remote and unimportant, beside the shadowy and elusive events emerging from her past and flooding her mind. Her tears were for the father and brother she'd been so desperate to see, so sure her world would become right once she was with them. For she knew—by the surety of the words that had almost fallen from her lips —they were lost to her forever.

Sofia felt paralysed by the realisation. Her health and happiness had rested on returning to her brother and father. And in helping her get there, Elizabeth was now exposed to the danger of Franco's advance. She'd never have undertaken this journey if not for Sofia's insistence that she needed to be home. How could Sofia now tell Elizabeth the father and brother she'd yearned to be with had been a figment of her imagination?

'Sofia, I promise you we will care for these paintings like they are our own children,' Lucien said, appearing to share Elizabeth's conclusion about her tears. 'Timoteo Pérez Rubio is one of Spain's leading artists, and just like you and me, he is passionate about our cultural heritage. He has supervised the movement of our art from

Madrid to Valencia, and then from Valencia to Figueres. If he trusts this latest plan, then we must, too. Like little *bebés*, these works cannot be left hidden in the mountains! They must be stored under special conditions. They need the right temperature and light. Even here, in this room, their boards and old canvas may become brittle or cracked, or damaged by mildew. Under the care of the International Committees' specialists, they'll be in good hands, I'm sure!"

'Yes—it is a good thing, I know, and I do trust your judgement. But so much has happened since I left Spain! It's a lot to take in.'

What Sofia wanted more than anything was to go to her room. She needed time alone to make sense of her life.

Concern furrowed Elizabeth's brow. 'Sofia, we have all had more shocks today than is good for us. I really think we should have an early night.'

'Yes, of course,' Laura agreed, sympathy in her eyes. 'Normally, Lucien and I have our dinner at about nine PM. It's the Spanish way, but far too late for you. How about I put together some huevos rotos, and perhaps a glass of wine, to help you rest? Tomorrow we'll see what plans we can make to get you away from this madness.'

Sofia agreed. Yes, the day had brought more shocks than she'd ever imagined. But the greatest of those had come in the last few minutes; the realisation her father and brother were no longer alive.

CHAPTER 24

*A*s they settled into the two single beds, Sofia remarked how calm Laura and Lucien seemed to be, even as they'd discussed the attack on Barcelona.

'I would say they are accustomed to the violence,' Elizabeth said. 'This war has been going on for years now. Bombings, killings—I suppose after a while, you get used to it. Mind you, from what I've heard, the Republicans have committed their own share of atrocities, though nothing on the scale of Franco and his band of thugs. I imagine people like Laura and Lucien just try get on with their lives as best they can, and avoid drawing attention to themselves.'

'Yes, but in getting on with their lives, they've gone to extraordinary lengths to keep the paintings safe. I am so grateful.'

'They've been marvellous, haven't they? And I imagine if you scratched the surface, Spaniards everywhere are doing their bit to support the resistance. It's the way of humans to try to survive and make the best of circumstances; to pray for better days ahead. Now let's get some rest.'

Rest did not come easily to Sofia, though. As she tossed and turned in a bid to get comfortable, her belly twisted and squirmed. It seemed as though her body was at war with her. She rubbed it, and rose several times to go to the bathroom, but nothing helped. However, her physical discomfort troubled her less than her mind, which was tied in knots trying to make sense of her life in Malaga.

As so often happened, the memories that had returned were like beads which had spilled to the ground and now needed to be threaded together again. Sofia felt exhausted as she worked to assemble them into a logical sequence. Playing with Andres among orange trees, lying on a bed listening to their father read to them, watching paint be applied to an enormous canvas on an easel—these were pleasant glimpses of her childhood. But then confusion set in. Was it her father painting, or Andres working alone in the studio? He and their father had always worked together, so why did the studio feel so empty? She remembered Papa smiling proudly as she'd reorganised their gallery, but in her memories of balmy evenings sitting in the courtyard or driving down the hill to Malaga in their car, his presence was vague. It seemed as if each time Sofia managed to connect her thoughts so they made sense, they fell apart, then tumbled and scattered beyond her reach.

Her memories of Andres were clearer. She felt the warmth of his teasing, saw the earnest way he viewed the world. She recalled a moment when they'd been thrilled with excitement when his painting won El Prado's portrait competition. What had happened to him and Papa? Had they really passed away? Why had she left them?

When Sofia finally drifted into sleep, her dreams were unsettling. In them, she sat with Andres under the magnolia tree in the finca's courtyard, drinking wine not with their father but with a tall young man —with laughing blue eyes and a teasing manner that made her giggle. Sofia struggled to make sense of the young man's presence at the finca. He said her name with a foreign twang, without the familiar lilt of her Spanish friends and family.

A phrase consumed her thoughts, repeating over and over like a drum's pulsing rhythm. *G'day, mate! g'day, mate! g'day mate!* The voice was utterly familiar. So lovely and cheerful. So close to her heart. Who was this man? Where was he now? A stifled sob broke the silence, and Sofia realised it came from her.

A soft murmur grazed her left ear and a firm hand stroked her shoulder. Sofia held her breath and listened—was it he? But it was Elizabeth who shushed her, crooning softly, Elizabeth's hands holding her close. No longer trying to control the gulping sobs that wracked her body, Sofia cried as if her heart would break. Andres and her father were dead, and they were not all she'd lost. Where was the tall, fair man who'd made her laugh? Had he, too, died? Elizabeth's voice drew her into wakefulness.

'Sofia, you are having a bad dream. Would you like me to make you a cup of tea?'

'No, thank you, I couldn't drink a thing.' A sob rose as she spoke, and she felt the movement of blankets and the bed springs shudder.

'I'll stay here with you. You must sleep, it is important. Please. You don't want to get sick again, do you? There now, shh… shh….'

Sofia succumbed to the warmth of Elizabeth's arms around her, Elizabeth's hands rubbing the swell of her belly. Slowly her tears subsided and the oblivion of deep sleep finally gave her relief.

The following morning, Sofia woke, somewhat refreshed, to the sound of voices in the living room. She found Laura and Elizabeth in the midst of a serious discussion. The clock read eleven AM.

'Oh, here you are! You must have been so exhausted, you poor thing.'

'I was. Thank you for letting me sleep in. I feel much better now.'

Sofia's words were a lie of the kind Louis Wain had recommended at Napsbury. *Play the game.* She felt numbed and shattered by events she had no words for. But until she could make more sense of her life, she decided it was best to pretend she was alright.

Laura's light-mannered mood of yesterday was gone. Grimly, she told Sofia how, when she'd slipped into Figueres that morning, the roads had been full of refugees, many loaded with everything they could carry. Old women, families, even young children were fleeing to the border. Laura had learned more details of the bombing in Barcelona, and it was far worse than she'd realised: dozens of houses damaged, and four hundred people killed. People had lost hope for their city and were abandoning it in droves, sure Franco and his soldiers would arrive any day. Rumour said they were advancing north, and people in Figueres had begun to panic.

Lucien did not arrive home for lunch, but when he walked into the lounge at five PM, he looked exhausted.

'Both the Catalonian and the Republican governments have now left,' he said. 'A good thing, for Franco's troops are bound to come north sooner or later. Almost everyone is trying to get to France. Mercifully, there is no reason for Franco to come in this direction,' Lucien's hand movement indicated his reference to their home. 'But without doubt, Sant Ferran will be a target.'

'And the collection? Is it still being moved?' Laura asked as she handed a glass of wine to him.

After taking a long sip, Lucien nodded. 'It's a big plan, Laura. I hope it goes well. The arrangements are far more than we could have hoped for! It's as if the whole world cares for our art and will do anything to help us protect it.' Lucien paused and mopped his face with the handkerchief he'd pulled from his pocket.

He looked at Sofia and smiled weakly. 'It seems our paintings will be safe after all, Sofia.'

'And what is to happen, Lucien?' Laura's voice was sharp, and Sofia considered how she was just like Elizabeth, who always adopted a no-nonsense manner when she dealt with problems.

'The works are to be transported by road into France—to Perpignan—and from there by rail to Geneva, Switzerland. Both the minister for Foreign Affairs, Julio Álvarez del Vayo, and the assistant director of the Louvre, Jacques Jaujard, have been at Sant Ferran all day working on the plan. There must have been a dozen phone calls back and forth with Geneva. At present, they are finalising the wording of the document. I am looking forward to seeing it signed tonight. They are calling it the Figueres Agreement.'

Lucien smiled again, and wiped his eyes, clearly moved to see Figueres recognised in the document that articulated this last step for the collection's protection.

'Once they're in Geneva, the paintings will be out of our hands. Curators from all over the world are travelling to Switzerland to prepare for their arrival. There is even talk of exhibiting the collection in Geneva! My apologies, ladies, but this has been a huge part of our life for over three years, and to think it's all coming to an end makes me extremely emotional!' Again, Lucien wiped his eyes.

'They are his babies.' Laura smiled fondly. 'Our babies! Ever since we were in Madrid, taking El Prado's works to its basement, the safety of the collection has consumed us. And then, as the number of works were added to from palaces and churches across Spain, the weight of our responsibility grew like a family does. Such a joy, but believe me, such a responsibility.'

'So when will you start moving the paintings?' Sofia asked.

'Today it has been my job to organise transport. I have managed to find over seventy lorries, and these will arrive at any time. Tomorrow, Timoteo and I will go to Peralada Castle and to La Vajol to arrange for loading the works that are hidden there. This must be done properly; I couldn't bear it if anything got damaged now! We have some good people at both sites, thankfully. After that is done, we will return to Figueres and help to oversee the movement of the collection from Sant Ferran.'

'How quickly are Franco's troops likely to reach Sant Ferran? Will you be safe?' asked Elizabeth.

'It will take more than Franco's army to stop Lucien from attending to the paintings. This I know!' Laura replied. She turned to him. 'But of course, Elizabeth is right... it's terribly risky.'

'Yes, certainly. Perhaps we might have a few days; a week at most. Some Republican soldiers have set up south of Figueres. They will warn us of any danger, and if that happens, you ladies must take the car and drive to the border.'

'Until then, we must help.' Sofia uttered the words without hesitation, knowing it was her duty to protect her country's artistic heritage in any way possible.

'That would be wonderful if you feel you are up to it. We are very low on volunteers here at Figueres. Many of our usual helpers were from Barcelona, but naturally, since the bombings, they are preoccupied with their own family's needs. You could oversee the movement of the collection from the basement here, where I am confident you'll be safe.'

'Are you sure you should do this, Sofia?' Elizabeth looked at her with alarm. 'You have not been well, remember.'

'I want to help. Spain's art means everything to me. Its safety is of the utmost importance!'

'It will not be hard for her,' Lucien reassured Elizabeth. 'You could work together, checking off the works as they are loaded onto the trucks. If you do that, Laura and I can supervise the collection's movement from Sant Ferran.'

'Yes, it would be wonderful if you can,' Laura added. 'We would be terribly grateful for the extra hands, and it should only take a few days. And it will be good for Sofia, yes? Something to do while you wait to return to London.'

'Alright then, if you are sure you can manage, Sofia,' said Elizabeth. She then turned back to Lucien. 'I would love to help. What a mission!'

'Perhaps we might go down now and assess the collection here. I have some work to do there before the trucks arrive.' Lucien said.

Sofia felt a shiver of thrill at the gravity of the moment as they descended the staircase to the stone vault below. As the room lit up, she again felt dazed by the sight of the crates leaning against the walls and set upon stands and tables. Over two hundred and forty-four, Laura had said yesterday. Some were huge! At least a dozen lorries would be required to move them all.

Lucien walked between the stacks of crates and beckoned. 'Come see, Sofia, Elizabeth.'

They crossed over to him and he gestured to a group of paintings set against the wall. These hadn't been here yesterday, Sofia was sure; Lucien must have put them there this morning.

'These are from one of the galleries in Barcelona. Timoteo received them last night—he thought they'd be safer with us than at Sant Ferran, with so many people converging there for shelter. As you can see, they need to be wrapped, but we can enjoy them for a few minutes.'

Sofia gasped as Lucien lifted the first painting into the light, revealing an image of a girl with skin as smooth as ivory, who was combing the long red hair that hung over her shoulder, assisted by a man who stood behind her, a mirror in each hand.

'This is over four hundred years old: Titian's *Girl Before a Mirror*. And this; Velázquez' *Retrato de niña*.' Sofia gazed at the painting of the solemn looking child with thick dark hair, set against the grey background. It seemed incredible to be standing in a basement of a private home just feet away from such wonderful treasures.

'They are beautiful!'

The paintings, three more Velazqes and a Ruben, were all marvellous. Despite the poorly lit room, their colours were rich, and the glistening brush strokes looked fresh, even though they'd been applied centuries earlier. Even their richly gilded frames were works of extraordinary craftsmanship. For over an hour Sofia watched as Lucien and Laura worked together, first applying padding to the outer frames, after which they used small lengths of timber to create a protective case before adding a layer of canvas, then tying the package with string and attaching the labels they'd arrived with.

Finished, and with a last look at the room, Lucien turned off the lamp, and they ascended the stairs. They shared a glass of wine accompanied by olives that had been marinated in sherry and herbs, and then, with a solemn voice, Lucien announced it was time for him to return to Sant Ferran. The ratification of the Figueres Agreement would occur that evening; the document granting permission for the jewels of Spanish art to leave their nation. His wry smile toward Sofia revealed to her that for him too, the movement of the artworks to Switzerland was a bittersweet moment; as much a loss as it was an accomplishment.

CHAPTER 25

*A*s it turned out, Lucien's belief that there would be a shortage of hands to help in the movement of the paintings was proven wrong. Certainly the people of Figueres were terrified, knowing Franco's troops could arrive any day. Already there had been an attack on the town's electrical supply, plunging half of it into darkness. As a result, the previous evening the Figueres Agreement was signed before the headlights of a motor vehicle in Sant Ferran's grounds. Despite the turmoil, news of the plan to evacuate the art collection had spread and numerous volunteers stepped forward to assist in any way they could. All offers of help were accepted.

Dozens of trucks arrived in Figueres throughout the following forty-eight hours, and were allocated between Sant Ferran, Peralada Castle, La Vajol and Lucien's and Laura's house. Early Saturday morning, they rose and, after a quick breakfast, headed downstairs to the basement where Laura explained to Elizabeth and Sofia the process for supervising the men loading the trucks, the first of which had arrived. They didn't see Lucien at all; he'd left before daylight with a load of blankets and quilts for padding. His and Timoteo's task for the next few days was to move between the sites, providing advice where a statue or a particularly large painting presented difficulties, and distributing ropes, tape, documents and additional pairs of hands as needed.

'You'll be right with Matias and his men,' Laura told them. 'They're experienced at moving works of art. All the trucks that will come here today are theirs. I wish I felt as confident of the drivers on the other sites. Of course, they may all be saints, but there could be an opportunistic rogue among them who wouldn't think twice about stealing a painting, if they could.'

Once Laura was confident Sofia was managing checking off the paperwork she'd given her as crates left the basement and Elizabeth repeating the process as the crates were loaded into the truck, she left for Sant Ferran.

'Do you think while you are in Figueres, you could send a telegram to my brother for me?' Elizabeth asked. 'I have no doubt the London papers are full of news about the bombing, and he'll be going spare for worry! Just a few words, so he knows we are fine.'

'Of course! I plan to get in touch with both Lucien's and my own parents for the same reason. Here, write down the details and I will get it away—if, of course, the post office is still open!'

For Sofia and Elizabeth, the work was straightforward. Each van waited at the top of the drive, and the men trekked up and down the steep steps alongside the house, first taking the larger pieces, which they loaded around the sides of the lorry, and then filling the middle with smaller works. Sofia was impressed by the care they demonstrated, and afterwards, when she and Elizabeth compared notes later that day, she was further reassured to hear how every piece, no matter how tiny, had been provided with additional padding and tied down to avoid any movement from the truck's jostling.

That night, Sofia was surprised at how well she felt following the long day's work. They had snacked throughout the day, but at eight

PM, with no sign of Laura and Lucien, she went into the kitchen and found onions and garlic. A cupboard held a cannister of rice along with some assorted herbs. Taking a frying pan from under a bench, she set to work.

~

'Sofia, thank you so much!' It was after ten when they shared the paella she'd made. 'It's nothing for me or Lucien to start cooking at nine or even ten o'clock,' Laura said, 'but after today's effort, I can't tell you how wonderful it is to arrive home to the aroma of good food wafting through the house!'

Lucien agreed, complimenting Sofia for the delicious meal, and she smiled, pleased to be of assistance.

He described how already twenty-five trucks had been loaded with artworks and left for Perpignan.

'Do the trucks all travel together?' Sofia asked.

'An interesting question, Sofia. Yesterday we spoke for hours about whether to send them in a convoy or not. The benefit of a convoy is that every driver keeps the vehicle in front in view, and hence supervises its movements, lest it take a side road and vanish into the hills. However, we decided too many vans and trucks travelling together would attract attention; Nationalist militants could stop them, examine their contents and undoubtedly confiscate the lot,' Lucien explained. 'Of course, if each vehicle travelled alone, a rogue driver may disappear, never to be seen again, along with a hoard of priceless masterpieces. So we decided that the vehicles should travel in small groups. They will travel straight through to Perpignan, where officials will meet them and officially receive the collection. Laura tells me all went well here?'

'Yes, no worries at all. Matias and his men were wonderful.' Elizabeth said. 'They took forever, selecting the right sized crates to best fit the space in their truck, and were ever so gentle as they moved them. I thought speed would be the imperative, and they'd throw the paintings in as quickly as they could and race them to the border!'

'Yes, they were careful in everything they did,' Sofia agreed. She'd been impressed with their patience as they'd stood beside her, crate in hand, checking off the works as they were loaded into the truck against the list Laura had given her.

'I knew they'd be good. Matias has driven for us right from the beginning, when we first moved the collection to Valencia, and he's never let us down.'

'You would have been horrified if the job had been left to me,' Elizabeth said. 'They'd have opened the doors at the other end to find a mass of smashed glass, broken frames and shredded canvas, I'm sure!'

Although she joined Elizabeth and Laura's laughter, Sofia shivered at the thought of paintings by El Greco or Velázquez lying in a tangle of canvas and glass.

Lucien gave a wry smile, then shook his head with a frown. 'Sadly, what you describe is not a joke. When the collection was moved from Valencia to Figueres, a truck was involved in an accident. Despite our careful packing, two of Goya's paintings were damaged.'

'Are they okay now?' Sofia's eyes were wide with disbelief.

'Yes, thankfully. You might know them, Sofia—perhaps one of Goya's most famous pairs: *The Second of May* and *The Third of May*. They were packed together, but the impact was great. *The Second of May* was completely torn through in a number of places.'

'How awful.' Sofia shuddered, remembering seeing these on the wall of El Prado. 'My father used to take Andres and me to see Goya's works every time we were in Madrid. He was obsessed with Goya's paintings!'

'Yes, they are extraordinary. I feel dreadful knowing they were damaged in our care. Fortunately, one of our best restorers was travelling with the collection at the time, and he did a wonderful job relining it. It is a terrible shame, though.'

'Sofia, you and Elizabeth could travel north with the first group of trucks tomorrow, if you wish,' Laura offered. 'At Perpignan station, you could catch a train to Paris. You'd both have to squeeze into the front seat with the driver, but it would only be for an hour or two. I could look out for one of the larger, more comfortable vehicles.'

'Alright, if you think so,' said Elizabeth, but she didn't sound convinced.

Laura turned to Sofia. 'Well, I'm thinking of you. We don't want to overtire you, and as it turns out, we have far more assistance than I had imagined.'

'Oh, no! Please let us stay and finish seeing the collection packed! Couldn't Elizabeth and I help at a different location tomorrow?'

'Are you sure? You are not too tired?' said Elizabeth.

'Of course, I'm sure. I'm fine! The art of Spain has been my whole life. From when I was tiny, our father taught us to cherish the paintings of the masters. He'd be thrilled to know I was here helping keep them safe.'

'Then it's decided,' said Laura. 'To be honest, even though we have only met, I trust you both more than I do some of our locals... They're not dishonest or anything, but they have a lot on their minds at present.' She looked at Lucien. 'Today, when I took the blankets for padding at La Vajol, Lopez was nowhere to be seen! Apparently, he'd left the truck driver to record the details of the paintings being loaded for over an hour, because he had to meet with his son! I am sure there were no mishaps, but it's a weakness in our system. In such lapses, a priceless work could be stolen or exchanged for another.'

'Certainly, we need to maintain our vigilance. It has served us well, so far. Thank you, Elizabeth and Sofia. We are very thankful for your help. There was a second attack on the electrical system in Figueres yesterday, and of course we know the castle could be next. Tomorrow we plan to empty a couple of storage rooms at Sant Ferran using a rear entry—this will provide us with an escape route should there be a serious attack. The works in those rooms are from the Royal Library; it is vital we get them out, and the more help we have, the better, if you are sure you don't mind taking a risk. I will have a car ready at the exit, should we get word to leave quickly.' Lucien's voice was quiet, but his appreciation for their assistance unmistakable.

'And then when Lucien and I leave for France on Thursday, you can come with us,' Laura offered. 'Perhaps you will join us for a night or two at our villa in Roanne before returning to England.'

CHAPTER 26

For three days, Sofia and Elizabeth worked tirelessly at Sant Ferran, assisting Laura and Lucien in every way they could as large lorries, small vans and assorted trucks were loaded with art and sent on their way north. Their work was not without risk, for each day saw an attack on Figueres, barely a mile to the south. As a precaution, a group of soldiers from the Republican Army were positioned along the roadway, ready to defend the castle, should one occur during the removal of the collection.

Despite the danger, Sofia found it immensely gratifying. As she worked, she imagined the contents of the crates being packed. The works they handled were indeed the crème a la crème, as Lucien had said, and although some of the titles of the paintings were unfamiliar to her, the labels revealing the artists: Bosch, Durer or El Greco would set her heart beating with excitement, and she tried to recall their contents from memory. She could barely believe it when she held a Rembrandt in her hands, and could almost hear her father's awestruck voice echoing out of the past: *'See, Sofia, look at the clever way he creates his hair—not painted, but scratched in using the sharp tip of his brush!'*

Papa would be proud of her, Sofia thought as she recorded each crate or parcel before it left the storeroom. She occasionally caught a glimpse of a frame where the packaging had been dislodged during its various relocations, and she'd peer at it, and marvel at the extraordinary task they had the privilege of undertaking. These were not merely crates—the larger ones jostled between two or even three men—and parcels, but the finest of Spanish cultural heritage; one of the greatest collection of extraordinary and valuable artworks in the world.

As she checked their tags and crossed items off her list, Sofia was reminded of the frequent conversations about various artists during her childhood. Increasingly, she was conscious of thinking about Papa and Andres in the past tense, which convinced her she was right: they were no longer alive. And while the details of their deaths evaded her, Sofia had become sure they occurred many years earlier.

Even as she came to terms with their loss, nothing prepared Sofia for the shock she received when Phillipe, one of the local men who'd been helping load the trucks, casually passed her a package. The rectangular parcel was small and light. Turning it over, Sofia glanced at the label and gasped. *Artist: Picasso/Blue Period. Woman in Street with Child, 1910.*

'One day you will know grief; then you will paint a masterpiece...'

It was as though the words came from immediately behind her, and Sofia spun around, but nobody was there.

Again, the words were repeated, *'One day you will know grief... one day...'*

A sob rose in her throat and she clutched her stomach.

'Are you alright, señorita?' Phillipe asked, his forehead furrowed in concern. Sofia nodded as she worked to control her breathing. *Inhale, exhale... and again, and again!*

Her fingers shook as she filled out the form before her. 'Yes, I am fine.'

'You should sit down, if you don't mind me saying. Really, in your condition, what with the bebé so close, you should rest your feet. We

don't want to have a birth here on the floor of the castle, do we praise
the Saints, for we have surely got enough going on!'

'No… there's no baby. I will be fine,' Sofia snapped as she fought
to regain her composure.

Phillipe's look of concern turned to one of surprise. 'Please accept
my apologies. One can't always be sure, of course!' He laughed self-
consciously even as he continued, 'I heard a lady went into labour this
morning, on her way through the border tunnel. Imagine walking from
Barcelona to France in an advanced state of pregnancy. Sweet Mary!
Hopefully, the poor woman managed to get a ride for some of the way.
Her bebé born in the tunnel, though—won't it have some stories to tell
its grandchildren!'

'And the woman, she is alright?' Sofia asked.

Philippe paused before replying. 'The child is a little girl, and she
is fine. The mother, I am not so sure. What about you, señorita? Are
you leaving Figueres soon, too?'

'Yes, when the lorries are all packed, then we will leave,' Sofia
replied.

'That is good… very good. Well, I had better get our lorries filled
so you can be on your way.' He tipped his hat and took the package
from her. Sofia saw him glance at its label, no doubt curious what
about it had caused her strange reaction.

Sofia felt a sense of victory as she watched the last truck start its
engine and then, at a snail's pace, inch forward, pass through the castle
gates, and turn north.

Over the week, seventy-one trucks were packed, Lucien told them.
An extraordinary feat, by all accounts. A couple of hours' driving and
the collection would be safely away from Franco's bombs, would-be
thieves and those who'd light fires and destroy property.

As it vanished from their view, Lucien offered a sense of
perspective in a mournful tone. 'Really, it is a tiny victory when

measured against all Spain has lost, the thousands of people murdered and left destitute. And now Catalonia, and very likely all of Spain, falls into the hands of Franco.'

Although she wholeheartedly understood Lucien's sentiment, Sofia believed his and Laura's commitment to the art was part of a bigger story. 'Yes, Lucien, but what you've achieved is incredible. Saving these paintings may mean nothing compared to the tragedy of so many lives lost. But still...' Sofia felt overcome with emotion and grappled for words. 'These treasures *are* Spain; they are our heart and soul. One day, they'll come back, and after all the madness, Spaniards will be thankful they survived. Then, your efforts will be appreciated.'

Finally, it was time to leave, and after breakfast on Friday, Sofia sensed both sadness and an air of resignation in Laura as she packed her cases and closed windows, ready for the drive to France. Wanting to assist, Elizabeth took a broom and swept through the rooms, while Sofia worked in the kitchen, emptying the refrigerator of its contents, packing sausage and cheese into a small bag, washing dishes and wiping benches.

Finally, the car was fully loaded, with small spaces remaining for Sofia and Elizabeth. She was glad to settle in her seat, where she leaned her head back and looked out the window. Lucien was not travelling with them after all, for yesterday he'd decided to go with Timoteo to Perpignan to see the last of the art unloaded from the trucks, then placed onto the train. Laura didn't expect to hear from him for days. With a wry grin, she exclaimed, 'Really, I'm certain a message will arrive saying he's accompanying Timoteo and the paintings all the way to Geneva!'

As they drove down the hill to Figueres, Sofia looked towards the mountains in the west, drinking in their snow-topped peaks and the dark slits which she knew were ravines plunging to the lower floor of forests. The sky was clear and blue—an almost perfect autumn day, when life should have been rich with laughter and bustling with people rising for work, children racing to greet their friends at school, donkeys hauling carts loaded with fresh produce to the village markets. In the distance, she saw the high walls of the castle where she and Elizabeth had worked for the last three days.

Though sad to be leaving, Sofia consoled herself with the knowledge that, little as it may have been, she had contributed to the war effort, given her best to her country at its hour of need. Poor Spain, bombed and torn, its people everywhere starving and homeless. Children denied the joyful childhood she'd known, one where food was plentiful, safety never a question, and she and Andres spending idyllic days racing around the finca.

While Catalonia wasn't the land of the Andalusians where Sofia had been raised, and there were variations in language and customs, it was still Spain. Her Spain! How dreadful it seemed to turn her back from the country she loved—fleeing alongside the tens of thousands of people on the roads, escaping Franco and his troops. Her heart ached at the sight around her: the weary man and woman sitting in a gutter allowing the three small children between them a few minutes' rest; the look of desperation in people's eyes as they trudged forward, pushing wheelbarrows and carts filled with their belongings, an elderly couple clinging together, encouraging each other forward as they struggled with an oversized suitcase. Sofia wished she could do something for them. Worse, as Laura edged the vehicle through Figueres' streets, she felt as if she was betraying them by having the luxury of leaving in this comfortable car.

'Good lord,' said Laura. 'There's five times as many people on the move today as there were yesterday. I hope the road won't be like this all the way to the border or we'll never get there.'

Thirty miles, Lucien had said. An hour's drive for the more

fortunate, a day's walk if it were on level ground, perhaps. But the route between Figueres and Portbou traversed mountainous terrain, ascending and descending in tight bends, and the distance was surely gruelling for the very young, or the very elderly, or those suffering from starvation and fear.

'I am so glad we met up with you, Laura!' Elizabeth was saying. 'Thank you for taking us under your wing. I hate to think how we'd have managed if not for your assistance! Mind you, I feel guilty taking space up where you could have loaded more of your things.'

'Good grief! Think nothing of it. We've been prepared for this move for months—most of our valuables are already in Roanne. And Lucien and I appreciate the help you've both been. Remember, you're welcome to stay with us for a few days if you'd like. We'd love to have you!'

'No, really, we should get home. A lot has happened in these last weeks, and the quicker we get back and into a routine before the...' Elizabeth's voice faded.

'I understand. I hope it all goes well.'

Even though she was in the back seat, the exchange between Laura and Elizabeth didn't escape Sofia, and she felt a flicker of annoyance. More than once she'd heard the two women pass secret messages through half-finished sentences and nods of shared understanding. Usually, Sofia tried to ignore them. If Elizabeth and Laura wanted to have their secrets, what was it to her?

Nonetheless, she was irritated enough—perhaps because her nerves had already been tried by the tragic scenes outside the car—that she asked, 'Why is it important we get back into a routine, Elizabeth? And what do we hope goes well? I don't understand.'

After a pause, Elizabeth answered, 'My wedding, Sofia—remember, it's now only two months away!'

'Of course, sorry. I wasn't thinking.'

'It's okay, love. We've had a lot on our plates this last fortnight. Sometimes I can barely remember Joseph's face, let alone that I'll be walking down the aisle with him. Sometimes he almost seems like a stranger to me!'

~

'Heavens!' Laura said as she braked for the dozenth time on their approach to the foothills of the Pyrenees. The hold-up was caused by an enormous truck—fully loaded with furniture, boxes and perhaps a dozen people hanging onto its frame—stuck in the middle of the road. Perhaps it was out of fuel, or maybe an axle had broken; it was hard to know.

As they waited for the vehicle to be moved, dozens of people surrounded their car.

'Please, can my child ride with you? I will pay you....'

Sofia jumped as a man loomed alongside the vehicle, tapping on Laura's window. 'Please, señorita, can you make a small space for my mama? She cannot walk another step!'

'No, no,' Laura replied, gesturing to the luggage filling every inch of the car's interior.

'Sí, here! Laura, I have space... truly, I don't mind.' Sofia shifted in her seat to reveal a few inches beside her. Surely the tiny woman could fit. It would be tight, but Sofia didn't mind.

'Thank you, God bless you...' The man's eyes filled with tears of appreciation as he opened the door beside Sofia and assisted his mother into the space she'd created, no doubt determined to see her safely on board before anyone could change their mind.

'I will see you in France, Mama! You are comfortable, sí? I'll be there later today, God willing. If I don't get there by dark, ask someone to phone Delfina. She will come and collect you!' Turning to Laura, he continued. 'Please, can you drop Mama at Portbou station? At least now her legs will be saved. God bless you!'

'No, that will not do.' Laura's voice was firm as she shook her head and frowned. 'We were in Portbou last week. It was bedlam then; I can't imagine what it's like now. You would never find each other. It's better you keep together. You stand on the side, see, and hold on to the mirror. I will drive slowly, and at least you can stay with your mama.' She put her foot on the gas pedal and called through the window. 'Now, hang on tight!'

Driving at a snail's pace, the man's right hand hooked through the open window, his left gripping the metal support of the side mirror, they wove their way towards the border. Looking outside, Sofia was stunned at the view of the human tide now snaking its way across the mountains. Every few minutes the man clinging to Laura's car ducked his head and looked at his mother, calling 'I'm alright, all good!' Though his words were all but lost to the wind, his thumbs-up and white-toothed smile of appreciation was reassuring. The elderly woman—Maria, Sofia discovered—didn't seem comforted by her son's gestures, for every few minutes her tremulous voice arose, with no chance of the words reaching their destination: 'Eliseo, are you alright? Hold on! We'll be there soon!'

The sweet sound of a mother speaking to her child, though he was a man perhaps forty years old, transported Sofia to her own childhood. Feeling the body of the woman against her reminded her of snuggling against her Tia Jovita, finding comfort in her soft curves. Until Maria's sharp elbow dug into Sofia's abdomen. She was thin where her aunt had been well covered, and her voice was barely audible where her aunt's had been firm and confident. Yet these differences didn't diminish the comfort Sofia felt with the old Spanish woman leaning against her.

CHAPTER 27

*I*f the roads for the past ninety minutes had seemed chaotic, the disorder at the border crossing was astounding. Not only the local municipal police, but the Gendarmerie—France's army police force—were everywhere, and they looked none too friendly in their attempt to bring order to the throng. Ahead of them, a man in uniform tried to control the flow of vehicles lined up to enter France, waving them to a checkpoint on the right of the road. Fortunately, there were far more vehicles than space to park them.

As the road opened ahead, Laura paused, then put her foot on the accelerator. Sofia held her breath, expecting they would be chased down by one of the armoured military vehicles parked along the roadside, but nothing happened.

'Eliseo!' cried Marie, and Sofia felt the old woman shudder as she called out over the roar of the vehicle's engine.

Sofia repeated Maria's cry, and Laura slowed down.

'Oops,' she said as she gently applied the brakes. 'Forgot about our passenger!'

A tap on Sofia's window, accompanied by the now familiar grin and a thumbs-up, revealed Eliseo had survived the charge, and their laughter diffused the nervous energy of the past few minutes.

Laura continued driving until they arrived at a small village shop about a mile or so on. There, they all alighted to stretch their legs and to farewell Maria and Eliseo.

'There is a phone box here,' he told them. 'I will call my cousin. She's waiting to hear from me. My mother and I are the lucky ones— we have a place of safety to go to. My heart grieves when I think about what will happen to most of those poor beggars on the road. I wish they could all be so lucky as to find three angels!'

Sofia hugged Marie. 'May God be with you both,' she said, the words overheard by Eliseo who turned back and reached for her hand.

'Gracias, señora, gracias, may the Lord bless you, too! Soon we will all return to our homes, God willing!'

Would she? Sofia wondered even as she smiled at him. She didn't know.

Despite what felt like hours of driving, it was barely midday when they arrived at Lyon. Laura assured them a train to Paris would be running at least every hour. Again she suggested Sofia and Elizabeth come home with her for a day or two first, but they declined.

'Okay, then, but while you are in Paris, please be my guest and stay at the Hotel Monge on the Rue Monge,' Laura said. 'It's in the Latin Quarter and utterly beautiful. Lucien and I stay there whenever we visit Paris. The manager's a friend of ours. I'll phone through from the station, if you agree, and arrange your stay.'

After unloading their cases, Laura escorted them to the ticket booth. There, in fluent French, she ordered their tickets to Paris, waving aside the notes Elizabeth thrust before her and paying for them with her own money. After taking them to the tea-room, she left the table to phone her friend.

'It's all organised,' she said as she returned. 'You will have room

314—it's the one we always stay in and offers spectacular views of the Seine. In the morning you'll be able to watch the sun rising over Paris.'

'Thank you so much, Laura,' Sofia said. 'You have been so very good to us!'

'Why, don't thank me—it is I who should be thanking you! Your help with the collection was incredible. It's hard to believe it will finally be safe. I know how much Lucien appreciated your help, too.'

Sofia smiled. By now, he would be in Perpignan, along with the jewels of Spain's cultural heritage, either seeing them loaded onto the train to Geneva or leaping aboard a carriage to accompany them. With Lucien in attendance, watchful as a father, the works were in safe hands, she knew.

Finally, the train appeared, and she and Elizabeth boarded, only just managing to squeeze their cases through the door before the sound of the porter's whistle pierced the air and the carriage lurched forward. Judging by the sounds of Spanish voices intermingled with the French passengers surrounding them, Sofia guessed at least some of the Catalonians who'd fled Spain had managed to cross the border.

'Here, madame! You must sit, please.' The man's eyes flickered toward Sofia's abdomen then returned to her face. He and his companion rose, vacating their seats and Elizabeth replied 'Thank you, gentlemen. You are very kind.'

Again, Sofia cursed her weight gain and felt like a fraud. She and Elizabeth had only been offered the seats because, like so many others had, the men thought she was pregnant. She prepared to correct them, but Elizabeth caught her eye and gave a slight shake of her head, before taking one of the freshly vacated seats. She patted the empty space beside her, beckoning Sofia to sit.

CHAPTER 28

*I*t was after five when they finally arrived at the hotel, and as
Laura promised, it was lovely. The suite looked fit for
royalty, with a sitting room and two bedrooms, each with a double bed
and a small balcony.

'Come on, Sofia, let's go sit out on my balcony while it is still
light. It is beautiful, isn't it?' insisted Elizabeth.

As Laura had said, the view of the Seine was wonderful, and Sofia
watched the fishermen lining its banks, and the small boats bobbing on
the water. The view across the city was lovely and they tried to identify
the sites within view. The dome of the Sacré-Coeur Basilica glowed in
the distance, while right before them the rays of the setting sun
reflected off the Eiffel Tower.

'It really is magical,' Elizabeth said. 'I can't wait to come here with
Joseph.'

'You didn't get your wedding shopping done,' said Sofia. 'I am
sorry. Why don't we go shopping tomorrow? We don't have to rush
back to London immediately, do we?'

'I think we probably do, Sofia. A lot has happened since we left,
and somehow, I have lost interest in shopping. I'll ring both Joseph and

Marcus later and fill them in on our adventure and let them know we are on our way home.' After a moment's silence, Elizabeth continued, her voice sombre. 'We couldn't get you home after all. Should we send your papa a telegram to let him know what's happened? '

Quietly Sofia gathered her thoughts. She struggled to control the tremor in her voice as she began, 'Elizabeth...'

'Yes, love?'

'My brother... My father... You know my illness affected my memories.'

'Of course, but you're much better these days, I can tell. Our trip to Spain seems to have been good for you, dreadful as the circumstances were.'

'That is true, but being in Spain helped me to remember a lot of things. Not clearly, but in fragments. More so than before. From these, I have tried to make sense of my past.'

'And that's been helpful?' Elizabeth sounded pleased.

'Yes... no. One thing I am sure of is...' Sofia faltered, for saying the words aloud was difficult.

'What is it, Sofia?'

'My father and brother are not in Malaga as I've claimed. In fact they are no longer alive.'

'What!' Elizabeth sat forward, gazing intently into Sofia's face. 'You think something has happened to them after Franco's bombing in Malaga? But you can't be sure. Your family are artists, not Republicans! They might have suffered some hardship, but surely they'd be no threat to Franco. Besides, didn't you say your family's home was on the hills beyond Malaga? They'd be away from danger, surely?'

'It's not that, Elizabeth. Actually, I think they passed away many years ago—long before Franco overthrew the Republicans. I now have many more memories of Malaga. Still more of our childhood; of Papa setting Andres and me before little easels. Him teaching us how to mix colours and helping us create our own little masterpieces. And of Andres and me filling baskets with oranges and carrying them to the house. But now, I also have recollections of being older. Of Andres and me sitting beside my father when he was very ill...' Sofia paused and shook her head, as if to shake the pain of the image from her mind. 'And I have a memory of Andres' himself, resting in a coffin; it is on the dining room table.'

'No! And so you were left by yourself? This is why you went to Australia?' Elizabeth asked, frowning in a bid to make sense of Sofia's memories.

'I don't know. I remember a man being with me. Someone I loved. I am very sure I wasn't alone.'

'Who was the young man?'

'I don't know. I see him sometimes. He was kind. He laughed a lot; like Andres—always teasing. He made me laugh.'

Elizabeth leaned forward in her chair and reached out, taking Sofia's hand in hers and squeezing them. 'Sofia, you know you were married, don't you?'

Sadness enveloped Elizabeth's face as she paused before continuing in a soft voice. 'You had a husband in Australia. You sent him a telegram on the ship. Marcus told me about it. Do you think it was him that was with you in Spain?'

Again, Sofia didn't answer. Certainly there were memories of a young man at the finca, and when she and Elizabeth had taken the Night Ferry, she'd felt she'd been there before, in the company of someone.

'There is so much that is unclear, Elizabeth, so many blank spots. I was certain when I got to Malaga, it would all come back to me. But now I know there isn't a home there at all. In fact, I suspect I sold the finca; the gallery. It would make sense, wouldn't it? That would explain why I have money in my bank account.'

Sofia squirmed under Elizabeth's sympathetic gaze and wondered if she believed her. 'I don't think I am imagining this; the pain I feel is so raw.' Tears pricked her eyes .

'You need rest, Sofia. Marcus told me he is sure your memories will return with time. He believes you've had some sort of shock.

Perhaps when your marriage ended? Perhaps on the day after you arrived at Tilbury? These things happen, love. You mustn't feel too bad. Rest your mind and don't try to force things.'

Sofia nodded, but couldn't stanch the tears rolling down her cheeks. 'I do remember being so happy. So loved. We laughed a lot, Jack and I.'

'Jack?'

'Yes. I am sure that was my husband's name.' Sofia squinted, as a vision unfolded before her. 'He was tall and fair. Very open and decent; quite innocent really. And he loved me very much. I think I met him here.'

'Here! At this hotel?' Elizabeth looked incredulous.

'No, no. Here in Paris. I look across to the Eiffel Tower and to Montmartre—we were here, together. I know it.'

'Oh, Sofia, come here. Sit with me. Let's not overdo this. Let's allow your memories to come back slowly.'

Sofia nodded and joined Elizabeth on the chaise lounge. Another memory was also vivid—a hotel foyer, like the one they'd been in an hour earlier. The place where she'd collapsed and the police had taken her to the dreadful hospital from which Marcus had rescued her. She didn't speak of it. Elizabeth was right. It was best to let the memories come to her rather than go chasing them.

'I think we should take a walk; the fresh air would do us both good,' Elizabeth said. 'And when we return, we can have dinner at the restaurant downstairs. I noticed they have chicken chasseur on the menu—hopefully they have crème brulée too! That and a glass or two of chardonnay would be a perfect ending to an extraordinary adventure, before we return to London.'

The walk was a good suggestion: it was beautiful outside. Yet as they crossed the road to the park Sofia had seen from their window, admiring its iron gates and trying to identify the stately figures on the statues within, again she was sure she'd walked these streets before, accompanied by a man named Jack.

~

Elizabeth didn't leave Sofia's side as they prepared for bed that night. They'd agreed to share the bed in Sofia's room, where the morning sunshine would wake them. Sofia squirmed for a while, trying to get comfortable, until finally Elizabeth intervened.

'Why don't you put a pillow in front of you? You can cuddle it, see?'

Elizabeth was right; the pillow tucked across her belly was somewhat comfortable, and Sofia fell into a deep sleep. She didn't wake until the early morning, at the sound of Elizabeth calling her.

'Come, Sofia, You must look at this! Our coffee will be here soon. Bring your blanket and we can sit out on the balcony and wait for it to arrive.'

Sofia joined Elizabeth, and together they leaned over the iron rail looking at the view. Dawn was breaking over Paris, casting a soft glow across the city. They watched as the sun's fingers crept over the buildings to their right, reaching through the alleys and onto the street below them. Rays reflected gloriously off the roofs, walls and the cobblestones set in shell patterns on the roads. To their left, the Seine glistened with sparkles of pure gold as sunlight bounced off the breeze-touched water, a thousand ripples dancing with flashes of light.

A knock at the door alerted them the breakfast they'd ordered the previous evening had arrived. Steaming coffee, fresh fruit and ham and cheese croissants were delivered on a silver tray by a friendly woman wearing a jaunty headscarf. After placing the tray on the balcony table between them, she insisted that if they needed anything more, they should press the buzzer on the bedside table, then bid them good-day.

'Isn't this the most perfect morning you could imagine?' Elizabeth asked between sips of the coffee, but Sofia's mind had returned to Catalonia and the events of the past week.

'I cannot believe Spain has changed so much,' she said. 'It used to be such a happy place!'

'Perhaps your memories were formed through the eyes of

childhood,' Elizabeth said with gentle tact. 'Children are often oblivious to the political troubles in their country, unless, of course, it's outright war! Those poor children in Figueres won't have much joy to remember, will they? For most of us, childhood was about playing with our siblings—climbing trees and making up ghost stories.'

'I think you are right. My memories are exactly like that... playing in the orchard with Andres while our father tended to the trees or planted vegetables in the garden beds.'

'It sounds beautiful, Sofia. My childhood was wonderful, too. Mostly riding horses and brushing horses and feeding horses. Marcus was far too studious to get his hands dirty in the stables. He spent his life with his nose in a book while I ran wild outdoors.'

'Do you think, after breakfast, we arrange to board tonight's channel crossing?' Elizabeth asked. 'I am keen to get home, suddenly.'

Sofia nodded in agreement; she didn't mind at all. However, despite sleeping reasonably well, she felt exhausted, and her back ached badly. All she wanted to do was return to bed and put her head down. Really, it was little wonder she felt tired and sore after all they'd been through. And beyond the physical activity and demands of their journey, she also carried the burden of knowing the trip she'd been so desperate to take was fruitless, that Andres and Papa no longer waited for her in Malaga. Strangely though, now that the illusion she'd held was torn down, Sofia found a degree of peace. Many of the obscure images that had haunted her now made sense; her past was a little clearer, and for this she was thankful.

'Elizabeth, would you terribly mind going down to the lobby and sorting out our tickets alone? I think I need to return to bed for a few hours, I'm utterly exhausted!'

'Not at all. We did wake very early. It was lovely to see the sunrise, though, wasn't it?'

'It was. Don't rush back, Elizabeth. I promise you I won't do anything silly. I feel much better than I did last time we were here.'

Elizabeth left with a promise to collect some pain relief for Sofia's aching back, plus some magazines and snacks for their journey to London.

~

The sun was high when Sofia woke to the sound of Elizabeth moving around in the sitting room.

'Sorry! I was trying to be quiet. I didn't mean to wake you!'

'Don't apologize, I am glad you did! I've had a good sleep, but it must be time to get up now.'

'No hurry. We don't have to be at the station until about eight-fifteen this evening; the Night Ferry leaves at nine o'clock on the dot. I was thinking this afternoon we could do something relaxing, perhaps a wander through the Louvre; after handling those crates and all that talk about great masterpieces, I'd quite like to see a few paintings. Or maybe we could go for a walk around Montmartre. I hear it's where the artists hang out.'

'No, not Montmartre. Let me take you to Montparnasse, to the Café Le Dome, where we can buy a cup of coffee and croissants for afternoon tea.' Yet again, Sofia was surprised by knowledge being unlocked from her mind. She spied half a dozen bags sitting on the table. 'Oh, good, you did do some shopping!'

'I ducked into Le Bon Marché; I couldn't resist. Lingerie and shoes! They are gorgeous. Like nothing I could ever have bought in London, I'm sure. Plus, I also bought us a couple of lemon tarts. They look delectable!'

'Good on you, Elizabeth!'

'Here, I bought you a present. I thought you must have something special from Paris to take home.'

'Thank you. How lovely.' Sofia removed the tissue to reveal a cream satin nightgown with a lace bodice and flowing sleeves. 'It is so beautiful, Elizabeth! I don't think I've ever owned anything quite like it. Mind you, I'm not sure it won't be a little tight—I am more of a pudding these days than the slim young woman I once was.'

'You'll slim down again soon enough,' Elizabeth said, and Sofia laughed at her confidence.

'Not if I'm to eat those lemon tarts you've bought!'

'Well, you will have to share one with me so it won't be too much!'

'What have you got in that gorgeous bag?' Sofia indicated one on the bench, striped gold, blue and black.

'It's for Marcus and Joseph—I bought them a tie each, as well as some nougat, which of course they will share with us!'

In the end, they did both, the museum and Le Dome, first catching a taxi to the Louvre, where they wandered through the beautiful rooms, gazing at the collection. Sofia was pleased to realize that much she'd learned as a young woman still remained with her, which she happily shared with Elizabeth.

'Oh, of course… at the end of this corridor is da Vinci's *Mona Lisa*. Thankfully it's quiet today. I remember clamouring for a place to see her, once. She's even smaller than I remembered her to be. You know, this is considered to be one of the earliest portraits where the sitter is positioned in front of a totally imaginary background. Usually, like the paintings of your ancestors, people were placed sitting at desks amid their belongings or in gardens or living rooms.' They gazed at the portrait of the woman bearing the famous enigmatic smile.

'So she is what all the fuss was about,' Elizabeth said.

'What fuss?' Sofia was surprised to hear Elizabeth knew something about the works in the gallery she didn't know.

'This painting was stolen! It was years ago, of course; I was only a child at the time, but our mother followed the story and I have never forgotten it. I remember her showing me a photo of this painting in the newspaper.'

After they left the Louvre, they taxied across the river to the Left Bank, then walked along Boulevard du Montparnasse, finally arriving at Le Dome. They claimed a table which had just been vacated. It was no surprise to Sofia that the cafe was full, the air ringing with the loud voices of diners, many of them foreign. Again she was overtaken by nostalgia; she may well have sat at the very same table, in the very same seat, smelling the same heady aroma of cigarettes mingling with the fumes of the vehicles sweeping along the road barely feet away from the patrons. Andres had been with her, but so too had Jack. She was sure of it and tried to fight the heartache that filled her chest.

Catching a glimpse of her expression, Elizabeth frowned. 'Sofia, are you sure you really want to eat here? I do have those lemon tarts back at the hotel. What say we walk for a bit, and then we hop into a taxi and return to the hotel? We can have a cuppa and a rest there, and then perhaps a snack for dinner before making our way to the station.'

Sofia was glad of the suggestion and immediately rose from the table. The sensation in her chest, caused by bittersweet memories of a time past, was growing—spreading into her throat and pounding into her ears. She breathed deeply, forcing herself to calm down, and took the arm Elizabeth offered her. Sofia was pleased when, rather than quiz her, Elizabeth chose to chat about the boats on the Seine and then led the way to the row of bookstores set up along the pavement. By the time they arrived back at their hotel, she felt normal again.

Three hours later, Sofia gazed though the train window watching the city lights recede into darkness. Here she was, returning to England. What next? She accepted that she wouldn't be going back to Malaga, or even Spain, any time soon. But she couldn't live with Marcus and Elizabeth forever. And although she had a sizable balance in her bank account, she probably should consider finding a job.

She inhaled deeply and leaned her head back against the rest; from experience she knew worrying too much would make her heart race and cause her thoughts to be muddled. Nonetheless, her efforts did nothing to eliminate the shadows at the periphery of her mind: voices and events, people's faces, flashing in snippets, all demanding her to make sense of their place in her life.

Sofia shook her head to rid herself of the intrusive thoughts and focussed on the words Elizabeth was speaking about her wedding: the caterers with whom she must meet, and the final fitting for her dress. Sofia found it hard to concentrate. After their recent experience in Spain and Paris, the wedding seemed to belong to another life. Elizabeth turned the conversation to the friends she'd invited, in particular her oldest friend, who now lived in Scotland. How she hoped Maggie would fit into the bridesmaid dress that had been made for her according to measurements sent by mail.

Maggie? Margaret...?

Sofia was thankful for the darkness, glad Elizabeth did not have to witness her shock again as yet more memories of her past crystalized. For as clearly as Sofia knew a man named Jack had once loved her and she him, she also remembered a woman called Margaret, one who'd played a significant role in their lives. Margaret had been stylish, strong and capable; a bit like Elizabeth, really. A vision came to Sofia of Margaret's arms around Jack. With the vision came a feeling: now Jack was safe. He, who'd once been hers, now belonged to Margaret, who would protect him in a way Sofia couldn't.

Protect him... Protect him from what? Sofia wondered at the strange notion.

PART V

Middle East

CHAPTER 29

t eleven thirty the following morning, Sofia and Elizabeth
finally arrived at St Albans. Marcus was already at the bus
stop, his greeting warm as he hugged them. For all of his expressions
of disappointment she hadn't made it home to her family, his beaming
smile told her he was ecstatic that she'd returned to Talonsgate.

'You will be able to write to them, Sofia, tell them what's
happened,' he said.

'Marcus.' Elizabeth's tone held the undercurrent of a warning, and
she shook her head. 'Let's just get home.'

Marcus had set up small tables in the lounge, where the fire blazed
cozily. 'You relax in here, Sofia. I want to see the horses before we eat.
How are they, Marcus?'

Sofia had no doubt Elizabeth's question was a cue for Marcus to
walk and talk with her. As they looked at the horses, Marcus would be
informed of Sofia's recollections about her family since they'd left
Spain.

What on earth would Marcus make of it all? She'd dragged his
sister halfway across Europe, distracted her from her wedding
arrangements and her horses and even endangered her—all to pursue a

figment of Sofia's imagination. Marcus might think she should be re-admitted to Napsbury Hospital, for clearly her mind was far from mended.

Even more troubling was a feeling that the revelations about her father and brother had only been half of it; deep within her was a foreboding of more to come. Memories which held the key to her illness—the events that led to her hospitalization. Her greatest fear was that should these return, her mind would once again unravel.

Looking around the room, warmed by the fire, Sofia realised she was glad to be back at Talonsgate, where all was so steady and solid in her surroundings, whatever happened within her.

'Alright, Sofia, time to eat!' Marcus exclaimed when he and Elizabeth finally returned.

Sofia opened her eyes; in the time they'd been away, she'd dropped off to sleep.

In his hands he carried a large pot of stew, and behind him, Elizabeth was carrying the butter dish and a plate holding bread rolls.

'Elizabeth tells me you two have had quite an adventure. You will have to tell me everything!'

Marcus filled their bowls and they passed the bread rolls around and, deciding against sitting at the table, they relaxed in the oversized chairs in the lounge. Lunch evolved into afternoon tea, and as the room darkened and lamps were lit, their tea and cake were replaced with cheese, biscuits and glasses of red wine. As they ate and drank the day away, Elizabeth and Sofia recounted the details of their journey. They bypassed any references to the setback Sofia had experienced their first night in Paris, and understated the severity of the bombing in Barcelona. However, their voices were filled with excitement as they told Marcus about their good fortune in meeting Lauren and Lucien and described how they'd helped to load the Spanish artworks for evacuation to Geneva.

'Good heavens! Good luck? What with Franco advancing northward, it's a wonder you weren't caught up in an attack! The papers here were full of the Barcelona incident—I tried to track you down, but didn't have a single lead to follow beyond learning you'd left Paris. I had my fingers and toes crossed that you'd got to Madrid before the bombing. If it hadn't been for that telegram you sent, Elizabeth, letting me know you were both safe, I would have been frantic!'

'Marcus, we were fine! Laura and Lucien's house was in the mountains, so we were well out of harm's way there. Besides, the opportunity to help; to be making history as Spain's artworks were evacuated was about the most thrilling thing I've ever done!'

'We couldn't have left, Marcus,' Sofia added. 'As Elizabeth said, the evacuation of the art was thrilling, and wonderful to be part of. But more than that, it was vitally important! The works we helped to move are of extraordinary significance. It would have been a loss to the whole world if they were damaged.'

As the chat continued, weaving between events in London and at Talonsgate, and their journey on the Night Ferry, visit to the Louvre and events in Figueres, Sofia's eyelids drooped, and the pain in her back returned. She shifted in her seat, reaching for a cushion to lean against.

'Time for bed, perhaps,' Elizabeth said. 'Marcus, have we got any painkillers? Sofia could barely sleep last night for her aching back, and from the way she's looking, she could do with some pain relief now. I managed to get aspirin in Paris, but perhaps you have something a little stronger?'

Half an hour later, Sofia snuggled between the cosy sheets of her bed, and—as Elizabeth had suggested the previous night—she tucked a pillow in front of her aching abdomen, appreciating the comfort it provided.

She fell asleep to the soft murmur of Elizabeth's and Marcus' voices drifting up the stairs from the lounge room, her back eased by the sedative she'd taken, her spirit soothed by the comforting atmosphere of Talonsgate.

~

The room was drenched by filtered moonlight when Sofia woke with a start. She looked around, thinking someone had entered, but all was still. Rising, she walked to the window and, looking out, wondered what time it was. The moon was full, illuminating the mist bathing the fields with a soft light. It could be near daylight, but again, it might equally be the middle of the night.

Sofia returned to her bed, and tried to settle into sleep again, but after a few minutes of rolling from side to side, she decided to go downstairs and get a glass of water. The house was quiet as she pattered along the hallway, glad for the moonlight which made navigating the stairs easy. In the kitchen, she found a glass and filled it. As she passed the lounge room where Marcus, Elizabeth and she'd been sitting a few hours earlier, a glow from the fireplace caught her attention, and she entered. The room was still warm, and the clock on the mantel ticked loudly; the illuminated hands of its face told her it was just gone one AM.

Sofia gazed at the glowing embers. Then, without thought, she poured her glass of water over them. She watched as the smouldering remnants of the fire sizzled and popped before fading into blackness.

A chill against her bare feet distracted Sofia from the dying embers —they were damp, she realized; a stream of the water she'd just poured had seeped across the tiled hearth and then onto the floor boards.

Without hesitating, Sofia went to the laundry for a cloth to soak up the mess. This room was in darkness, and she reached for the switch. As light filled the room, a vice-like cramp took hold of Sofia's abdomen with a force that made her gasp. *Good heavens*, she thought, breathing heavily and gripped the tub for balance, for her legs felt as though they might collapse under her.

Just as she steadied herself, a second cramp took hold of her, this one more vicious than the first, and her legs folded. Sofia sank to the floor trying to fight the light headed sensation now filling her—was she going to pass out? The ancient flagstones were freezing and hard beneath her, and a sticky warmth seeping from between her legs made no sense at all. She wrapped her arms around her belly and rolled onto her side, her knees drawn up as waves of pain racked her body in rapid succession.

She was somewhere else. In another time. In a kitchen, with her belly rhythmically tightening until she was sure it would crush her. However, she was not alone, but surrounded by a group of women. *'Here's another one... come on, Sofia, breathe deeply. Jack will be here soon, then you can go to the hospital!'*

'Oh, there he is now! I think we have a baby coming, Jack!'

Sofia, was overwhelmed by an urge to push. She forced herself to sit up, leaning against the wall, only to slide back down as the ache in her back grew stronger. She heaved and gasped.

'Scotty, Scotty,' she cried. He was coming, she knew it, for she felt the pressure low in her pelvis. Again, she pushed.

'Come on, Mrs Tomlinson, one last push... your baby is nearly here...'

Sofia drew a deep breath, and holding it, she grunted and pushed down. It wasn't one last push though. Rather it was half a dozen, each leaving her more exhausted than the previous. The voices repeated their calm commands, urging her to breath deeply, pause, push just one more time. Suddenly the whimpering cries of an infant filled the room. As the sound became a roar, echoing in the hard-surfaced room, Sofia looked down.

'Oh, he's beautiful, Mrs Tomlinson—a baby boy, and look at all of that hair! How lovely.. Congratulations!'

But it wasn't a plump baby boy with a shock of black hair on the floor between her legs. It was a different child, tiny and angular with a pale rounded head. Through the smears of blood and mucous coating it, Sofia saw no hair to speak of. She reached out and pushed it away from her, and the baby's wailing escalated with a shrillness that pierced the air. Sofia shuddered. This child was not Scotty—it was a girl! Where had she come from? But more than that, where was Scotty?

'Scotty, Jack! Did you get him? He was asleep in his bed!!'

Fighting the exhaustion in her legs, Sofia pedalled faster. But it wasn't fast enough, and climbing off her bike, she tried to run. Her legs were so heavy could barely move them. In the distance, Sofia saw smoke, and as she got closer, the faces with shocked expressions turned towards her. No words were necessary; their faces said it all. And then she began screaming.

CHAPTER 30

*S*ofia had a vague memory of Marcus hauling her into his arms and carrying her up the stairs to her bed, of the rustling movement as her sheets and blankets were tucked in around her.

She awoke to the greyness of early dawn and saw Elizabeth at the door, her face white, holding a bundle wrapped in the small crocheted rug which belonged on the back of the lounge room couch.

She walked toward the bed. 'Are you alright, Sofia? Good heavens, that was a shock for us all, wasn't it. The baby needs a feed.' Elizabeth lowered the bundle into Sofia's arms.

Sofia looked down to see the wrappings unravel, revealing the waving of tiny hands. A red face scrunched into a wrinkled frown appeared, its mouth widening to release a roaring cry that pounded her ears.

'No, no...' Without thought, Sofia pushed the bundle back toward Elizabeth, dreading its closeness. The baby's cries intensified.

'Sofia, stop this. You are terrifying her!'

'No, take it from me... Please...' Again, Sofia pushed it away, and at the risk of it landing on the floor, Elizabeth scooped the screaming infant into her arms and hugged it to her.

'Do something, can you?' she said to Marcus, who had entered the room behind her. 'The baby needs to be fed! Can't you give Sofia something to calm her?'

'It's alright, Elizabeth. This is not altogether a surprise.'

'What? Not a surprise that Sofia has a baby on the laundry floor in the middle of the night, and now she refuses to feed it? In what way were you prepared for this, Marcus? Because I wasn't, and quite clearly, neither was Sofia!'

'Elizabeth. Shush…. The baby came early. It has caught us all off guard, but it appears to be alright.' Marcus leaned over and glanced at the child now whimpering in Elizabeth's arms. 'Take her away for now. Perhaps we can call one of the women from the village. There's a Mrs Davis, a midwife. She may be able to help.'

'Good lord! It would have been good of you to prepare us for this, Marcus. It's one thing dealing with a newborn foal, but a baby!'

'Elizabeth, there is no woman in the world more capable than you! Come on now. Do what needs to be done. I'll attend to Sofia.'

Sofia watched Marcus settle into the chair at her bedside, and lean forward to take her hand.

'You poor thing,' he said. 'You've had a terrible shock, haven't you?'

Sofia gazed back at him. What did he know? Had she spoken of the horrific images which had descended upon her? The memories so vivid, she'd felt as though she'd relived them? Had she mentioned the fire?

'I don't mean just now, though of course, giving birth alone on the laundry floor must have been awful! I am so terribly sorry. I should have been ready for this, but you've delivered much earlier than we'd anticipated.'

'You knew a child was coming?' Sofia's words came as a whisper.

He stroked her forehead, pushing the damp hair out of her eyes. 'We tried to prepare you, but you weren't ready to know.' I am guessing something happened last night to set labour off? And now you've had more memories?'

Sofia sobbed and turned her face to the ceiling. What could she say? How could she tell Marcus about the smoke, the flames? Her baby boy, gone? But not just him. There was all the loss—her mother, her father, her brother. Everyone. Every single person closest to her, dead. A curse hung over her, she had no doubt. And now there was another child to fear for. A baby had been forced upon her. No. She wouldn't have it. She couldn't bear to cause another death.

'Shhhh…' She felt his hand smoothing her forehead and closed her eyes. His voice was calm, as he spoke in a quiet steady tone. 'It is critical that you rest, now. I can't imagine what sort of trauma you've relived in these past few hours, let alone the shock of giving birth all alone. Your head must feel it is about to explode. I want to give you something to make you sleep—an injection—and then I will sit here with you. We need to quieten your mind. I don't want you to worry about the baby… not anything. We can talk later, but for now, sleep is best. In a few hours, I will contact Doctor Spencer. I will also get a general practitioner; Doctor Jardine. He's experienced with obstetrics. It would be good for him to check there's been no complications caused by the delivery.'

'Do I need to go back to Napsbury?' Sofia's voice emerged husky from her dry throat. At the terrifying idea of returning to the asylum, she felt as if she was plummeting into a nightmare. Had she really lost her mind? Was she going to be like Louis Wain? Would she too, need to be institutionalised for the rest of her life?

'No, I don't think so. Not at all. But I do think you need to talk with Doctor Spencer and see what he recommends.' Now, if you'd just relax, this needle won't hurt at all.

The injection Marcus gave her did its work, and when Sofia woke next, the sun was high in the sky. Without even rolling over, she sensed he was by her bed.

As she turned towards him, he reached out and took her hand.

'Feeling a little better, dear? You've slept for nearly twelve hours.'

Sofia nodded. She did feel better, though groggy, and a restlessness infused her—a feeling there were things she needed to attend to. And then it came back to her:

Montsalvat.

Jack.

Scotty.

Her eyes filled with tears of despair as she recalled how it had all gone so dreadfully wrong.

When an infant's squeals filtered from the hallway, Sofia looked up. The door opened, and Elizabeth entered, the baby in her arms. Sofia trembled. Marcus nodded, and Elizabeth crossed the room to the bed.

'See your baby, Sofia,' Marcus said quietly. 'A little girl! Look at her. She's lovely, don't you think?'

Sofia couldn't bring herself to look at the child.

'No, Marcus. No… You don't understand!'

'I think I do. Something happened back in Australia, yes? You were married. You left your husband, and you caught the ship. You wanted to go back to a place where you felt loved and safe and cared for: back to your father and brother. Am I right?'

Sofia nodded. What Marcus said was true, even though she now understood her plan had been fuelled by an aberration of her mind.

'It must have been terrible for you to find yourself in a strange country, alone, when your marriage broke up. Would I be right in guessing you hadn't known you were pregnant when you left Australia?'

'I had no idea. None at all,' she whispered. 'Not until the pains started. When the baby was coming. That is when I knew… when it all came back to me.'

Marcus squeezed her hand. 'Doctor Spencer and I are convinced you've suffered a rare condition, Sofia. It's called "pervasive denial of pregnancy"—where a woman refuses to accept she is pregnant, despite all evidence to the contrary. As strange as it seems, this does happen. From what you told me on the ship, my guess is when you found your husband with another woman, you were distraught, with no one to turn to. And because you were isolated from the people you loved and shattered by the man you trusted, you went into a shell. Sort of like a hibernation—a safe place—where you protected yourself from things that were impossible to bear.'

Sofia shook her head. 'It wasn't like that! Jack didn't cheat on me!'

'No? On the ship you mentioned he was with another woman.'

'Not at first. He loved me, and I loved him. But our baby...'

'This little girl?'

'Our little boy! I should have put out the fire...' Sofia began rocking, her head shaking from left to right. The memories were unbearable.

'A fire! You lost a child in a fire? Good heavens, how dreadful! You poor dear. I am so, so sorry.'

Shame swept through Sofia at Marcus' words. She doubted he'd be so kind if he knew how reckless she'd been; how she'd ignored the live coals in the campfire at Montsalvat despite knowing their potential for destruction. She closed her eyes in a bid to shut out the memory of Jack's agonised expression when she'd revealed what she'd done, but that only intensified the shock in his eyes.

'Everybody is gone, Marcus. My parents. My brother. My baby. I am cursed!'

'No! These things happen. It's not your fault! As hard as it is to understand, God has his own plans.'

'What, to take the people I love from me? Is that His plan? And who will be next, Marcus? Jack? This child?'

'Sofia, please! Remember, Jack is fine. He tried to find you, went to the police. He must have been terribly worried when you left.' Marcus paused and shook his head, wincing, as though he, too, felt the pain she felt. Clearing his throat, he continued. 'The thing is, Sofia, you've suffered too many losses for one person to bear. You've been traumatized and are not thinking clearly.'

'What is not clear? Mother, dead. Papa, dead. Andres... my brother.... my twin..... dead! And my baby, Scotty! Gone, too!' The air echoed with the shrillness of Sofia's words as she spelt out the depths of her sorrow. Marcus squeezed her hand, and she felt it tremble, as if by very force, he might transmit his strength to her.

'Should we contact your husband—Jack? Let him know where you are?' Elizabeth asked quietly.

'No! No… He received the telegram we sent from the ship. He is with Margaret now. She will look after him.'

Again, Sofia closed her eyes as she recalled the past. How the loss of Scotty was more than Jack could bear. His grief had sent him to Margaret, and as much as it hurt, Sofia knew if anybody could mend him, Margaret would. Not her; the woman who'd caused their child to die.

'Are you sure, Sofia?'

'I'm sure. They were always very close. I always thought if it wasn't for me, they would probably have come together.'

'And the baby? This little girl, here?' On cue, the child burst into a lusty cry, reminding them she was very much alive.

'Please, Elizabeth, take her away!'

'But who will care for her if you don't?'

Although Elizabeth spoke gently, Sofia felt pressured to take the baby. Its cries were ones of hunger—just like Scotty's when he needed the breast. Staring at the wall, Sofia's eyes filled with tears. How could she possibly explain to Elizabeth that if she touched this child, it would surely die too?

She felt the squeeze of Marcus' hand on her shoulder. 'Elizabeth, for now, let's see if Mrs Davis will come again. She might even know someone who could help out for a few days,' he said.

'No. Not just for a few days.' Sofia spoke with all the resolution she could muster. 'The baby needs to be adopted.'

'Really? Is that what you want for the child?'

'Yes! Please, Marcus, will you arrange it?'

'I don't think you should be making such a monumental decision at present, Sofia. Yesterday you didn't even know you were having a baby, and now that it's here, you want it adopted. It's a little hasty to finalise such a step, don't you think?'

'No, Marcus. I can't keep it. It will not survive if I keep it.'

'Sofia, where is this coming from? The best thing for you now is rest, not worrying about the future. You've had a terrible shock, and you've lost a lot of blood. Try to drink a cup of tea and then get some more sleep. We can talk more about the baby tomorrow.'

Sofia knew all the tomorrows in the world would not change her mind. She would not keep this baby, and no one could make her.

CHAPTER 31

*O*ver the next few days, despite both Marcus' and Elizabeth's efforts to persuade her to hold her baby, Sofia refused to touch her. And when they told her how the baby had fed or burped or slept, she maintained a polite smile, but said nothing. Anyone listening would have assumed she was a disinterested bystander rather than the child's mother.

Sofia did give in to Marcus' wish for her to be examined by Doctor Jardine, but during his prodding and poking, she barely spoke. His manner was gruff, and Sofia couldn't dispel the feeling the older man believed the child was the product of an illicit encounter.

While he offered no words of comfort, he confirmed the baby was fine, though perhaps a little small for a newborn, at five pounds nine. Just before he left the room, he turned to her and added that although there was no evidence of physical problems, he recommended she rest as much as possible, sit in the sun each day and avoid intercourse for at least four weeks. Fifteen minutes later, when Marcus returned to her room, Sofia wondered if perhaps he had experienced some of the doctor's gruffness, for he looked embarrassed and apologised for the man's manner.

Talonsgate seemed to ring with a new energy, one generated by the squeals of a newborn infant demanding attention at all hours of the day and night.

When Doctor Spencer visited, three days after she'd given birth he was full of apologies. He'd been on a walking trip in Scotland, but had returned as soon as he'd heard about the delivery. After a lengthy series of questions, to which Sofia barely responded, he advised Sofia to take small steps towards caring for the baby: to start by holding her for a few minutes at a time, perhaps, giving her a bottle of warmed milk. Sofia shook her head. She knew what they were up to, he, Marcus and Elizabeth, and she was determined not to be coerced into keeping the child.

She repeated to Doctor Spencer the same message she'd given Marcus: the child must be offered for adoption as soon as possible. There would surely be a couple somewhere who were unable to have children of their own and who would love to have her. People who would keep her warm, fed and safe.

His reply was the same as Marcus' and from his words Sofia knew Marcus had given him an account of her most recent memories. 'Yes, but Sofia, please give it some time. You don't want to relinquish your baby to another woman and then, too late, discover you've made a dreadful mistake. Give it a month or two. We will review your medication and continue your treatment. I will do whatever I can to help you to make peace with the awful events you've been through. These memories of losing your first child in such terrible circumstances is traumatic and very raw. But, although it will always be painful, in time you will learn to live with the loss. You will get stronger and then, perhaps, you will realise you need to love this little baby as much as it needs to be loved by you.'

To refuse to follow Doctor Spencer's advice seemed unreasonable. Sofia knew she was far from well. Every time she closed her eyes, she was swept away; a floodgate of memories had been opened with the arrival of the baby on the laundry floor. Memories of Jack and Scotty —memories of the fire—replayed over and over in her mind.

As the days went by, despite her inner turmoil, Sofia adopted an appearance of normality. She'd learned much during her time at Napsbury: how to control her breathing and shift her mind from the pain of the past to the simple pleasures of the present; to wonder at the sight of an eagle circling high in the sky and to feel the softness of grass beneath her feet; to chew her food carefully, absorbing its texture and taste; to carefully select her clothing and brush her hair and rub the cream Elizabeth had bought for her onto her forehead and cheeks and neck.

In this way, Sofia managed to prevent traumatic thoughts from overwhelming her. If she was careful, she could ensure her hands didn't tremble and ensure her features were relaxed in an appearance of calm. What she couldn't control was the nervous energy flowing through her, a feeling she needed to be active, for if she sat for too long, her thoughts shifted from the eagle in the sky and the taste of the food she carefully chewed to the crackling of the fireplace and the hungry cries of the infant. These thoughts caused her hands to shake and her chest to heave and a battle within her to suppress the pent-up sobs that filled her throat.

As she expected, the baby did fine without her. Through conferring with Mrs Davis, the local midwife, Marcus had found a woman in St Albans, barely five minutes from Talonsgate, whose own child had been in a breech position and, for all the interventions attempted, it refused to rotate and enter the world in a timely manner. After eighteen hours of labour, the baby was pulled from her exhausted body, clammy and blue, and it took neither a first nor last breath. It was the woman's fifth pregnancy, and though grieving for the loss of her child, she agreed to take Sofia's each day, nursing the child from her own breast and tending to it while Marcus worked and Elizabeth cared for the horses.

In the late afternoon, Elizabeth then collected the baby and continued with its care, offering a mixture of condensed milk diluted with water in the evening before settling it into its crib, and then again in the night and the early morning. After initial resistance, the baby's hunger overcame its screaming demands for the comforting aroma and sweet taste of a mother's warm nipple, and accepted Elizabeth's offering of reheated milk delivered through a rubber teat.

When Joseph arrived, which he did most weekends, he loved to carry the child around the estate, talking non-stop to her as he pointed out colourful flowers, prancing horses and airplanes in the sky, even though the infant could barely focus on anything more than two feet in front of her face.

These activities did not matter to Sofia. They couldn't, for to be interested in the child was to care. Instead she maintained an impenetrable shield of indifference which kept the baby's sweet gurgling and hungry cries from tugging at her heart.

CHAPTER 32

*A*s the weeks passed, Sofia held to her conviction that the less she had to do with the baby, the better. And as she maintained distance by creating her own routines, her thoughts were filled with planning for her future.

Taking both her doctor's and Marcus' advice that fresh air would aid her recovery, Sofia walked into town after breakfast each morning, the day's shopping list in her hand. On returning with vegetables, meat and bread, she set to work in the kitchen, first making sandwiches for herself and Elizabeth for lunch, and also for Marcus on the days he was home. After lunch she'd go into the garden with gloves and a small spade and tackle the neglected beds, pulling the yarrow and ivy which grew in a tangled mess, then digging out the invasion of dandelions and chickweed. As she worked, Sofia considered her options. Perhaps she'd go to London and find a job. She was good at cooking; she might find work in a restaurant. Or, with her knowledge about art, she might get work at one of the galleries as a tour guide. Clearly she could not remain here at Talonsgate forever, living with Marcus and Elizabeth, even though they insisted they were happy to have her—accepted her as part of their family, even. And not only did

Marcus and Elizabeth accept her, they also accepted the baby as one of their own.

And as it emerged, they too had been thinking and planning.

It was the hour immediately after dinner but before the baby woke for its evening feeding, and they'd just sat down in the lounge when Marcus and Elizabeth adopted serious expressions. Sofia knew something important was about to be said. *Do they think it is time for me to leave?* Or perhaps, finally, Marcus had found a couple who were keen to adopt the baby, which would be wonderful news.

He cleared his throat and turned the fullness of his gaze upon her. 'Sofia, Elizabeth and I have been talking.'

Sofia restrained the chuckle threatening to erupt. As if she didn't know they'd been talking; they barely seemed to know how not to talk! The air echoed with the inflection of their voices every second of the day, sometimes sharp or loud in disagreement, other times muted in murmured conversation. Often their words drifted into silence or made a sudden turn in direction when she walked in on them unexpectedly. Oh yes, she thought. They'd been talking, alright—in the mornings just before she'd arrive in the kitchen; in the stables at noon, their voices urgent and intense; and in the evenings after she retired to bed. Sofia knew their thoughts were occupied with concerns and arrangements for both the baby and the upcoming wedding. She had other things on her mind.

Marcus continued with a quizzical if not somewhat worried expression—doubtless wondering what he'd said to rouse her amusement. 'The wedding is barely four weeks away, and then Elizabeth will be moving out of the house. Not that she's moving far, of course…'

Talk of her and Joseph's wedding and their proposed move to the lodge was one conversation Sofia had been privy to.

Their marriage would take place at the tiny stone church Sofia passed each day going into the village for the grocery shopping. Following the ceremony, there would be a reception with over eighty guests here on the lawns of Talonsgate. Sofia had assisted in planning the menu, thrilled when Elizabeth agreed she make a range of tapas: small rounds of bread topped with creamy cheese and salmon, marinated peppers and olives, which would be served as appetizers to accompany the glasses of chardonnay the guests would receive when they arrived at the house.

The preparations for the newlyweds' move to the lodge, barely twenty yards from the main house and connected to it by the glass room, had been less consuming. Because it had been occupied by the Edmunds' aunt until quite recently, it was in quite good order. All it had needed was a good airing, a bit of paint on the walls to freshen the bedrooms and living room, and a new electric stove to replace the slow combustion agar their aunt had used for the last two decades. For a week, Sofia had taken the lead in sorting through the kitchen cupboards, cleaning and relining the shelves.

'Elizabeth and I have been thinking about how all of this will affect Andreanna.'

The baby! What does the wedding have to do with the baby? Sofia wondered, even as she ignored the use of the name Elizabeth had decided upon after repeated encouragements for Sofia to choose one. Eventually, given Sofia's total lack of interest, Elizabeth had come up with the unusual combination of *Andre* for Sofia's brother and *Anna* for Sofia's mother. Joseph's mother's name was Anna, too, Elizabeth had explained, pleased with the happy coincidence. Plus, she'd suggested, the name offered plenty of scope for Sofia to change in the future if she wished. Andrea, Rean, Anna were all possibilities should Sofia prefer them. But Sofia was determinedly disinterested. It was wrong for her to name the child she had no intentions of raising. Surely the adoptive parents would want the pleasure of selecting a name for a girl they were taking into their lives.

'You know I love Andreanna like she was my own,' Elizabeth said.

'I was thinking—Joseph and I were thinking—perhaps she should come and live with us... for a while at least.'

'But don't you think a permanent solution would be better? For her to go to people desperate for a child?' In truth, this was Sofia's preference. To have the baby's future decided once and for all by settling her with a loving couple, and in doing so, eliminating the lingering expectation that she would rise to the occasion of motherhood and want to keep the baby for herself.

Marcus cleared his throat. 'The thing is, Sofia, I think we should be open to all future possibilities. Elizabeth and Joseph love Andreanna as though she were their own. They will lavish her with attention, and Talonsgate is a wonderful place for a child to grow up, don't you think? Plus...' Marcus paused and took a deep breath before continuing. 'In truth, I am fond of Andreanna! If the circumstances were different, I would be hankering to keep her right here, in this house. One thing's for certain, none of us want to see her banished from our lives and handed over to strangers. We wouldn't be able to sleep for worrying about how she was getting along.'

Sofia's face remained blank before these declarations of affection for the child to whom she'd given birth. She turned to Elizabeth. 'So, you and Joseph plan to adopt her?'

'We have discussed this, and we think you should remain as Andreanna's mother. You wouldn't need to make decisions for her or worry about her daily care. But, in time, as she gets older, she will know you are her mother. And should things ever change for you, should you decide you want to take care of her—have her live with you, even—it wouldn't be a shock for us all.'

Marcus continued explaining their proposal. 'We'd have no secrets about Andreanna's parentage. Elizabeth and Joseph could be called Aunt and Uncle, and they will be her guardians. Hopefully, you might allow her to call me Uncle, too.' Marcus' expression reflected the tenderness he felt for the baby, and as uncomfortable as Sofia felt with the arrangement, she could find no argument. It was undeniable, there could be no more lovely environment to raise a child than here at

Talonsgate, with its open spaces, the horses and the loving care of Elizabeth, Joseph and Marcus.

'I guess so,' she replied evenly. She would leave them all to it, if that's what they wanted. They could continue as they'd been managing over the last month, the baby spending weekdays with Mrs O'Neil, then coming home in the afternoon and being cared for by Elizabeth and Joseph overnight and on weekends. In time, she would find a job and leave, and the child would be safe in their care.

A month later, on the day of the wedding, without doubt, Andreanna was the star of the show. She was passed from guest to guest, cooed over, her pink cheeks kissed and gently squeezed, her little satin gown and slippers admired.

Out of respect for Sofia's privacy, very little information had been shared about the circumstances of the baby's arrival. She was sure more than one distant relative believed Elizabeth to be its true mother. Certainly, between smiles, photographs and greeting guests, it was Elizabeth, assisted by Joseph and Marcus, who constantly checked on Andreanna to ensure she was clean, fed and napped, while Sofia focussed on the distribution of tapas and the passing of napkins, then assisted the caterers in serving the three-course meal to Elizabeth and Joseph's wedding guests.

CHAPTER 33

*E*lizabeth's, and hence Andreanna's, move to the lodge scarcely changed the dynamics at Talonsgate, except the nights were considerably quieter without the baby in the main house. Also, Sofia was alone with Marcus for dinner and the hours afterwards, when they'd sit before the fire and make conversation—a situation less comfortable than she and perhaps Marcus had bargained for.

Sofia had never doubted Marcus's affection for her, though with Elizabeth's presence in the house, this had been easy to ignore. In fact, Sofia had always felt she, Marcus and Elizabeth made a comfortable trio, sharing meals and settling in the living room in the evenings to read or chat about daily events. Now, she looked forward to the nights when Joseph stayed in London for his work commitments so Elizabeth joined them for dinner, or better still, the weekends where they'd all share dinner after which they'd play cards till midnight.

Increasingly, Sofia sensed that Marcus was biding his time, that he believed a day would come when she would return his feelings and they would have a future together—a hope that was out of the question. Never again could she chance being responsible for losing someone, to endure such excruciating pain and guilt would surely break her. So when Marcus' conversation became a little too serious, Sofia became adept at turning his thoughts to ideas for planting more herbs in the garden, or discussions about her thoughts for finding employment— perhaps there might be a job to be found in St Albans or even in London.

Marcus agreed a job would be a good idea for Sofia, and even offered to inquire at the hospital, which employed vast numbers of people throughout their offices, on the wards and in the kitchens.

'How about we get you a driver's license? Then you will be able to use the Austin to get around. Elizabeth doesn't seem to drive it much these days since Joseph has bought the Wolseley.'

'I would love to have a license! I used to drive in Spain all the time, although the roads there were not as busy as they are here. I'd probably have to learn the road rules again.' Sofia remembered Suzie, the lumbering Hispano-Suiza she'd learned to drive in and often held firm conversations with to ensure it didn't let her down.

The next day, Sofia went to the news-agency where she bought a book of road rules for learner drivers. She studied it for hours at a time and in the evening, Marcus quizzed her. After she'd successfully gained her Learners License, Marcus took her driving in the Austin at every opportunity. One Thursday, a few weeks later, instead of Marcus beside Sofia, there sat a burly inspector with sharp eyes and a calm voice, assessing her ability with a view to granting her a driver's license.

Sofia carefully followed his instructions as he directed her to drive here, turn there, pull in behind a lorry parked on the roadside and reverse into a driveway. Finally, he asked Sofia to turn back towards Talonsgate.

'Flying colours,' he said as Sofia settled the vehicle in the driveway, returned the gear to first, pulled the brake handle and turned the key to stop the engine from shuddering.

Proudly, Marcus beamed as the inspector expanded on her capabilities. 'I couldn't fault Sofia at all. Looked hard, mind you— there's way too many women drivers on the road, as far as I'm concerned,' he added with a cheeky wink, 'but I found no reason to fail her.'

Marcus insisted they celebrate Sofia's success with a special dinner. Although she agreed, Sofia was both disappointed to learn Elizabeth and Joseph would not be joining them and intimidated by the grandeur of the restaurant Marcus chose. When the waiter turned to her and asked Marcus, 'And what would your lovely lady like?', Sofia paled. What was happening here? Did Marcus think now she'd gained her driver's license, she was ready for their relationship to change in some way? That she was ready for romance?

Looking across the table at him, Sofia knew without doubt Marcus would be a dream catch for any young woman. He was as handsome as he was pleasant. In addition, he was witty, intelligent, and very caring. But he was not her. She'd been both loved and married, and had no intention of returning to either state.

In the intimate confines of the restaurant, Marcus' attention suddenly felt overwhelming, and Sofia's mood was dampened. What might have been an enjoyable evening of light chatter in a less formal environment was stifled by the white linen and candles and the hushed tones of the room. When the piano began tinkling and a couple rose to the dance floor, Marcus looked at her inquiringly, but accepted her small shake of the head with a disappointed smile.

The disappointing mood of the dinner lingered at breakfast the following morning, after which Marcus busied himself with paperwork in his study, while Sofia attended to the kitchen, first cleaning the stove then slicing dozens of peaches into fine slices and stewing them in a large pot. At about eleven, a sound through the window caught her attention. Elizabeth and Joseph, dressed for the warmth of the spring day, emerged from the main entrance of the lodge. Held in Joseph's arms, Andreanna looked sweet, with a pink bonnet and matching dress, white stockings and tiny soft leather shoes. Sofia knew they were driving to a horse show in Aylesbury, where Elizabeth was keen to see a young stallion being exhibited.

Viewing the normality of the scene, the happiness of the small family prepared for an outing, Sofia felt as though she'd been whacked in the chest. A memory emerged of her and Jack walking along the streets of Eltham, each holding a hand of their tiny boy between them. Scotty had been about eighteen months old, and the three of them had laughed as he'd lisped, "One, two, three!" On his prompt, they swung him forward, lifting his feet off the ground. Sofia gasped, remembering how the dry Australian air held the crisp aroma of eucalyptus, how the fallen leaves had crackled beneath their feet. They'd jumped on them so innocently, never knowing this same crisp tinder would fuel the destruction of their lives.

She leaned against the bench and fought to breathe against the cutting pain in her chest.

'Sofia! Are you alright?'

She hadn't heard Marcus come into the kitchen, and the concern in his voice was tangible. When she didn't answer, he crossed the room and took her into his arms.

Tears coursed down her cheeks as she fell against his chest, and he rocked her, making a soothing sound.

'Come on, sweetheart… it'll be okay.'

Sofia nodded and her breathlessness subsided. The feel of Marcus' hands rubbing her back replaced the sense of loss which had overwhelmed her minutes earlier. This wasn't fair on him, she knew; she needed to take control of herself.

Forcing a smile upon her face, Sofia stepped out of his arms.

'Yes, I know; I *will* be alright. It's just occasionally it all creeps up on me. The tiniest, most unexpected event sets off a memory, and then I feel the sadness. But I must look to the future. I am fine, I promise you. Now for those biscuits burning in the oven! I thought I'd make a risotto for dinner. Elizabeth and Joseph might join us, and my chicken and chorizo risotto is their favourite. And you know how pleased Elizabeth will be if she doesn't have to come home and cook!'

Although Marcus smiled encouragingly, he lingered. Sofia sensed the battle within him; knew he longed to fuss over her, to offer her his comfort and strength rather than walk away.

Again she smiled. 'Off you go! I am fine. I'll make us cheese balls to go with our gazpacho for lunch—you've never tasted those! You will love them, I promise you.'

That evening, as Sofia hoped, Elizabeth and Joseph arrived with a sleepy Andreanna. Sofia even found it in her to smile at the baby and offer her one of the biscuits she'd baked that morning. But when the child returned her smile with a solemn look, Sofia felt as though she was being reproached, and she looked away, rising to help Elizabeth gather their plates and take them to the kitchen.

Their conversation after dinner took on a serious note, for at the horse sale, Elizabeth and Joseph had run into Joseph's friend, Samuel Golberg, also of Jewish heritage, with family in Berlin, who'd shared his concerns about Germany's leader, Adolf Hitler.

As Joseph and Elizabeth recounted their conversation, Sofia discovered how, during the time she'd been ensconced in Napsbury Hospital the previous year, a political crisis had all but taken Britain to the brink of war.

'It was dreadful,' Elizabeth explained to Sofia. 'That horrid man threatened to take Czechoslovakia for Germany. Both the British and French prime ministers were utterly against it, even prepared to go to war if necessary. Joseph was on standby—ready to be called up at two hours' notice! Each day we expected to wake to the sounds of German planes flying overhead.'

'And what happened?' Sofia asked, astonished to realise she'd been oblivious to these events while confined to hospital.

Joseph took over the story, scathing in his description of how Chamberlain and Daladier had folded to Hitler. 'Even though that man had shown his hand two years before when he took both the Rhineland and Austria!'

'I don't understand,' Sofia said. 'Are you saying the British and French stood by and allowed the Germans to take Czechoslovakia?'

'No, they didn't give him Czechoslovakia, but they compromised with him to avoid a war. They said he could have the Sudetenland, since it was largely populated by people of German heritage, anyway.'

'Well, isn't that good?' said Sofia. She'd seen how Franco had devastated Spain, and felt sure a war was best averted whenever possible.

'Not at all,' said Joseph. 'Men like Hitler are never appeased. Barely six months after agreeing to accept the arrangement; to take the Sudentland for Germany and leave Czechoslovakia alone, he marched in and took Czechoslavakia anyway, and nobody raised a finger!'

'Which brings us to now,' Elizabeth continued. 'Samuel insists Hitler is planning his next move. And not just Hitler, but also the Italian dictator, Mussolini.'

'So, it's time to prepare the basement again,' Marcus said wryly.

'Prepare the basement! Whatever for?' Sofia asked, wondering if Talonsgate's basement was to be used as a hiding place from invaders or for storage.

'For us to hide in, should there be an air strike,' Marcus said. 'Just like in the bombings of Guernica and Barcelona, everyone expects that should Germany choose to strike at us, the attack will come from the sky—airplanes will fly across the Channel and drop bombs on our towns.'

It all seemed too unbelievable to Sofia. 'What, you think there could be an attack on St Albans? Surely not!'

'Well, that's what the government was saying last year. Towns all over Britain have already put preparations in place. They aren't sitting back and relying on the military, although I am sure Joseph and his military mates will do their bit for us.' Marcus gave Joseph a teasing glance. 'Last year dozens of Civilian Force Initiatives were implemented across the country; bunkers for people to gather in, people trained to sound warnings and apply first aid—all that sort of thing.'

Sofia listened, amazed. Elizabeth gave her an assuring nod.

'Sofia, don't feel too bad. You did have a bit going on! In honesty, it was all terribly disturbing, so perhaps you were lucky to be oblivious. I spent my whole time gazing into the southern sky, and every time I saw a speck in the distance, I'd wonder if we were about to be blown to smithereens! I completed the first aid training, so my job was to report to a first-aid post should there be an attack. I should be going to the meetings, I suppose.' Elizabeth gave a wry look and shrugged her shoulders. 'I imagine the Air Raid Precautions group and the First Aiders still meet each week.'

Marcus must have thought Sofia had heard enough, for he tried to bring levity into the discussion. 'Of course, Elizabeth, how could I forget being bandaged up like a mummy every night for a fortnight?' He and Joseph laughed.

'You know the Red Cross and St John's Ambulance Service have just combined their resources to form a Joint War Operation. They are now running courses together,' Marcus said. 'One's coming up at Shenley very soon, I believe.'

'So, they're training the hospital staff?' Sofia asked.

'Well, yes. Not for the doctors and nurses; should there ever be an attack, they will be busy enough providing medical treatment. The training is for the wardsman and the like. The kitchen staff, members of the community... anyone who wants to sign up for it.'

'I had no idea all this was happening.' Sofia said, shaking her head. I suppose with trying to get to Spain, and then Elizabeth's wedding...' No-one mentioned that she'd also given birth to a baby, for which Sofia was thankful.

'It would be negligent if we didn't prepare,' Joseph said soberly. 'How much warning do we need? We already know these dictators— Franco, and now Hitler and Mussolini—are determined to exercise their muscle. I just don't understand why we have to wait for them to strike us first. We always seem to be on our back foot.'

'I'd like to be trained...'

The words were out of Sofia's mouth before she realised as her images of the thousands of people walking to the French border, starving and desperate filled her mind. She recalled the story of a woman who'd given birth in a tunnel. As shocking as her own experience had been, Sofia knew it would be awful to give birth out on the road, amid fear and chaos and surrounded by strangers. If what Joseph was saying was true, and a war were to erupt, she wanted to be armed with skills to offer assistance in any way she could.

'Sofia, do you think so?' Marcus frowned.

'I do, Marcus. I saw what happened in Spain after Barcelona was bombed. I know how dreadful a war can be. Elizabeth and I were lucky to be taken in by Laura and Lucien. Lucky for the opportunity to be helpful rather than just swept up in the confusion we saw on the streets of Figueres. If there is any chance of an attack occurring here, I want to help in any way possible.'

Marcus looked thoughtful. 'Yes, and in truth, you would be marvellous. You are such a practical person and you have excellent organisation skills. Look how you've sorted the household here! The St Albans First Aid Group would be thrilled to have your help. If you like, I'll find out what I can when I am at Shenley next Friday.'

'There's not just First Aid courses, Sofia. You might want to look into the Royal Volunteer Service. I heard Stella Isaacs speak about it in London last September—she's a powerhouse! She's a marchioness or some such thing, but has no truck with titles. She wants action, and was on a recruitment drive, getting women to sign up for training so they would be on their front feet should Hitler cross the Channel. I was so impressed with her attitude. Despite her social status as a bit of a hob-nob, she doesn't care if women are duchesses or charladies; if they can knit, drive an ambulance or manage an air raid shelter, she wants them. I'd already done my First Aid training but I did seriously consider joining her group and learning how to drive an ambulance after I'd heard her speak. But with the wedding arrangements and you coming to Talonsgate, then

Christmas, and now Andreanna, I hadn't given it another thought. Not until now.'

'To be honest, Elizabeth,' Joseph said, his expression grim, 'I think everyone should be giving it a thought. I have to agree with my friend Samuel—it's only a matter of time before Hitler makes his next move, and it could very well be a strike on British soil.'

True to his word, Marcus arrived home with the pamphlet describing the First Aid course being offered at Shenley Hospital, as well as an enrolment form for Sofia. She filled it in immediately and posted it to the address provided. Enthused by the thought of training as a first aid officer, Sofia started to find her days long; beyond basic cooking and cleaning, she yearned to do more.

Over the following week, Sofia poured over the newspapers, both from London and St Albans. Each contained a multitude of references to brewing troubles in Europe. One article expressed fears Hitler might develop an atomic bomb, another discussed the signing of a non-aggression pact between Germany and Russia. Amid the articles were many tiny advertisements offering training for volunteers in First Aid and Air Raid Response. And when she went into St Albans, Sofia saw posters for a whole range of meetings she'd never noticed: women's auxiliary groups, the local Red Cross and even the Royal Volunteer Service Elizabeth had mentioned.

With eyes wide open as she searched for information, Sofia discovered a number of articles about Spain. In this way, she learned that an exhibition of artwork was being held in Madrid. On closer examination, she discovered the collection of cultural treasures so carefully protected by Lucien, Laura and their committee throughout the years of the Spanish war had been handed back to Franco, who was now being recognised as the official leader of Spain.

Dumbfounded, Sofia described the events to Marcus and Elizabeth over dinner.

'Yes, Sofia. It's true.' Marcus said.

'You knew all the artworks were returned to Franco? That the League of Nations has agreed it belongs to him?' Elizabeth sounded as astounded as Sofia felt.

'No, Elizabeth. They have not given the treasures to Franco. They have returned them to the people of Spain! Remember, millions of Madridians love their art as you do, Sofia. And although many may hate Franco, at least they have got their treasures back. It is not such a bad thing. Franco has promised he will see that every piece is returned to its rightful owner. The violence and destruction are ended now, so they will be safe.'

'He may hold a big exhibition at El Prado and pretend to the world he is honourable. But is he going to restore works to the Republicans? The collections of the Catalonians? Return the paintings owned by the people of Barcelona and to those in the Basque country?'

'I don't know, Sofia. In truth, does anyone know what he'll do? Certainly, the damage to Spain has been awful. It is a lesson to all of us of how terrible war is, sadly

'Do you think steps are in place to protect London's galleries, should there be a war? And here at Talonsgate, perhaps you should get your paintings from the stairwell and put them in the basement.'

'What? The ancestors!' Marcus shrugged his shoulders and laughed. ' I don't care too much what happens to those old rogues, but I would hate to see my lady of Boreas come to grief, so thanks for reminding me! Anyway, nothing is going to happen to us, I'm sure.'

'Well, hopefully all of this war talk comes to naught, but I'd rather be prepared than caught unawares like they were in Barcelona. I can't wait to start training on Monday.'

CHAPTER 34

$\mathcal{T}$he following week, Sofia discovered Joseph was not alone in believing that a war with Germany was eminent. When she arrived at the classroom at Shenley Hospital, she found it packed to capacity. Listening to the men and women surrounding her, she heard the anxiety in their voices as they discussed the various courses being offered as a consequence of the rising tensions across Europe. Besides the first aid and air-raid precautions courses, a form was pinned on the wall requesting expressions of interest in training as a civilian ambulance driver. Already several attendees had signed the form.

The conversation switched to one about war preparations in general, and their trainer, Bob—a font of information—shared all he knew. He reinforced the view that an attack on Britain would come from the sky, as Joseph had claimed. Using the blackboard, he outlined a potential scenario and the flow of actions each town would take should they be unlucky enough to be targeted. First, the Air Raid Response team would sound an alarm, warning townspeople to precede to the safety bunkers. Simultaneously, those trained in first aid would present for duty at their posts, and man them—or woman, he added with a chuckle—for the duration of the attack. Civilians with abrasions and minor wounds would receive treatment at the post, while casualties bearing serious injuries were to be transferred via ambulance to the nearest hospital.

A man within the group spoke in a loud, critical tone. 'Beyond training us mugs to sort ourselves out when Adolf unleashes his bombs, what has Chamberlain got in place to prevent these attacks from occurring?'

'Oh, he's got things happening, alright.' Bob's answer came quickly, and returning to the blackboard, he sketched a rough drawing of the British coastline. He then added details of the heavily fortified anti-tank line, which included pillboxes and trenches, beginning from the south of London and continuing through to York.

'This line—the General Headquarters Line—will protect London and our industrial sectors from German tankers in the unlikely event that our coastline defences fail.' Turning back to the board, he added a few more dashes and a second line, which he labelled the Taunton Stop Line.

'Similar to the General Headquarters Line, this here will provide defence should the Jerries get in from the southwest.' Adding chalk marks and dots to his scribbles, Bob explained how if the need arose, major cities would also be surrounded with similar defence lines. So too would airfields; their security was of paramount importance, for they were a prize target for an enemy to capture.

The discussion continued, and it was as if everybody in the room had a story, or knew somebody who was witness to—or directly involved in—defence activities. For almost an hour, Sofia listened quietly as tales were shared: the woman sitting near her explained how her son-in-law was supplying coils of barbed wire to the Army, which were being strung along the foredunes of the Channel to deter enemy soldiers. A man across the room spoke of his uncle in the concrete business, now consumed with making huge blocks ready to be set up as obstructions on roads and airfields at a moment's notice. A man sitting just in front of Sofia was outspoken in his indignation that the army had requisitioned a portion of his parents' farm. They'd taken the position offering the best view of the Channel to set up an unsightly artillery battery. The conversation, led by a couple of men who clearly saw themselves as experts, tilted to military weapons: various guns, bombs, and land mines.

'It makes it hard to sleep at night, doesn't it. I mean... it could be tonight Hitler makes his charge, and here we are, pawns in the grand scheme of things, dependent on the actions of our military, and all we can do is just try to survive and help each other.' The comment came from the lady beside her, and Sofia couldn't help agreeing it did seem rather depressing. She suddenly wondered how a few well-placed bandages could make a difference to the bigger picture of Britain being over-run by an enemy.

'Yes, but we can all do our bit to help the military!' As if he'd read her mind, the man whose uncle was making cement blocks spoke up. 'As soon as Gerry's here, we can work from the ground so to speak. You know; protect our towns, confuse the enemy.'

'How so?' the cynical reply came from an older man sitting toward the back of the room, who, like Sofia, hadn't spoken before.

'In all sorts of ways. For a start, we can turn road signs in opposite directions so any German patrols who make it across the channel are disorientated. Imagine the chaos this would cause.'

Not to be outdone, another man described how common objects could be used to fool the Germans into believing British defences were stronger than they actually were: shop mannequins could be dressed in uniforms and positioned as though on guard duty; strategically arranged pipes, chains and tin would look like they were bombs—the ideas were endless.

The chatter continued through the lunch break, with a degree of enthusiasm for citizen warfare that chilled Sofia. The discussion had resurrected a vision of thousands of Spaniards walking to the French border, hungry and destitute. What would happen if, like Barcelona,

London was attacked—its buildings destroyed, the electricity and water supply cut off, trains and buses brought to a halt? Millions of people would be forced onto the streets. A cruel enemy could take control of the nation.

When they returned to the class after the break, an aura of sobriety had infused the room. It was as though everybody had exhausted themselves from the excitement of planning for war and they were now ready to get down to the business of being trained to respond to one. As she waited for Bob to start, Sofia looked through the window and saw vehicles entering the carpark. Men and women emerged with flowers in their arms, arriving to visit sick relatives. In contrast to the normality of life outside, Sofia felt party to privileged information of an impending disaster; how at any minute, all of their lives could be flung into turmoil. Strangely, her thoughts turned to Jack and Margaret, to his parents and to those at Montsalvat, and she imagined them utterly oblivious to the events unfolding across the world. She was glad they were well away from it all.

Sofia returned her attention to Bob. For all of his talk of war preparations, he was no fearmonger. In fact, he was quite the opposite: a man full of pride for the might of the British, confident of their military's resourcefulness, sure an attack would be rapidly quelled. They were the British Empire, after all, and although he acknowledged The Great War had taken its toll, the British had been victors then. Should an enemy rise, they would stoically face it and win again.

The opening topic in the first aid course focused on basic skin injuries that might be caused by flying debris of a bomb blast. Although some of the trainees looked squeamish, Sofia gave the lesson her full attention. She learned how skin tears, punctures, lacerations and embedded foreign bodies all required different methods of cleansing and bandaging, and was determined to master the techniques in case she was called upon to use them. It was a topic Bob made interesting and memorable by adding dozens of anecdotes. However, Sofia was less sure of his tendency to punctuate the lesson with a steady dose of nationalistic fervour in order to make them feel victorious. She too had once believed her nation was safe, that nothing would ever threaten it. Yet in barely a decade, the face of Spain had been transformed, with almost half a million people killed, hundreds of thousands forced to leave, and important monuments, century-old churches and whole cities devastated. Nobody could be assured of a British victory.

A week later, having completed the first aid course, Sofia undertook the two-day ambulance driver training. After that, she enrolled in Hospital Training—a course teaching volunteers basic skills to support nurses: how to roll bandages, fold linen, polish floors and clean spillages. Helping with these tasks would free up the nursing staff should hospitals be swamped with casualties. Sofia hoped that by acquiring as many qualifications as possible, she could assist the war effort in a range of circumstances.

Each afternoon, on returning to Talonsgate, Sofia popped into the lodge to see Elizabeth and, over a cup of tea gave an update on the day's lessons. Most days she arrived before Elizabeth picked up Andreanna from Mrs Whyte. However, occasionally the infant was home, and Elizabeth would find excuses for Sofia to hold her or leave her with the baby for a few minutes while she tended to her horses.

Each time this happened, Sofia was uncomfortable. She might have given birth to Andreanna, but motherhood was a role she had no intention of assuming. Elizabeth and Marcus had decided on this arrangement for Andreanna's care despite her apprehension. Though thankful the child was well cared for, Sofia felt it best to maintain her distance.

Of all the training, Sofia enjoyed first aid the most. Learning about contusions and abrasions and how to check for pulses and recognise when a person was going into shock fascinated her. She was glad to know how to identify life-threatening symptoms—the hisses and wheezes of abnormal breathing, blueness of the fingernails and lips, excessive blood loss—all indicators to hurry the victim to hospital. Such knowledge might not prevent a war, but it could save lives, and Sofia was thankful for the sense of purpose she gained over the weeks of study.

After the final course was completed, Sofia enlisted with the local Voluntary Aid Detachment and attended meetings with members of the St Albans first aid team. Weekly, they discussed their fears about a shortage of resources and identified creative ways to add to their stock of bandages, gauze, and slings. Sofia's favourite part of the meeting was when they practiced their techniques on each other, responding to hypothetical scenarios. She took the meetings seriously, and soon the others looked to her for confirmation that their treatments were correct. Sofia found she had extraordinary recall for the correct techniques to treat the most obscure of injuries.

For some members of the team, the weekly meetings were a social event. They had completed their first aid training over a year earlier, and their sense of urgency for a pending war had long passed. Not for Sofia. To her, the threat of war was very real, and each day she read horrifying news articles suggesting Hitler was making a nuclear bomb and revealing how he'd created a pact with Russia. Thus, on the nights of their meetings, after the bandages were rolled, the makeshift splints stored away, and the paperwork completed, she'd go home, leaving the others to drink tea and share the biscuits they'd brought while they talked about their weekend activities. Sofia had never been an unfriendly person, but since her illness, it was as if her capacity to make small talk or to banter and joke with strangers had vanished.

Sofia's commitment to her training was not in vain, for on September 1st, Hitler finally made the move they'd all been dreading. It was an advance on Poland, and this time neither Chamberlain nor Daladier was going to be fooled by the German Chancellor. They gave Hitler two days—if he didn't withdraw his troops by nine AM, September 3rd, war would be declared. Whether Hitler thought they were bluffing or not was unclear. However, he didn't retreat, and as a consequence, Britain was at war.

CHAPTER 35

*W*ith Chamberlain's declaration of war, it seemed every level of Britain's government, industry and civilian life burst into action. Plans which had been in the making for over twelve months were activated, and Sofia, along with the forty-five million British citizens, could only hope the preparations would be adequate. In St Albans, men in uniform were everywhere as Army, Navy and Air Force units were mobilised. Women gathered together in shops and on street corners, where they bravely wiped away tears as they consoled and encouraged each other. Hundreds of husbands, sons and fiancés were being assigned to bases across Europe at short notice. The mood wasn't helped by revived memories of fathers, grandfathers and uncles who'd left for the Great War barely three decades earlier, and not returned.

London's hospitals discharged patients to their homes or relocated them to regional centres. Throughout Britain, many country manors had been seconded by the government, their rooms converted into wards to house the discharged patients and, in time, injured soldiers and even prisoners of war.

The newspapers advised householders how to conceal their

266

presence from Luftwaffe pilots: light bulbs should be painted blue to diminish their glow, windows taped to minimise shattering glass and black curtains draped to shield the glow of interior lamps.

Thankfully, Joseph was staying in England—for now at least. His unit was stationed to the south, working on coastal defence, where they were maintaining a twenty-four hour watch on ports and open beaches where an enemy vessel might land. When Marcus, Sofia and Elizabeth travelled to London to purchase black fabric to make curtains for Talonsgate's windows, its changes stunned them. Sofia had read about the hydrogen-filled barrage balloons operated by the Women's Auxiliary Air Force to deter German Stukas from dive bombing the city. However, the enormous silver fish-shaped structures billowing across the skyline, anchored by straining cables, were a sight to behold.

A second surprising spectacle was the lines of children—dozens of them weaving along the pavements, many with gas masks dangling from their tiny necks and carrying small suitcases. They made for the train stations; Sofia guessed they were being sent away from London to smaller towns where they'd live with strangers until the danger passed. She wondered if some of these same children might show up in St Albans; for weeks, representatives of The Women's Volunteer Service had been canvassing suitable homes for children, pregnant women and mothers with infants to live in relative safety should war break out. Seeing these children on the move was sobering.

When they returned to Talonsgate, Elizabeth unearthed a sewing machine and for three days, she and Sofia made curtains while Marcus taped the windows. In the evenings, they were careful to keep both the house and Elizabeth and Joseph's lodge in darkness. They took to congregating in the lounge room of the main house, where they sat by candlelight, playing cards or chatting.

Their conversation, fuelled by radio reports and newspapers, concerned the taking of Poland, Russia's alliance with Hitler, and an attack on Finland. When Joseph was able to join them, they bombarded him with questions. Closer to home, there was an air attack on Scapa Flow, a naval base near Scotland, and in April the Nazis invaded Denmark and Norway. Soon after, Holland surrendered. Some accounts of events in Europe were so dreadful that Sofia couldn't believe them, especially one saying the Nazis were euthanizing the sick and disabled in Germany. Then there were stories about the Jewish people. How they were forced to comply with curfews and wear yellow stars on their shirts, and how thousands were rounded up and transported to Poland to live in vast ghettos; it appeared the stories Joseph had heard were true. Then came the chilling news that France had been taken, supported by a surreal image of Hitler standing in a triumphant pose before the Eiffel Tower.

Nonetheless, the events of the war seemed confined to distant places, and the fears for Britain remained unrealised. As days turned into weeks, and then months, life at Talonsgate as across Britain, lapsed into those of a pre-war footing; windows remained uncovered, and the urgency to stockpile toiletries and medicines subsided. Marcus, Elizabeth and Sofia's conversation reverted to social events, work and household matters, and across St Albans voices lost their anxious tones. Increasingly, Sofia heard discussions that questioned what all the fuss had been about, and the phrase 'phony war' became commonplace.

'Do you think the war will really come to England,' she asked Joseph on one of the rare occasions when he got home for a weekend.

'Sofia, I don't think he will. I know he will. It's just a matter of time.'

Most people seemed to doubt this however, and Sofia couldn't help thinking one or two members of the first aid team seemed disappointed that their commitment to being trained as volunteers had so far come to naught. Sofia said nothing as they grumbled about Chamberlain, then their new Prime Minister, Winston Churchill, and repeated the complaints now prevalent everywhere: how the millions of pounds dedicated to building defences, thousands of hours spent mobilising citizens, and the disruptions to London and beyond had all been an overreaction.

All doubts regarding the extensive preparations for war were put to rest when, in mid-July, dozens of German Stukas, He111s and Do17s soared across the Channel. Although St Albans remained unaffected, the London newspapers offered vivid outlines of the panic created when high-pitched whirring sounds had filled the air, followed by deafening explosions; how shocked citizens leapt to their feet and rushed to dampen lamps, close curtains and race to their allocated shelters.

The attacks on London were a startling reminder to the residents of Talonsgate of the need to be diligent, that the Germans could attack at any time. Marcus led a serious discussion about their response at Talonsgate should there be a strike on their home or heaven forbid, if German soldiers arrived there. Food, water and bedding were taken down to the basement as well as a spare cot for Andreanna.

Sofia attended a meeting of the various civilian response teams in St Albans, including the Bomb Shelter Team, First Aid Team and the Women's Auxiliary and they reviewed their plans in the event of an assault. It was agreed the ringing of the church bell was limited to one purpose: to call the townspeople into the shelters in the case of an air attack and posters would be made to remind people to check on their neighbours, particularly the elderly and infirm who might need assistance. Alongside the other First Aiders, Sofia checked their stock of bandages and refreshed the protocols they would follow in readiness for casualties.

The attacks continued with the Luftwaffe arriving nightly, swooping through the searchlights, impervious to the tracer bullets that ricocheted off their armour plating. They came by the hundreds and unleashed their devastating loads onto the streets of London and beyond, killing and maiming soldiers and citizens alike. Every few nights, St Albans was a target and as soon as the sound of the church bells were heard, Marcus and Elizabeth descended to the basement while Sofia dressed, raced from the house, and with the Austin's lights on low beam, drove to the town bunker to join the First Aid team.

Over a hundred people gathered there, and although emotions ran high, the First Aiders' work was usually confined to treating minor wounds. Not always though—when a young girl arrived with dreadful injuries to her eyes, the team looked to Sofia. With care, she padded and bandaged the wound and then sent the child to Shenley Hospital. A fellow officer whispered that the girl's mother was dead, killed in the blast. No first aid could save the seven-year-old girl who was riding her bicycle in broad daylight when a single plane roared overhead and dropped its load upon her.

As dreadful as they were, these were isolated incidents; London was doing much worse than St Albans. Photographs in the newspapers showed whole streets of England's capital where every building had collapsed, and articles described injuries of a scale and nature far beyond the capacity of London's first aid posts. As the weeks passed, hospitals became swamped by the number of casualties arriving nightly, and with injured men, woman and children clogged the waiting rooms, the situation was dire.

Sofia read an article entreating retired doctors, surgeons and nursing sisters to return to work and describing the implementation of a new strategy for London's volunteer First Aiders—no longer would they man posts at bomb shelters; instead, they would be attached to operating theatres, emergency departments, and wards to support the nurses.

After reading this, Sofia knew she had to act.

'Marcus, have you seen what's happening in London,' she asked him.

'Of course. It's dreadful. Thank God we are away from it. We are very fortunate.'

'I think I will volunteer to help there.'

'What do you mean, Sofia. You are already working for St Albans.' Marcus looked at her as though she'd lost her mind.

'No Marcus. Most nights we have far more staff than casualties. I could be far more helpful in London.'

Marcus shook his head, with a frown upon his face.

'But really, where would you live? It is so dangerous there! You'd be putting your life at risk.'

'Thousands of people's lives are at risk, Marcus and the hospitals are in a desperate state. They are begging for volunteers! I really have no excuses not to go.'

Marcus must have pondered her decision overnight, because the following morning, he offered an alternative.

'Sofia, you love caring for people—why don't you train for the Civilian Nursing Reserve? Then you can work in the wards alongside the registered nurses. You would have set shifts and greater responsibility. You would even be paid a weekly wage.'

'The nursing reserve? To be a nurse requires four years of training. I need to do something *now* to support the war effort!'

'No, the military urgently needs staff for their hospitals and has implemented special courses for axillary nurses; to my understanding, the training is not long at all... perhaps two weeks or thereabouts.'

'How do you know so much about this, Marcus?' she asked

'I heard about it at Shenley; it's been reallocated as a military hospital and there have been lots of changes. I'll see what I can find out next time I am there.'

Sofia didn't know what to think, beyond suspecting Marcus was looking for ways to keep her close to home, where she would be safe, and more precisely, close to him.

'Marcus, I can't hide away here in St Albans, stay safe while people in London are suffering and unable to get the support they need.'

'London has plenty of first aid posts and hospitals,' he argued.

'No, they haven't. Not enough by any means. Didn't you read how the first aid posts are being shut down, how the VADs are now reporting directly to the hospitals?'

Nonetheless, Marcus did not give up easily. The following Monday, he arrived at Talonsgate with a flyer outlining the training for civilian reserve nurses offered by what was now called Shenley *Military* Hospital, as well as an application form. In addition to the documents, he presented a persuasive argument.

'You would barely recognise Shenley, Sofia. Since it's been reclassified for the military, they've converted the basement to create more wards. These are packed with soldiers from northern Europe and France. Today I walked through them and truly, it was astonishing. Beds wall to wall, nurses run off their feet. I am sure they would be glad to have you.'

Sofia rolled her eyes as she accepted the papers he passed to her. She was sure he exaggerated the needs of Shenley Hospital. Nonetheless, after studying the information, she decided to enroll. The training period was only two weeks, and there was nothing to lose by acquiring the skills to work in hospitals, although she hoped the status of general nurse would offer more scope than merely rolling bandages and folding sheets as taught in the hospital training course she'd completed months earlier.

CHAPTER 36

inally, the day arrived. Standing in the foyer of Shenley
Military Hospital with three other women—all much
younger than her—awaiting the arrival of a Sister Levant, who they'd
been told would be their guide, Sofia's heart beat with nervous
excitement. All around, people poured in and out of the hospital's
entrance with serious faces and purposeful gaits. The women beside
her were full of chatter, and when Sofia smiled at them, they
introduced themselves. She discovered that of the four, she was the
only one who'd undertaken previous training. The others—all friends
from Hatfield, a town nearby—were shop assistants, two from the
same frock shop while the other worked in her father's butchery.
Mavis, Ruby and Thelma were a happy bunch. From their heavy
mascara, red lipstick, and shared nudges and giggles each time a man
crossed the foyer, Sofia suspected their motivation to become nurses
was more about finding a husband than tending to 'those poor lads
who'd put their lives on the line for their country.'

They didn't have to wait long for Sister Levant to arrive. She was a
pleasant woman of about thirty, with a rounded figure, plump cheeks,
smiling eyes and a chuckle to finish every sentence.

'Pleased to meet you,' she said, offering her hand to each of them in turn. 'Welcome to Shenley. Let's start by getting you up to the uniform room. The girls up there should have something for you to slip into today, and hopefully by 4 PM they'll have you fully kitted out, ready for service.'

While Mavis, Ruby and Thelma found the whole process of being fitted into the plain blue dress with the badge of the Red Cross on the upper left breast hysterical, Sofia felt self-conscious. The slim-fitting uniform was totally unlike anything she usually wore. After donning it, then slipping her hair under the matching blue cap, she barely glanced into the mirror before following Sister Levant into the corridor.

For over an hour, they were led on a tour of the hospital, veering along corridors and up and down stairs. As they visited the sterilizing units, operating theatres, the rehabilitation centre and the mortuary, Sofia wondered how she'd ever remember to navigate the meandering layout. Finally, they ventured down the stairs where Marcus had told her the basement had been converted to wards, and Sister Levant informed them they'd undertake their training.

The six rooms were enormous, with over fifty beds jammed together and offering little privacy beyond thin walls of curtain strung on a frame. At the end were the sluice rooms, storerooms, kitchenettes and a nurses' station, which consisted of a large desk, bench space and a filing cabinet.

On completion of the tour, Sister Levant steered them to a room at the end; a dining room for the nursing staff, where pots of tea, coffee, and biscuits were set out.

'So, nurses, what do you think?' she asked when they were settled around a wooden table.

'I think if I have to walk another step, I will need to climb into a bed myself,' said Thelma. Sofia smiled as the younger woman kicked her shoe off and stretched her stockinged foot, rubbing where her footwear had left an impression.

Ruby and Mavis nodded in agreement and released their own shoes.

'Don't worry. You three are not the first girls to turn up with your dancing shoes on, and I doubt you'll be the last,' Sister Levant said with a chuckle. 'Tomorrow you'll be wearing something more sensible, I'm sure.' She gave Sofia a conspiratorial wink, glancing at her feet, which were clad in a modest laced leather shoe.

∼

Fifteen minutes later, they stood, ready to return to the wards. However, Sister Levant suggested she take them through the hospital's kitchen, which was close by. Often nurses were sent there to fetch a special meal for a patient on a restricted or sugar-free diet, or when the ward trolley arrived short of food.

Through the open door, Sofia could see a lively, bustling group of men and women, their chatter accompanied by tinkling crockery and rattling cutlery. A wonderful aroma of roasting meat and baked vegetables, blending with the sweet smells of stewed fruit and custard filled the air. Just as they were about to enter, a red-faced nurse in a uniform similar to the one Sofia now wore appeared.

'Sister Levant, you are wanted up at reception immediately!' The girl's voice was breathless with urgency.

'Oh—right, then.' Sister Levant looked around as if seeking for a spot to settle her new recruits.

'We can wait back there if you like,' Mavis offered, pointing to the little alcove they'd just passed, where half a dozen chairs and a small table formed a neat arrangement.

'No, that is a visitor's waiting area; we can't be seen sitting there,' Sister Levant said. 'Here's James. He's the orderly for the medical ward. I'll see if he's got a minute to look after you.

'James—I've been called upstairs. I don't know how long I will be caught up. Can you look after our new nurses, please? Perhaps take them down to Sister Casey. I daresay she'll get them going.'

Sister Levant vanished as if she'd been whisked away by a magician's wand.

'Come along, ladies,' James said, 'though I must say, I feel like I am escorting you to an executioner... She's a bit of a dragon, is our Sister Casey. But don't take too much notice of her—her bark is far worse than her bite.'

Sofia and the Hatfield girls, as she found herself referring to them, dutifully followed James through the wards. Halfway along the second ward, he was distracted by greater imperatives than taking them to meet with a charge nurse still three wards away.

'Nuss, nuss... here, please.' The call came from a young man whose hands were bandaged, and it took a second for Sofia to realise he was asking for a nurse.

'Burns,' James explained as he led them over to the bedside. It was immediately evident the man had tried to drink from the cup which now lay upturned in his bed linen, beyond his reach. A pool of brown fluid was soaking through the layers of blankets and sheets.

'Frank, couldn't you have waited another minute? I would have got to you.'

'Yes, and Christmas is coming, too,' Frank replied with a rueful grin. 'You have more than enough to do without feeding me like a baby.'

Sizing up the situation, Sofia followed James, and together they helped Frank to stand and then to step toward the chair by his bed. He had a sweet nature and apologised for creating unnecessary work with his foolishness. They chatted with him while James swept the bed linen from the mattress and fetched a fresh set of sheets and blankets.

When he returned, Sofia went to the opposite side of the bed and tried to keep up as James shook the linen with brisk snaps. After a fold here and a tuck there, they had the bed remade in no time.

'Looks like they are a bit short of hands, girls. You might do better to stay here; Maria's looking after the ward today, and she's much kinder on the ears than Charge Sister Casey, if you know what I mean. How about you give these men a hand with their morning cuppas? Sister Levant won't mind, and I'll tell Marie you're here. She'll be thrilled to have the help.'

Plainly, Frank was not alone in needing assistance to access his morning tea; cups rested on saucers alongside beds throughout the ward, beyond the reach of the patients they were intended for.

Following Sofia's initiative, Mavis, Ruby and Thelma stepped into action. For the remainder of the morning, they responded to a continuous cycle of requests, assisting men to sit, stand or drink and fetching urinals, extra blankets, or nursing sisters when needs of a medical nature presented themselves.

'Nurse, can you help here for a minute?' called a female voice from behind a closed curtain and looking around her, Sofia realised it was she who was being summoned.

'Certainly, Sister, if I can,' she replied, cautiously peeping behind the screen. Before her, a man lay on his back. The wound dressings on his chest had been removed, revealing a nasty gash of about three inches.

'I need you to pass me the swabs... in the jar there, see? Perhaps if you give your hands a quick wash first—the tap's over there.'

Recalling her first aid training's emphasis on maintaining sterile environments while dressing wounds, Sofia followed the sister's directions. She used the tweezers on the side of the tray to lift half a dozen swabs from the container. The sister deftly grasped these between long, curved tweezers one by one and cleaned the wound before applying gauze, a wad of cotton wool, and a pad. Without being asked, Sofia passed a strip of dressing adhesive to her so the pad could be secured.

'It looks very sore,' she said to the man.

'I am happy to say it is indeed very sore,' he replied with a grin. 'If I wasn't feeling the sting of Sister here's iodine, I would probably be gazing at the lid of a coffin right now. A bit of pain is a reminder of just how lucky I am.'

After they'd completed the dressing and left the bedside, the sister turned to Sofia. 'Your name, Nurse? I don't think we've met before.'

'No, today is my first day. I arrived for General Nurse Training this morning. My name is Sofia.'

'And I am Marie. Training, huh—well, you will get trained here alright. Very quickly, believe me. It's called on-the-job training. If you've got two hands and two legs, you will be an enormous help, and if you have a brain and don't mind a bit of blood, so much the better. Good job just now, by the way. Want to help me with a couple more? I've got some stump dressings where a second pair of hands would be most welcome.'

'Certainly, Sister,' Sofia said, trying to recall what a stump dressing might involve.

'Marie's fine... unless the charge is about. Then we'll be back to Siss and Nuss.'

Although she'd never seen one, her training sessions for dressing a stump came back to Sofia when she followed the sister to the bedside of a young man with a pale face, whose left leg ended mid-thigh.

'Morning, Bernard,' said Marie. 'I've got Sofia with me today. She's new, but I have to say, I think we've got a good one. Don't you go chasing her around the ward when I'm not looking, will you now? Or you'll have me jealous and all.'

Sofia was horrified by what she thought was an insensitive reminder of his lost leg, but to her surprise, Bernard broke into a broad grin and laughed.

'You jest, Sister, but be warned: the physio's already talking about the wooden leg he's got planned for me. When I get my peg-leg on, I'll be dangerous. You'll need your jogging shoes on then, let me tell you!'

Sofia gulped when he lifted what remained of his upper thigh, a flabby, bloated mound of tissue with a blazing red slash across it and large welts where stitches had recently been removed. Bernard and the sister continued their banter as she attended to the wound, then expertly criss-crossed a bandage over the blunt protrusion where, barely three weeks earlier, a knee and shin and foot and toes had been, before the blast of a land mine had robbed him of them.

~

Sofia remained alongside Marie, helping to complete their final dressing for the morning. Again, it was an amputation, but sadly, this one was bilateral. The lad—Edgar—was barely twenty, Sofia guessed, and he'd lost one leg above the knee, the other below it, when his lower limbs had been trapped beneath a collapsed concrete wall following a night of bombing in London. Rather than applying the humour with which she'd approached Bernard, Marie used a soft tone as she asked Edgar how well he'd slept the previous night and encouraged him to ask for morphine if his pain was too unbearable.

When he winced and reached toward Sofia, she did not hesitate to take his hand, squeezing it gently as a tear rolled down his face. Clenching his jaw, he stared at the ceiling.

Marie's fingers were deft and her tone reassuring as she described what she was doing and explained that his wound was healing well. After they completed the dressing, she fussed around Edgar's bedside, plumping his pillows, filling up his water cup and advising him to accept the offer of a wheelchair to take to the shower the following morning; a week of bed baths would have anyone feeling awful, she told him.

Having extracted Edgar's promise that he would try a shower, they left his bedside. Out of earshot, Marie explained to Sofia the pain Edgar experienced did not come from his wounds. Rather, it was phantom pain—a knifelike stabbing sensation in his left foot, even though the source of it was long gone.

Sofia admired Maria's wisdom, and marvelled at her ability to move between the patients and judge their emotional states, laughing and teasing one, consoling the other. Her manner was surely comforting to the men whose bedsides they'd just left, whose lives had been transformed so completely. Sofia considered their future options. Bernard would have the capacity to hop from bed to chair to bathroom, dress independently. He would be fitted with an artificial limb and perhaps feel secure as he moved around the town, and his optimistic disposition would certainly stand him in good stead. The years stretching out before Edgar offered a much bleaker picture. He would be significantly dependent on others to do everything from dressing to transferring between bed and chair to climbing steps and stairs. Little wonder the lad was so depressed, Sofia thought, for in losing both his legs, the young man would never play football or run or dance again. Edgar had paid dearly for a war that was proving more dreadful than anyone had imagined.

Over dinner, Sofia told Marcus about her first day at Shenley, but she felt no thrill for her new role as a General Nurse. Rather, she had been sobered by the rows of beds containing dozens of men, many of whose lives had been utterly transformed by lost limbs, facial scarring, burns and eye wounds.

She told him about Sister Marie and how she'd helped with the dressings and how, if the men who served in the military forces were heroes, then those in the nursing profession were surely saints; how wonderful it was to have the opportunity to work alongside such a skilled and capable woman as Marie.

Marcus smiled and nodded at her enthusiasm, and Sofia knew he was pleased her aspiration to go to London had been curbed.

That night, she barely slept for thinking about the needs of the soldiers on the ward, and the next morning she arrived at the hospital soon after seven AM. At the end of the day, when the Hatfield girls left, Sofia decided to stay a little longer. There were men who were keen for a walk outdoors, but needed assistance to manage their crutches, and a spilled cup of tea beside one bed urgently required attention.

Just as Marie had warned Sofia when she assisted with the dressings on the first day of training, Shenley Hospital was extraordinarily busy. Every hour patients were admitted—many, soldiers who'd returned from the distant fields of Northern Europe—others, civilians wounded on British soil. Rather than through formal teaching, her nursing skills were mostly acquired by the hour as she got on with the job of being useful. Sofia's admiration for the nursing sisters increased daily. If they weren't rushing for injections of morphine for a man writhing with pain, they were tending to someone vomiting, or haemorrhaging, or climbing out of bed when he should be in, or refusing to leave his bed when he should be up and walking. They accompanied cranky surgeons and diffused the emotions of harried relatives, their calm manner a balm to emotional crises of all dimensions. More than anything, though, Sofia admired the sisters' brusque no-nonsense style, their capacity to gaze unflinchingly at wounds most people would turn away from, their tones always matter of fact. It was as though they believed excessive sympathy would crack the spirit of the toughest of soldiers.

However, there was much Sofia did not admire at the hospital, and more than once she was chastised for applying what she considered common sense.

The first event happened during her second week when she was working on the surgical ward.

'Nurse!' The oft-repeated call came from Charge Sister Casey, and its quaking volume all but rattled the iron beds as the single word travelled the length of the room.

Looking up, Sofia realised there were no other nurses in the ward —she was the target of the charge's ire. She moved toward where Sister Casey was standing with her hand on her hip, and with each step, Sofia's mind sifted through her actions of the last hour as she wondered what had gone wrong.

'Tell me, Nurse, what on earth are these towels doing, hanging out here?'

Sofia looked at the row of towels, limp despite the wintery breeze, clearly as damp now as they'd been thirty minutes earlier when she'd found some pegs and hung them there. Surely the reason for their presence on the balcony was obvious.

'They were damp, Sister. I hung them there so they could dry.'

'Have you not observed towels belong on the bedside lockers, Nurse? They must be folded neatly and set there so as not to get mixed up with those of another patient. We can't have cross-infection, you know. Come, let me show you.'

There was nothing for it but to follow the irate charge sister to a locker, where an amused-looking man winked at Sofia from the chair beside it. She squirmed with embarrassment as, with a loud voice using the tone of one speaking to a naughty child, Charge Sister Casey demonstrated the army's protocol for setting a towel on a bedside locker. She folded it in half, then folded it again, and finished with a trifold before setting the neatly packaged and sodden towel on the bedside locker. Then, on top of it, she placed the damp face washer, soap and razor.

'But, Sister—the towels are all damp after the bed baths.' Sofia was still convinced the charge had misunderstood.

'Nurse, did I not make myself clear enough? Come here!' Her cheeks burning, Sofia followed the charge to the nurses' station at the end of the room.

'If you still can't fathom what is required, I have a poster to guide you,' Charge Sister Casey snapped as she rummaged amongst the papers on her desk. She passed Sofia a sheet bearing a diagram of the towels laid out on a bedside locker, then gave a loud humph and swept off—a woman with far more important things to do than waste time with the lowly nurses.

And if the absurdity of military protocol around the folding of towels, wet, dry or in-between, was not enough, the Saturday morning ward inspections were the height of madness. Sofia only learned about them in her fourth week at Shenley, where, having completed her training, she'd been rostered onto a Saturday shift.

Arriving early, Sofia listened to the night sister's report about the new admissions and updates on each patient's condition. At the end of her report the sister added a reminder that Lieutenant Cameron would arrive for his weekly ward inspection at eleven AM, as usual.

Sofia thought nothing of the ward inspection other than resolving that today, of all days, wet towels would most certainly be folded according to the poster; bed covers would be pristine, their corners folded to an eighth of an inch of perfection, the pillows plumped and inviting; the floor would be waxed and polished till it gleamed; and the patients would be freshly shaved, their hair combed, their pyjamas buttoned and their bandages spotless.

Sofia followed the lead of the more experienced nurses as with a flurry of activity, all men—both bedridden and ambulant—were indeed shaved, washed and changed. What Sofia had not expected was the manner they were presented to the Senior Officer, each man sitting upright, his legs neatly arranged with feet together, alongside an immaculately tidied locker. On the dot of eleven, the impressively uniformed officer walked the length of the room, nodding and addressing each of the men with the same greeting: 'How are you today, Private?'

The replies were almost identical, variations of, 'Very well, sir,' regardless of the soldier's condition.

Sofia shook her head in disbelief. She wondered whether the body of Private Marsh, who'd died the previous evening from an internal haemorrhage, might have been propped in a seat for the inspection had they not transported his body to the morgue in time.

Apart from the slip-up with the towels, Sofia received regular praise for her work. Not only did she regularly show the intelligence Marie had so highly valued at their first meeting, but she also showed an aptitude for interpreting the needs of the men. She was skilled at repositioning men to make them comfortable and prodding them to drink or eat or walk. But she was also intuitive; quick to notify the sister when a man's face seemed unusually pale, or when red lines radiated beyond a dressings indicating an infection. In addition, she possessed a fearlessness to tackle any job, and a total lack of queasiness for blood, vomit or any other bodily emission she faced.

Most VADs who worked at Shenley mopped floors, cleaned the sluice room, took patients for walks, or assisted with the meal rounds. However, frequently Sofia was singled out by Sister Marie or the other registered nurses to check whether intravenous drips were flowing correctly, to assist with the dressings of complex injuries and to give men their medications. The stream of ambulances bringing seriously injured casualties was never-ending, as was the steady stream of men being returned from the operating theatre, and the registered nurses barely had a second to rest.

While many of the nurses approached their work with enthusiasm, teasing the men and joking with each other, Sofia worked quietly, fixed on the healing of patients, particularly those whose lives were forever altered by the wounds they'd received. Although she smiled at the amusing anecdotes of the VADs or junior nurses, and wished them well when they announced engagements or expressed excitement about events in their personal lives, Sofia rarely joined in the banter that came so naturally to them.

Occasionally, their attention turned to her and they would ask about her personal life. They seemed to assume Sofia was a refugee, her presence in London a consequence of Spain's civil war, and she rarely corrected this. Never did she divulge how she'd spent years in Australia, or mention a loving husband now lost to her, or speak of a child who had died and another whom she'd relinquished. Sofia's conversation was always about the tasks on hand, and in the meal breaks she kept her own company.

For her, the greatest satisfaction was to see a man who'd believed he would never walk again don the wooden prosthesis he'd received and take first two steps, then a dozen, and then walk the length of the ward. Or how a combination of rebuke and hope could force a depressed man to view his future more positively. In return, Sofia knew she had the men's respect and gratitude. Sure, they complained when she pushed them to walk an extra yard or two, or sit out of bed a little longer, or try to manage their forks and spoons with hands rendered all but useless after being shattered by exploding ammunition on the battlefield. Nonetheless, they greeted her warmly when she arrived for duty and seemed pleased when they learned it was she who'd been assigned to care for them for the day.

'You might be a dragon, Nuss, but I know it's for my own good,' they'd say as she prodded and cajoled and pushed them to their limits. Her vision was fixed on their future; they must strive to be as independent as possible, regardless of their injuries, before they were discharged.

Four months had passed when Sofia received a call to work in the operating theatres. There she was placed at the beck and call of the surgeon and team of registered nurses. Her task was to fetch sterile instruments, swabs and gauze as well as to keep a record of each item passed across to the operating table. Just before the surgical excision was closed and the stitching commenced, every item was accounted for to ensure no clamps or blood-soaked swabs were left inside the patient's body.

As always, Sofia applied a quiet, methodical diligence to the task, and she felt a huge sense of pride for the work done by the theatre staff as she arrived for her shifts and donned the scrubs worn by everybody, from the most senior surgeon to the most junior nurse. There was a strong sense of camaraderie in the theatre, and Sofia enjoyed being part of a team in a way she hadn't felt in the wards. There, the nurses had seemed much younger than herself and often the charge sisters— especially Sister Casey—could be tyrannical as they shouted orders and fussed over the most trivial of matters.

In time, Sofia learned there were considerable variations in the way the registered nurses she worked with had gained their qualifications. Many of them had completed their four years of training in the various hospitals across London and, when the war broke out, had enlisted with the British Army. Another group, which also included surgeons and doctors, had been called from retirement. Some of these older men and women had served in the Great War and, although advanced in years, they appeared to thrive on the unexpected opportunity to re-enter their respective professions. However, the vast majority of the registered nurses at Shenley were referred to as QAs. These were military nurses who'd been trained by Queen Alexandra's Imperial Military Service, and as such, held the rank of non-commissioned officers in Britain's Army, Navy and Air Force.

Sofia discovered that a couple of the registered nurses had previously been nursing assistants in roles much like her own as a Voluntary Aid Detachment general nurse and they were happy to share their experiences with her. And in the course of one discussion, she discovered her own status as a VAD could be designated as either 'mobile' or 'non-mobile'. Curious, Sofia made enquires, and discovered her status was 'mobile'. With a stirring of excitement, she realised this meant that should the Army need VADs to work in the military hospitals overseas—places like France or Northern Europe or even the Middle East—she was eligible to serve.

CHAPTER 37

Once Sofia realized she was eligible to serve overseas, she could think of little else. Saying nothing, she kept her ears open whenever a discussion about distant war fronts arose. She noticed how the paperwork which accompanied the casualties returned from overseas service bore references to British General Hospitals, usually identified by a number. Cyril Shepherd had been transferred from BGH36, while Freddy Riley, with his amputated left foot, had initially undergone surgery in a field hospital described as BGH138.

Although soldiers rarely discussed the battles they'd endured, they didn't mind talking about the field hospitals. From them, Sofia heard about the rustic conditions where beds were camp stretchers, often laid out in the open; how the nurses worked fifteen-hour shifts, and just when they'd finished and could finally grab a few hours' sleep, a fresh wave of casualties would arrive. Sofia pictured these medical stations, overflowing with soldiers direct from the battlefield, their wounds raw, their lives hanging in the balance, and she wanted more than anything to be there doing what she could to help. She could do nothing to save her parents, or Andres, or Scotty, but by applying the skills she'd gained in the VAD training, she might help save the lives of young

British serviceman who were risking so much to halt the German army's advance across Europe.

~

Two weeks before Christmas, Sofia showed Marcus a newspaper article which described how members of the QUAIMNS were leaving for overseas service in astonishing numbers.

'Yes, they are extraordinary, aren't they. As if the demands of nursing weren't enough in a regular hospital, without choosing to be a military nurse and serving right in the midst of the fields of battle.'

'Yes, but it's not just the Military nurses who are heading overseas. Lots of VADs like me are also going. I am eligible too, you know. In fact, I am thinking of volunteering.'

'No, please! Don't even think about it!'

'Yes, Marcus, I want to.'

'But why? You are doing good work here. You love your job at Shenley. Why on earth would you want to go anywhere near the battlefields?'

'Because men are dying there.'

Unable to argue her logic, Marcus next asked, 'And what about your daughter? You know how she'll miss you.'

'No, Marcus. Andreanna is not my daughter. How many times do I have to say this? She is Elizabeth and Joseph's child. They've chosen her and she has chosen them—don't you hear Andreanna calling Elizabeth 'Mumma'?"

It was true. The previous weekend, Joseph and Elizabeth had joined Sofia in the glass room, where they'd chatted for a few minutes before setting off for a Sunday drive. Andreanna, who'd been crawling around the floor, had clearly said "mum-mum-mum," her voice firm and expectant as she waved her hands toward Elizabeth, insisting she be picked up.

They'd all laughed at the demanding infant, but it had been a telling moment when nobody had corrected her. If Sofia felt anything, it was relief. She was glad the pressure to reclaim Andreanna had subsided over recent months; happy to see Elizabeth and Joseph take full responsibility for all aspects of Andreanna's care.

Marcus' opposition to Sofia's intention to volunteer for an overseas posting ran out of steam, and for days nothing more was said. A week later, Sofia was stunned when he announced his intention to join the military.

'Whatever for?' she asked, sure Marcus was enlisting in order to follow her, and not sure whether to be pleased or annoyed by his news.

Her own decision to enlist had nothing to do with her life at Talonsgate, her relationship with Marcus or the unusual situation around Andreanna's parenting arrangements. For Sofia, volunteering to work on the war front was a calling. Something she believed had purpose. From the day she'd started her training, her practical skills and common sense had been appreciated, and on the wards and she'd learned much from working closely with the nursing sisters. She thrived on the challenge of caring for patients with diverse needs, pushing them to achieve greater independence in readiness for the time they'd be discharged. And now, having gained insights into the role of military hospitals situated close to the battles, she had to be there.

But Marcus enlisting! What on earth was he thinking?

'What about your work here? Your patients?' she asked.

'The thing is, Sofia, daily now I am called to assess fellows who have returned from the front—men who bear emotional scars I barely understand. I know they are suffering shell shock, but how can I possibly understand what they have been through? How can I treat them effectively when I have no understanding of the demons haunting them? I spoke to the senior psychologist at Shenley, and he agrees; first-hand experience on the field by qualified psychologists could only benefit the men we are trying to help. By volunteering myself to serve *alongside* the men, experience the realities of the battlefield, I will be able to record my experiences and make recommendations.'

'But what if you... get injured?' Sofia didn't want to say *are killed*, even though it was the phrase which first came to her mind, accompanied by a tremor of fear. What if, because of his affection for her, Marcus was the next person to die?

Sofia shook her head as though to eject the thought from her mind. She imagined Sister Marie listening to this conversation. *'What is this nonsense, Sofia? What on earth are you talking about?'* would be the practical nursing sister's impatient response if she'd known Sofia blamed herself for the death of the people who loved her.

But was it nonsense? God only knew. The God Sofia had grown up with had given her comfort and peace through her deepest losses. But the day Scotty was taken, God had become a stranger. No longer loving, but cruel. However, with the war now raging, and little peace or happiness on offer to so many people, Sofia decided it was time for her to pray. She'd ask God to look after Marcus and she'd pray for the health and wellbeing of the soldiers, that their wounds—both physical and mental—would be healed and the war would end. She would pray for the protection of Andreanna, and Jack and Margaret too.

Over the next few weeks the conversations at Talonsgate fluctuated from tense exchanges about Sofia's and Marcus's respective decisions to enlist for overseas service, to periods of time out, where in a civil fashion Marcus, Elizabeth and Sofia discussed daily events around Talonsgate such as meal preparations, the needs of the horses or Andreanna's antics.

When, over dinner, Sofia mentioned how she'd discussed her interest in volunteering overseas with Sister Lewis, the Operating Theatre's Charge Sister, Elizabeth's encouragement for Sofia to follow her passion to serve had been met with unveiled anger from Marcus.

'What are you saying, Elizabeth. Sofia shouldn't be thinking of going overseas!'

'Why ever not! Sofia loves nursing; can't you see how good it is for her.'

'Because it's dangerous. Why on earth would a woman—would

anyone—want to go across to where a war has erupted if they didn't have to?'

'Marcus, sometimes people just have to do things. Its inside them. I say, if Sofia is passionate about going, she should. She's not a child you know!"

Sofia listened to the exchange, as if she were a fly on the wall. It was no surprise to hear Marcus being so protective of her, but interesting to see Elizabeth so passionate in her defence. It made Sofia wonder if it were personal for Elizabeth; if perhaps she'd once forsaken a dream and regretted it.

The table was turned when two nights later, Marcus said he intended to enlist with the British Army at the end of February. This time it was Elizabeth who was furious.

'What are you trying to do, Marcus. You are no soldier, for heaven's sake. You are an academic. A doctor!'

Sofia felt equally concerned by Marcus' decision, but in no position to tell him he was making a mistake, given her own plans. Worse, she felt responsible, sure he was only enlisting because of her.

Christmas and New Year came and went, and although they did their best to celebrate the occasions, life at Talonsgate was very subdued, especially when Elizabeth received news that Joseph, who was serving in the south of England, would not be released for leave as she'd expected. It seemed that Hitler was determined to take England as quickly as he could, for the attacks over London were relentless, and more than once Sofia had driven to the First Aid Post ready to offer treatment, when the pealing of the church-bells in St Albans rang through the night. Thankfully, though a number of buildings were struck, few were hurt.

Shenley's operating theatres continued to operate day and night and throughout the hospital all staff—from the most senior administrator to the most junior nurse—were run off their feet, with barely time to have meal breaks.

And then, on a Wednesday morning, while Sofia was changing into the gown she wore for her work in the operating theatre, Sister Lewis called her to her office and, with a wink, told her Shenley's matron wished to see her immediately. Surprised at the unusual request, Sofia had been even more astonished when Captain Fairly, the matron of Shenley, asked if she was available to join a team of medical staff— mostly doctors and QAs—who were leaving for the Middle East the very next day. She explained how she faced a shortage of QAs to nominate, and given Sofia's expression of interest in overseas service, there was an opportunity for her if she wanted it.

Without hesitation, Sofia thanked her for the offer, filled out a brief acceptance form, and accepted the matron's good wishes. She returned to the operating theatre in a daze; with barely twenty-four hours' notice, she was being sent to a military hospital on a foreign shore, and she could not have been more pleased. Sister Lewis was thrilled for Sofia, and suggested she go home early so she could prepare for the journey, but Sofia elected to stay. It would not take her long to pack her bag that evening and she had no desire to extend the hours at Talonsgate defending her choice.

Sofia was both surprised and relieved when Marcus reacted calmly to the news of her posting. 'If you are sure it's what you want, Sofia, then I am pleased for you. You just stay safe and don't attempt any heroics!'

'Marcus, I am going to be nursing, not charging the enemy with a bayonet,' she replied.

'Yes, but some of those hospitals are very close to the action. You need to be careful.'

'I will, Marcus. I promise!' Sofia decided since he'd accepted the news of her departure so well, the least she could do was graciously respond to his warnings.

Elizabeth joined them for dinner, and their conversation was surprisingly light.

'You will be wonderful Sofia. The hospitals there are lucky to have you!'

Marcus agreed, adding he expected the war would be over soon enough, and she'd be home in no time. Neither Elizabeth, nor Sofia asked him what source had inspired his optimistic belief that the end of the war was in sight; it certainly wasn't the impression the news reports were giving.

The following morning, Sofia was surprised to hear the soft whinnying of horses before daylight, and looking out her window, saw the stable light was on. At six AM, Elizabeth appeared in the kitchen with a bright-eyed Andreanna in her arms and announced they were coming to Tilbury to farewell Sofia.

And an hour later, standing at the docks, hugging Elizabeth and Marcus and then offering a kiss to Andreanna before turning to where the ship waited, Sofia felt tears prick her eyelids. They really were her family, she thought. For a brief moment, she questioned the wisdom of her decision to leave the safety of Talonsgate and travel to a war zone in a foreign land. There were many ways she could support the war effort without leaving St Albans, and certainly there was no real need for her to leave England. What was she doing, leaving a lovely home, living among good friends who cared about her? Was it about serving as a nurse, or was it about something else? Was she putting distance between herself and Marcus so that he wasn't lulled into believing they might have a future together, or was she trying to fill a hollowness within that never really left her? Sofia didn't know.

PART VI

The Middle East

CHAPTER 38

*A*s she stood among the men and women waiting to board the ship, Sofia felt a thrill of excitement. Despite questioning her motives for accepting the overseas posting barely an hour earlier, she knew she'd made the right decision.

The *Atlantis* was enormous, painted white and trimmed with green stripes. Once this ship had transported passengers and cargo across the globe, but with Europe at war, the British government had requisitioned it for military service. Now it wove across the northern seas, and in place of its original flag, another fluttered; this one white and bearing a large red cross. The flag's symbol matched the red crosses painted on the ship's sides, and announced to friend and foe the *Atlantis* was a hospital ship and not to be attacked.

Sofia watched half a dozen men wrestle the last of the trolleys up the gangplank—supplies for the hospitals in the Middle East, they'd been told. She considered the irony of life: how it had taken the horrific circumstances of war to draw her out of the disconnected chaos she'd dwelt in for almost two years. Now her path seemed clear. And even though there were moments where it took every ounce of her strength to resist pangs of overwhelming sadness for all she'd lost, she'd found a purpose and dedicated herself to fulfilling it.

Already she and the two dozen recruits alongside her had been addressed by a smiling woman who'd introduced herself as Sister O'Neil, otherwise known as Tessa, Matron of the *Atlantis*. Her most important question for them was whether anyone had thought to bring a violin or perhaps a trumpet in order to provide their nightly entertainment as they travelled to Alexandria, at which they laughed. On a more serious note, she then explained how the *Atlantis* had just returned from Norway. On board were almost a thousand men who'd been injured in the Battle of Narvik—perhaps they'd heard of it? Sofia had, of course. For months the newspapers had been full of stories about the Allies' attempts to resist the German invasion in far-flung locations such as Norway, Denmark, Belgium and the Netherlands.

However, for Sofia, even though the wards were filled with men who'd returned from these northern European battlefields, it was as if their history began from the day they'd received their wounds; the events causing them in far flung place had never felt real, perhaps more so because the soldiers never spoke of their battles.

Tessa outlined the plan for the day, explaining how they'd soon board the *Atlantis*, where they'd be taken to the ship's lounge. There, they'd leave their suitcases—for the next few hours, the priority was to disembark the soldiers on board. The ship also held over thirty German prisoners of war, men whom they needn't concern themselves with. These would be guarded by the military police and transported to Grizedale Hall, otherwise known as U-Boat Hotel, where they'd be held until such a time when they'd be relocated to Canada.

Just after nine AM, they were requested to proceed up the gangplank. Sofia felt odd as she stepped forward. The women in the group wore the grey dresses, scarlet capes adorned with medals and white veils of the Queen Elizabeth Imperial Military Nursing Service like the QAs she worked with. Most possessed the calm bearing Sofia had so often admired, especially those with years of experience. She wondered if one or two of the older of the nurses had served during the Great War. Others fidgeted with the nervousness of new graduates, and if their white faces and wide eyes weren't enough evidence of their inexperience, further proof could be gleaned by the brightness of their badges and the creases of the newly assigned uniforms they wore. Regardless of their experience, each QA bore the rank of lieutenant, and to Sofia, they may well have had halos hovering over their veil-clad heads, for she was in awe of their status as four-year-trained registered nurses and would give anything to share their rank. As the only VAD present, a volunteer general nurse with barely five months' experience standing alone in her blue uniform, Sofia fought down her feelings of inferiority. Nonetheless, she remained at the periphery of the group while the captain, a friendly man named Mark, welcomed them aboard the *Atlantis*, and she trailed at the back as they walked through a maze of corridors to the ship's dining room.

Here Tessa shared details of the plan for disembarkation of the men on board. There were two exit ramps in place. The first would cater for those who were bedridden to be carried off in stretchers, the second for men who could walk with minimal help. They would then be distributed to the waiting ambulances or military buses according to their mobility. Some had significant wounds which required further treatment, others needed rehabilitation, and the remainder would likely be formally discharged, the nature of their injuries rendering them unfit for further service.

Sofia smiled at the sight of the men eagerly shuffling into line to leave the ship. One, struggling with a single crutch was grateful when she took his free arm and assisted him down the ramp. The air was filled with both laughter and tears as the men exited and many of them turned to her and even though she'd only met them a few minutes earlier, many farewelled her with such gratitude it was as though she represented every nurse who'd ever cared for them.

'Best of luck, soldier,' she repeated a dozen times over and smiled as a group of men burst into song, first singing "It's a Long Way to Tipperary" and then "The White Cliffs of Dover," to the delight of the cameramen and reporters who waited on the dock. Returning to the ship, she entered the corridors where the stretcher-bound men waited. There, she worked for over three hours, fetching drinks, rubbing backs, repositioning legs in casts and adjusting pillows.

Sofia considered how these men, fresh from active duty, seemed to be far more soldiers, war heroes, than patients in bed for nurses to tease and boss as she'd been used to at Shenley. Walking among them, she noticed how their moods varied. Some soldiers could barely conceal their excitement at being home; they laughed loudly, called good wishes to their departing friends and making jokes—offering to go dancing or even to marry the nurses assisting them.

Other men couldn't wait to get off the ship, expressing fears for loved ones whom they hadn't heard from in months. Still others were despondent, expressing irritation at being forced to leave the front lines and insisting they'd get themselves back to their units at the first opportunity. Worst, Sofia felt, were the men with scarred faces, disfiguring burns or missing limbs—their livid, drawn expressions reflected their anxiety for the homecoming they'd receive from their fiancées and wives.

'She won't be wanting me anymore,' she heard several times from men who looked at her with appeal in their eyes. Her heart broke for them. Their words were difficult to respond to, especially since she wasn't sure if they formed a question or a statement of fact.

A number of the men were Polish or Norwegian and spoke very little English. Many were agitated, and Sofia gleaned that for them, the relief of arriving in England was shadowed by fears for the friends and family they'd left behind in the hands of the Germans.

～

As the only VAD, Sofia was left to her own devices, and she reverted to what she did best—singling out those men whom she recognised needed encouragement. They were easy to spot: ones who stared at the ceiling, lost in their own thoughts, or who battled in a silent rage to grasp mugs beyond their reach, or writhed in frustration, unable to reposition themselves while hampered by bandages, casts or missing limbs.

While many nurses might have offered a sympathetic ear or tried to diminish their fears with a cheery *'Come on, lad, it won't be so bad,'* Sofia had developed her own approach. It was geared towards encouraging the men to reach further, try harder, and break through their pain barrier to achieve a little more.

'You are so tough, Sofia,' her workmates often said when Sofia had encouraged men to sit out of bed or walk for an extra five minutes at Shenley, but to this, Sofia would just shake her head.

'It is not I who is tough. It is the world they'll soon find themselves in. These men must strive for independence. Mollycoddling them and pretending they don't have a battle ahead will not help. We need to help them face their future, and conquer it. The less sympathy and more encouragement we give them, the better their lives will be!'

It was after one PM when the last stretcher case was loaded into a waiting ambulance. Immediately after, Sofia and her comrades received a flurry of warm farewells and best wishes from the group of nurses whose overseas postings were now completed before they, too, left the ship to return to the families awaiting them on the docks.

Over the rail, the reporters packed up their equipment. Sofia could also see the retreating backs of the hundreds of people who'd arrived to welcome the soldiers home. The morning's work had been satisfying, but now it was done. A shiver of thrill ran through her as she thought of the days ahead. Her own adventure was about to start.

Sofia went to the dining room, collected her suitcase and made her way to the cabin she'd been allocated, glad to have a few minutes alone. After changing her clothes and freshening up, she joined the others in the common room, where they'd been told sandwiches, sponge cakes and pots of tea awaited them.

As well as the QAs on board, the team travelling to Alexandria included four doctors, a surgeon and an anaesthetist. Having worked together throughout the morning, a congenial atmosphere had already pervaded the group. Joining their friendly banter over lunch, Sofia was confident the ocean crossing would be pleasant. That is, as long as they didn't attract the unwelcome attention of a stray bullet from a German ship, or a torpedo from a U-Boat below, or a bomb from above, as one of the doctors who'd boarded that morning reminded them. The morbid comment led to a moment of subdued silence which Tessa broke.

'Well, yes, it's always a possibility of course. Heaven help us, we are in the midst of a war, after all. But if we follow all of the rules, we will be safe.' Her voice was firm and resolute and Sofia suspected the only way the charge sister could endure months at sea where enemy attacks were a real possibility was by having faith in the protocols designed to protect hospital ships.

No-one mentioned that while the Geneva Convention declared an attack on a hospital ship to be a war crime, it hadn't saved Britain's *Maid of Kent* or the Norwegian's *Dronning Maud*. Sofia had read of the events; the newspapers had been full of them, as had conversations at Shenley, for the lives of dozens of doctors, nurses and patients had been lost. They were a sober warning that the red crosses blazing on the sides and deck of the *Atlantis*, the flags hanging from its mast and the special lights which would be shone at night to signal their status as a Hospital Ship were no guarantee of a safe passage.

After lunch, Tessa took the new recruits on a tour of the ship, and once again, Sofia was amazed by its size. Although they'd disembarked nine hundred men that morning, the ship was designed to carry over sixteen hundred patients. As they followed Tessa along the narrow corridors, Sofia realized it was every bit a floating hospital:

although the wards shared by the men were cramped, its radiology unit, sterilizing facilities and operating theatres were fully resourced.

The evening gathering was as pleasant as Sofia could have hoped. The new arrivals, along with Tessa and her group of QAs, gathered at the captain's table, where Mark gave a brief speech, once again welcoming them aboard his ship, after which they were served one of the finest meals she had eaten in months. The fillets of fish bathed in a creamy white sauce had been caught by one of the crewmen, a Scottish man called Keith who was mad for fishing and whose catches often graced their table, according to Mark.

In addition to the fine food, Sofia found the dinner conversation fascinating. It started with an informative discussion about life aboard a hospital ship. While Sofia was traveling to Alexandria, four of the QAs who'd boarded that morning would remain on the *Atlantis*, continuously crossing the Atlantic Ocean and North Sea, caring for wounded soldiers in transition between the war fields, military hospitals and their home countries.

Tessa answered all manner of questions about her war-time experiences with cheerful enthusiasm. Her commitment to her work shone out, as did Mark's admiration for her and their compatible working relationship. He insisted it was Tessa who should be Captain, claiming she'd barely stepped off the *Atlantis* since she'd accepted the role of Charge Nurse eighteen months earlier. He was sure that, should the ship take a hit and start sinking, she'd refuse to abandon it before he did.

For almost an hour, Mark and Tessa shared stories with their enthralled audience. Tales of stormy seas, close shaves with enemy fighter planes and prisoners of war who were intent on continuing their fight, needing to be locked in cabins and supervised by military guards for the duration of their journeys sounded thrilling rather than frightening. To Sofia's surprise, she learned that should the Germans,

Italians or indeed Russians wish to inspect the *Atlantis* to ensure it was operating as a hospital and not a battle ship in disguise, they couldn't be refused. Additionally, beyond the prisoners of war captured on the battlefield, Mark could also be asked to receive their enemies injured soldiers, for the *Atlantis*—like all hospital ships—was neutral. Such an incident had not arisen and he assured them it was unlikely to occur; most enemy forces were close to their own hospitals, which would manage their casualties until they could get them home.

Sofia also discovered that, despite the absence of patients, there was work to be done over the next few days; nothing too arduous, Tessa assured them. A few hours a day would do it, but it was important the *Atlantis* be made ready for the next influx of patients— its cabins tidied, dressing stations stocked, and each of theatres prepared. In addition, they would sort through the freshly loaded medical supplies. Half would be retained on board to serve the needs of the *Atlantis*, while the remainder would be distributed to the hospitals across Egypt and the dressing stations and military hospitals operating near the battlefields.

The conversation turned to the temporary military hospitals operating in the Western Desert. One of the QAs who'd boarded that morning, Marcelle, was returning to British General Hospital 261, and was full of information. She explained how her team followed the front lines of battle, continuously setting up and pulling down the canvas hospital, and laughed at their shocked expressions when she described dirt floors, bush showers, the constant battle with sand and the poor sanitation. After just having left the sterile atmosphere of Shenley's operating theatres, Sofia could not imagine nursing her patients amid such unhygienic conditions.

'Sofia, it's wonderful that you have volunteered for overseas service. Where did you do your VAD training?' The question from Tessa caught Sofia by surprise, as did the sensation of having all eyes turned towards her.

'Yes, thank you. I look forward to serving overseas. I did my training at Shenley Hospital.'

'Oh, Shenley! Then you would have met Captain Fairly. She used to be Matron at Millbank. She can be quite the tiger at times, but then again, I suppose you might have to be when you are responsible for the wellbeing of hundreds of young nurses as well as the running of a large military hospital!'

'I met her for the first time last week. She called me to her office to offer me this posting. I found her very helpful and encouraging. I couldn't believe my good fortune in being chosen.' Sofia's voice sounded loud in her ears as she battled self-consciousness.

'Well, good on you. I'm amazed to think you are so new to nursing. Your help today with moving the men off the ship was wonderful. It is very hard for some of those poor fellows to face coming home. They need as much support as we can give them. Not everyone is cut out for the job, but I am sure you will do fine.'

'Thank you,' Sofia replied, hoping her cheeks didn't look too pink, and she was glad when Tessa shifted the conversation away from her.

Just after eight PM, Tessa clapped her hands, calling everyone to attention, and asked anyone who could sing or play an instrument to show their hands. Within minutes, one doctor collected a trumpet, and another produced a guitar. Although, like Sofia, most of the nurses were bashful when asked to sing along, Tessa and two of her QAs proved to be seasoned performers. For over an hour, they entertained the group with a repertoire of modern numbers styled on the popular American band, the Andrews Sisters. By the end of the evening, everyone was joining the choruses and even performing actions to one or two of the songs.

It was after ten when Sofia went to bed, and she felt relaxed, warmed by the camaraderie within the group. She'd been surprised when Tessa had singled her out across the dinner table, but appreciated her welcoming manner, and felt further encouraged that her decision to accept the posting overseas was the right one.

∼

The next morning, the *Atlantis* set forth on its journey to Alexandria. Sofia enjoyed the days at sea, working alongside the cheerful medical team to prepare the ship for its next influx of patients. In between sorting supplies and stocking cupboards and shelves, there was plenty of time for sitting with a cup of tea. At night, hours were spent chatting across the dinner table about wartime experiences, the various hospitals staff had worked in during the pre-war years, and the people they'd crossed paths with during their careers. Each evening, Tessa insisted on their sing-songs, and these became more hilarious, and cheeky, as the days passed.

For as much as Sofia enjoyed the friendly company, she couldn't shake her feelings of guilt for being cocooned from a world overloaded with suffering. Immersed in ship routines, with hours of free time after they'd completed their work duties, they dwelt in the surreal comfort of the ship, floating across the beautiful shimmering seas; life beyond the *Atlantis's* steel hull seemed to belong to another world. Occasionally they saw land, glimpses of the coastlines of Portugal and Spain, followed by distant blurs on the horizon which the Captain told her were Italy and then Greece. Dozens of ships and small fishing boats were visible in the distance, and the crew watched these attentively lest they presented a threat.

Twice on the journey, small squadrons of Italian planes flew overhead before dipping their wings and retreating. On one such occasion, while Sofia stood with Tessa on the deck, watching the retreating planes, she mentioned her guilt for being so removed from the war. Tessa's response had been reassuring.

'Sofia, there will be plenty of days ahead where you will be run off your feet, despairing at your inability to save every man carried to you on a stretcher, and so sleep deprived you'll be staggering to remain upright! Don't you go feeling guilty because you are not knee-deep in agony alongside those men every minute of the day. You must seize opportunities like this to relax, to keep your spirits up and reserve your strength, for that is what the men will need from you when they are carried off the battlefield wondering whether they are going to live or die. Believe me, once my team receive our next shipload of casualties, we will not have a minute to scratch ourselves for weeks on end. For this reason, so I insist we make the most of our down-time when we can.'

Sofia realized Tessa was right; their sing-songs and civilised evenings weren't about entertainment. Rather, Tessa lifted the weight of the war off them, if only for a few days. She demonstrated that it was not just permitted, but vital for them to allow themselves moments to feel happy to be alive, despite the bloodshed surrounding them.

Finally, the *Atlantis* arrived at Alexandria. With mingled excitement and sadness, Sofia farewelled Tessa and those QAs and doctors who were remaining on board to staff the hospital shift. She then farewelled a second group of nurses who were reporting for duty at the British Military Hospital in Alexandria. She, two QAs—Betty and Moira—and two doctors, James and David, were yet to be advised of their postings, and climbed into awaiting sedans that would transport them to the Cecil Hotel, the Headquarters for the British Military in Alexandria. There, they'd be provided with accommodation until details of their postings came through.

On the drive through the streets of Alexandria, Sofia was amazed by the sight of a beautiful bay, its blue water edged with yellow sand where dozens of men, woman and children relaxed in the sunshine. Approaching the centre of the town, the vehicle turned into a broad street lined with multistorey buildings, many with distinctive canvas awnings flapping in the breeze. Hundreds of vehicles bearing gleaming paintwork and glistening chrome sped through the streets, sharing the space with cyclists and pedestrians, many of whom wore full-length robes and head coverings. The sight caught Sofia by surprise, for in truth, she'd expected Egypt to be a land of deserts, pyramids, palm trees and camels rather than a modern city.

They reached the Cecil Hotel, a six story building with charming balconies overlooking the streets below. Its foyer was stunning, with enormous stone columns, waxed timberwork and colourful rugs scattered across gleaming marble floors. Small tables bore impressive arrangements of flowers and gold metal lampstands, and the floor-to-ceiling curtains looked like they'd been spun from threads of gold.

The nurses each had their own rooms, and Sofia was delighted to find hers had French doors leading out to a balcony which overlooked the bay.

'Isn't this just too much?' Betty called from the next balcony.

'It sure is,' Moira, who had appeared on a balcony further along, called back. 'Let's meet downstairs in half an hour and we can walk along the foreshore.'

For three days Sofia, Betty and Moira indulged in the delights of Alexandria, crossing the road to sit on the sandy shores of the Mediterranean Sea; walking the streets crowded with vendors offering all manner of interesting produce; sampling spicy meals of kushari, falafel and kofta fingers and in between, filling themselves with fresh dates, figs and loquats. In the evenings, they joined dozens of expatriates—mostly males in uniforms or suits—who gathered in the hotel bar where beer and wine flowed freely.

There, a friendly group of British soldiers introduced them to the latest fad, a cocktail invented in Cairo called The Suffering Bastard. Made from equal parts bourbon, gin, and lime juice, with a dash of Angostura bitters and topped with ginger beer, it came with a promise to leave imbibers with a clear head the next morning. Although Sofia had no intentions of drinking so much that she'd have a sore head, she was happy to sample the cocktail. The lively gathering created a surreal atmosphere; it was as if there were no war at all and Sofia travelled three thousand miles to attend a party, complete with live music, abundant food, alcohol, laughter and dancing.

The party did not last forever, though. On Sofia's fourth day in

Alexandria, news arrived that she, Moira and Betty were being posted to a general hospital in the desert. With no further information forthcoming, they were advised to pack their bags and meet in the foyer of the Cecil Hotel the following morning. They'd be transported to their new destination by bus.

'Good Lord, are we going to cross the desert in this? We'll be killed before we travel a dozen miles!' Moira exclaimed. They all studied the vehicle, which was more like an army jeep than a bus, complete with a large dent on one side, chipped paint, a flapping canvas roof and hard bench seats. The driver, a cheerful man called Barry, must have overheard Moira's comment, for with a cheeky smile, he assured them the vehicle would get them to their posting safe and sound, and without being bombed, in time for their morning tea the following day. After settling their cases in the back, he produced some cushions to serve as padding, and soon they were on their way.

It emerged that the general hospital to which they'd been appointed was over four hundred miles west, a military hospital being established in readiness for a battle that was expected to erupt at any time. Barry told them his plan was to drive as far as possible before the sun sank below the horizon—hopefully he'd reach Bardia, a seaport on the Libyan coast which had recently been taken by the Allies.

'There, you girls can get your beauty sleep—not that you need it,' he hastened to add, before reverting to his cheeky self. 'We'll get away at daybreak, but if you're up early, you'll be able to shower and freshen up your lipstick before we leave. All being well, I'll have you reporting for duty at eight AM tomorrow.'

As they exited the city, streets and buildings were replaced by vast stretches of rolling dunes, reflecting yellows, golds, oranges and scarlets. Sofia watched, fascinated by the play of the sun and shadows on their surface and intrigued by the formations of jagged-looking rocks interspersed across the landscape.

She laid her head back, listening as Betty and Moira plied Barry with questions about the hospital they drove towards—how big was it? was it well resourced? were they likely to be in danger? what were the showers like?—and a dozen other obscure details.

Sofia could not help marvelling at the changes in her life over the last fortnight. Two weeks ago, she'd been living at Talonsgate. Then, she'd crossed the ocean in an enormous albeit almost empty ship. Once in Alexandria, she'd been ensconced in a beautiful hotel with grandiose rooms and views across the Mediterranean. Now, here she was: in a rattling jeep driven by the cheeky Barry, accompanied by a pair of women who were pleasant, but essentially strangers, travelling through the desert where she'd be living and working in tents, within a couple of miles of a battlefield.

She wondered what had happened at Talonsgate since she'd left, and whether Marcus had, in fact, joined the army as he'd said he would. She hoped he'd change his mind.

When Barry mentioned the large number of Australians and New Zealand soldiers who were serving in the Middle East alongside the British, Sofia's thoughts turned to Jack; at this minute he seemed further away from her than ever. As usual, a vision of him with Margaret came to her, and she wondered what they might be doing. Shaking her head, freeing her thoughts from futile imaginings, Sofia hoped they'd discovered some sort of happiness. Of late, as she closed her eyes in prayer before sleep, Sofia cast her thoughts to them both, along with Elizabeth, Joseph, Marcus and Andreanna, whispering to a distant God to keep them all safe. Lastly, though it pained her to envision the beautiful little boy Scotty had been, Sofia found comfort in picturing him sleeping, like a little cherub on a cloud in a place she imagined to be heaven and she prayed to God to keep her baby safe.

As Barry had promised, after hours of driving—sometimes in silence, at other times chatting—they arrived at Bardia just on six PM. The coastal town was small and rather quiet. By the last of the sun's rays, Sofia saw buildings which had been reduced to piles of debris and half-standing walls perilously close to collapse. The damage, Barry explained, had been caused the previous month, when Allied troops had wrested the garrison town from the Italians. In itself, Bardia offered no real value to the British, but in the hands of the enemy, its location was far too close to the Egyptian border for comfort. Presently, it was inhabited by a unit of British soldiers stationed there to warn the British War Office should either the Italian or German army return. In the meantime, they occupied themselves by repairing the damaged infrastructure for the sake of the Libyans, to whom it was home.

Sofia, Moira and Betty were shown to a room which they were to share, then directed to a second building which offered amenities for showering. Just after seven, Barry arrived at their door and escorted them to a small inn where dinner was served.

While Moira and Betty were keen to join the officers for a few drinks following the meal, Sofia preferred to have a quiet night and left them to it. Returning to her bedroom, she was pleased with the bed she'd chosen, situated beside a small window which opened to a star-filled sky. She leaned against the glass and gazed into the night, looking down onto a steep shelf below, where the sea glistened in the moonlight. As her eyes adjusted, she could spot the movement of people—perhaps fisherman—on the rocky foreshore.

Turning her attention to the sky, Sofia gazed into its vastness, a pitch-black blanket dotted with thousands of twinkling stars. And when she searched the patches of darkness between them, still more tiny specks emerged, their distance from her beyond imagining.

Usually, Sofia found the sight of the night sky marvellous, but tonight it only made her feel insignificant. Who was she, and what was she doing here? Deep within her, an emptiness stirred, the unfathomable ache that often arose when she least expected it.

'Sofia, enough.' She whispered the words aloud. 'Look forward, chin up. You have friends who love you and...' She paused, unable to finish the sentence. Tonight, her self-talk wasn't working, and she could feel the ache expanding in her chest and tears prickling her eyes. She took a deep breath, considering her options. Should she get dressed and go to the crowd at the bar? Join in the chat? Laugh and have a glass of wine or two?

Deciding not to, she turned from the window, where the night sky had betrayed her by highlighting the deep emptiness in her soul, and faced the wall. She resolutely pummelled the hard pillow, rested her head, and was asleep in minutes.

She didn't hear the girls come in that night, but she heard their cursing in the morning and laughed at them.

'I take it you weren't drinking Suffering Bastards last night, ladies,' she teased as they groaned complaints of their aching heads when called to rise at six AM.

'Gin and tonic… and, I must say, not too much tonic,' Betty said. 'It was after three when we came in! I hope we didn't wake you!'

Grabbing coffee and bread rolls for breakfast, they were on their way by eight, and, within an hour, the jeep weaved towards a stand of tents which all but blended into the landscape.

Assisted by Barry, they collected their luggage, and as they walked through the camp, he pointed out its various features—the Casualty Clearance Station, the acute treatment tents, and the facilities for staff to gather for meals and relaxation. To the far right, a row of large tents formed staff living quarters. Three for the men—a dozen doctors, two anaesthetists and half a dozen camp orderlies, plus the cooks and general assistants in their own tent—and further along, a single large tent for the women: the nine QAs and Sofia. She, Betty and Moira were greeted by a group of QAs who'd been attached to the Field Hospital for the last three months. They were a friendly bunch, and after showing the newcomers spare bunks, besides which they left their suitcases, they explained the facilities within the camp.

'We are pretty well set up,' said a tall redhead, who introduced herself as Christine. 'Most of the camps we've been in over the last couple of months have been pretty rough. Here, we girls have our own bathing and toilet area, which is nice.'

Looking where Christine pointed, Sofia saw a length of green canvas draped around tent posts, with an overhead bucket and shower rose; close to it was a similar arrangement, within which sat a can with a wooden cover.

Three jeeps were set in a line along the edge of the camp, and beside them two large tray-backed trucks and half a dozen ambulances, all tired-looking machines which had undoubtedly seen a fair share of travel across the sandy desert.

To the north, rising dust preceded the arrival of a military truck loaded with dozens of camp beds, quickly unloaded beside the canvas wards where men would soon be housed. A shiver of fear rippled through Sofia as she realised they were barely three miles from the proposed battle site, Tobruk, a garrison town similar to Bardia and which the Allies also intended to take from the Italians. Christine told them that according to the latest information from Army Headquarters, the ensuing battle would engage as many as sixty thousand troops; they should expect to be busy.

CHAPTER 39

*W*hile the rustic conditions of the field hospital might have reminded Sofia of those early days at Montsalvat when she and Jack had wallowed in clay, making mud bricks under Justus Jorgensen's direction, nothing else did. Certainly, there tents had been commonplace, as were meals shared while seated on logs and baths in the bucket shower or tin tub behind the flimsy seclusion of canvas strung from trees.

However, at Montsalvat the air had been rich with organic matter, lively with birdsong, and the chatter relaxed and full of excitement about the world they were creating. Montsalvat's atmosphere had abounded with vigour and a sense of purpose. In addition to expanding their painting skills under Justus' guidance, the artists had turned their hands to stone-masonry and carving as they constructed solid and timeless buildings which would stand for centuries. Montsalvat had been a world to itself, its activities confined to the property's boundaries, its ethos defined by Justus and adhered to by the community who, for the best part, were happily devoted to his vision.

Here at Tobruk, the earth was barren and sand constantly invaded Sofia's hair, eyes, and throat, especially when an afternoon breeze lifted the fine grains and dispersed them into every available crevice. Although the medical team laughed and chatted as they set up the hospital, the underlying mood was sombre, for the gravity of the job ahead of them was inescapable. Their conversations looped back to global politics, the consequences of war, and the killing and maiming of men.

This tiny, fragile outpost was no retreat, as Montsalvat had been, but rather a place of service, where everybody's focus was on mending the bodies of strangers—men drawn into the war whose efforts were rewarded with wounds which might prove fatal or have lifelong consequences.

For the first twenty-four hours, Sofia had little to do but walk around the camp, familiarise herself with the resources on hand, anticipate what might happen when the battle began, and drink tea. She met with the camp's head cook, a man called Simon, and listened, intrigued, to his account of preparing meals for the medical team and wounded soldiers. Sensing Sofia's interest, he showed her around his cookhouse. Not only was Simon a cook by trade, she learned as they chatted, but he'd also served at Gallipoli in the Great War. Looking into his tired eyes, she suspected that painful experiences from the battles of three decades earlier had been revived by the carnage of the present war. Being too old for active service, he'd still wanted to help the war effort, he explained, and he was thankful for the opportunity to serve the war in the best way he knew how: by cooking. Sofia nodded, fully appreciating how Simon felt. While there was little he could do to assist the medical teams in their work, he could strengthen them with the pleasure of good food so they might better perform their jobs. And as for the soldiers, his bully beef and stews, service biscuits and hot black tea would be shared liberally to those who were allowed to consume them in the hope they might find some small comfort despite their injuries.

As someone who also loved preparing food for others, Sofia understood exactly how Simon felt. Far too often, meals were an under-rated commodity at Shenley Hospital, and Sofia had been convinced good food would help improve both the patients' physical wellbeing and their mental health. It was the same theory Marcus had applied to his own patients, herself included, at Napsbury Hospital.

She, Betty and Moira were amazed by the calm manner of the doctors and nurses, who all seemed quite at ease working within the limitations of the tent hospital.

'You all seem very relaxed,' Moira said to Christine.

'Well, there is really no other way to be,' was Christine's reply. 'As I see it, our job is like any other day in an operating theatre, except here, once we get going, we are ten times as busy.'

'And at risk of having a stray bomb drop on our heads at any minute,' added Moira, at which they'd all laughed, including Sofia, although she wasn't sure why.

'How will we know when the battle has started?' she asked.

Another of the nurses, Bernice, whose voice was surprisingly light, with a sweetness which seemed incongruent in their rugged surroundings, added, 'All the battles are a little different, but they generally unfold in the same way. We'll either hear the rumbling of airplane engines approaching or the whistle of the Moaning Minnies dropping from the sky. Sometimes we can feel the ground move beneath us when they explode. We know, then, within an hour we can expect the first of the casualties to arrive. Depending on how serious the fighting gets, within a few hours we'll be utterly flooded and barely have time to pee!'

'It sounds like chaos!' Sofia said, but the nurses shook their heads.

'Certainly, it can seem like Bedlam, but in fact we've developed a straightforward process to stick to. Come on, we'll walk you through it.'

Moira, Betty, and Sofia rose and followed Christine and Bernice to the large tent at the front of the camp.

'This is where the men will first arrive, to be assessed by the Casualty Clearance team. Unfortunately for the CCS, they have to make the tough decisions: choose between who is critical, or serious, or just in need of a patch up. The men whose wounds can be easily treated are sent directly to the dressings tent.' Christine pointed to the large tent to their left. 'There, they will be bandaged or stitched, and then sent to Cairo or Alexandria for further treatment, should they need it. The bleeders, or those with gunshot wounds or broken limbs or head injuries—they are brought over here.' Christine led them to a second tent, where two dozen beds were set out. 'The men here are usually in a bad way; we have to monitor them until the surgeons are ready for them. Martin—he's in charge of the medical team—looks after the damaged limbs.' She waved across the central opening towards a man with heavy eyebrows and a bald head who sat with a group of men. 'He's a magician when it comes to saving arms and legs, although it's not always possible. Chester is the expert with abdominal wounds, and Fred oversees the head injuries. Those men are all brilliant, especially when you consider the circumstances under which they are working.'

'*We* are working, Christine!' Beatrice added. 'Remember, *we* work in impossible circumstances, too! But you are right; the surgeons are remarkable.'

Sofia looked around the tent, at its dirt floor, canvas walls, trestle tables loaded with green drapes, and the racks where stainless-steel trays and cotton wrapped parcels held surgical instruments, and she nodded. It was extraordinary to imagine complex surgical procedures taking place here.

'Once the men have been put back together again, they are taken to the wards, where they are monitored. As soon as transport is available and they are stable enough to be moved, we get them off to Cairo or Alexandria.'

They returned to the trestle table where coffee and tea had been set out, along with milk, sugar and a tray of oatmeal biscuits.

'Hi, ladies. Not quite like the London hospitals you're used to, I'm guessing?' Martin asked.

'Not even nearly,' Moira replied, shaking her head.

'Give it a week and you'll forget you ever worked in a place with running water, septic systems and shiny linoleum floors,' a second doctor said with a chuckle.

'What I still can't get used to,' said Christine, 'is leaving the critical men untreated. I am sure we could come up with a better plan.'

'What are you thinking?' Martin asked her.

'Well, we've got a few extra hands here. I think we should set up an emergency section at the CCS and see if we can't try to stabilize the *criticals*, move them to *serious*, and then follow through with surgery.'

Sofia was intrigued. 'Are you saying we don't treat the men with critical injuries?' she asked Christine. This couldn't be right, surely soldiers bearing such wounds would be the highest priority for treatment? Martin intervened.

'No, nurse... Sofia, is it? I know it's a tough call, but we are dealing with limited resources and can only do our best with what we have. Time spent treating the men with little chance of survival means our second group, the *seriously injured* men, are placed at risk.'

'Think of it like putting out a fire in a row of buildings,' said a tall man with greying hair, a doctor named Paul, who Sofia later discovered had worked in the field hospitals of the Great War. 'If you approach a row of houses where the first is engulfed in flames, and the fire is spreading to the second, what is going to happen if you put all of your attention and resources into the first building?' He answered his own question. 'The first is already as good as lost, and while we try to save it, so too would the second be lost, and likely the third and fourth as well. We must put our resources—our time, and energy—into where they can have the greatest effect.'

Sofia nodded. His point was made, but his reference to fire startled her, and she fell silent.

Sofia woke just after five the following morning. As she'd been warned, the thundering sounds of hundreds of bombs exploding in rapid succession, so close earth the shuddered beneath her, revealed the battle had begun. Glancing at Bernice, she mimicked her actions, quickly replacing her cotton pyjamas with a crumpled blue uniform before exiting the tent. Already, a dozen or more of the team had gathered in the common area, and when Sofia joined them, Simon handed her a steaming cup of coffee and pointed towards a table where slices of toast and scrambled eggs were set out.

'Eat, Nuss. You will need all the strength you can get. It's going to be a long day.'

'Gracias, Simon,' Sofia said, and tasting the eggs—smooth and well salted—she hoped the medical team appreciated how fortunate they were to have such an excellent cook.

Barely an hour had passed when the ambulances, which had left for the battlefield as soon as the bombs were heard, returned to the camp. They quickly unloaded a dozen stretchers bearing men in blood-soaked clothes, before charging off in a cloud of dust for more.

Seamlessly, the surgical team and the QAs gathered at the CCS, where they assessed the injuries of the soldiers before distributing them to the various stations.

'Sofia, you work here with me,' Christine said, calling her to the dressing tent. 'Most of these men need basic first aid. You and I can make a start patching them up. Hopefully, we'll be able to get them off to Alexandria later today.'

Sofia was glad of the instructions, for all about her the doctors, nurses and orderlies were running. Ambulances arrived throughout the day and the orderlies emptied them of men, most of whom were covered in blood, groaning and clutching at their wounds, or lying still, silent and pale. The CCS staff seemed to barely cope with the influx, and Sofia heard them shouting instructions to one another while shuffling men in various directions. The operating theatre was a different version of chaos, its four tables continuously occupied and over a dozen staff filling the room. Nurses passed swabs, needles and kidney dishes to the surgeons, who deftly worked their scalpels. Often, they worked on two patients at a time. Too frequently, a less urgent case was abandoned mid-surgery to respond to the call, 'Doctor, we're about to lose him!'

Perhaps worst, though, was the post-operative tent, where men had begun waking out of the battle they'd been rescued from to a second version of hell. Their stomachs heaved in reaction to the ether or sodium pentothal circulating through their systems, and far too many were confronted by the reality of lost limbs or bandaged eyes. More than one cried, apologising for their tears, but overwhelmed by the world gone mad. Sofia wondered if anyone, even a professional soldier like Joseph, was ever truly prepared for the horror of the battlefield.

Throughout the following forty-eight hours, Sofia barely slept; time became a blur of cups of tea she barely sipped, mouthfuls of steaming stew from the bowls shoved into her hands by Simon at the oddest of moments, and sleep grabbed as one or another of the QAs insisted it was her turn to take a nap.

The state the soldiers brought into the camp was shocking, unlike anything Sofia had ever encountered. At Shenley Hospital, the men had arrived onto the wards with their wounds cleaned, dressed and bandaged, their initial treatment already dealt with at first-aid stations and in operating theatres.

Here, she was witnessing the injuries at their worst. Her stomach heaved at the sight of torn flesh, merged with blood, mud and bone fragments even as she pushed pads to stanch bleeding, applied bandages and checked tourniquets. And despite the process of triage, often the treatment given to those designated *serious* wasn't enough and they too slipped into the *critical* category, only to finally join the dozens who rested in the makeshift morgue at the back of the camp.

On the third morning, Sofia held her stockings up; there was no way she could repair the runs. Seeing her plight, Beatrice threw a pair of men's trousers and a shirt onto her bed.

'Here—you will find these much easier to work in,' she said. Sofia didn't have to think twice, donning the pants and then, at Beatrice's advice, using her stockings as a belt to hold them. She slipped on the shirt and pulled her hair into a bun, but discarded the VAD cap she'd been wearing and reported to the operating theatre, where she tied a cotton scarf around her hair.

It too was a long and exhausting day, with hundreds of men arriving at the hospital with injuries from minor lacerations to life-threatening haemorrhages requiring immediate surgery. Sofia was thankful to be relieved of duty at nine PM. Her hopes of having a shower—cold would do her—then tumbling into bed were quickly dashed. Arriving at the nurse's tent, she discovered another battle taking place within its canvas walls.

Ants, entire armies of them, had converged, each bearing nippers that bit into any flesh they could find as they invaded the women's clothing, toiletries and beds. With irritation, Christine and a Scottish nurse, Helen, were at work stripping sheets and calling for containers, preferably Player's cigarette tins. By the light of kerosene lanterns, Sofia helped them fill the tins with water, then place them under the legs of each stretcher bed. They might not rid the tent of the ants, but at least they would sleep easy without them biting through the night.

As Paul had suggested when Sofia first arrived, by her fourth day she could barely imagine the time when she'd worked in a hospital built from bricks and mortar. However, with wry humour she recalled the ridiculous Saturday morning Captain's rounds at Shenley: the farcical process of folding towels, wet or dry, and then setting them atop the bedside lockers; the beds presented in pristine order, with snowy white sheets and pillow slips arranged according to regulations. How alongside each bed, the men were propped upright with their feet neatly together, and when asked, they'd pretended they were fine. Here, packing cases served as bedside tables, shaving gear and belongings were almost non-existent, anything which may once have been white was now a dirty grey, and nobody made any pretence about the severity of the men's condition.

The battle to take Tobruk was over within the week, and though it was deemed a victory for the Allies, the fact barely registered for Sofia and those at the General Hospital. Their work continued for another ten days as soldiers in their care were stabilized before being loaded into vehicles and sent to hospitals in Egypt.

While the final group of soldiers was being prepared for transportation, accompanied by a group of QAs, Sofia sat at the table with the remaining nurses and scribbled letters to both Marcus and Elizabeth, summarising the beauty of the desert, the chaos and exhaustion of the field hospital and the remarkable skills of the nurses and doctors in her unit. She finished with a series of hastily written questions about a world so vastly removed from her present circumstances she could barely remember it: Elizabeth's horses, Andreanna's well-being, Joseph's safety and Marcus' status regarding his decision to enlist in the army.

Sofia handed her letters to the QAs as they boarded the truck to Alexandria, farewelled with hugs and promises to stay in touch. Then, along with the remainder of the camp, she prepared for the move to their next destination, Benghazi, where it felt the days were a repeat of Tobruk.

By the time the General Hospital was set up in Sidi Bashir, Sofia was more sure of herself, for this was her fourth camp. However, since her arrival in Tobruk, there had been a large changeover of nursing staff; to her surprise, the newly arrived QAs, fresh from London, looked upon her as an experienced nurse, one from whom they sought advice regarding the routines of the camp. Here, Sofia's status as a VAD nurse meant little. Helpful and experienced hands were all that mattered, and while she knew when she must defer responsibilities to those more qualified, most of the time she was treated just like the QAs and quickly stepped up to perform whatever tasks presented without question.

After ten months of working behind the western desert war front with a number of British General Hospitals, Sofia received the news of her recall to a hospital in Cairo, The Scottish General Hospital. Her interest in the posting increased when a couple of the QAs expressed their excitement for her, thrilled to see her hard work being rewarded by such an exotic posting.

'Exotic! What could be exotic about a Scottish General Hospital in Cairo?' she asked.

'Lucky you! It's on the Nile; you'll live in a houseboat with servants and be given the most incredible meals. The hospital itself is spectacular, all marble and columns and sheer luxury! You've never seen anything like it!'

Sure the QAs were joking, Sofia prepared herself for something possibly worse than the conditions of the desert hospitals.

CHAPTER 40

*D*ropping her bag onto the bed she'd been allocated, Sofia could barely believe the changes in her life. The scent of salty water and view of palms edging well-tended lawns, their large fronds wavering in the breeze, while people strolled along the foreshore dressed in well-fitted suits and white uniforms, seemed fantastic after months of living in the desert.

How luxurious it was to have her own room, one with a cupboard —small as it may be—after months of sleeping on camp stretchers in tents! Right out the window, an enormous sea bird dipped its bill into the water then glided upward, its wings flapping gracefully. A fish squirmed within the grasp of his large beak and Sofia watched, wondering if he might drop it. She had no doubt now the QAs had been speaking the truth when they'd said the Scottish General Hospital was a dream posting.

'Come, Sofia, let me show you around,' offered Jenny, an Australian nurse who had the cabin next to her own. Sofia followed the young woman down to the lower deck of the barge, to a dining room where platters of fruit were laid out on a bench and a thin, pale-faced man was setting out plates and cutlery for the evening meal.

'Good afternoon, ladies,' he said. 'Can I offer you some fresh mandarins, or perhaps you might like some pineapple juice?'

'Thanks, Olaf. That sounds lovely! Meet Sofia; she's just arrived from the desert. I am telling her how much she's going to enjoy it here!'

'Welcome, Sofia. Yes, I would say you will like it here, especially since you have me to wait on you hand and foot!'

'He does, Sofia! It's true! Anything you need, just ask Olaf and he will help you find a solution. The bus timetables or where to buy items for good prices—Olaf knows everything!'

'Wonderful! Thank you, Olaf. I'm pleased to meet you!'

Sofia could not shake the feeling she was living a dream. Beyond the fact there was so much to take in, she was trying to suppress the sense of being flung back in time as she adjusted to Jenny's accent. It was certainly not the first Australian accent she'd heard in Egypt; the field hospital had been full of Australian and New Zealand soldiers, however, her melodic voice stirred memories, particularly ones of Sonya Skipper. Like Jenny, she'd expressed a similar enthusiasm for life in the same confident tone.

'Would you like to go for a wonder into town?' Jenny suggested after they finished the tour of the barge.

'That sounds lovely, but I feel a bit of a wreck.' Sofia smiled, tugging self-consciously at the wrinkled grey excuse of a uniform she'd donned for the long drive to Cairo.

'Don't worry about that! I'll take you across to the laundry; they'll get you sorted with replacements. Was the desert awful? The nurses who come back from the General Hospitals are full of stories about the horror of it all! The dreadful wounds of the poor soldiers, the scorpions and ants, and the nasty POWs. We don't get too much of that here. Mostly, our patients have been through the worst of their treatment on the field.' Jenny said. 'You might even recognise some of them!'

Though they returned to the barge from the laundry armed with half a dozen dresses and three veils, Jenny insisted there was no need for Sofia to be in uniform yet.

'They'll give you a few days off, for sure. We are only halfway through the current roster; I expect your name will appear on next week's, so you should have at least four days of freedom. Lucky for you, I'm off for two days, so I will be your tour guide. You are going to love Cairo!'

Taking Jenny's advice, Sofia had a quick shower and changed into some civies—a dress, stockings, shoes and a cardigan. Refreshed, she enjoyed being dragged from pillar to post, listening to Jenny chat excitedly about the wonders of the city.

They started with the hospital itself, which was indeed as beautiful as she'd been told, with gleaming marble floors, enormous windows and modern equipment.

'Why is it called the Scottish General Hospital when it's here in Cairo?' Sofia asked.

Jenny laughed. 'Everybody asks that! The reason it is called the Scottish Hospital—so I've heard—is because it was built *by* the Scottish *for* the Egyptians. Apparently, the Egyptians never put it into use, and so the British reclaimed it when war broke out.'

'Are any of the staff actually Scottish?'

'Yes, there's a group of nurses here from Edinburgh. Truly, they are wag; they laugh about anything and are full of mischief. They live on the second houseboat, but we get together all the time. I've learned all their dances: the Eightsome Reels, quadrilles, two-steps and Strip the Willow. And then there's the Brown's Reel, waltzes, Flowers of Edinburgh, Dashing White Sergeant and the Gay Gordons. I am sure they make half of them up!'

For two days, Sofia, Jenny and any one or more of the nurses on the houseboats wandered through Cairo, weaving through the tiny lanes of the bazaar filled with colourful silks and embroidered cloth, and then along the Nile to the Mad Mile. There, they watched hundreds of melons being unloaded from barges and bought bananas, dates and large slices of the lush melons, cut for them by Egyptian men with flashing eyes and broad smiles.

At the first opportunity, Sofia purchased half a dozen postcards on which she wrote messages to Elizabeth and Marcus as well as to staff at the Operating Theatre at Shenley Hospital. As she recorded updates on her overseas adventure, described the wonder of Cairo, and asked how they were faring, Sofia couldn't help feeling how distant she felt from the world she'd once known.

Despite the beauty of the Scottish General Hospital, Sofia's work did not differ much from what she'd done on Shenley's wards. If anything the routines of sponge baths, dressings and post-operative care for the soldiers proved bland after serving in the desert, where she'd been given extraordinary levels of responsibility. Some days were busier than others, particularly when large numbers of men were brought in from one battle or another. Sofia enjoyed the challenge of juggling the demands of those busy shifts.

Another thing she appreciated about her posting was that she now had days off, dictated by the ward's weekly roster. Mostly, her shifts were ten-hour stints; only occasionally was she asked to work a dreaded double shift. Usually she smiled when nurses complained about busy shifts and tired legs, for to Sofia the work was easy compared to the eighteen-hour straight shifts she'd often endured at the desert postings. Now, her days off were not measured by episodes between skirmishes on battlefields, but by the promise of visits to extraordinary places. Sofia was excited by the nurses' enthusiastic descriptions of tours to the Pyramids, camel rides in the desert, and barge trips down the Nile.

In her second week at the Scottish General Hospital, the administration office sent a message to the medical ward where she worked, advising Sofia that a parcel of letters awaited her in the Mail Room. She could barely wait to collect them, and in her lunch break she raced downstairs. As she expected, a parcel had arrived from Talonsgate.

As Sofia read through more than a dozen letters by Marcus, she

327

conceded that his words were not the rapturous tones of a lover, as she frequently heard read aloud by the nurses she worked with, but his sign-offs—*Sofia, dear, please tell me you are okay. I couldn't bear it if anything were to happen to you* and the variations thereof—exceeded the tones of brotherly affection.

Through these letters, she discovered Marcus had indeed enlisted with the British military, although to his disgust, his attempts to gain a posting to the Middle East, to gain the experience of life as a soldier on the battlefield had been futile. Instead he'd been retained in Britain, sent to Yorkshire for training as a reconnoitrer. Marcus' job was to gather tactical information about the battlefields and screen the flanks of the proposed advances. He'd been trained to use the wireless set, he added, though he'd much prefer to work with the homing pigeons held by the unit who were trained to gather intelligence and carry messages across Europe.

Sofia couldn't help smiling with relief, even as she imagined an irate Marcus entreating the military hierarchy to send him overseas. Far better for him to be away from the firing line, even if he was frustrated! She imagined he wasn't used to being told what to do, but it was comforting to know he was working in an administrative position rather than suffering the horrors of the battlefield for the sake of research.

Elizabeth's letters, which Sofia opened in chronological order, were written in the same manner she spoke. Short and to the point, she coupled her inquiries into Sofia's wellbeing with reassurances that all was well at St Albans. Even though London was beset by rationing and bombing, her references to simple things like Andreanna's sleepless nights caused by teething and days caring for horses whose owners were caught up in the war served as pleasant, poignant reminders of the timelessness of Talonsgate. Her most recent letter, however, held news of Joseph that was less comforting.

Dearest Sofia,

So wonderful to finally hear from you, although I can well imagine getting mail out of those far-flung military hospitals is difficult. I was so pleased to hear of your posting to Cairo, and hope you are getting some rest away from the dust of the desert. Though you didn't say as much, I am sure confronting the horrible injuries suffered by our young men is as awful for you as it is for us to hear of it; good on you for the work you are doing!

On a more positive note, you will be amazed to hear Andreanna has found her legs. She is now running here, there and everywhere and loves nothing better than to sit on the back of a horse. I've chosen Spirit for her—a quiet old gelding who prefers eating to walking and who barely notices a squirming toddler impatiently 'giddy-upping' on his back. I am sure Andreanna thinks he is a rocking horse!

I have had a few messages from Marcus, and each time he writes he includes a letter for you, with instructions I must post them at the first opportunity, so if you are reading this, then no doubt you have his letters in your hand also!

As you may know, he did of course enlist, and thankfully he'd been given a safe posting in Yorkshire. However, the fool's not happy with that! He's constantly applying for a posting overseas, demanding he be given a gun, a tin hat and an appointment with Hitler. Really, if he were here I'd save the Germans the trouble and knock him on the head myself, for all the worry he is causing me! Why on earth he didn't enlist with the British Army to serve as a psychologist, I'll never understand!

As if I didn't have enough to worry about! Joseph, is (as far as I know) somewhere in Italy. I haven't seen him since April; he writes when he can, but as you know, mail is ridiculously unreliable at present. I have to be happy with whatever updates arrive from the other men in his unit; they all band together to look out for each other's families, which is an excellent arrangement under the circumstances.

Talonsgate is still standing, although I don't think a biscuit has been baked or a floor washed since you left... Well, the second might be a joke, but the first is definitely true!

Lots of love, hugs and kisses from me and Andreanna. Keep well,
and come home soon!

Again, Sofia was reassured by knowing Marcus was in England, this
time for Elizabeth's sake. It was enough for her to worry about Joseph,
and he a trained soldier, without having to be worried about the safety
of her brother. Like Elizabeth, Sofia knew the battle field was no place
for Marcus. He was an intellectual with a gift for reaching deep into
the minds of troubled souls. A man who was kind and intuitive. He was
not built for marching for hours on end in heat and dust with a pack on
his back and a gun in his hand. But then again, were any of the men
who fought in the desert designed for the war fields?

Cairo was every bit as exotic as Sofia imagined. The weather was
warm and the nurses were a pleasant group. Jenny, along with a nurse
from Wales called Paula, quickly became firm friends with Sofia, and
the three of them seized every opportunity to gad about, sight-seeing in
the manner of tourists or joining in with the others, mingling at the
various hotel bars for drinks and meals. Sofia remained quiet by nature,
but always accepted invitations to join the others on tours of the town
or to swim at the beautiful pools at Mena House or the Heliopolis, or to
dine at the Shefford Hotel.

Of all Sofia's experiences in Cairo, none was so startling as what
occurred one afternoon two months after her arrival, when she was
walking through the bazaar with Jenny and Paula. They'd worked a
night shift on the medical ward, but rather than going straight to their
cabins for some much-needed sleep, they'd agreed to walk into town
together. Paula wanted to buy stockings, and Jenny planned on keeping
her company. Sofia decided she'd go along with them and see if she
could find some shampoo and hair pins.

Wandering amid the bustling crowds in the bazaar, Sofia was once again fascinated by the assortment of wares on offer. Spicy aromas of food mixed with the pungent odour of carpets woven in bright coloured patterns. Carvings, jewellery and ornaments vied for the attention of shoppers. They turned into a small store where every shelf was filled to overflowing with all manner of items: miniature pyramids and tiny grotesque looking sphinx'; milk, yoghurt and cheeses in an ice storage; assorted books and magazines set beside oddments of stationery; and an array of scarves, stockings and even a bin filled with shoes. Very likely, she would find a pile of mismatched stockings tucked away in a back corner. After a couple of minutes perusing the shelves, she decided to ask the old man at the counter, clad in the striped robes common to elderly Egyptian men.

'Sir, I am looking for some ...' her eyes landed on a drawing that had been pasted behind the counter and she was stunned into speechlessness. It was an ink drawing of a small boy standing on the rim of a fountain, his hand stretched towards the cascading water, his laughter-filled eyes gazing towards her, his mouth fixed in a broad grin. The portrait had been beautifully executed, its lines a masterful interplay of shadow and light that had been created by a very talented artist.

'May I see that?' she asked, gesturing towards the drawing.

'No, no... My grandson. It is not for sale!' He shook his head, his mouth set in a firm line, and she knew this was one sale he would not be talked into.

'Please, I just want to look at it...'

'No, not for sale.' His frown deepened; Sofia imagined he was used to deflecting the demands of tourists who might think that anything was for sale at the right price.

Attempting to look docile, Sofia stepped forward, holding her hands up to demonstrate that she wouldn't touch the picture; her intention was just to look.

As she got closer, her eyes moved to the lower right of the portrait, where a swirling letter made her heart race.

Surely not!

Leaning closer, she read the one word of the signature. However, even without seeing that, Sofia had recognised the artist by the formation of the lines, the pattern of shading and shadowing, the looseness of the background features. The word only confirmed what she knew. This portrait had been drawn by Jack!

Sofia's heart beat as though it would jump out of her chest. 'Who drew this?'

'My grandson. See? He is a cheeky boy! He should not be climbing on the fountains!'

'Yes, but Jack—the artist—where is he?'

'I don't know... Jack... soldier artist....'

Again Sofia examined the paper. Yellowed, with curled edges, it was quite a few months old.

'Your grandson? Is he here?'

'Yes, yes. Doing his homework. He is a good boy, when he is not cheeky!' The man smiled at his joke before turning to a large curtain which partitioned the shop. 'Lateef, come here!' he called into the rear area. 'This English lady, she likes your portrait!'

The boy emerged from behind the curtain, his eyes widening in fear as Sofia gazed upon him.

'Hello. How are you?' she asked, trying to make the child feel relaxed.

He didn't reply, and she tried again.

'I am wondering... I'd like to know, who drew this picture?'

'Soldier man,' he replied. 'Soldier man, at the square.'

'When?' she asked.

The boy shrugged.

'Is he still here, in Cairo? Have you seen him again?'

The boy looked back at her, but did not seem to understand.

'Thank you,' she said, unsure of where to take the conversation. Again, she looked at the drawing, overwhelmed by a feeling she might grab it and run from the store. But of course, she didn't. If she wanted, she could come back again and ask more questions.

As she retreated, Sofia found Jenny and Paula staring at her, no doubt surprised by the intense interest she'd shown for the drawing.

'What was happening there?' Jenny asked. Her voice was soft, her eyes filled with concern. In the three months they'd spent together, she'd been a caring and supportive friend. And on a couple of occasions where the girls probed into Sofia's past, Jenny had been quick to divert the conversation. It was as if she'd known Sofia's life was complicated, and not a subject for gossip around the breakfast table. Now, Sofia felt it was time for at least some of the mystery to be revealed.

'That drawing was done by my husband.'

'Your husband! You never mentioned you were married!'

'Well, I *was* married. I *had* a husband. His name is Jack. He's an Australian, and it would appear he's been here, in Cairo.'

Sofia's words hung in the air, and it seemed nobody knew what to say. It was rare to hear a cheerful story when a marriage was described in the past tense.

'He could still be here, now,' Jenny stated..

Sofia nodded, even as her heart hammered in her chest. Jack was here in Cairo! How could he be? But of course, there were dozens, no, hundreds—of Australians soldiers posted to the Middle East.

'But you don't know? You haven't been in touch?' Paula asked.

'No. I haven't seen Jack in years. Not since I left Australia.'

'You lived in Australia! I thought you were Spanish.' Paula said.

'I am. Both... I met Jack in Paris and he came home with me to Spain, where we were married. Later, we went to Australia.'

'But what happened?' Paula asked. A brief pause followed, as Sofia struggled to find the words. What happened? How could she begin to explain? After a brief pause, Jenny intervened.

'Well, the thing is, he's here. Or at least he *was* here. Do you want to find him, Sofia?'

'Yes. I do. I definitely want to find him. I need to know that he is well.'

CHAPTER 41

*I*magining where Jack might be filled Sofia's thoughts every waking hour. Was he walking through the streets of Cairo, wandering through the bazaar with his sketchbook in hand this very minute? Might he be seated at one of the bars where soldiers gathered in the evenings?

Jenny and Paula also became caught up with the idea of finding him, and then as the story of Sofia's missing 'husband' spread, the nurses on the barge also became consumed with the mystery of where Jack might be.

Within twenty-four hours, Sofia had accumulated a list of the places in Cairo which Australian soldiers frequented, from the hotels to the training camps. She had four more shifts until her days off, and on each she asked the men she cared for if they'd heard of a man named Jack, an Australian soldier who was a talented artist. One or two thought they'd heard of him; one had even seen him sketching in the town, but she heard nothing conclusive about his whereabouts.

The following weekend, Sofia had leave. Both Jenny and Paula were rostered on, and they wished her luck as she rose early to catch the bus to the Casa training camp, where many Australian soldiers were stationed. Once there, she made her way to the Administration Office.

The officer who spoke with her was kind, but when he requested Jack's battalion and unit number, Sofia could not provide either, and immediately she sensed a coolness enter his responses.

'Mrs *Tomlinson*, thousands of men from the 2ndAIF pass through this camp on their way to the battlefields. Unless you can give me more details, I can't really help.'

'So, you cannot tell me anything about him? You can't tell me if he's here, right now?'

'I am sorry, but no. I am sure your husband will try to get a letter to you as soon as possible. He knows you are with the nursing corps, I take it? You are working as a VAD with the British Military?'

It was then Sofia realised the officer did not believe she was Jack's wife at all. Why should he? She was a Spanish woman working with the British Army's medical corps in Egypt and claiming to be the wife of an Australian soldier! He very likely assumed she'd met Jack at a bar in Cairo, and was trying to pursue a relationship with a man who might not wish to be found.

Despairing, she returned to the barge. As supportive as Jenny and Paula were, she wondered if they too doubted her claim to have been married to an Australian soldier who'd sketched a drawing of a small boy standing on a fountain and signed with just four letters, *Jack*.

Over the following days, Sofia felt a veil of darkness descending over her as she grappled with knowing Jack could be close, yet having no way to be sure. She rejected the other girls' invitations to join them for dinner at the Shefford Hotel, to visit Mena House, or to go shopping. She preferred to take long walks through town, gazing into the faces of Australian soldiers gathered at the cafes, and sometimes approaching them to ask if they knew of Jack.

It was on one such walk Sofia received news, both good and bad.

She'd approached a table outside a café where a group of Australian soldiers were seated and asked if any of them knew of a Jack Tomlinson; a soldier they might have noticed because he liked to sketch. She was amazed when a red-haired officer with a clipped moustache nodded; he remembered how, months earlier, there had been a morning muster where a private was promoted to Captain; the poor fellow had been given the questionable privilege of becoming a war artist, and the drill sergeant had a bit of fun with him. The man had been attached to the 2/5th, and very likely he'd gone to Bardia and Tobruk.

Armed with this information, Sofia returned to Camp Casa and met with the same administration officer. She shared her findings, sure that mentioning her husband had been appointed as a war artist would make him more helpful.

It made no difference. Again, the officer reiterated the difficulty the army was having trying to account for troops once they'd left the training camp for the battlefields. Certainly, Bardia and Tobruk had been victories for the Allies, but from there the battalions had been sent to Greece, and although he didn't spell out the outcome, Sofia understood his dilemma: the Greek campaign was fresh on everyone's minds, for it had been a crushing defeat.

Sofia could barely function for worrying about Jack. To think after all these years, the war had brought them both to this tiny portion of the world, this place of desert skies, sandy plains and exotic cities. Had he been one of the men who'd passed through the hospital at Tobruk or Sidi Barrani? Had he been a patient at the Scottish General Hospital? Sofia kept picturing him, and always, she could only visualise him injured, for that was how she understood the soldiers best, as men who arrived at casualty clearance stations to be sorted into groups of *critical*, *serious* or *first aid*.

In the disastrous Greek campaign, had Jack been one of the men sent to the back tents of a field hospital, offered a sip of water or maybe rum, given a blanket and a dose of morphine, then left to die? Or had he been one of those who'd made it to the operating table? No, no, no. Not Jack. She shouldn't think like this, Sofia told herself. Rather, she should picture Jack as a victor. He was a war artist, not a combatant. Why would he be injured, or indeed killed?

But where was he?

On Sofia's third visit to Camp Casa, instead of the gruff officer who was reluctant to give her any meaningful information, a young soldier with sorrowful eyes and an open manner, bearing a badge on his chest labelled Private Haslow, listened to her story. He nodded when Sofia told him she believed Jack had gone to Tobruk.

'The thing is, ma'am, if your husband survived Greece he was likely separated from his unit during the evacuation. To complicate things, he might have been dropped off at Crete, which again... well, Crete was a total disaster if you don't mind me saying, but nobody will admit it. Thousands of men—no, tens of thousands of men—were dumped on the island. They were expected to take on the Germans, but the poor chaps had nothing left in them. The whole operation was a mess, with far too many Indians and very few chiefs, not to mention shortages of food, weapons and practically anything else needed to win a battle. That's not to say they weren't impressive. They very nearly had Jerry running. But once the Germans took the airport at Meleme it was all over for our boys. The British made an attempt to evacuate them, but only a handful were taken off the island. Those who remained had to surrender.'

'Surrender? Be taken prisoner?"

'Sorry, ma'am. My guess is your Jack is now a guest of the German Command. Probably behind barbed wire in Austria or Yugoslavia. We have a few lists floating about with names of those who surrendered, but they are so unreliable, you couldn't get your hopes up either way. If you don't mind waiting, I'll see if I can find something.'

Sofia could barely believe she was seconds away from receiving news of Jack's whereabouts. She was not sure if she wanted to learn he was a prisoner of the Germans, but at the same time, she hoped he was, for the alternative was possibly worse.

Fifteen minutes later, the lad returned, shaking his head.

'So you are saying my husband is not on the list?' *My husband, my husband, my husband*; the phrase drummed through Sofia's mind. In a matter of weeks, knowing Jack was so near, that very recently he'd been walking these same streets, sketching the sights around her, he'd become her husband, she, his wife. And for whatever that meant, she had to find him. Had to see him and know he was safe. And though she could barely hope it, Sofia knew more than anything, she had to see if the love they'd once shared before the tragedy of Scotty's death might be rekindled.

'No, ma'am. There is neither a Private nor a Captain Jack Tomlinson on any list.'

'So, where is he, then?'

'Ma'am, I am sorry, but we don't know. He could still be in the hands of the Germans. Like I said, our lists are unreliable. Perhaps he escaped. Perhaps he is still on the island... heaven forbid. News is so sketchy at present, we really don't have all the pieces of the puzzle together.'

What Private Haslow didn't say was Jack might be one of the hundreds of soldiers who'd been killed on Crete, and for this Sofia was thankful, even though she knew this may be the case.

Sofia felt hollow as she left the camp. She'd learned so much, and yet so little about Jack's whereabouts, and felt no wiser than she'd been a month earlier when she'd discovered the ink drawing taped to the back wall of the store in the bazaar.

She considered writing to Marian and William, or even to Margaret, to see if they'd heard anything of Jack, but in the end, she did neither, for shame surfaced with a vengeance that almost knocked the breath from her. There was no way she could put pen to paper. Now, not only was she heartsick from worrying about Jack's whereabouts, but also consumed with guilt for the sorrow she'd brought to Marian and William by losing their grandchild and then leaving their son. What could she say, if she was to write to them? Offer them the news she'd learned, tell them Jack had gone missing and upset them yet again? She concluded there was nothing to gain by writing, so didn't.

Instead, Sofia continued calling weekly at Camp Casa's administration office, asking for Private Haslow, and each week he gave her the same reply: no news. Then in early April when she returned, this time accompanied by Jenny, they were called into a side office. There, they were greeted by both Private Haslow and a man bearing blue and gold stripes on his shoulders and a badge on his left breast stating his name was Captain O'Neil. After inviting Sofia and Jenny to take a seat, the captain drew his chair from behind the desk and settled in it across from them. Wearing a serious expression, he cleared his throat.

His voice was quiet and impassive as he spoke, as though seeking to remove all emotion, any inflection which might add to the pain of the news he was delivering.

'Mrs Tomlinson, five days earlier, our data from the Crete offensive was updated. Your husband, Captain Jack Tomlinson, has been recorded on this list; he has been identified as missing, presumed dead. I am very sorry.'

Sofia shook her head, as if by the movement she might be freed from the unbearable news. No, surely not! It was too much. Gasping in disbelief, she clutched her handkerchief to her mouth. Had she done this to Jack? Was this more evidence of the curse she carried? If she'd left him alone—not even tried to search for him—might he still be alive? It was too, too awful.

Inhaling and exhaling frantically, Sofia sought control of her body and mind. If her emotions ran havoc, her illness might take hold; at any second her mind might shatter into a thousand fragments.

She fought against the feeling of being swallowed in a chasm, the desire to sink to the floor and beat her fists. To howl for Jack, who'd seemed so close, and now he was gone! At the unfairness of it all: her parents, her brother, Scotty and now Jack!

No, no, no! Breathe, breathe, breathe…

A sting pierced her right hand; it was from Jenny's nails biting into her flesh as her fingers squeezed Sofia's hand. The pain was a feeble reminder of the room she was in, the people she was amongst, her present circumstances, but it was enough. Sofia knew she must grasp on to reality. Hold on to the world where men lay in hospital beds, thankful for the ministrations of nurses like herself. Where friends cared for her. Where a daughter, albeit relinquished, did not deserve to have her mother institutionalised in Napsbury. *No, no, no! Inhale, exhale!*

'Sofia, are you okay?' The words came from Jenny. *Okay*, of course, was the only option to choose, and the tough talk she often gave to the men she nursed flashed forth. *Stand up, take a step—endure the pain of the present in order to gain your future.*

But the question arose. *Did* she want to live? *Could* she bear this loss? Over the last few weeks, Sofia had felt so close to Jack, it was as though they'd survived the dreadful loss of Scotty; their hearts hadn't been ripped apart. And now he was gone for once and for all, and the ache was dreadful. Sofia wondered now if she'd been wrong when she'd pushed her patients towards their unknown futures. Perhaps sometimes living was worse than dying: facing what lay ahead was simply too hard, too painful, too empty, the incentives too few. *In, out, in, out… breathe, breathe, breathe.*

Feeling a second squeeze from Jenny, and then the arm of her friend reaching around her, Sofia nodded.

'Sofia, Jack is *missing*, presumed dead. *Presumed* dead. Nothing is absolute here. Miracles do happen, you know. He could well be tucked away on Crete, biding his time until the opportunity to escape arises.' Jenny's fingers gripped Sofia's arm as if they might squeeze a sense of hope into her.

'That's right, Mrs Tomlinson! You mustn't lose faith. Our lists are constantly being revised. As yet, your husband is listed as missing.'

The words came from the Private Haslow, and the captain echoed his agreement, though did not conceal the flatness in his tone.

Sofia shook her head and when she replied, her voice was both firm and resigned.

'No. He is gone. I feel it. You said the list of prisoners has been updated a number of times, so we know he is not in the hands of the Germans. It has been ten months since the Germans took Crete, and now they control the island. How could he possibly survive there, without weapons or food or shelter?'

'I don't know, Sofia. It wouldn't be easy, but I say, don't stop hoping.' The waver in Jenny's voice made Sofia wonder if she truly believed Jack might be alive.

But clinging to an unlikely thread of hope was futile. Why would Jack survive against the odds, when no one else had? These days, she chose to be a realist. Her work as a nurse had confirmed that to survive in this world, you had to face the facts, accept the hand you were dealt and make the best of it. To cling to dreams only led to disappointment.

Jenny held Sofia's hand as they made their way back to Cairo, and neither spoke.

CHAPTER 42

*G*rieving the loss of Jack took a heavy toll on Sofia, but somehow, she survived with her sanity intact. It was the third time she'd lost him: the first time was when, following Scotty's death, sick with grief, she'd chosen to leave Jack rather than inflict the curse of her love on him. The second time had been after the birth of Andreanna, when she'd emerged from the depths of her illness to the realization that the life she'd had with a caring husband and a beautiful child, was gone. This time, losing Jack did not induce the tormented heartbreak of the first two occasions, but instead led Sofia into a deep depression, which was no easier to bear.

For almost two weeks, she barely spoke. She rose from her bed, completed her shifts on the wards, and then, exhausted from the effort, returned to her cabin. There she lay down and, assisted by the gentle lull of water lapping the houseboat's sides, she easily succumbed to the refuge offered by sleep.

At Jenny's insistence, she joined the other nurses for dinner, but the loveliness of the houseboat, the beauty of the Nile, the grandeur of the hospital, the richness of the bazaars and the energized chat of her companions was lost on her.

For all of her silence, Sofia's thoughts were in constant turmoil. A shattered twist of disconnected thoughts, memories, visions and plans shimmered across her mind the way light danced off the surface of the Nile as the sun sank over the horizon. Memories of the fire, Jack's anguished expression, the tiny coffin at the front of the church, Jack finding comfort in the arms of Margaret returned to haunt her. There were new images, too, collages her mind created from her recollections of a thousand wounds in the soldiers she'd nursed: critical head injuries, protruding bones, shattered limbs. But for each of them, the face was Jack's.

By the third week, Sofia managed an appearance of normality. *Get up, breathe, move.* Go to work, follow instructions, speak to the patients. *Play the game*, as Louis would say. It wasn't so hard, she discovered, and she marvelled at her body's capacity to respond to the ebb and flow of routines, how she could arrange her face to look calm, force her voice to speak without quavering—even adopt a pleasant tone, make a joke, crack a smile.

But Sofia knew degrees of her illness had returned, that her mind was out of sync with her body. When she spoke, her voice sounded disconnected from her soul. It was as though a puppet master had taken possession of her and was guiding her arms and legs through the motions demanded of her—washing patients, tending to their dressings, assisting them to drink their cups of tea—while Sofia, the real Sofia, watched from a place far away.

Sanity was a fragile thing, and it made Sofia think about those around her. If she was able to put on a show of being normal, how many others around her were playing the same game? What was normal? Was anyone normal?

She became drawn to those patients who did not play the game, those who could not even try to pretend they were normal. Men whose minds were utterly broken, and they'd speak disconnected words, or sob uncontrollably, or see things that were invisible to others. These were the men Marcus hoped to understand better, Sofia realized, and was thankful he cared.

And as Sofia spent more time with those men with head and brain injuries, with the psychological traumas which couldn't be seen, her work became interesting to her. Waking up each day, a sense of purpose returned to Sofia. In having purpose, her mind reconnected to her body, and her thoughts became cohesive. No longer did Sofia have to remind herself to breathe.

Sofia's interest in nursing patients with brain trauma was recognised for when a Mobile Neurosurgical Unit dedicated to the care of head injuries in the field was posted to the Scottish General Hospital, she was assigned to work with them.

The unit was led by a vibrant young doctor, Kenneth Eden, barely thirty years old. A Londoner, he was inspired by an Australian, a Doctor Hugh Cairns, who in turn had been inspired by the work of Doctor Harry Cushing, a remarkable surgeon who'd treated brain injured soldiers during the Great War. Three decades earlier, Doctor Cushing had insisted that of all injuries inflicted in battle, those which affected the brain must be given immediate treatment.

A man of ideas, Hugh Cairns had taken Harry Cushing's theories to the British Army when war erupted, insisting on the life-saving potential of specialised surgical units manned by surgeons experienced at opening the cranium, separating the meninges from the soft grey matter, and using fine scalpels and tweezers to remove shrapnel and bullets within hours of the injury occurring. A year earlier, Cairns' ambitions had become a reality; half a dozen Mobile Neurosurgical Units had been created, including the one Sofia had been asked to join, though teething problems still needed to be addressed before they returned to the field.

Everything about the idea of brain surgery being performed on the battlefield thrilled Sofia. How wonderful it would have been if such a unit had operated at the General Hospitals out in the desert! Of all the casualties which arrived at the CCS, the head injuries were always most dreadful and often delegated to the *critical* group, deemed unlikely to survive and thus left untreated. And those who did survive had to deal with tremendous deformities to their faces or scalps, as well as the effects of brain swelling and lacerations, from blindness, to dullness of the mind, to paralysis.

Sofia found the work on the neurosurgical ward intense. Dr Eden, or Kenneth, as he encouraged everyone to call him, fanatically championed the administration of penicillin, certain the new wonder drug to fight infections, in combination with early treatment, was critical for saving lives.

To this end, he was exacting about the data they must collect to monitor the effectiveness of penicillin, and he trained the nurses on the Neurosurgical Ward to observe and record everything. Sofia became adept at noticing symptoms like slurred speech, loss of strength in a patient's hands, weakness in legs, restlessness, tingling and visual disturbances.

She was passionate about her work and thrived on the increased responsibility she was given. Each day, her patients expressed their pleasure at having her assigned to them, which surprised Sofia, because she knew she pushed them much harder than the other nurses.

'Oh, no! We've got the merciless matron again,' they'd say, when she appeared at the bedside, but she knew they were joking.

Often they would ask her to write letters home for them, and she'd sit by their beds, scribing the words they dictated to parents, brothers and girlfriends. One young fellow, Jimmy, had terrible facial injuries, and feared his fiancé's reaction. Sofia was fastidious as she cleaned his wound and each week, recorded words of his love for Mary, and mailed his letters. Jimmy was looking forward to December, when he planned to send her a beautiful silver compact he knew she'd love.

Sadly, it proved that the deep laceration to his face was the least of Jimmy's worries—symptoms of a brain abscess appeared. The afternoon, before he went to surgery Jimmy again asked Sofia to write to Mary for him. She tried to hold back her tears as, through slurred speech, he dictated words of love. Entreating him to rest, Sofia promised she'd write a special message on his behalf at the end of her shift. But Jimmy did not survive the surgery and according to hospital policy, his belongings must be sent to his parents.

Sofia was beside herself with worry, imagining a dozen scenarios in which the compact Jimmy had bought for Mary failed to reach her. She discussed her concerns with the Charge Sister, Amy Dunnett, who said break the rules: for Sofia to take the letter and the compact and send them directly to Jimmy's girlfriend.

In mid-November, Sofia arrived on duty to learn her MNSU team had been given clearance to enter the field. Doctor Eden's unit, as well as five new MNSUs would be attached to various infantry battalions. Each would have their own team of doctors, anaesthetists, QAs and orderlies. Additionally, they would be provided with an electricity generator, tentage and water supply, operating tables, suction apparatus, diathermy and illumination. The QAs were to be recruited from the neurosurgical ward at the 15th Scottish Hospital; they would, of course, be registered nurses.

As excited as everyone was to see the MNSUs join the field hospitals where they would have the most effect, Sofia was disappointed by the realization that it was time for her to return to the general wards. It didn't seem fair. For of all the nurses, whether QAs, Reservists or VADs, who worked with the neurosurgical team, she was sure no one was more dedicated to caring for the men with head injuries than herself.

Thankfully, her diligence had not gone unnoticed. When Kenneth Eden learned Sofia would not be joining the team, he asked her why. And when she told him it was because she lacked the training of a registered nurse and thus wasn't qualified to join the MNSUs on the field, he'd shaken his head and immediately approached Sister

Dunnett. The Charge Nurse had laughed when she'd described to Sofia how Kenneth had strode into her office and insisted Sofia remain with his unit. 'I would take Nurse Tomlinson before I'd take a dozen QAs,' he'd said, and on the spot created a position on his own team for her. Henceforth, Sofia would join the No. 4 Mobile Neurosurgical Unit, which was attached to the 8th Army.

CHAPTER 43

*R*eturning to the fringes of battlefields, first in Tunisia then Souk Ahras and Thibar, Sofia felt as though she had joined a travelling circus, albeit one whose troupe shared extraordinary skills. Kenneth had not been happy with the small tents he'd been provided with. Rather than complain, he'd found an 11-tonne Italian motor coach and had it converted into an operating theatre, and then added two huge, colourful tents, distinguished by bold Indian patterns, which they used as reception wards.

Initially, their Mobile Neurosurgical Unit was set up alongside the 71st General Hospital, where they diverted men with head wounds from the CCS to their own operating theatre. Sofia's task was to work alongside Joe, a neurosurgeon who assessed the men at the CCS, she recording notes while he prodded wounds, gazed into eyes and checked reflexes before selecting those to be taken into the motor coach for surgery. When she was not working with Joe, Sofia worked with the post-surgical care nurses, monitoring their patients and ensuring the men's conditions were stabilized before transferring them to Cairo or Alexandria. She also helped to collate the data they'd gathered measuring the effects of penicillin.

Nonetheless, for all of their innovations, Kenneth still wasn't satisfied that the unit was working as effectively as it could, and he made a decision to split it into forward and rear sections. The forward section would move even closer to the battlefield, while the rear section would remain well behind the lines. Sofia was thrilled to learn he wanted to keep her on the forward section, where she assisted in both assessing the head wounds and working in the van's operating theatre.

Thanks to their tireless work, many more young men survived their wounds, aided by swift treatment—always within 72 hours—and the penicillin. Abscesses, the complications of infection, and necessity for further operations were all significantly reduced.

In early July, the team returned to Cairo for a two-week spell before their next posting, which was to be in Italy. Sofia knew Jenny had long returned to England, but looked forward to the opportunity to catch up with Paula and the other girls who still worked on the medical ward at the Scottish General Hospital. On her second day in Cairo, Sofia was thrilled to discover a pile of letters being held for her in the hospital's mail room. Two were from Elizabeth: a belated Christmas greeting which included two photos of Andreanna—the first of her sitting on the back of a horse, a second of her feeding ducks alongside a large pond. The second offered more news of events at Talonsgate but in it Elizabeth revealed her fears for Joseph; news was the fighting in Italy was particularly intense, and she hadn't heard anything from him in weeks.

The other letters were from Marcus, and unintentionally Sofia opened the latest first, a letter which had only been written a week earlier. She held her breath as she read the words on the page before her.

. . .

Dearest Sofia,

I need to tell you we've had bad news at home. Joseph took a bullet wound to his spine in Italy, which, as you may imagine, is very serious. At present he is in the Queen Alexander Military Hospital in London awaiting surgery. He is receiving the best of care, but we fear he faces a lengthy rehabilitation, and I don't like to say it, but his mobility might be affected in the long term.

Elizabeth, of course, is staying in London with him. Fortunately, Andreanna is young enough to be oblivious to the ghastly toll this war is taking, and she is happily ensconced in the household of Mrs O'Neil, who will care for her for as long as is necessary. Given the circumstances, I have taken leave and am back at Talonsgate, doing what I can to manage the property and to support Elizabeth and Joseph.

Please let me know how you are. It's times like this when it helps to be reassured the people you care for most in the world are well. It is far too long since we last spoke.

My love, always,

Marcus

Good grief! Poor Joseph. Poor Elizabeth. Such terrible news. It wasn't hard for Sofia to imagine the wound he had sustained. She'd seen enough gunshot injuries, including those which interfered with the fragile spinal tissue, to know the devastating damage bullets caused.

She needed to go to Talonsgate and offer what support she could. Elizabeth and Marcus had been wonderful to her; she needed to repay the same kindness to them, in their hour of need.

Sofia had never asked for leave in her whole time in the Middle-East, and her request for one month's was granted without question.

CHAPTER 44

'hank God you are safe!' Marcus hugged her tightly, and the moistness in his eyes revealed to Sofia how glad he was to see her.

He looked handsome in uniform; his shoulders seemed squarer than she remembered, and he appeared to be taller, but of course, he hadn't grown. Rather, his body was leaner, his features weather worn—he now bore the familiar hardened look she observed on many of the soldiers after hours spent training outdoors. Marcus' mood was both elated and sombre, and Sofia felt conflicted in her response. This was the thing about war. The most dreadful situations often became the cause of reunions, and the sheer joy of laying eyes upon friends and family was combined with tears for lost homes, shattered lives and far too often, the deaths of loved ones.

At least Sofia's reunion with Marcus at London Station was not overshadowed by death. Nonetheless, Joseph's condition was both complicated and extremely serious, and his future health very uncertain. Without letting go of her hand, Marcus explained how the Gewehr's bullet had entered the left side of Joseph's abdomen, passed through his stomach, and then lodged against one of his lumber vertebrae. The stomach wound alone had been truly dreadful; infection had spread through his abdominal cavity, causing peritonitis, a condition Sofia knew was often fatal. Treatment for it, by necessity, had taken precedence over the bullet now resting in Joseph's spinal column. To keep it from shifting dangerously he'd lain flat on his back for the last three weeks.

Thankfully, they'd received the news that the infection was now under control; Joseph's condition was stable enough to withstand surgery and he would go to the operating theatre any day. Sofia was glad to hear Joseph had received huge doses of penicillin, sure the wonder drug was responsible for saving his life.

Marcus led her out of the station and to its busy carpark, where he placed her bag in the back of his Austin.

'Are you up for a visit to the hospital now, Sofia? Elizabeth and Joseph are dying to see you.'

'Yes, please,' Sofia replied. She'd always liked Joseph, not only because he was an extraordinarily kind man who made Elizabeth happy, but also because he was the sort of man who'd accepted the role of father to a tiny baby girl who wasn't even his own.

Arriving at the ward, Sofia embraced Elizabeth. She had lost weight since Sofia had left, two years earlier, and the lines on her forehead and dark shadows beneath her eyes revealed the depths of her fatigue. Still, her smile was broad and her welcome cheerful.

'Sofia! How wonderful to see you! Thank you so much for coming! I would much rather have you back to celebrate the end of the war, but so be it...' Elizabeth faltered, a helpless look replacing her bravado, and Sofia patted her shoulder.

'How is Joseph? Marcus tells me he will go to theatre any day now. That is wonderful news, don't you think?' Sofia's questioning tone was intentional. As when she spoke with her patients, she believed it was far better to resort to practicalities than emotions. The upcoming spinal surgery offered as much risk as it did reward, and she could well imagine the anxiety Elizabeth must be feeling. There was little alternative, though; Joseph could not remain immobilized on his back forever.

'Up and down. Glad to be alive one minute, cursing himself for being foolish enough to walk into a bullet the next. He feels terrible for me and Andreanna. Blames himself for letting us down, the silly man!'

Entering the surgical ward, an enormous room with perhaps twenty beds lining each side, Sofia realised she'd forgotten the sturdy feel of hospitals built with bricks and mortar; the luxury of simple things like spaciousness and cleanliness, compared to the dusty conditions of the Indian tents and the operating theatre created in the bus that had been her workspace for the past six months.

Yet despite that, as she followed Elizabeth and Marcus through the ward, Sofia noticed the trays of coffee and biscuits sitting beyond the reach of their intended patients, the soiled bed jackets needing changing, the pillows which could do with plumping and the blankets needing to be rearranged. As conscious as she was of these lapses in care, Sofia held no judgement. This was a front-line hospital in a battle-besieged city, and despite the demands to present a picture of order for the weekly Captain's rounds, sometimes it was all the nurses could do to keep up with the men's pain relief and ensure their wound dressings were clean.

Joseph's bed was in a side room, one of three reserved for more serious cases. Its door was closed, and through a small window, Sofia saw no less than three nurses in attendance, one at the head of the bed, two along the side. They carefully rolled Joseph over and rubbed his back.

'Poor Joseph!' Elizabeth whispered. 'He hates this!' She explained how every two hours, day and night, the nurses turned him, rubbing his bony shoulders and lower spine, his heels and even the back of his skull, which lay upon the pillowless bed.

'Truly, Elizabeth, for as awful as it is, the consequences of not moving him are far worse!' Sofia had seen bedsores more than once, the awful ulcers which ate into the flesh of those bony prominences that rubbed against the bedsheets when men could not move themselves. Indeed, it was a point of pride amongst the nurses Sofia worked with that the men in their care did not develop bedsores. They all knew the pattern: first the skin developed red patches, which then became white, then black. From that point, quickly, the surface tissue broke down, exposing the flesh below. In a matter of weeks, the ulcer could eat through to the bone.

'I know, and so does Joseph. Really, they are marvellous here, the way they care for him. I don't know how they do it. I don't know how you do it, Sofia! I've often thought of you as I watch them at work.'

Finally, they were allowed to enter the room, although Sofia noted the frown of the senior nurse when she realized there were three visitors. Hospitals and their rules! It was a decidedly unique experience to be a part of an anxious family, worrying about a loved one, rather than the bossy nurse who was protective of her patient's need for rest.

Joseph smiled weakly as she approached the bed and she took his hand, squeezing it.

'Joseph, I am so sorry! I can't say it is good to see you like this— however, you are looking mighty well, given the circumstances!'

'I decided I'd had enough of the battlefields. The company of men becomes monotonous after a while. I thought I'd go for a little downtime, that lying in a nice clean bed with sweet nurses to wait on me hand and foot would be a pleasant change.'

They laughed at Joseph's attempt to make light of his circumstances. He turned to Elizabeth. 'Sister Donaldson just told me the surgeon's putting me on his list for tomorrow. He wants me first... She expects they'll take me down to the theatre just after seven-thirty AM.'

'Joseph, that's wonderful. It's been a long time coming! At last! Soon he'll have you out of bed and gadding about.'

He smiled wryly. 'Perhaps he might. As long as they don't carry me out of here in a pine box, I don't care.'

'It won't be in a pine box. Don't be silly. This is a great step forward!' Elizabeth's sharp rebuke revealed the stress she was feeling.

Sofia nodded in agreement. Under the circumstances, what else could they say? She felt sad to see Joseph in such a dreadful situation and sorry for the anxiety Elizabeth suffered. From her work in the neurosurgical ward, she knew the outcome of the surgery could not be assured, and even if successful, Joseph might require months, if not years, of rehabilitation.

After fifteen minutes, Sofia could see Joseph was tiring, and although they hid it well, both he and Elizabeth were emotional about the prospect of the pending surgery.

She and Marcus bid the couple farewell. He took Sofia's arm as they left the ward.

'You must be wrung out. Would you like to stop for coffee, or shall we head home?'

Without hesitation, Sofia suggested they go home to Talonsgate. It had been a long journey first on the ship and then on the train to London. What she saw as they drove through the streets leaving London shocked her. Of course, she knew of the Blitz. It had begun even before she'd left for the Middle East; indeed, at Shenley she'd nursed dozens of casualties from the bombs which had fallen over London. But as Marcus steered his vehicle, taking detours where none had been required before she'd left, Sofia could not believe the changes to the once vibrant city. Whole streets were lined by buildings which were no more than heaps of rubble, and everywhere she looked, boards covered windows where glass had been shattered.

She was glad when they arrived at St Albans, pleased to see the town seemed much the same as when she'd left.

'Would you like us to collect Andreanna?' Marcus asked. 'Mrs O'Neil is happy to keep her, but of course, it's up to you.'

Sofia considered the options. It felt strange to be returning to the large, empty house with Marcus. What was he to her? Brother-like? Dear friend? Would-be boyfriend? A hopeful wartime lover? Andreanna might offer a buffer between them, a point of interest beyond themselves, easing the awkwardness.

Sofia chided herself. How awful of her, to be thinking of the little girl in terms of usefulness to herself. Was that all she thought of the child who was her own flesh and blood? Second, why on earth did she think she needed a buffer? Marcus had always been an utter gentleman, and for as many times as Sofia knew he'd have liked to, he'd never pushed for their relationship to be anything more than she wanted. Her thoughts turned to Andreanna, and Sofia decided she did want to see her. It was the least she could do to ensure the child was safe, well, and happy.

'How about for today we just call in and say hello? I am sure Andreanna is best left where she is, but I would like to see her just the same.'

Sofia felt the pace of her heartbeat escalate as Marcus pulled up outside a neat two-storey red brick home with dormer windows overlooking the street. It suddenly seemed strange to be paying a visit to the child she'd given birth to, and she wondered how she should greet her. There were a dozen or more children ranging from very young to about twelve years old, all playing together on the grassy verge in front of the house. They chased a hoop, keeping it upright with a short stick. How fortunate it was for them to be enjoying each other's company, finding pleasure in something so simple as a hoop and stick, despite the war raging across the globe. Andreanna was easy to spot. Perhaps the youngest of the children, she was wearing a red dress, small black leather boots, and a blue jacket. She squealed with excitement when one of the older girls picked her up and swung her around. Sofia's eyes met Marcus' and they smiled at the sound of her giggles.

As they approached the children, silence fell, and then the oldest child, who was still holding Andreanna's hand, spoke.

'Andreanna, it's your mumma!'

Sofia was as surprised by the words as Andreanna appeared to be.

'No, that's not Mumma,' she said. 'It's Uncle Marcus and a lady. Hello, Uncle Marcus! Did you see Mumma today?'

A lady! The impersonal phrase sounded odd, but of course, Andreanna was quite right. Sofia was merely "a lady" to her. A lady she barely remembered. One who'd given birth to her, but who'd relinquished her care to others. Sofia shook away the thought that she'd abandoned her child. Elizabeth and Joseph were far more suitable parents for Andreanna than herself. When they'd chosen to raise her, nobody could have expected the impacts of the drawn-out war, or that Joseph would be injured.

At that moment, Mrs O'Neil came outside and greeted them. She invited them into the house to join her for a cup of tea, but they declined. It was getting late, and Marcus needed to get home to feed the horses before sunset. They did have a brief chat on the doorstep while the children continued their game. Of the dozen children playing in the yard, four belonged to Mrs O'Neil, one of course was Andreanna, four were from a neighbouring house, and the other three children were siblings; some of the six thousand child refugees who'd been sent to St Albans two years earlier.

'They are sweet little mites,' she told Sofia. 'Never caused a moment's trouble.' She explained how when they'd first arrived, they'd been so nervous they'd barely spoken until her own wild things had livened them up. Now they gave as good as they got in the noisy, jolly family. Mrs O'Neil looked pleased, and Sofia could see she was a woman with a big heart, happy to support her country in the best way she knew how: by opening up her home to a few frightened children forced to live apart from their parents while enemy bombs blasted their neighbourhood.

Changing the subject, Mrs O'Neil explained how all the children loved having Andreanna at the house—spoilt her rotten, indeed. If they weren't carrying her around, they were giving her biscuits or apples, or rummaging through their toy boxes for books and dolls to entertain her.

As Mrs O'Neil spoke, she directed frequent glances towards Sofia, ones that made her uncomfortable. Sofia knew Mrs O'Neil was aware that she was the natural mother of Andreanna, and yet she'd volunteered for the war effort and been absent for over two years. She would also know Andreanna called Elizabeth Mumma, and Sofia made no move to correct her. All this must seem terribly unnatural to the maternal woman.

Their conversation turned to Joseph's health, and Mrs O'Neil tutted when she learned of the surgery which would take place the following day. 'Dearie me. Poor Elizabeth! She's going to have a lot on her hands when he's discharged, isn't she?'

On the drive to Talonsgate, Sofia's mind buzzed with thoughts about the future. About Joseph, and the dreadful, but very real possibility he may never walk again, and how it would affect the arrangements at the house. It didn't seem right to speak of such concerns at present, but Joseph's surgery could prove life-changing.

Marcus removed Sofia's suitcase from the Austin and set it on the back doorstep before opening the kitchen door and encouraging her to settle herself while he parked the car in the garage. Every passing second seemed loaded with anticipation, and Sofia analysed the feelings of awkwardness that made her stomach flutter.

Unlike many women she knew, who found men endlessly mysterious and fascinating, for most of Sofia's life she'd been surrounded by males. Her childhood in the company of a brother and father, the time she'd shared with Jack and Andres in Malaga, followed by years in the masculine world shaped by Justus Jorgensen. And then, during this war, although she lived in close quarters with the army nurses, much of their conversation and purpose had been about the men around them: the doctors they worked with, the soldiers they cared for, the men they were attracted to, or for some, the fiancés and boyfriends they missed and whose letters they impatiently awaited.

If the discomfort she felt wasn't about being alone with Marcus as a man, it was likely caused by the fact she was not used to being alone with anyone. She'd invariably lived her life in spaces shared by others. She chuckled, considering how, even in the womb, she'd been denied nine months of solitude, and then in all instances since, from her family, to the community at Montsalvat, to the women's refuge, to Napsbury, and virtually everywhere she'd ever gone, she'd lived in one form of community or another.

Now, here at Talonsgate, utterly alone with Marcus in the large house on the extensive acreage without Elizabeth and Joseph's presence in the lodge, Sofia felt unusually self-conscious. How could two people fill such a space so even their tiniest actions were noticeable, their voices sounding loud, their movements clumsy, their hands unsure of where to be?

An hour later, the wine Marcus poured to accompany the roast beef he'd prepared for their dinner helped Sofia to relax, as did the small glass of port he offered her when they left the dining table and moved to the lounge.

All the while, as they discussed first Joseph and their concerns for his future, then Andreanna and how happy she seemed in view of the change of circumstances, next the awfulness of the war, and of course, their own experiences—Marcus' frustration at being retained in England before being posted to Scotland, and Sofia's work in the Middle East—she could not forget for a moment that he was a man bearing a deep interest, no, a deep attraction for her.

Sofia confided in Marcus about the discovery she'd made in Cairo. Her tears flowed as she described how she'd found the ink portrait of the child and instinctively known it was drawn by Jack. How she'd done everything she could to locate him, only to learn he'd been missing since the battle in Crete.

Marcus squeezed Sofia's hand as she spoke, his face grave, sad for all that she'd lost. She sensed the change in his tone as he manoeuvred the topic from the awful experiences of the present to what their lives might be like after the war. He was clever, she mused, as she settled into the ebb and flow of his words; he was a far superior conversationalist to herself, but then he was a psychologist!

Sofia was not surprised when Marcus' hand reached towards hers and he laced their fingers together. She held her breath, preparing to extricate herself, suspecting he was about to speak words she wasn't ready to hear.

'Sofia, I know you are not yet ready to think about your future, but can I please just say one thing?'

She nodded, unsure of what else she could do.

'I love you. I think I have since the first time I saw you sitting alone at the dining table on the *Strathnaver*.'

She winced. Love! Her family had loved her, and look at what had happened to them. Scotty! He'd loved his mummy with every ounce of his being, as she had loved him! Jack had loved her, and even though she'd tried to move far away, still he'd met an untimely death.

'Marcus, everyone who ever loved me has died. Do you know that? Everyone!'

'No, Sofia. We have discussed this before and it is nonsense. The world isn't like that. People are not cursed. They don't bring bad luck to others. Life just happens. Some people have lots of good luck, other's get more than their share of bad luck, but it doesn't mean people are cursed. My heart breaks to think of all you have been through. But don't you think it's time you allowed something good to come back into your life? Please!'

Marcus settled back into his chair, and held his hands up, as if to stem her reply. 'You don't have to answer now. I am hoping you might consider what I'm suggesting… *imagine* a life here at Talonsgate with me. Obviously, with Joseph's injuries, Elizabeth is going to have quite a job on her hands. We could all live together, as we did before the war. Only this time, Andreanna could live here, in the house, with you and me. She is very young. She'd adapt well, and she has always known you are her mother. We've never kept that from her.'

Sofia absorbed his suggestion. Certainly, Marcus was a good man. A nice, attractive man who'd be a dedicated husband and a wonderful father to Andreanna. And unquestionably, he loved both herself and the child.

She shifted uncomfortably, unsure of what to say, but before she could speak, Marcus intervened.

'Again, Sofia, I don't want you to answer now. I'm just asking you to spend the next few months imagining how lovely our life might be together—to allow the idea of a future with me to grow on you.'

Perhaps it was the wine which relaxed Sofia's resolve, or maybe it was the madness of a world now quaking in uncertainty, or the stirrings of maternal responsibility towards the baby she'd borne, whose life was about to change. Sofia didn't know why, but she nodded. There was nothing to lose by agreeing to at least think about a life where she, Marcus, Elizabeth, and Joseph lived together in harmony, to imagine raising Andreanna in the world she loved, surrounded by people who adored her. To imagine being married to Marcus. Yes—Sofia promised she'd think about it.

CHAPTER 45

*A*lthough Marcus' suggestion was not mentioned again, Sofia noticed a distinct shift in their relationship: a deeper sense of closeness, perhaps a foreshadow of the companionable life they may one day share. And as they travelled into London to visit Joseph, discussed the requirements for the stable with Elizabeth, and took Andreanna home to Talonsgate every few days, the promise she'd made to Marcus was never far from Sofia's mind.

The surgery proceeded without complication, and four days later, Sofia and Marcus took Andreanna into London with them. The child had been fretting for Elizabeth and worrying about Joseph, and they all thought a visit would do everybody good. The hospital agreed to bend their rules which normally forbade entry to children and allowed a fifteen-minute visit. It was hard to say who was more thrilled, Joseph or Andreanna.

When Sofia, Marcus and Andreanna arrived at the hospital, Elizabeth was waiting for them in the foyer. At the sight of the little girl, she flung her arms open and with a squeal of excitement, gathered her up and whirled her about. Sofia did not know whether she felt pleased at the sight of their uncomplicated relationship, or envious for what had been lost to her. As they rode the elevator to the third floor where Joseph awaited them, Elizabeth provided a quick update on their news. She and Joseph had been told his surgeon was expected on the ward immediately after lunch. Apparently, he wanted to perform some tests on Joseph and discuss the outcomes of the surgery.

When they arrived at Joseph's bedside, he was far more interested in teasing Andreanna than discussing himself, and he insisted Elizabeth prop her up on the bed beside him.

'By golly! Who is this young lady with the pretty ponytail?' he exclaimed, reaching out to ruffle her hair.

'Andreanna!' replied the child.

'No, it isn't. My Andreanna has a baby lisp and carries a ragdoll called Popkin.'

'I'm Andreanna!'

'You can't be! Here, come a little closer and let me get a good look at you... ahh... You smell like Andreanna.... Let me see... Do you giggle like Andreanna?' He began tickling her and their laughter filled the room.

Too quickly, a nurse arrived at the door of Joseph's room. It was time for Andreanna to leave.

'Marcus, do you think you might be able to stick around for the meeting?' Joseph asked. 'It shouldn't take long.'

His words seemed pointed, and Sofia gleaned from his request Joseph was hoping Marcus would be there to support Elizabeth while the surgeon delivered his findings, lest the news be bad.

'Certainly, Joseph. Of course I will.'

'Andreanna and I will go down to the foyer. We can wait for you there,' Sofia offered, but Elizabeth shook her head.

'The surgeon is not expected until about one; it's only eleven forty-five now. Why don't you slip Andreanna and Sofia into town, Marcus? It will only take you a few minutes to drive them to Brampton Road. Is that okay, Sofia? You could have a walk around the shops, and perhaps have lunch at Harrods—Andreanna would love that. And then, if the surgeon is delayed, it means you won't be left trying to entertain Andreanna in the hospital foyer for hours on end.'

It was a sensible idea, although Sofia had to admit an hour spent walking around London's streets with a tiny girl was no less intimidating than spending an hour with her in the foyer.

The look of shy appeal Andreanna directed towards Elizabeth when she heard the plan revealed she also felt uncomfortable. Feeling a stab of remorse, Sofia resolved to make the next few hours as pleasant as she could for the little girl.

The outing was more enjoyable than perhaps either of them expected. By nature, Andreanna was a chatty little girl, and the liveliness of the London streets fascinated her. She asked dozens of questions. Many of the shop windows were covered in boards, a response, of course, to the bombing, but their doors were open; weaving in and out of the shops and looking at the goods they offered proved fun for both of them. When they came to the toy department of Harrods, Sofia led Andreanna to the shelves. A little toy, perhaps a jigsaw puzzle or a doll, might be a nice gift during this time of upheaval in the child's life.

Half an hour later, they lined up at the cafeteria and purchased tea, scones, and a milkshake for Andreanna. The tables were all but full; however, Sofia found a quiet spot in the corner. No sooner had they settled into their seats than a small fair lady with an Irish accent, wearing the blue uniform of a VAD, approached them.

'Miss, it's terribly busy here. Would you mind if I gave my feet a rest and joined you?'

'No, that will be fine,' Sofia replied, glancing at Andreanna, who was now playing with the baby doll they'd purchased. Pulling the child's seat closer to herself, she made room for the woman, who certainly looked harried. Sofia sympathised. She understood how tired one's legs became, dashing back and forth on busy hospital wards. She wondered if the nurse worked over at the Queen Alexandra Military

Hospital, where Marcus and Elizabeth were waiting with Joseph to hear the specialist's report.

'You are a VAD? Where are you working?'

'Orpington Hospital; it was set up here by the Canadians. Really, though, I'm just waiting for the call up for an overseas appointment. It could come any day now, they tell me.'

'I don't suppose you know where they will send you? No, how silly of me. You won't know where you are going until the ship is all but departed. And with the war extended to the Pacific, you could be sent anywhere.'

'You are familiar with the overseas postings? Are you a nurse, too? But you're not British, are you?'

Sofia laughed at the run of questions. 'No, I am Spanish. Sofia Tomlinson, by the way. I'm a VAD like yourself. And yes, I am familiar with overseas service. I have been working in the Middle East for the past two years. Trust me, VAD or registered nurse, for most postings, it makes no difference. If a job needs to be done, any hands will do!'

'How wonderful! I can't wait to be sent off—I'm willing to go anywhere! The Middle East, the Pacific, Europe—I don't mind at all. So glad to meet you, Sofia! My name is Genevieve! Nuss Winters, if you please!'

Sofia smiled her understanding. If you weren't Siss to the patients, you were Nuss. And if you were male, you were invariably called Doc!

'I understand just how you feel. It is satisfying to know you are doing something important, helping the wounded men who are so far from home. Mind you, it can be quite awful too. It's heart rending to see so many young men being brought off the battlefields, their lives hanging in the balance, and the wounds are like nothing those we deal with in the wards. In some locations, you can hear the gunfire and feel the ground shaking when the bombs explode. Your heart is in your mouth, waiting for the casualties to arrive and hoping you can save them all.'

'But it must be wonderful to be there and offer comfort, to see their pain relieved and treatment applied so quickly!'

Returning Genevieve's gaze, Sofia recognised the call to serve the soldiers she'd felt all those months ago, when she'd awaited an appointment close to the front line of the battlefields, convinced that by being there, she could make a difference. Had she? Yes, Sofia believed. Many a time she'd argued for a soldier to be placed on the *serious* list, where they'd be treated, rather than *critical*. Furthermore, her relentless expectation that her patients should sit and stand and walk and eat, despite their cries of resistance, had pushed them along, and by achieving these milestones they'd gained their best chance for recovery.

But Sofia's experience had also been confronting. The proximity to the battlefields exposed her to the worst of the injuries. She'd listened to men screaming in agony, with horrendous wounds. To men's stertorous breathing that fell silent, and when she'd checked them, she'd found glazed, lifeless eyes staring into an unfathomable distance. Perhaps the worst of serving in the field hospitals was seeing what every nurse with a brother or boyfriend or fiancée who served in the military experienced as dreadfully injured men arrived. These nurses were wonderful at work, efficient and caring, giving their very best to ensure their patients would survive, but when night came and they thought of their loved ones, their tears fell and they divulged their deepest fears. Would their Johnny or Frank or Henry get off lightly, or would he be one of the unlucky ones delegated to a makeshift morgue? Sofia understood how they felt; every time she looked into the eyes of a young man robbed of his life by the war, she'd thought of Jack, and her heart broke with the tragedy of it all.

None of this was a conversation for this young woman though, and Sofia did her best to answer Genevieve's questions about the conditions at the desert hospital, and how much luggage she should take, and applauded her decision to go overseas.

❦

An hour later, when Marcus joined them at Harrods, Sofia saw from his grim expression that the news from the specialist had not been good. They said little as he led them to the car, but on the drive home, with the sleeping child resting against Sofia, the doll tucked under her tiny arm, Marcus updated her on the surgeon's report. Apparently, the bullet lodged in Joseph's spine had torn through two vertebrae, shattering the fine bones encasing the delicate spinal column. Thus, the surgeon offered little hope Joseph would ever walk again, explaining how the damage to the spinal cord was extensive, news Joseph accepted with remarkable calm. From experience, Sofia guessed the surgeon's words had been anticipated. He'd likely prepared himself for the worst weeks earlier. Many a time, she had discovered her patients knew, without being told, the state of their body: of the leg that was dead to them or the bandages encasing eyes whose vision would never return. Often the soldiers were incredibly stoic about their circumstances, and that Joseph's concerns were for Elizabeth rather than himself did not surprise Sofia.

Marcus told her how after the surgeon left, he, Elizabeth and Joseph had talked for more than an hour, and it had been as if Joseph was reassuring them rather than the other way around. The surgeon had recommended Joseph be transferred to Queen Mary's Hospital for rehabilitation as soon as it could be arranged. There, he'd be fitted with a wheelchair, which the surgeon was confident Joseph would adjust to very quickly. Marcus described how, although deeply dismayed, Elizabeth had taken the news well. Sofia nodded.

'They are both brave, Marcus. Joseph for her, and Elizabeth for him. They are fighters, and I have no doubt that together they will make the best of the situation.'

'Yes, but before Joseph comes home, there is much to be done. I am going to apply for a release from the army and return to my work as a psychiatrist. By doing that, I can live at Talonsgate and help to oversee the modifications that will be needed.'

～

During the final days of her leave, Sofia joined Elizabeth and Marcus in making a list of the adaptations for the lodge so Joseph could move about in the wheelchair. Elizabeth raised no argument when Sofia gave the kitchen a thorough clean and then vacuumed the entire lodge's floors. As she worked, Sofia discovered dozens of drawings tacked to Elizabeth's kitchen wall, along the hallway, and in Andreanna's bedroom. She was impressed by the child's instinct for blending blues and greens when drawing water in a lake, and looking closely, she wondered if she was seeing a duck tucked against a patch of reeds? Was Sofia simply deluded by a latent maternal pride, or was Andreanna showing signs of an artist in the making? As she examined each of the drawings, Sofia couldn't help thinking of the artistic family who was lost to her. How proud Jack would have been, seeing these pictures drawn by his daughter. Sofia inhaled deeply and wiped away the tears that sprang to her eyes.

Each morning, Marcus collected Andreanna and brought her home to Talonsgate for a few hours. As they worked, she played among them, or stood at the table in the kitchen chattering non-stop to Sofia and helping her to make batches of chorizos and croquetas. These would then be packed in a basket for her to take to Mrs O'Neil's house where they'd agreed was the best place for Andreanna to be until Joseph was home and settled.

In early October, Sofia travelled to the station with Marcus. Taking her suitcase in one hand, her hand in his other, he walked her to the platform. It was a sweet gesture, and that she permitted his overture of affection revealed the healing that had taken place within her since losing Scotty and hurting Jack so very badly.

However, Marcus was not at all happy with Sofia; for day's he'd tried to convince her to seek a posting in London, rather than join a group from the International Red Cross and embark on the dangerous journey through France to Italy where she'd once again endure the danger of the battlefields. But Sofia was committed to resuming work the Mobile Neuro-Surgical Unit team.

'Marcus, hundreds of young men—boys, really—are putting their lives on the line to resist the Germans. Don't you think they deserve the back up of sound medical treatment in a timely manner—especially men with head wounds,' she insisted.

'Yes, but Italy is a mess. Don't forget, it's where Joseph was injured.'

'All battlefields are a mess. But Italy has turned; its people are our friends now Mussolini is gone. Their new government has signed an agreement to support the Allies—they are as keen to see the Germans out of Italy as we are. We must help them.'

As if realizing he had no hope of dissuading Sofia from abandoning her duties to the MNSU, Marcus changed the subject. His voice was quiet as he turned her to him.

'You haven't forgotten what I asked you, Sofia? You will think about a life at Talonsgate? This is not a proposal, by the way—I'd prefer to think of it as a pre-proposal. You've been through a great deal, and as I said before, I don't want you to feel any pressure, but rather, be assured that you are not alone. At Talonsgate you have a home where people care very deeply about you.'

Sofia nodded. Marcus loved her, she had no doubts, and in many ways, marrying him would be easy. Did she love him? Not in the way she'd loved Jack. Marcus was kind, and their companionable closeness had increased over the last few weeks. But Sofia did not feel joy or excitement about their future, and knew they lacked the spontaneous smiles, the moments of silly laughter she and Jack had once shared. But then again, much had happened in her life to rob her of her natural joy. Not only was she burdened by the numerous losses in her life, but it was war time and the world was in pain. Perhaps nobody would ever really feel joy again.

In weighing up the circumstances, Sofia felt she owed it to Marcus to take his offer seriously. 'Yes, I will think about it. I promise you.'

He smiled, and she realised she'd been half wrong. For while she did not feel a sense of excitement for the future, the glow in his eyes and the tenderness with which he touched her face revealed his truth: Marcus felt joy. For all of his calm demeanour, he yearned for a time when they'd be together! Marcus adored her, and suddenly, the strength of his feelings terrified Sofia, and she needed some space from him. With fifteen minutes before the train was due to leave, she decided she'd make a dash for the ladies' restroom, which was situated close to the platform.

As Sofia rushed through the crowd, the sound of an Australian voice caught her attention. Glancing towards a fair-haired man speaking loudly and garrulously, Sofia was startled. It was Colin Colahan, the charming rascal who'd often arrived at Montsalvat with one woman or another clinging to his arm and a witty story on his lips. She'd always viewed Colin as a rogue, but a likable one nonetheless.

Bits and pieces of Colin's past came back to her: The cloud of suspicion which had hung over him when his girlfriend, Molly Dean, had been found murdered. His broken marriage which had produced a son, after which he'd turned his attention to Sue Vanderkelen. Sue had loved him deeply, but to her despair, Colin became besotted with a married Frenchwoman. Everyone had said her boys belonged to Colin rather than her husband. Yes, certainly Colin had been a rogue, but nonetheless, he'd always been very friendly to Sofia. What's more, to his credit, he'd been especially fond of Lil and had often argued with Justus about seeking the correct treatment for her malady.

Perhaps he felt her gaze upon him, for he looked up, and when his eyes met hers, they widened in recognition. 'Sofia! Fancy seeing you here! What a surprise! Are you living in London? Is Jack with you? And what is this uniform you're wearing? Surely you are not a nurse?'

Colin's exuberance was warming, despite the memories of her old life that he brought with him.

'Well, I was living here in London, but now I'm nursing; a VAD with a Mobile Neurosurgical Unit. I'm leaving now to join them in Italy.'

'And Jack?' he asked.

Sofia shook her head, and her voice fell as she spoke. 'He's gone, Colin. The Germans got him on Crete.'

Immediately, he pulled her into a hug. 'I am so very sorry. I hadn't heard. Jack was a fine man. How dreadful for you!'

As he squeezed her, Sofia suspected he knew nothing of the death of Scotty, who'd been born after Colin left for London, and with minutes before the departure of her train, it was not the time to mention the tragedy.

It was easier to change the subject. 'Thanks, Colin. It is awful. And you? Are you well?'

'Can't complain... I'm married now, with two daughters. I was getting a few good commissions, too—that is, before the war started. I painted the Astors, which was quite a coup. Ursula and I purchased a wonderful place on the Embankment... well, not exactly wonderful; it does need a lot of work, but I am quite chuffed, because since we bought it, I've discovered it was originally built for James Whistler. Do you know him? He's quite a famous nineteenth-century American artist. I'm thrilled to think I now work in the very studio where he painted his famous *Nocturnes*. Not that I am home much. For the last year I've been all over the UK painting for the Australian War Memorial Board. I just got back from Scotland, where I've been painting Australians who are supporting the war effort by milling timber, of all things.'

'So you are a war artist?' For a second Sofia wondered if Colin had met up with Jack, but imagined he would say if he had.

'I suppose so. They renew my contract every few months and send me a monthly cheque, plus they've given me a Ford to get around in, which is very nice. I just paint what I feel like and pass my paintings to Australia House here in London, and they take care of them for me.'

'And David?' Sofia suddenly remembered how it was Colin's son by his ex-wife, Vi that had taken him to London. She had abandoned the boy and headed to England, leaving David in the care of his grandmother, who'd subsequently placed him in boarding school. Colin had been furious when he discovered what Vi had done, and he all but abducted the child, arriving at his school under the pretext he was visiting and whisking him off to England before anyone could react. There had been much laughter at Montsalvat when Colin's letter had arrived, outlining how he'd turned up on Vi's doorstep with David and demanded she take her responsibilities to their son seriously. Colin's face fell at her question.

'That's a sad story, Sof. Just a few months ago, David was killed. He was serving with the British, of course, a dispatch rider up in northern Ireland, when his motorcycle crashed. Shocking.'

'I am so sorry, Colin. How awful for you!'

'It was awful. I think, if only I'd left him in Australia, this wouldn't have happened, but then, thousands of young Australians are over here dying anyway, so you have to ask, is anywhere safe? Not that I have to tell you that... I mean, poor Jack!'

'It will be all over soon,' Sofia said. It was the phrase on everybody's lips—a hope millions of people across the world were desperate to see fulfilled.

'Sure, sweetheart. It will be! You look after yourself, and be careful over in Italy. I'm sure all of those poor soldiers appreciate having you to tend to their wounds!'

'Thanks, Colin. You take care, too!'

Leaving him, Sofia looked at the station clock; in five minutes the train would arrive. She returned to Marcus; she'd have to find a restroom on the train.

CHAPTER 46

*A*s Sofia looked through the windows at the Italian landscape passing in a blur, she grappled with memories of Montsalvat that had been enlivened by her meeting with Colin. She wondered about Sonia and Helen, imagining how their children would be scampering around the grounds of the retreat, getting into mischief. She thought of Lena as a grandmother and wondered how Lil's and Helen's relationship had developed over time, given they each bore children to Justus. Her mind turned to Matcham, and her heart ached as she wondered what sort of man he'd grown into. He'd been like a younger brother to her and Jack. *Oh, dear God, please keep him safe from this carnage!* And she thought of Jack, picturing how he and Matchum would throw off their shirts, their backs tanned and their hair bleached in the hot Australian sun, always laughing and teasing each other. Of Jack leaning back on his chair in their cabin, his long legs extended, bouncing Scotty on his lap, smiling towards her, his eyes alight with joy. She and Scotty... their little family been the most important thing in his life and she'd robbed him of Scotty, and left him to Margaret. And now Jack, too, was gone!

~

Seventy-two hours later, meeting her MNSU in Naples, Sofia discovered that in the weeks she'd been away, significant changes had occurred. A new group of doctors and QAs had joined them to support the Allied troops advance through Italy, and although they were friendly enough, from her inferior rank as a VAD, Sofia knew she'd have to prove herself to earn their trust. Worse, Kenneth Eden, the leader she admired so much, who'd demanded Sofia join his unit, insisted on the benefits of penicillin and led their bus-based operating theatre and Indian tents near the battles, was extremely ill with polio-encephalitis. As soon as she heard, Sofia visited him at the Naples hospital and was horrified to see the once vibrant young man waxen and limp in his hospital bed. She feared for his life. Unfortunately, her fears were well placed, for not even the skill of his medical peers could save him. It was with a heavy heart that her unit advanced north with a Canadian doctor, Major Slemen, in charge.

The winter of 1943 was gruelling, and the MNSU was as busy as ever treating head-injured men as they came off one battlefield and the next. Like Kenneth, Doctor Slemen also decided to split the MNSU, and he took one group forward while leaving the second group, including Sofia, to serve in the rear. The staff was pleasant, though there was little time for recreation—fortunately they worked well together as they were overrun with men who bore the most horrific of injuries. The men transferred to them from the forward MNSU were numbered in the thousands, and in addition, the rear unit received hundreds of Yugoslavian men who were ferried across the Adriatic Sea, in desperate need of treatment. The days were long and exhausting, and Sofia had to resist her tendency to view each man carried into the receiving tent as bearing the face of Jack. As exhausted as she felt, she was relentless in her efforts to ensure the men who might be deemed '*critical*' were assessed instead as '*serious*' wherever possible. Sadly, hundreds of the troops were beyond saving. Often her tears flowed as she offered sips of water, and held the hands of dying men even as they spoke their last words and took their last breaths.

How utterly meaningless this all was, she thought, sickened by the endless stream of injured men and the hundreds of bodies of both Allied and enemy soldiers carted to the morgue. To her, they all looked the same: young men with smooth faces and set chins, each determined to defeat the enemy, to play his role in achieving victory for his nation.

Every few weeks, mail came through, and Sofia was glad to hear Joseph was home and coping with the challenges of life in a wheelchair. Each letter included a drawing from Andreanna, which she analysed with interest before attaching to the canvas wall beside her bunk.

Rubbing her forefinger over the outlines—the horses, sometimes with a rider, sometimes grazing in a paddock; the house with its many chimneys; the people in Andreanna's life—Sofia pictured the child, her tiny lips pursed in thoughtfulness, her little hands moving between her pencils as she selected her colours, forming lines on the paper, revealing the ideas in her head. At the bottom of each drawing, a sentence described the picture, the letters most likely reproduced from an original draft by Marcus. And on the back, the message was always the same. Here, the handwriting was not that of a child, but Marcus, although the voice was intended to be Andreanna's. However, Sofia had no doubts the simple phrase was an understated personal message to her, coming from the depths of his heart, and his kindness and love warmed her.

Dear Mumma Sofia,

Hope you are well. I miss you and look forward to seeing you again!

With love from Andreanna xxxooo

. . .

As well as the personal letters from loved ones, news from beyond the Italian campaign came frequently, though it often proved unreliable. It seemed the world was aflame with battles, with the United States, the AIF and New Zealanders fighting the Japanese in the Pacific while the Allies fought the Axis nations in Europe. There seemed to be as many victories as defeats, towns fallen and others liberated, and Sofia often wondered if peace would ever be found. There was some good news, though. By mid-1944, Paris was retrieved from the clutch of the Germans, and there was hope that Belgium and the southern Netherlands would be freed.

Sofia barely observed the Christmas of 1944; the MNSU team endured freezing conditions while they tended to soldiers sent first from Rimini, then Loreto, as the Allies pushed to expel the Germans from Italy. The 8th Army approached from the southwest while the Americans advanced from the east. The intention was that, by using a scissor-like manoeuvre, they would close in upon the German army and force it northward.

For a period the rear guard was stationed in the town of Barletta, where Sofia relished the comfort of a bed that wasn't a camp stretcher and enjoyed the luxury of bathing in the tub set up in front of a large open fire.

Sofia could barely believe it when in mid-January, a tattered parcel made its way through to her within which were two smaller parcels and a bundle of letters. She wept with the longing for the war to be over as she read the Christmas cards Marcus and Elizabeth had written and hung the drawings Andreanna had made on the wall of her room. Included in one parcel was a box of luxuries: chocolates, fruit cake, mince pies and dried fruit. And when Sofia opened the second, she blushed at the sight of the half-dozen sets of camisoles and panties as well as talcum powder, face cream and soap. She wondered if it had been packed by Marcus or Elizabeth.

As the new year wore on, cold weather and a recall of troops to Greece caused a break in the fighting, which provided a welcome respite to the field hospital, but by February northern battles were once again in full swing. A tenuous sense of optimism pervaded the camp with the news that Warsaw and Krakow had been liberated from the Germans; they'd long learned such victories did not mean the end of the war. The effort to expel the Germans from Italy was enhanced in mid-April when thousands of troops, including Brazilians and Australians, joined the British and US forces, and this time everyone sensed the tide was finally turning in the Allies' favour. The catch-cry went out: the German army is in retreat! The morale of the Allied forces leapt to new heights.

'Perhaps we'll be home for Christmas, after all!' It was a phrase which never failed to amuse everybody, for of course they'd be home by Christmas! The question was, as always: which Christmas?

Reporting for duty in early May, Sofia wondered at the shouting she heard from the CCS, barely a hundred yards away. And when a second wave of noise erupted, this time cheering from the MNSU's quarters, she knew good news must have arrived. Had the Germans finally retreated from Italy?

She approached the dining area, where the head QA from the adjoining General Hospital, a feisty old nurse who'd fought in the Great War, met her gaze.

'Sofia, love! It's over!'

'The Germans have left?' Sofia wondered where their next posting would be.

'No, no, no! It's all over. Hitler's dead—or so they are saying! The German army has officially surrendered! We're going home!'

Laughter mingled with tears of joy as the doctors and nurses moved around, hugging each other, their mouths almost splitting with the broadness of their smiles. They accepted mugs of scotch, or rum, or anything else they could find and raised them high in toast after toast to the news, all amid an air of disbelief.

Nonetheless, seriously injured men still required their attention, poor souls still arriving from the north, unlucky enough to have received wounds on these last days. The doctors and nurses attended to them with mixed feelings, relief and concern side by side.

That night, after a celebratory dinner and a last check on the men who lay bandaged and resting post-surgery, Sofia returned to her bed. There she gave in to tears, not happy ones of relief for the war's end, but deep sobs for five years wasted, millions of lives lost, and a world that might have found peace, but which Sofia was sure would never be the same. Her mind tallied her own personal losses: Jack, gone; Joseph, confined to a wheelchair; hundreds of young men she'd befriended as she'd treated them, with physical injuries and shattered minds.

But no, she told herself. *Be glad for now—the war is over!* It was time to pick up the pieces and move forward. Time to rebuild their towns and cities, strengthen their international bonds, and pray that such dreadful circumstances would never overtake the globe again.

PART VII

Home

CHAPTER 47

*W*ith the fighting over, soldiers and auxiliary staff all over Europe pulled down their camps and returned to their homes in the United Kingdom, Australia, New Zealand or the United States. However, the MNSU's first duty was to care for the injured men who, despite the defeat of the Germans, remained ensnared in a different battle. Although perhaps half of their fifty patients would likely tolerate the journey to the military hospitals, two dozen were too ill to be moved. Sadly, four of those men did not live, but the remainder were stabilized and then transported at a painfully slow pace, all the while being monitored by members of the medical team who were quick to stop the vehicles at the first sign of concern. Of the thousands Sofia had treated over the past five years, none had seemed so precious as these lads, whose families must not be denied the joy of celebrating the end of the war with their men returned to them, whole.

It was the end of June before Sofia stepped off the carriage at London Station. Looking around, she saw the station platform lively with a bustling crowd, smiling faces now freed from the heavy lines of anxiety caused by years of war, and heard the air ringing with chattering voices. A surge of pleasure coursed through her when she spotted Marcus under the station sign where they'd agreed to meet, his left hand waving a large bouquet of roses towards her, his right arm holding Andreanna close to his chest, the child covered in a pink ball of frothy lace and shyly waving at Sofia.

Taking the roses he offered, Sofia kissed Andreanna on the cheek and accepted Marcus' hug, and as his arms encapsulated them both, she fought to control her emotions.

'Sofia, at last you are home!'

'Thank God, it's over! I can barely believe it, but it is wonderful just the same!'

'No one can believe it—We keep expecting to hear the air raid sirens going off.'

She turned to Andreanna. She'd grown since Sofia had last seen her, and her hair fell in soft waves to her shoulders.

Sofia leaned towards her. 'Andreanna, sweetheart, I loved the drawings you sent me—thank you so much! And isn't that a beautiful dress!'

'Joseph's in a wheelchair,' Andreanna replied in a quiet voice. 'And Emily has twelve babies, but one died.'

Sofia looked at Marcus, puzzled.

'The chook!' He laughed. 'I pity any poor woman who has twelve babies! That's not to say I haven't treated a few who have done so, poor things. Little wonder they need to seek my services… looking for some peace and quiet, I imagine!'

Sofia returned her attention to the child. 'How lovely! I can't wait to see Emily's babies!' Marcus set Andreanna down between them, and reached for the case Sofia held. Relinquishing it, she took Andreanna's hand, then accepting Marcus', the three walked towards the carpark.

Driving through St Albans was strange for Sofia, and the feeling increased as they approached Talonsgate. Although no words had been spoken, she was acutely conscious of the promise she'd made to Marcus two years earlier, when he had spoken of their future. Very likely, this place would be Sofia's home forever.

Fifteen minutes later, walking up the staircase to her bedroom, Sofia paused on the landing and gazed at the painting of the woman in the blue cloak, who'd always made her feel as though she was looking at a version of herself—the woman she'd been when she'd first arrived at Talonsgate after being discharged from Napsbury Hospital. Unlike Sofia, the woman in the painting remained unchanged—she stood clutching her shawl, buffeted by Boreas, the North Wind god, and looking as lost as Sofia had felt when it had seemed her mind was at once pushing and pulling at her, and it was all she could do to stand upright when to collapse on the ground would be so much easier.

Thankfully, although she'd always grieve for the loss of Scotty and Jack, she no longer felt tormented by her past. She knew how fortunate she was in having Marcus discover her, both for the manner in which he'd cared for her and for the life he now offered. Studying the wistful expression on the face of the woman in the painting, Sofia wondered if she'd been so lucky.

'She's still here,' Marcus said, arriving to stand beside her.

'I wonder how her life ended,' Sofia murmured. Hearing the note of sorrow in her voice, she felt silly.

'Oreithyia? Why, she had a wonderful life! Boreas, that blustering god of the North Wind, carried her off to Hyperborea, a mythical land of eternal spring, where together they raised their family. Fine sons and daughters, some of whom became gods themselves. Oreithyia had a very happy ending, love, and so will you!'

Sofia smiled at him and laughed, encouraged by Marcus' optimistic view of her future—their future!

'When you are ready, we'll go over to the lodge. Andreanna is already there; she was keen to help Elizabeth and Joseph, who are preparing a welcome-home dinner for you.'

~

Sofia entered the kitchen to cheers, and Elizabeth greeted her with a hug while Joseph gave her a rueful wave from his wheelchair, parked behind the large bench where the two of them had been preparing vegetables. Sofia immediately went to his side and laughed as he pulled her onto his lap and kissed her cheek.

'Thank God you're home, Sofia, sweetheart,' he said and unashamedly wiped the tears running down his cheeks. 'I've been praying for your safe return every day, and that says a lot from a man who never prays! We couldn't have borne it if anything happened to you.'

'I was fine, Joseph. It was all you poor men who copped the worst of it.'

'I don't know about that…'

Sofia hugged him again before standing. Joseph might have lost the use of his legs, but indeed he was lucky, and they all knew it. Millions of men worldwide had lost their lives over the past six years, and in hindsight, one had to ask, for what gain?

Elizabeth produced glasses of lemonade, and for the next hour they chatted as dinner was prepared. Joseph, with Andreanna sitting on his lap holding a tub of cutlery, pushed his chair through to the dining room to set the table.

'How are you, Elizabeth?' Sofia asked quietly.

'I'm good, thanks for asking. That's not to say we don't each have our moments. But Joseph does his best to hide his from me, and I hide mine from him. What else is there to do but to stay positive for each other?'

Sofia nodded. 'I can imagine it's not easy, but if anyone can make the most of the circumstances, I know you and Joseph will! Let me know if I can do anything to help.'

The meal was lovely, and Sofia enjoyed being back in the company of her friends—friends who'd be her family soon—analysing the war now past, hearing about Andreanna's drawings, the new horses delivered into Elizabeth's care, and both the humorous and the more frustrating times Joseph had experienced while he'd adjusted to the wheelchair.

It was barely nine when Sofia and Marcus walked through the glass room from the lodge to the main house, and Sofia was pleased to discover how relaxed she felt with him. When Marcus suggested they share a nightcap in the lounge, she agreed.

He moved a small table closer to the sofa before beckoning her to sit next to him. Unsure whether he was going to choose this moment to ask the question hanging between them, Sofia was thankful when he did nothing more than take her hand and tease her fingers with his own, all the while chatting about Elizabeth and Joseph, and how pleased he was to see them managing so well. To Marcus' admiration, Joseph had enrolled to study law at the University of London, after which he intended to specialise in international law. They spoke of Andreanna, who was still spending five days a week with Mrs O'Neil, an arrangement which worked well for everyone given the present circumstances.

'I was thinking we could set up a room for her here, and then she could stay at Talonsgate for most of the week. There are four spare rooms—all of them quite nice. Perhaps you might like to pick one for her?'

'That would be a good plan. Perhaps tomorrow we can look at the rooms and choose one for Andreanna together.'

Marcus smiled at her response, and Sofia felt as if she'd passed a test of sorts, as if he'd been assessing her thoughts for their future, and her agreement to accept Andreanna into the house suggested the possibility they might marry, resume the care of the girl, and build a life as a family.

Marcus returned to work the next day, but before leaving, he walked Sofia to the shed where a car was parked.

'I picked this up for you to use. See, it's very similar to the old Austin, only a newer model. You might like to drive it around the yard here for a bit to get used to the gears and steering. With it, you'll be able to go to town whenever you wish. You might even want to pick up Andreanna and bring her home for a few hours, when you feel up to it.'

'Thank you, Marcus! How very thoughtful! I did drive occasionally while I was away—only in the desert, and the vehicles were mostly jeeps. Once or twice, I drove an ambulance. However, I'm a little out of practise with navigating the ordinary world. Once I am used to driving again, the car will be wonderful for ducking into town.'

The following Friday, Marcus advised Sofia that he'd be late home from work, and suggested she might join him for dinner in town.

The Boot was a lovely restaurant. The building was almost seven hundred years old, and although it had undergone a number of renovations, it still retained a medieval charm. The atmosphere was pleasant, the air filled with the murmur of diners' voices and a light tinkling of piano keys, and the tables were set with beautiful embroidered linen, polished silver, and fine crystal.

The waiter led them to a table towards the back of the room. Weaving through couples dressed in their finest clothing, Sofia was relieved she'd decided to drive into town to purchase a flowing dress with a broad belt that cinched her waist for the occasion. They both began the meal with bowls of a delicious smoked haddock soup, after which Sofia chose the venison shank in a tangy red wine sauce while Marcus selected the rump of Herdwick lamb served with tiny roasted potatoes. To finish, they both ordered a fluffy golden syrup sponge, served with a sweet custard. Without discussion, it was as though they both knew it was a night for champagne and Sofia giggled as the cork released with a celebratory pop, and enjoyed the rare opportunity to savour its sparkling fruity flavour.

Following dinner, they strolled along the streets of Market Place hand in hand, looking into the windows of the shops. As the evening cooled, Marcus suggested they go for a drive; he wanted to take Sofia to one of his favourite spots in Hertfordshire.

'Ah, Marcus. The place where you take all of your sweethearts, is it?' she teased.

'Yes, all two dozen of them, ever since I was sixteen! Truly, it will be lovely tonight. It's worth seeing, I promise you!'

It was a mild evening and Sofia enjoyed the feel of the car purring along the road, a ribbon illuminated by the car's headlights, surrounded by darkness. After driving for fifteen minutes, Marcus turned the vehicle into a parking bay. He walked around to open the door for Sofia. The night was black, but Marcus proved resourceful, for a beam from his torch lit the gravel path before them. After they'd walked perhaps a hundred yards, Sofia sensed before she saw a large structure looming before them, and she turned to Marcus in surprise.

'Come on,' he said. 'This is one of the last sections of an ancient city wall: the Roman Wall of St Albans, to be exact. It's an easy climb —I'll light up the path for you. I'm glad you aren't wearing stilettos, or this might have proved a bit tricky!'

'Marcus! I am a nurse. Nurses would never wear such foolish shoes!'

The edifice before them was made from hundreds of rocks bonded together by centuries of dust and wear. As Marcus had promised, with his assistance to steady her, the ascent was quite easy. Reaching the top, she realized they were on a flat, albeit uneven surface.

'Isn't it incredible to think this wall has stood for almost seventeen hundred years? It was built in 200 AD, and once surrounded all of St Albans, back in the days of the Romans when it was called Verulamium,' Marcus told her.

The sky was clear, and the glistening stars against the inky sky formed an enchanting cover above them. Gazing upward, Marcus placed one arm around Sofia's shoulder, and with the other, he traced a constellation called Draco.

'It means the dragon in Latin,' he explained. 'Its job is to guard the pole star—see, the brightest of those stars to the north. In ancient times, people believed the pole star was the doorway between the mortal world and eternity.'

As she examined the mystery of the night sky with Marcus beside her, Sofia felt at peace. She felt his arm tightening around her shoulder, and he pulled her to face him.

'Sofia, my sweetheart, I know so much has happened over the last few years, but more than anything, I am hoping we can make the years... the decades ahead of us happy ones. Happy ones, together! Would you do the honour of marrying me?'

A younger Sofia, perhaps a more carefree and happier Sofia, might have squealed with delight, thrilled at the proposal from this kind, intelligent, handsome man.

However, that young, exuberant Sofia was long gone, replaced by a quieter, more thoughtful woman. One who'd been deeply loved, but who'd also been terribly scarred by an accumulation of losses which had all but broken her. In all honesty, these words from Marcus tonight did not surprise Sofia, and what was more, she'd planned her answer: a definite yes. But now that the moment had arrived, she couldn't help expressing the fear in her heart.

'Marcus... I want to say yes, but I am worried. I fear you will suffer the same curse as everyone else who's ever loved me.'

'Sofia, no! I have loved you since the minute I laid eyes upon you when we travelled from Australia to London, and no harm has come to me. I survived that fearsome storm we encountered on the *Strathnaver*, endured the York Blitz, and over the past few years, with Elizabeth so busy with Joseph, I've even taken the reins of some of those wretched horses she has, and I am still alive! My heart aches for the pain you have suffered in losing so many loved ones, but believe me, I have no intentions of dying... at least not until I am old and grey!'

'Well, if you are sure, Marcus, then yes, I will marry you.'

In the darkness, he pulled her towards him, and she felt the roughness of his jacket against her face and then a raspy stubble against her cheek.

'Thank you, Sofia! You don't know how happy you have made me! And in return, I promise to bring you and Andreanna all the joy I possibly can. I know we are going to have a wonderful life together!'

Marcus searched for her lips, and finding them, he kissed her slowly and gently. His lips felt soft against her own, and his arms were warm and comforting.

Though Sofia had not expected it, perhaps it was no surprise that this moment raised the memory of when Jack had kissed her for the very first time, on the doorstep of her aunt's apartment in Montmartre. It had been at the end of their first day together, when they'd walked the streets of Paris hand in hand, laughing and teasing and smiling at everything. That kiss had been one of fumbling inexperience, but full of promise for what lay ahead for them, and it had left Sofia tingling with heat and desire. That night, she had lain in her bed, reliving Jack's touch, her arms encircling her own body in the way she'd imagined Jack might hold her, and she'd shivered with delight.

This kiss with Marcus was devoid of fanciful longing, nor did it set waves of heat pulsating through Sofia's body. Perhaps those emotions only accompanied the kisses of young lovers. After all, she was almost thirty-six years old, and Marcus was about to turn forty.

CHAPTER 48

$\mathcal{W}$hen Sofia and Marcus shared the news of their engagement with Elizabeth and Joseph the following morning, Joseph smiled broadly as Elizabeth squealed with delight.

'I am so happy for you both! When are you planning to get married? Perhaps, Sofia, you and I should go down to London for a night and get you a dress.'

Elizabeth's excitement was exactly what Sofia would have felt if it had been Andres getting married, the thrill of seeing her brother had found the woman he wanted to spend the rest of his life with.

'Why don't you?' Marcus agreed. 'Joseph and I can fend for ourselves for a day or two. I am sure the White Hart would appreciate our patronage for an evening.'

Marcus and Sofia agreed there was no sense in delaying their wedding. Perhaps they could plan for the end of August, barely six weeks away.

'Church, or celebrant?' Elizabeth asked. Sofia hadn't considered this, and looked at Marcus, wondering what he would prefer. Elizabeth had a suggestion for them. 'You realize the courthouse does a very nice ceremony. I have attended quite a few weddings there over the last few

years, and honestly, it's worth considering. Then we could follow with
a meal at The Boot, or if you prefer, we could do a reception here at
Talonsgate. We could decorate the glass room and open the doors into
the garden if the weather is nice.'

By the time they'd finished lunch, it was decided: Sofia and
Elizabeth would catch the bus to London the following Wednesday;
they'd spend the day shopping, after which they'd stay a night at a
hotel. Joseph had an appointment with his specialist on the following
afternoon and Marcus suggested the two of them drive down in the
Austin; they could all meet for lunch at The Dog and Duck, following
which Joseph would attend his appointment, and then they would
travel home to Talonsgate together.

Sofia couldn't help but feel excited by the wedding plans. She and
Marcus had called in at the courthouse, where an old school friend of
his, a jolly fellow named Seamus, would be performing the ceremony.

'Just treat the day as if it is the fanciest wedding in London,' he
said. 'Come along in all of your finery, bring your bridesmaids and
flower girls and whatever else you like, and I'll have you tied up in no
time! I'll even be happy to share a glass of champagne and a bite of the
wedding cake when it's all over!'

Marcus and Sofia had laughed, appreciated Seamus' enthusiasm,
but in truth neither of them wanted to have a fancy wedding. Joseph
and Elizabeth would be their witnesses, Andreanna would be their
flower girl, and one or two of Marcus' work colleagues and their wives
would be invited, but that was all.

Sofia made a list of some things she would purchase in London. A
dress and shoes, of course, as well as some lipstick, face cream and
mascara.

'Do you think I will find a black lace dress in London?' She
maintained a serious expression as she turned to Elizabeth. 'That is
how we Spanish dress for our weddings.'

'What? No! Marcus would get the fright of his life if you appear in black lace—so would I, I'm sure!'

Sofia laughed. She knew that like the Australians, English brides favoured white gowns.

'What on earth are Spanish women thinking?' Elizabeth continued. 'That they are going to their funerals? I mean to say, knowing some men my friends have married, perhaps wearing black might have made sense! But honestly, Sofia, we want you to look happy, not grief-stricken.'

Both women were silent as Elizabeth's words settled upon them, a reminder of Sofia's tragic past. However, Sofia was determined to resist morbid thoughts about the upcoming wedding.

'Do you know what I would like to wear? A nice knee-length dress. Perhaps a skirt and jacket. You know, how a lot of brides dressed during the war. I would like something simple, with a handbag and matching shoes. Something I can wear again.'

Elizabeth nodded enthusiastically. 'What about a very straight, fitted dress? You would look stunning in satin. I know a couple of shops where we might find something.'

Elizabeth seemed to know all the shops in London, and a week later, as they looked at one dress after another, weaving in and out of dozens of establishments, Sofia realized she had not had so much fun in ages, possibly even years.

The war had been over for two months, and Londoners were still celebrating. Everywhere they went, the stores were full of assistants and customers who were quick to express their excitement for Sofia's upcoming wedding. They were enjoying themselves too much to stop for lunch, instead preferring to focus all of their attention on shopping, and eventually, they discovered three simple satin dresses, each equally lovely. Forced to choose between them, Sofia settled on a mint green dress with a beaded bodice and a matching jacket. With the dress wrapped in tissue paper and then placed in a large box, she and Elizabeth went to the store recommended by the shop assistant, where they found a pair of satin slingbacks with a tiny heel and a handbag to match.

Having found her dress and shoes, all Sofia needed to do was purchase stockings, garter belt, undergarments, and with a reminder accompanied by a suggestive wink from Elizabeth, a negligee for her bridal night.

At four PM, Elizabeth recommended they save the rest of their shopping for the following morning, suggesting for now they collect their luggage from the locker at the station, check into their lodging for the night, then eat at the Café Royale, which was close to their hotel.

'It's half café, half wine bar, and attracts all sorts of interesting people,' she told Sofia.

It was just after six-thirty when Sofia and Elizabeth arrived at the Café Royale. Although it was early, the room was full, and the air thick with smoke—and not only from tobacco. They squeezed along the edge towards an empty table at the far corner. All around them voices chattered, laughter resounded, and wine glasses clinked.

Once seated, Sofia looked at the small stage where a singer tapped the microphone. 'Good evening, ladies and gentleman. My name is Cherie, and I am here to entertain you, so let's be entertained!' Without pause, she began a melodious humming which emerged from deep within her throat, her eyes closed, her arms moving as though she was reaching out for a lost lover who was just beyond her grasp. Just as Sofia felt certain she couldn't wring any more emotion from the stirring sounds, Cherie's voice broke into a powerful ballad, accompanied by a double bass, a trumpet, a saxophone and a piano player.

'Miss, can I get you a drink?' A waiter broke into Sofia's reverie, his pencil poised over his pad to take their order. With a giggle, she agreed the occasion called for cocktails and they each ordered a Bloody Mary along with fish and chips from the menu.

As they ate and sipped cocktails from the tall glasses, complete with sticks of celery, Sofia felt contented with the direction her life was taking her. It was nice, being here with Elizabeth, and she wished Marcus and Joseph were here with them, too, enjoying the music and sharing their meal. How lucky she was for this family she'd soon be part of: Marcus, Elizabeth, and Joseph and of course, Andreanna. Sofia had much to be thankful for.

They had just ordered their third drink each and were contemplating whether to finish the meal with a slice of pecan pie when a loud voice echoed from a table nearby, catching Sofia's attention. Not just because the voice was Australian, but because it sounded familiar. Rising up, Sofia peeped across the tables, seeking a glimpse of its owner. It didn't take more than a few seconds before a fair-haired man's eyes returned her gaze. Colin Colahan, of course! Surrounded by a table full of women, he looked relaxed, and Sofia sat down, hoping he hadn't recognised her. But he had.

'Sofia, is that you?' He approached her, eyes wide, arms extended, and she stood and accepted his hug. 'Amazing! How are you? So nice to see you again.'

'And you too, Colin. Sorry, I didn't mean to disturb you, but your Australian accent caught my attention.'

'Australian accent, my foot. I don't have an accent! It's all these pommies who have strange accents. It's wonderful to find you here! I've been thinking about you... indeed, I've been hoping I might run into you.' Colin's words were slurred, and Sofia suspected he'd already spent a few hours at one of the other taverns before arriving at the Café Royale.

Thinking about her! Whatever for? With Colin's history as a ladies' man, Sofia felt wary. She wondered if the wife he'd mentioned at London Station was with him. Sofia had dealt with many men in her life, but the likes of a drunken Colin Colahan lay beyond her experience. Elizabeth, however, remained nonplussed, extending her hand in greeting.

'Good afternoon, sir. I am Elizabeth, soon to have the pleasure of being Sofia's sister-in-law. Very pleased to meet you!'

Sofia felt like giggling at Elizabeth's manner. Her words sounded like a warning, a *don't mess with Sofia* message, and she suspected Elizabeth was wondering about the intentions of the inebriated man before them.

'Uh... very pleased to meet you, too,' Colin stuttered, clearly disconcerted by Elizabeth's imposing manner. 'So now the war's over, you're back in London, Sofia? Living here?'

'Yes, I am living north of London. At St Albans.'

'Oh, very nice. I have some friends out that way. Perhaps we could catch up sometime?'

'Yes, Colin, maybe we could.' Sofia doubted this would ever happen. Despite sharing acquaintances from the past, she and Colin had nothing in common. Marcus was sensible and stable, not to mention an utmost gentleman. She couldn't imagine what he would think of a frivolous charmer like Colin.

'So you are getting married... Really, Sofia? Are you sure?'

'Of course I'm sure.' Sofia laughed, suddenly feeling lightheaded from the vodka-laced cocktails she'd been sipping all evening.

'And you are not going back to Australia?'

'No Colin. My life is here now.'

'Okay. And when are you planning for the happy day?'

'In about a month. Late August. Just a simple affair at a registry office.' Sofia hoped Colin wasn't expecting an invitation.

'Well, good on you. I wish you well.' He stood up, preparing to return to his table, then paused for a moment.

'The thing is... I don't know if I should tell you this, or even if you want to hear it, but...' he shrugged and shook his head.

'What, Colin? What shouldn't you be telling me?'

He returned Sofia's gaze, and then, looking from her to Elizabeth, he shook his head. 'No, it's okay. It's nothing, Sofia. You just be happy.

It's been a shitty war, and we all deserve some happiness, don't you think?'

For a moment she felt sorry for him. Yes, the war had been awful, and Colin too had paid dearly, losing the son he'd loved.

'Colin, wait. Sit down. What do you mean? What did you want to tell me?'

Still eyeing Elizabeth, Colin opened his mouth, then closed it again and shook his head.

Sofia felt bewildered and again wondered what Elizabeth was thinking. She hoped Elizabeth did not assume Colin had been a past lover.

'I tell you what, you two. I have a nose that needs powdering, and a glass which needs refilling. It's time I attended to both.' Elizabeth winked at Sofia before mouthing, *I'll be back in a minute*, then left them.

Even now remaining cagey with the news he'd seemed so keen to share, Colin groped for Sofia's hand, but she moved it away from him. *Good heavens, whatever is wrong with him?*

Colin transferred his nervous empty fingers to the paper serviette and began tearing it into shreds. 'Sofia, I don't know if you want to hear this news. War does strange things, of course, and who am I to judge? But I think you should know... Jack isn't dead, like you told me. Now... perhaps you were only saying that... If so, it's your business. I know there are people who've used the war as an opportunity to make new lives for themselves. But like I said, I thought you should know.'

'What on earth do you mean, Jack's alive? How could you know this?' Surely the drunken Colin had his facts skewed.

'From Lil. We correspond, you know. Every few months I exchange letters with the Jorgensens.

'I received a letter from Lil a few weeks ago. She mentioned Justus had bumped into a face from the past at The Latin: Jack Tomlinson, who was there with his friend Margaret and her Yankee boyfriend. Lil wrote how pleased she and Justus had been to see Jack doing so well after the dreadful state he'd been in a few years earlier. Apparently, he is living in the city, and the very day Justus saw him, he'd submitted an entry to the Archibald Prize. Of course, I immediately thought of you… been thinking about it all ever since, given what you'd said that day at the station, about Jack being dead and all. And now, here you are! It's like I was meant to see you!'

Sofia paled as Colin's words washed over her, running together into a blur.

Jack was alive! He hadn't died in Crete?

'Is everything alright, Sofia?'

The words came from Elizabeth, who was standing at the table, two drinks in her hand. Sofia shook her head.

'Sofia…' Colin frowned. 'If you'd like to talk some more about this, you will find me here most evenings. If I'm not here, ask the barman for Aussie Col. They know where I live. Look, I am sorry if I've upset you with this news! Perhaps I shouldn't have told you. Truly, you do what you want. I won't say anything more. What happens in London, stays in London, if you know what I mean.'

Standing, he glanced at Elizabeth before reaching out hugging Sofia, and then he returned to his table.

'Sofia, what is it? Are you okay?'

'He's alive!'

'Who's alive, Sofia?'

'My husband, Jack.'

'Jack the scoundrel?'

'No, Elizabeth. I told you, Jack was never a scoundrel. He always loved me. It was I who left him after the accident… after Scotty died. Jack's pain was so terrible, I could barely face him, and then I started adding up the deaths. My parents, my brother, Scotty… and I was sure I was cursed. I was sure if I stayed, Jack too would die. When I saw him with Margaret, I was half mad with grief. I told myself Jack would be better with her. She would care for him. She would bring him happiness.'

'But you thought Jack had died?

'Yes—in Cairo, I found a drawing signed *Jack*, and I knew it was his. So I asked about him. I asked everyone, the AIF administration, the soldiers on the wards. All I could find out was Jack had been to Bardia and Tobruk, and then to Greece. The information from the battlefields was confusing. I kept returning to the Admin, trying to find out more, and finally, they said he was missing in action, presumed dead following the German invasion of Crete. It was terrible news. Jack had been missing for over six months by then and his name was not included on any of the lists coming from the German P.O.W. camps. No one had heard from him. I was sure he'd died!'

'And now, you find Jack's alive. Good Lord! What a pickle! What do you want to do, Sofia?'

'I don't know. Heavens. I was so happy, so sure of everything half an hour ago, and now this!'

'Well, you don't have to do anything. You can go ahead and marry Marcus if you wish. I will never speak of it again, if you want to do it that way.'

'But how can I, Elizabeth? How can I build a marriage with Marcus upon a lie?'

Elizabeth was silent, and Sofia felt dreadful for her, with her brother's happiness at stake.

Oh, oh, oh…. How could she do this to Marcus? All he'd done was offer kindness to her, bringing her into his family home and helping to make her better.

'Truly, all I seem to do is cause unhappiness to the people who care for me!'

'Nonsense, Sofia. Listen. I think it comes down to this: Who do you love? If you love Marcus, then choose him. We might have to delay the wedding and get you a certificate of divorce or something… We'd need to get some legal advice. Alternatively, I beg of you, if it's Jack you love, then don't marry my brother! Too many times I have seen marriages where one party is in love with someone else, and the outcome is always disastrous.'

'But Marcus will be devastated if I tell him I can't marry him.'

'Yes, but better for him to be devastated now than destroyed by you leaving him later. Please, Sofia. Love is about the heart, not the head. Listen to it, and do what it tells you to do. Otherwise, you will be forever heartsick for Jack, and Marcus will know.' With a sigh, Elizabeth collected her purse. 'Let's head back to the hotel. We've both had too much to drink for clear-headed decisions. Let's sleep on this, and we can talk about it more tomorrow.'

Of course, they didn't sleep. For hours and hours, Sofia spoke to Elizabeth, crying buckets of tears. It was all clear now. She started at the beginning, her childhood in Malaga, with Andres, the wonderful brother who'd been so funny and clever, then the trip she'd taken with him to Paris after he won the Prado's competition. How she'd fallen in love with the young Australian. She and Elizabeth both laughed when Sofia described how Jack had leapt on the train, joining her and Andres as they returned home to Spain. There, they'd married, and then, after the death of Andres, Jack had taken Sofia to Australia. She told Elizabeth about his family, and Montsalvat, and Justus Jorgensen's dream, which had been so alluring until it had all gone so horribly wrong.

'We were happy for most of the time, Elizabeth. The people were good, like family really. I loved working in the garden and when Scotty was born, our life was perfect!' Sofia sobbed as she recalled the happiness she'd once had.

'But Justus... he was so controlling. I hated the way he treated people. My dislike for him was like poison, I couldn't bear to look at him. I had to go. It was only for my sake, that Jack agreed to leave.' Again, Sofia took a breath and wiped her eyes, and Elizabeth squeezed her hand, for she already knew what was coming next.

They cried together as Sofia spoke of the house they'd found in Eltham and about the day they were leaving. Of the fire, and how guilty she felt for ignoring the red-hot coals that had been stirred by the breeze, then picked up by it and carried to the dry leaves.

'I was mad with grief, Elizabeth! So many of the people I loved were dead. All of my family, and then Scotty! I couldn't even keep him safe! I was so frightened for Jack. So scared for him, and overcome with guilt, for the pain I'd caused him. Somehow, I convinced myself he'd made a life with Margaret. But Colin mentioned she had an American boyfriend, so even in that, I was wrong! It is all so dreadfully awful.'

'Sofia, it is not all sad. Jack is alive! That is wonderful news, isn't it?'

'Yes, of course! Thank God he didn't die, like so many others. But what to do now? Should I go back to him? He hasn't seen me in years! Would he even want me back? Maybe it was the hand of fate keeping him away from me in Egypt. Perhaps that's the reason he is alive!'

'Nonsense, Sofia. Why do you let these ideas haunt you?' Elizabeth squeezed Sofia's shoulder as if she might crush some common sense into her. 'Sometimes terrible things just happen.... And think about this: regardless of what happens between you and Jack, Andreanna is his daughter. Don't you think he has a right to know about her? No wonder she is such a little artist! Honestly, there is no choice. You must take her back to her father. That poor man. What he must have been through!'

'But poor Marcus!'

'Yes, poor Marcus. But he is a strong man, and he will be fine. You can't feel responsible for the way the hand of fate chooses to deal its cards. Ha... listen to me, now, you've got me blaming everything on fate! However, it seems clear to me the meeting with your friend Colin was no accident. How much better to find out that Jack is alive before you marry Marcus, rather than after!'

~

The following morning, with all thoughts of shopping abandoned, Sofia and Elizabeth left the hotel at noon to meet Marcus and Joseph for lunch.

'I don't know how I am going to tell him, Elizabeth! It all seemed so straightforward last night. But now, in the cold light of day, I feel truly awful. Marcus thinks I have just bought my dress for our wedding!'

'Listen, Sofia. For a start, none of this is your fault. You left Jack because you were ill and your sense of reason was confused. Marcus fell in love with you long before he knew even half of your story. Today, he will learn the other half, and he will still love you—believe me! But he will also know you are making the right choice, even if it's not the one he'd want you to make. I suggest we break the news down for him. We go to lunch and you confess something has come to light, tell him you will speak to him about it this evening. That way, he'll be ready to hear a problem has developed.'

Sofia considered the strategy. Certainly, Marcus would be curious, but he wouldn't press her; most likely he'd anticipate she had some bothersome paperwork to attend to regarding her Spanish heritage or something. She knew in Marcus' eyes, no problem would be insurmountable. Nonetheless, she agreed with Elizabeth; she couldn't possibly endure lunch pretending everything was fine, nor did she want to share the news at the restaurant.

Sofia rehearsed the lines in her head as they approached the restaurant, and walked towards the table where Marcus and Joseph sat waiting for them.

However, what Sofia hadn't prepared for was the look upon Marcus' face as they arrived at the table, the warmth in his eyes when he turned to her, his features alight with pleasure. Seeing him bursting with happiness at the mere sight of her, Sofia's heart ached, and her plan to defer the dreadful news until tonight was forgotten. Her eyes filled with tears as she stood wordlessly beside him.

'Sofia, my love, what has happened? Are you alright? Heavens, sweetheart! Surely buying a dress wasn't that terrible!'

Sofia tried to smile at Marcus' attempt at humour but was overcome with sorrow for the disappointment she was about to inflict upon him. Through tear filled eyes, she looked helplessly at Elizabeth.

'Joseph, come with me. Sofia and Marcus need some time together. Marcus, can I have your keys? Joseph and I will have a bite to eat elsewhere, then I will take Joseph to Dr. Townsend. We'll wait downstairs in the foyer at about three-thirty.' She stepped toward Sofia and gave her a hug.

'Sofia, honey, everything is going to be alright. Don't worry.'

As she gazed at their retreating backs, Sofia felt like she'd leapt off a high-rise building. There was no going back. She wiped the tears from her face and sat down beside Marcus, leaning into him, searching for strength from this kind, steadfast man even as she knew she was about to break his heart. He stroked her hand and looked down at her, his forehead furrowed in puzzlement.

'Marcus. I heard some news yesterday…'

'Good news, or bad news?'

'I guess it depends on how you look at it. I bumped into an old acquaintance at the Café Royal. An Australian named Colin.'

'Yes…' Marcus' eyes didn't leave Sofia's face as he waited for her to explain.

'Colin told me Jack is in Australia, Marcus… he is alive!'

'Jack's alive! But you were informed he'd died on Crete! Where did this friend of yours get his information?'

'From Australia, Marcus, from friends we had in common. He's the same Australian man I met that day you took me to London Station to re-join my unit in Italy, Colin Colahan. At the station, he'd asked me about Jack, and naturally, I told him Jack had died on the battlefield. Yesterday, Colin appeared at the Café Royale, where Elizabeth and I had dinner. He had drunk a lot, but nonetheless, I am sure he was speaking sense when he told me he'd received a letter from one of our friends from Montsalvat. That's where Jack and I lived… where the fire happened. In the letter, Lil mentioned her husband had bumped into Jack, and he is living in Melbourne. Of course, Colin was confused, given I'd said Jack had died, and he wanted to be sure I knew Jack had been seen... that he is alive!'

'But how can you be sure...' Marcus grappled with his words.

'Marcus, I am sure. I know Jack is alive...' Her words dropped to a whisper.

'And you think you should go to him?'

Sofia nodded, tears again filling her eyes. How she hated doing this to him!

'Sofia, my dear... You have had so many awful things happen to you. Jack is your husband, and I know despite all that's happened between you, you loved him very much. Very likely, he loves you.' Marcus paused and squeezed her hand before continuing. 'As hard as it is for me to say it, I agree... You need to go to him. Try to make sense of what has happened between you. Perhaps you and Jack might even put your marriage back together. And of course, if you find you can't, there will always be this heartsick Englishman, waiting for you!'

Sofia smiled through her tears. 'Marcus, I feel so terrible for you... for us. I know you would have been a lovely husband, and we would have been happy together! It seems so unfair to you.'

'I will be alright, Sofia. I do love you, my sweet Spanish lady! I will always love you. But it's time for you to do what is right for you.'

'You realise, I have to take Andreanna with me.'

'Oh, Sofia, now you are breaking my heart!' Marcus smiled at her, attempting humour, but tears glistened in his eyes for the loss of a dream which held so much promise.

'Thank you, Marcus!'

'Thank *you*, Sofia. My life has been all the richer for having you and little Andreanna in it. Can I ask you something?'

'Of course.'

'Andreanna has never been baptised. Do you think, since we aren't going to have a wedding, we could have a baptism instead? Then I, Elizabeth and Joseph could be named as her godparents, and we would always have some claim upon her, even if you are both in the Antipodes!'

～

The logistics of baptizing a child born of Protestant and Catholic parents, and with Anglican and Jewish godparents, proved complicated. To simplify things, Sofia suggested they have a naming ceremony instead—an event in Andreanna's honour which would forever connect her to the people who'd raised her in those early years when her own mother had been so unwell. Although it was a mouthful, the name Andreanna Elizabeth Marian Tomlinson was formalised at the registration office, and Marcus, Elizabeth and Joseph were named as her official aunt and uncles.

And the following day, Sofia embarked on the third ocean crossing of her life, this time accompanied by Andreanna.

CHAPTER 49

*S*ofia did not know what to expect when six weeks later she disembarked from the *Orontes*, clutching the hand of the little girl who finally felt like a daughter to her.

The ship had been loaded with hundreds of British families, all taking advantage of the opportunity for a new life offered by the Australian government, who were determined to expand the size of its workforce and populate the land's vast open spaces. The adults had only to pay ten pounds, and children travelled free. Optimistic about their new life, Sofia's fellow passengers had been full of humour, laughingly referring to themselves as "ten-pound Poms," and excited to be travelling to a country where they were sure they'd see kangaroos hopping through the streets.

Each day Sofia and Andreanna had played together, eaten together and read books together. Hand in hand, they'd walked the decks, looked at birds swooping, whales breaching, and waves crashing against the bow of the ship. Finding paper and pencils, Sofia had smiled as Andreanna drew pictures to send to Aunt Elizabeth and Uncles Marcus and Joseph. Although Andreanna didn't mind playing games with the other children, she was clearly happiest making marks on paper.

She told Andreanna of Australia: of cute little koalas nestled in trees and flocks of kangaroos all bearing long, powerful tails, which they used along with their legs to bound across the countryside, and the kookaburras who cackled like they were laughing at you. She described the lovely yellow sandy beaches where they could go swimming, the steaming hot days of summer when the sky was as blue as the pencils in Andreanna's drawing set, and how beautiful and clear the air was. And she told Andreanna about Jack, the man they'd visit, who also loved to draw and paint pictures. But, in view of the uncertainty of the outcome this long sea journey might bring, Sofia kept her stories about Jack simple, as if they were visiting a friend, rather than possibly the most important man in Andreanna's life.

Sofia's stomach fluttered as they left the ship in Port Melbourne and she flagged a taxi to transport her and Andreanna to Copelen Street. She wondered how Marian and William would receive her. They'd be quite old now, Sofia reflected, and without doubt they'd have been hurt by the way she'd left Jack, how she'd vanished without a word to anyone.

But Andreanna was their grandchild, and they had a right to meet her. The cab slowed as it rounded the corner and came to a stop before 14 Copelen Street, and Sofia couldn't help thinking about the last time she'd arrived here in a taxi. She glanced behind them, at the empty space where she'd once glimpsed Jack in the arms of Margaret. Shaking the memory from her head, she looked at the house. To her surprise, three children were playing in the front yard, and a large pale blue motorcar rested in the driveway. A woman with a red scarf tied around her hair was leaning over a garden bed. She looked up at the taxi, her head tilted as if wondering who the visitors were.

'Sorry, but the people who lived here must have moved,' Sofia said to the driver.

'Well, what would you like to do, ma'am? Perhaps a hotel in the city until you can locate them?'

'No. Please take me to Montsalvat...' It was all Sofia could think of.

'Montsalvat?'

'Sorry—Eltham. Montsalvat is the artists' retreat. I will direct you when we get there.'

Sofia snuggled Andreanna against her. It had been a long day, and the child was sleepy. She gazed at the fields as they drove and decided to wind down the window. The day was warm, the sky a clear blue, and Sofia inhaled the pungent aroma of eucalyptus, which would always spell Australia to her. Suddenly, she felt overwhelmingly pleased to be here. When she'd left London, it had been a cold autumn day, with barely seven hours of daylight sandwiched between a long bleak dawn and the heavy fog of an early sunset. Here, the days would be long, the heat of the sun chasing residents out of their beds in the early morning. At the end of the day, evenings would be spent outdoors until the houses cooled, and people would sit beneath the shade of trees drinking glasses of icy cold beer or lemonade before turning in for the night.

Arriving at Montsalvat, the driver set Sofia's belongings on the gravel carpark, and looking around her, she marvelled at how little had changed. Piles of bridge timber still lay in neat stacks, ready for Justus' next project, and the familiar storage shed, which had been erected by Jack, Matcham. and a group of Justus' art students years earlier, caught her eye. The row of students' quarters where she and Jack had lived was barely recognisable, and the scattering of chairs, clothes hanging on rails, and tables set beneath a newly added veranda, indicated they were inhabited.

Sofia caught sight of movement near the Great Hall. It was Lil, standing with her hand on her brow, squinting up towards the carpark. She called inside, and then a second woman appeared. Sue Vanderkelen's long hair had greyed, but she looked as stylish as ever. With a squeal, she raced to Sofia and drew her into a tight embrace.

~

Throughout the afternoon, it seemed a constant stream of tears ran down Sofia's face as she was greeted by Lil, the Skippers, and later Justus. Within minutes of their arrival, Andreanna had been claimed by Sonia's daughter, Saskia, who was thrilled to have the company of another girl close to her own age, even if it was one who spoke with a funny accent.

'Jack's in Sydney,' Lil told Sofia. 'In fact, it's lucky you arrived at Montsalvat today—in two days' time we'd all have been gone! He's a finalist for the Archibald, and we plan to be there with him for the opening night.'

After seven long years away, there was much to catch up on. Although disappointed by the delay in seeing Jack, Sofia was captivated by the excitement the Montsalvat residents shared as they prepared for the trip to Sydney—excitement no doubt doubled by the arrival of her and Andreanna. Not only were they planning to surprise Jack on his big night at the New South Wales Art Gallery, but now they were arriving with treasures beyond his imagining—his long-lost wife and a little girl he didn't know existed!

'My, my! He's going to be so surprised, Sofia,' they repeated one after the other. 'To think you and Andreanna are here is all quite incredible!'

Even as they squeezed into three vehicles—Justus', the Skippers' and Matchum's—Sofia felt sure they were keeping a secret from her also, but after twenty-four hours in the company of the eccentric community, she felt relaxed in their presence. After all, the Skippers and Jorgensens had been her family for almost five years; she'd lived amongst them, cooking, cleaning, washing and building during the early days of Montsalvat's creation.

CHAPTER 50

Sofia should have been tired when they entered the outskirts of Sydney the following afternoon. Their convoy of vehicles had been travelling for near twenty hours, with the Skipper's car in the lead, holding Lena, Mervyn, Arthur, Sonya, Saskia and Sigmund. Following had been Matchum, who drove Sofia, Andreanna, Helen, and Sebastian, and then bringing up the rear was Sue with Lil, Justus and Max. The journey had been arduous, broken by an overnight stay in Albury, a flat tyre on the Skipper's vehicle as they'd traversed the Blue Mountains, and what seemed like dozens of toilet stops to cater to the unpredictable bladders of four small children. Now, with only two hours remaining for them to find a place to stay, have a quick wash and reach the gallery in time for the opening of the Archibald prize, Sofia's stomach was doing somersaults.

Her restlessness was every bit like that she'd felt over fifteen years ago when she and Jack had been married: a combination of joy and nervousness. She wondered what he would think of her after all of these years. Would he even recognise her? Of course he would, she hadn't changed that much! Her main question, though, was would Jack be happy to see her? But despite her fears, Sofia felt at peace, and she was reminded of Elizabeth's words. *Love is about the heart, not about the head.* And if there was one thing Sofia had always known, Jack loved her. She'd known it in Paris and in Spain. She'd known it when he brought her to Australia and when they'd lived in their tiny van, and then the cabin at Montsalvat.

What had possessed her to leave? Sue had asked, and Sofia had tried to explain. She'd left Jack because she loved him, and out of her love, she'd feared for him, feared that like her family and her son, he would be taken from her. Sofia now recognized how misguided she'd been when she decided to hand Jack over to the care of Margaret, how illogical her reasoning had been in thinking he'd be safer and happier.

But she was strong now, and ready for whatever their future might bring. And whenever stirrings of concern arose regarding Jack's reaction when he saw her, Sofia looked to the excitement of the Montsalvat residents, accompanied by the warm hum of her own heart, and her fears were alleviated.

As it turned out, Lena and Mervyn took a wrong turn, leading them west towards Parramatta, and an hour was lost as they negotiated the route back into the city. It was quarter to seven when they arrived outside the Art Gallery of New South Wales, but its carpark was full, and they were forced to park blocks away. With only a few minutes to spare, Sofia ran a comb through her own and Andreanna's hair, and then she used her dress to wipe the tired child's face. She nodded encouragingly, and pulled her into a hug, whispering, 'It will be alright, Andreanna,' before taking her hand and entering the crowded building.

It was the first time Sofia had been inside an art gallery in years, yet everything felt familiar, from the foyer with its posters promoting the current exhibition, to the attendants seated at the entry, to the excited babble of attendees in the crowded room beyond the foyer.

This evening the guests were all dressed in their finest clothing, typical of an important opening night, and many held wine glasses. The air was thick with the aroma of cigars and the sound of voices commenting about the quality of the paintings. As a hush descended over the crowd, Sofia realised the exhibition's attendees had been called to attention. She paused, expecting the group from Montsalvat would wait until the official presentations were over before finding Jack, but Matcham had other ideas.

He stood tall, glanced around, and with a confident motion, beckoned for them to follow as he proceeded to weave across the room. The Jorgensens trailed him, and then the Skippers. Sonia reached out to take Sofia's hand, and she laughed, realising how eccentric they must appear as they pushed through the crowd in their colourful outfits and handcrafted jewellery. Not everyone was thrilled by the disruption they created, and when the man standing on the stage with a microphone raised his hand and called for silence, Matcham replied in a loud voice, 'Excuse me! The catalogue says formalities begin at seven-thirty. It's only seven twenty-five! We're not late! You're early!'

Reaching the centre of the room, he veered left and, ignoring the disapproving tuts, he called out over his shoulder, 'Hoy, over here!' He swept his arms to clear the path ahead and gestured for Justus, accompanied by Lil on one side and Helen on the other, to proceed. The trio were followed by Lena, clutching Sebastian's hand, and Mervyn, clutching Saskia's and carrying Sigmund high on his shoulders.

Holding Andreanna's hand tightly, Sofia allowed herself to be led forward by Sonia, all the while scanning the crowd. Every few seconds she gained glimpses of the paintings on the walls, whose subjects gazed into the room—paintings chosen as finalists for Australia's most prestigious portrait prize.

Suddenly, a stunning portrait made her stop. It was an image of herself, and yet not herself. A Spanish woman with a glint of joy in her eyes and a smile on her lips. A woman who stood tall and proud. Sofia gasped, for the painting was wonderful. Perfectly executed, it was more than just a representation of a woman. Rather, it was a stirring insight into the mind and heart of a woman steeped in liveliness and joy, and who seemed to be lit by an internal light. A true masterpiece.

As she gazed at the portrait, Sofia felt the eyes of the Montsalvat residents upon her. She realised they'd found Jack. Sonia was hugging him, then Sofia saw her whisper into his ear. She watched as he turned, his eyes upon her widening in confusion. She smiled as he shook his head, for the motion was so familiar to her. She knew he was thinking his eyes had deceived him; that surely this couldn't be real.

She nodded, and gave a cautious smile as she stepped forward and reached out to touch his shoulder. Her lips quivered and she wondered if she could trust herself to speak.

'Sofia?' Jack's voice was low, as if he didn't wish to be overheard, for fear he was going mad.

'Jack. I am so proud of you. You have made a wonderful painting!'

'Sofia? It's really you?'

'Yes, Jack. It's me. At least, I think it is. I can barely believe I am here myself!'

Sofia closed her eyes as his hands reached out to her. Inhaling deeply, she relished the touch of his fingers gently sweeping down the side of her face. She opened her eyes and looked into his when he took her hands, gripping them tightly. His face was the same, yet different. Lines had formed across his brow, and faint white creases fanned from the corners of his eyes. How many of those lines had she caused? Sofia wondered, and her tears threatened.

'Jack!' she whispered, and her voice cracked as she continued. 'I am sorry I left you. So very sorry! I was confused. It was all too terrible!'

He shook his head at her, as if to hush her thoughts, and pulled her close. 'I have missed you, so much, Sofia. Every single day, I have thought of you! Wondered where you were!'

Sofia nodded, realising the agony she'd put him through. He turned his face away from her, looking down and fixing upon Andreanna, who now cowered behind her legs. Sofia stood aside, and reached to gently pat Andreanna's shoulder, assuring her all was well.

Bending down on one knee, Jack sought the little girl's attention.

'And what is your name, young lady?'

'My name is Andreanna,' she replied. 'Andreanna Marian Tomlinson.'

'Andreanna... Andreanna Marian Tomlinson? Well, I am very pleased to meet you, Andreanna.'

Sofia's heart ached with both joy and sadness as she watched Jack take Andreanna's hand, turn it over and, to the little girl's delight, kiss her fingers.

Guilt, which seemed to be so much part of her life, again surged through her as she realized just how much she'd robbed from both of them. Had she known she was pregnant at the time of Scotty's death, she might have made very different decisions.

Standing, Jack looked into her eyes. 'Sofia?'

'Jack, Andreanna is our daughter. She is yours; I am so sorry.'

Jack shook his head, reaching out, and their tears merged as he pulled her to him his arms almost crushing the breath from her. When Andreanna tugged at Sofia's dress, he leaned down and lifted her up, and pulled Sofia against him with his free arm.

'My Sofia,' he whispered. 'I can hardly believe you are here. Please tell me this isn't all a dream! I don't think I could bear it if this isn't happening!'

'No, Jack, it's not a dream. It is real. Finally, I have come home to you, and I promise, I will never leave you again.'

EPILOGUE: 1961 MELBOURNE

'*M*um, where do you think this should go?'

The painting Andreanna held was a scene depicting a deep blue sky set above turquoise water. Colourful small boats dotted the still water. Her face glowed with excitement. She was loving seeing the gallery they were putting the final touches upon take shape. Andreanna's love of drawing as a child had culminated to the point where, under Jack's tuition, she'd become a very competent painter and hoped to make a living from her work.

Sofia smiled. For years, Andreanna had enthusiastically supported her dream to establish an art gallery in Melbourne. Up to now, her life had been busy with rearing children and home building, but that hadn't stopped her mind from straying to thoughts about the gallery she'd have one day. The painting Andreanna was holding was one of more than a dozen which had arrived from the framers earlier in the week; surrounded by a generous three-inch matt in deep yellow, the painting's vibrancy was as fresh as if it had been painted yesterday.

'How beautiful, Andreanna! See what a wonderful artist your uncle Andres was! He painted that scene at La Malagueta which was near to where I grew up. Just seeing it takes me back to my childhood. Look, Jack! Isn't it wonderful? Shall we put it on the back wall?'

'You're the curator, Sofia! But I agree, it would look wonderful there. Come on, Elizabeth, how about you and I set these down against the wall, and Mum can decide where they should go? Look at this: it's a Matisse, and those four are Picassos. They might be fifty years old, but they're worth a small fortune now! We can thank your grandfather for his foresight when he began collecting the artwork of his peers, for these paintings may well make you a very wealthy lady one day!'

'Wonderful. When we are rich, we can make another trip to Paris!'

'Paris, Paris! Why does everyone want to go to Paris?' Jack asked.

'You can't talk, Dad. That's where you met Mum.'

'What, now you are saying you want to go to Paris and find yourself a husband? I don't think so!'

'No, Daddy. I am only ten. I want to go there and be an artist!'

Elizabeth's giggles were infectious. It seemed as if their youngest child and Jack were always just a few feet apart and forever teasing each other. Sofia smiled as she watched them working together to lift each painting from the bench and carry them through to the main room.

Jack, Andreanna and Elizabeth were the artists in the family, endlessly immersed in conversations about their paintings and burying themselves in the studio at the back of their house. Their third child, Robbie, now fourteen years old, had no inclination to paint. Rather, beyond a passion for playing football each weekend, his love was for food; the pleasure of eating Sofia's almendrados and polvorones and risottos had led him to an interest in cooking. He'd become a connoisseur of the tomato sauces they enjoyed making together. Tall like Jack, Robbie had matured into a strong young man who was always happy to wield the hoe in their garden. He and Sofia spent many happy hours working together, expanding their vegetable patch to include dozens of varieties of tomatoes, which, once ripe, they experimented with in the kitchen. At this minute, Robbie was at home slicing the Black Krims they'd picked in the morning, which he would blend with brown sugar, vinegar, and parsley. When he'd done that, he'd prepare pastry, ready for toppings for the dozens of tapas they would serve tomorrow night at the grand opening of the Galleria Toulousie.

Sofia walked from room to room, satisfied with the what they'd achieved. The spaces were large, and with the addition of half a dozen stands, Sofia hoped to build her display to about one hundred paintings. Thanks to her father's collection, as well as his own and Andres' works, they had a unique display which was guaranteed to draw the interest of the public. Despite the continuing conservatism of Melbourne's art world, there was a growing appreciation for both impressionist and post-impressionist pieces. In addition, Jack and Andreanna would continually add to their stock with landscapes and seascapes, which were always popular if the price was right.

She went to the counter where her sketchbook lay. Unlike Jack's and Andreanna's drawing books which held preliminary outlines for their paintings, Sofia's contained her ideas for the gallery she'd dreamed of; for years she'd recorded details of everything from the front entrance, to the walls where she'd group the various works, to a tea room just like she'd once had at Malaga. This gallery's location in what was once a small warehouse in Flinders Lane did not allow for the garden tea room Sofia had hoped for, but it was a wonderful space just the same. It included five rooms with large windows offering plenty of natural light, and an enormous shed to the side where Jack planned to set up a new studio where he and Andreanna could work.

Not all of the paintings were for sale. Her father's works and those of Andres would form a permanent display, along with the Picassos and the Matisse, which, as Jack had noted, were now rising in value. Sofia would place them in the light-filled side room as a permanent display of early twentieth-century European art.

Also on the not-to-be-sold list was Jack's *Sofia*, the painting he'd entered in the Archibald Prize over fifteen years earlier. Recently set in an ornate gold frame, it was the most beautiful of paintings. Certainly, it was comparable to those painted by Joaquin Sorolla, which Jack had always loved. For the dozenth time that morning, Sofia walked into the main exhibition room, where it was mounted, holding pride of place in the centre of the far wall. This portrait may not have won the Archibald Prize, but it had inspired dozens of commissions for Jack, and for every portrait he'd painted, even more commissions followed. These days he earned a sound income from his work which, along with their savings, had financed the purchase of the large, if somewhat rundown, two-storey house within walking distance of Marian and William's home in Beaumaris.

Sofia smiled as she remembered when she'd first viewed this portrait, hanging on the wall of the New South Wales National Gallery. That night, after seven long years, she'd been reunited with Jack, and after seeing the love in his eyes and his relief at her return to him, Sofia had finally been released from the guilt which had haunted her after the death of Scotty. And despite the time which had passed and all that had happened, from the minute Jack had taken her into his arms, she'd melted into the familiar warmth of his embrace and knew it was the only place she ever wanted to be. The remainder of that extraordinary week in Sydney had been like a honeymoon, albeit one shared with their dearest of friends and family. And, just like when they'd first met, Sofia's heart had beaten with excitement a dozen times a day when Jack had smiled at her, taken her hand, or laughed with pleasure as he'd spent hours getting to know his daughter.

There had, of course, been lots of catching up to do as she and Jack shared stories of what they'd seen and done while apart; many of the stories had taken years to unfold. But for all of their lost time to make up for, they had a little girl who'd needed their love and care as she adjusted to a new life in a foreign country with parents she'd scarcely known. Marian and William had been ecstatic to see Sofia again, and their lives had been enriched by the joy Andreanna brought to them, then enriched again when, a year later, Robbie had arrived, and three years after that, Elizabeth. The subsequent years had been busy and happy, filled with bay side walks with Grandma and Grandpa, raising children, and transforming the old house they'd bought into a home filled with love.

'Hey, there you are! You better tell us what you want to do with these—I'll have to get them up by midday if I'm to pick up the trestle tables for tomorrow's supper. And we're expected for dinner at seven, aren't we?'

'Yes. They should be at their hotel by now. They were driving down from Ballarat this morning.'

Sofia had been thrilled by her English friends decision to come to Australia for three months, timed to include her gallery opening as well Andreanna's twenty-first birthday in the following month. Already, Marcus and Sara, the woman he'd married three years earlier, as well as Elizabeth and Joseph had been in Australia for three weeks. After staying with her and Jack for the first week, they'd travelled to Ballarat, where Marcus' friend lived. Now, returning to Melbourne for the gallery's opening, they'd refused her invitation for them to stay with Jack and her. "You'll be far too busy," Elizabeth had declared, and had booked themselves into a hotel in Beaumaris. Tonight, they were treating the Tomlinson's to dinner at a nearby restaurant, and Sofia looked forward to it. It had been wonderful to see them again, although not for the first time since she'd left, because five years earlier, she, Jack, and the children had made the crossing by ship on a pilgrimage of sorts. They'd stayed at Talonsgate for a month before travelling to France, where they'd visited Laura and Lucian, and then they'd travelled through Spain, staying at Barcelona, Madrid and finally Malaga. She sensed Jack standing at her side as she gazed upon *Sofia*.

'It's still my favourite of all of your work, Jack. Such a beautiful painting!' Sofia looked into the eyes of the woman, a much younger version of herself, with laughter-filled eyes, glowing smooth skin, and slim waistline, she thought ruefully, even as she felt Jack's arm reach around her.

'She's still my favourite, too—so very beautiful!'

Sofia smiled as he bumped his hip against her, warmed by his joke, and they stood, arms entwined, gazing at the work.

The painting was indeed the portrait of a beautiful woman, but it was so much more. Jack's command of realism had rendered both joy and thoughtfulness in the younger Sofia's expression, and her lips bore the secret smile which she recognised was the one she had for him alone. And though Jack had portrayed her with a slenderness long gone, he'd shown strength in her bearing. Then there were the items he'd included in the painting, set on the shelves beside the window. Things she'd brought from Malaga in the chest Jack used to call her Spain. Scotty's death had revealed to her the chest never held her treasures, and she'd hated it for the way it had deceived her. But when Jack had taken her to his apartment and she'd again looked at its contents—her father and Andres paintings, the candlesticks that had sat on the dresser in her child home, her mothers hair combs and mantilla —she found peace. Of course the items were not her truest treasures. These were the people in her life; those around her now, and those she had lost. But the items were valuable because they unlocked her memories. Seeing them, the laughter of voices long gone, the perfume of orange blossom that had infused her childhood, the heat of the summer sun, and the softness of her babies' hair became enlivened. For that reason, the contents of the chest were precious.

Sofia did not only depict items from the chest she'd brought from Spain; on the shelf Jack had recreated a framed photo; the actual one sat at home on their dressing table. Sofia looked at it, her hand going to her chest as if to hug him. Scotty, sitting in a pedal-car, his dark eyes meeting the camera and now looking into the gallery. He would be twenty-six now; older than Jack was when Sofia had first met him. For the thousandth time, she wondered what sort of man her eldest son would have been; what he'd be doing if he were here, today. It seemed incredibly fitting that Scotty was here, in the painting.

At that minute, Andreanna appeared carrying another of the paintings delivered from the framer. Setting it down, she joined them.

'It's beautiful, Mum,' she said. 'That painting has always been my inspiration; one day I will paint one of you and it will be even better than Dad's!'

Sofia smiled, and looked at Jack. She doubted even the greatest painter who'd ever lived could create a better painting of her. The magic of *Sofia* sprung forth from Jack's love for her; from the years of joy and heartbreak they had shared, and from the deep place he'd held her in his heart for the years they'd been apart.

'I wish Scotty was here,' said Elizabeth. 'He'd be tall and strong, and could help us to hang the paintings.'

'He is here,' Jack said, and Elizabeth shook her head, as if convinced her father was mad.

Sofia looked at him, with a sad smile, as Jack explained what they both knew.

'Scotty's always here, Elizabeth.' He raised his hand to his chest, and then to Sofia's, tapping her on her left breast.

'Our little man is never far away from us. And you know, he is watching down on all of us: Mummy, Daddy, Andreanna and you and even Robbie while his is working in the kitchen at home. And today, he is incredibly pleased to see all of this.' Jack waved his hand to encompass the rooms of the gallery.

Sofia felt his arm squeeze her waist again, and he looked into her eyes.

'And I know he is particularly proud of mummy, so pleased to see all she has achieved, just like we are.'

The End

Acknowledgements

Thanks to the many people who have read and critiqued various drafts of the *Portraits in Blue* series. For Sofia's Story, a huge thank you to Susan, Nevin, Janetta, Aly and Kathie for your keen eyes as you pre-read *Sofia's Story*, and helped me give it a final polish.

A special thanks to Michel for pushing for depth in my stories; from Book One when you told me to strengthen my characters to Book Four when you insisted on a bit more, then more, and then even more. *Sofia's Story* definitely gained from your input.

As always, a special thanks to Jacques-Noël Gouat for your unfaltering enthusiasm for The *Portraits in Blue* series. Your time spent reviewing Book One's French components and your enthusiasm for my work ever since has been encouraging.

Thanks so much to Tarkenberg for bearing the grunt work of editing *Sofia's Story*. Your attention to detail is incredible, and the mini lessons you teach me along the way are much appreciated and hopefully leading me to become a better writer.

To my readers, for supporting me by buying my books, providing ratings and reviews, and for emailing me to tell me about the things you like, and also those things you don't like. I will always endeavour to write the best book I can for you.

To my husband and children, thank you for your encouragement, time spent reading drafts and listening to my author-world thoughts that invade so much of the real world. Your support is immensely valued.

AUTHORS NOTE TO THE READER

Dear Reader,

This is the last book in the Portraits of Blue Series. I feel a great sense of satisfaction in seeing Jack and Sofia rediscover their love and create a joy-filled life, true to their passions which they share with their children.

I am not sure whether I wrote Jack's story or whether he whispered in my ear as I typed. Certainly his physical and emotional journey fell onto my pages with ease. I wish he'd been a little more helpful with the editing, timelines and perhaps a little fact checking here and there! Nonetheless, wherever it came from, the Portraits of Blue Series has been a joy to write, and I have relished acquiring knowledge of the art world, events of WW2 and learning about various locations across the globe.

Having experienced Jack's journey in Books 1-3, I felt it was important to hear Sofia's voice; to know more about her following the tragic death of Scotty, hence *Sofia's Story* emerged. Even though I always knew her departure from Jack was borne of a tormented mind, I had no clear idea of the direction she would take. I hope you found the people she met and the events that unfolded as fascinating as I did.

Beyond the writing and publishing journey experienced as Portraits in Blue Series came to life, I have loved the opportunity to make connections with readers across the world through emails, social media comments and reviews. Your contact is highly valued. Hearing about your enjoyment for my books inspires me to keep writing. And for those who have shared criticisms, I am inspired to learn and do better! (A big shout-out to the reviewer whose comment inspired the epilogue in Sofia's Story!)

I have a couple of projects that I will be working on in 2022 plus three stories plotted out and ready to write for my next novel! Eeny, meeny, miny, mo... I can't wait to immerse myself in the process of breathing life into new characters once again. If you would like to keep in touch with me, please go to http://www.pennyfields-author.com and subscribe to my newsletter and receive a copy of my quirky short story titled 'The Young Guitarist' based on a moment of time in the life of Picasso.

Alternatively, you might like to drop me an email at pennyfieldsschneider@gmail.com or catch up with me at:

Facebook.com/PennyFields-Schneider
Instagram.com/pennyfieldsschneider

BOOKS BY PENNY FIELDS-SCHNEIDER

PORTRAITS IN BLUE SERIES
(Available in paperback and ebook)
Book One – The Sun Rose in Paris
Book Two – Shattered Dreams
Book Three – Searching for Sofia
Portraits in Blue - Book Four - Sofia's Story

SHORT STORIES
(Available free to Penny's newsletter subscribers!)
The Young Guitarist
Framed (coming soon)

Made in United States
North Haven, CT
31 October 2022

26152966R00257